A LIFE'S M

Other novels by George Gissing
also published by Harvester

ISABEL CLARENDON
Edited and Introduced by Pierre Coustillas

THE NETHER WORLD
Edited and Introduced by John Goode

THYRZA
Edited and Introduced by Jacob Korg

SLEEPING FIRES
Edited and Introduced by Pierre Coustillas

THE UNCLASSED
Edited and Introduced by Jacob Korg

DEMOS: A STORY OF ENGLISH SOCIALISM
Edited and Introduced by Pierre Coustillas

IN THE YEAR OF JUBILEE
Edited by P. F. Kropholler, and Introduced by Gillian Tindall

OUR FRIEND THE CHARLATAN
Edited and Introduced by Pierre Coustillas

THE WHIRLPOOL
Edited and Introduced by Patrick Parrinder

THE EMANCIPATED
Edited and Introduced by Pierre Coustillas

THE CROWN OF LIFE
Edited and Introduced by Michel Ballard

DENZIL QUARRIER
Edited and Introduced by John Halperin

BORN IN EXILE
Edited and Introduced by Pierre Coustillas

WILL WARBURTON
Edited and Introduced by Colin Partridge

THE PAYING GUEST
Edited and Introduced by Ian Fletcher

THE TOWN TRAVELLER
Edited and Introduced by Pierre Coustillas

THE PRIVATE PAPERS OF HENRY RYECROFT
Edited and Introduced by John Stewart Collis

A LIFE'S MORNING

George Gissing

Edited with an introduction by
PIERRE COUSTILLAS
Professor of English,
University of Lille

and with historical and topographical notes by
CLIFFORD BROOK

THE HARVESTER PRESS 1984

THE HARVESTER PRESS LIMITED
Publisher: John Spiers
16 Ship Street
Brighton, Sussex,
BN1 1AD,
England

'A Life's Morning'

First published 1888 in three volumes by
Smith, Elder London

This edition, reproducing the text of the
one-volume reprint of 1890, first published
in 1984 by The Harvester Press, Brighton

Introduction © Pierre Coustillas, 1984
Notes © Clifford Brook, 1984

British Library Cataloguing in Publication Data

Gissing, George
  A Life's morning
  I. Title
  823'.8[F]   PR4716.L/

  ISBN 0-7108-0651-5

Printed in Great Britain by
Whitstable Litho Ltd., Whitstable, Kent

This book has been published with subsidy from
The Arts Council of Great Britain

Contents

v

Acknowledgements

I wish to express my thanks to P. F. Kropholler, whose textual notes on *A Life's Morning* have, as on many similar occasions, been most useful, and to Lieutenant-Colonel D. C. H. Shrubsall, without whose disinterested assistance the fragment of the original MS of the novel might have remained unknown to Gissing scholars for many more years. I also wish to acknowledge my gratitude to Dr. G. O. Morse. His familiarity with and enthusiasm for this story have proved most stimulating.

P. C.

Bibliographical Note

Originally entitled *Emily*, *A Life's Morning* was first published serially in monthly instalments from January to December 1888 in the *Cornhill Magazine*. Smith, Elder & Co brought out the novel in three volumes on 15 November 1888 at the standard price of 31s.6d. The most part of the first edition (500 copies) was bound in brown cloth with gilt titling, but there is a later, and much scarcer, variant binding in light blue cloth. The same firm published a one-volume edition of 2,000 copies in pictorial boards in August 1889. A new impression of 1,000 copies issued in August 1890 was bound partly in red cloth, partly in boards; so was the next one, again of 1,000 copies in July 1892. These editions sold at 2s. (boards) and 2s.6d. (cloth).

In June 1914 Smith, Elder published a shilling edition of 7,500 copies in blue cloth, and John Murray, who took over the stock from Smith, Elder in 1917 when the latter firm closed down, brought out an edition of 8,000 copies in 1919. Nash & Grayson reissued the book at 7s.6d. with an introduction by Morley Roberts in 1928, but some copies printed the year before are dated 1927. The Nash & Grayson copies are in red cloth while the copies offered by Grayson at the reduced price of 3s.6d. in 1938 were bound in green cloth. In October 1947 Home & Van Thal published a new edition in red cloth at 12s.6d.

The first American edition was printed from British plates by the J.B. Lippincott Company of Philadelphia and published in late November 1888 in paper covers at 25 cents. The volume was no. 91 in Lippincott's Series of Select Novels. In the 1890s the book became available in cloth at one dollar (see *The Publishers' Trade List Annual* for 1896). By arrangement with Nash & Grayson, E. P. Dutton & Co published in 1929 the edition introduced by Morley Roberts, and the AMS Press reprinted the original three-decker in one volume in 1969.

In Japan Apollon-sha of Kyoto published an abridged edition of the story in 1961. The excerpts were edited with notes by N. Jimbo.

An abridged Russian translation by E. N. Akhmatova appeared under the title *Utro Zhizni* in a Petersburg periodical, *Zhivopisnoe Obozrenie* (May-June 1890). There is no mention in the Smith, Elder ledgers of any translation rights having been paid to the English publisher; nor did Gissing apparently ever hear of this translation.

Only Chapter III of the manuscript seems to have been preserved (see 'The Manuscript').

Introduction

Writing in January 1907, some three years after Gissing's death, the distinguished American critic Paul Elmer More called *A Life's Morning* 'one of the most passionate stories in English of love striving against degraded associations.'[1] A highly favourable judgment, but not so easy to contradict if one knows how powerfully Gissing could analyse human struggle against adverse circumstances. It is no accident if such novels as *The Nether World, New Grub Street, Born in Exile* and *The Odd Women* have slowly achieved the status of classics — their author is an authority on the influence of poverty — and his most characteristic books have no equivalent in the literature of his country. Of course *A Life's Morning* cannot claim a place on the same level as these later titles, but it is nevertheless vintage Gissing and the scenes laid in Yorkshire belong to his best work of the 1880s. The book has indeed many endearing features and, as we shall see, its first publication has in retrospect become a signal instance of Victorian conflict between author and publisher, ending naturally in the defeat of the former. Modestly though it ranks among Gissing's novels, it has always enjoyed the good opinion of critics and readers. Early reviewers gave the story a warm welcome because they mistakenly viewed it as a successor to *Demos* and *Thyrza*, two books which had made their mark. The dramatic fate of James Hood, the heroine's father, was deemed by Ernest A. Baker, one of Gissing's discriminate supporters, to be 'representative of a small group of [his] characters, worthy and capable, whose life-work is ruined by the conditions into which they are born.'[2] When William Plomer, in 1947, was asked by Herbert Van Thal to choose a Gissing novel which was intended to be the first volume of the long-awaited collected works, he fixed upon *A Life's Morning* because it belonged to Gissing's lighter vein. But the experiment was not a happy one — the book did not sell and the

xi

long-term project was dropped — and no attempt worthy of the name has been made since to revive the story. It is therefore high time to give it a new lease of life.

I

Gissing was not quite twenty-eight when he wrote this novel and, although it ultimately became his sixth published title, he was still a comparatively new hand at the trade in those days. Only two of his stories were in print at the time of composition, the very interesting but immature *Workers in the Dawn* (1880) and the better semi-realistic, semi-romantic tale of *The Unclassed* (1884). *Mrs. Grundy's Enemies*, notwithstanding its acceptance by Bentley, was still unpublished (and fated never to appear), whilst *Isabel Clarendon*, after a thorough revision and cutting down at George Meredith's request, awaited Chapman's decision to publish. At this stage of his career Gissing already felt the need to renew his inspiration and it was therefore natural that after half a dozen tales set in London (*Isabel Clarendon* was his first departure from this line) he should wish to write a story of provincial life, actually a story set in his own hometown. The idea had been for a couple of years in his mind. When his brother Algernon was still only nursing his ill-advised project of becoming a professional novelist, George had sketched out for him a story of Wakefield life entitled *Pastures New*.[3] Algernon had made a brave attempt, but he had failed to complete, let alone publish, the story, and when George himself had finished writing what was to be *Isabel Clarendon*, he felt free to use the Wakefield setting — under some other name as he had urged Algernon to do. As chance had it, he had no opportunity to carry out his plans immediately after finishing *Isabel Clarendon* in late March 1885, but it was then, however, that the first idea of *A Life's Morning* began to take shape, only very tentatively in the beginning. Between 25 March and 8 April Algernon visited George in his Marylebone lodgings, at 7K Cornwall Residences, and the project was debated by the two brothers. A letter from George to his sister Margaret of 10 April reflects his uncertainty: he wanted to tackle another novel but he thought it was 'really useless until we know whether there is going to be war or peace,' an allusion to the current political tension between Britain and Russia. His original plan consisted in having the story start in Wakefield, which he would call Vicarsley; the protagonist would more or less closely resemble his brother Algernon and the provisional title was 'Walter Wyvern', a surname which was eventually to emerge in *Demos*. But this first plan was not to fructify for in early May Chapman suggested that *Isabel Clarendon*, written for publication in three volumes, be recast in two. Such was indeed the advice of Chapman's reader, Meredith, who had previously demanded alterations in *The Unclassed*. Revising *Isabel Clarendon* consumed most of Gissing's time until about mid-August.

It was, however, early in that month, even before the end of Volume II of *Isabel Clarendon* was in sight, that he turned again to 'the first chapters of my new book, which I think will be called "Clara Wace"', as he told his sister Ellen. His cultural enthusiasm of the period was to find its way into his novel. 'Because you are a woman, and living at present in an out of the way corner, that is no reason why you should not keep before your eyes an exalted aim, and should not acquire more of real insight into literature and art than the majority of people can get.' In the novel Emily Hood was to act as though she had been given this advice, which was penned for Ellen Gissing's benefit. He was determined to write only two volumes this time and he reckoned that with an average of six pages a day the narrative would be reached in two months. Planning the new book took about a fortnight and it involved some correspondence with Algernon about the social position and wages of the clerk to the Board of Guardians in Wakefield as well as about a mill owned by one Briggs. The clerk, he explained to his brother, was to be 'a man of 45, with wife and daughter, and the poorer the better. But his intelligence has won for him the respect of the better townspeople.'[5] He was elated by the 'glorious ideas' he had for the story and intended 'to go at it forthwith'.

A working title, 'Emily', soon appeared in the correspondence. On 24 August he told Ellen that he had written the first chapter and was now rewriting it. 'It always requires some labour to get the first chapter satisfactory, especially when, as in this case, it contains a rapid survey of many years.'[6] Concurrently he was reading *The Divine Comedy* in Italian and *Marius the Epicurean*, which Walter Pater had just published, as well as studying the art of the Renaissance. His novel contains traces of his intellectual interests of the moment, but its progress did not suffer from his manifold pursuits. By 9 October the first volume, that is half the story as we have it, was completed, but he felt the necessity of rewriting some pages. The need for money speeded his pen. Chapman had not yet notified him of his final acceptance of *Isabel Clarendon* and he was painfully aware that he would presently be out of his wits 'to provide cash', which meant 'stoppage of all work'.[7] The £2.10s. brought him weekly by the lessons he gave to his only pupil, Walter Grahame, would not be paid until the end of the quarter. Half-jocosely he predicted that when the spring sun returned he would probably be in 'Marylebone Workhouse over the way'. Straightaway he passed on to the second volume, toying with the notion of sending his manuscript to Macmillan when it was ready. Chapman's dilatoriness, together with his unfair dealings, made him an impossible publisher for an impecunious novelist. 'The blessed certainty of progress in the achievement of a fixed daily task!' he sighed with some pride. 'The end comes before one knows of it.'[8]

Few if any of his twenty-two novels were composed with greater ease. On 22 October he wrote to his brother that he was past the middle of the second volume. Already he had the skeleton of his next novel fairly clear in his head. The socialist agitation in the East End had revived his old idea of writing *Demos*. He recorded his failure to produce more than twelve poor lines one very bad evening, but he carried out his plans successfully. 'Emily' was completed in the first few days of November. Then it was that he had one more interview about *Isabel Clarendon* with Meredith, an interview which shook his self-confidence and caused him to turn again to novels of working-class life for a few years. 'Meredith tells me I am making a great mistake,' George wrote to Algernon the day after the interview, 'in leaving the low-life scenes; says I might take a foremost place in fiction if I pursued that.'[9] Besides being Chapman's reader, Meredith was the only novelist whom he almost unreservedly admired and the master's judgment on *Isabel Clarendon* seriously affected his view of 'Emily'. Furthermore this new book, which he had written with so much ease, turned out to be ready at an awkward moment. Had he known that *Isabel Clarendon* was not to appear until June 1886, he would have been even more concerned with the bottleneck effect his own speed and Chapman's remissness had produced. As he could not contemplate having two novels brought out at the same time under his own name by two different publishers, he chose to send 'Emily' to Smith, Elder under the pseudonym of Osmond Waymark, the protagonist of *The Unclassed*. His friend Mrs

Gaussen, the great lady of Broughton Hall, Lechlade, was enthusiastic about 'Emily' — yet he was lucid enough not to trust her judgment. 'She will be enraged if I don't publish it in my own name,' he confided to his younger sister, who had been petted by Mrs Gaussen earlier in 1885 during a visit to London, 'but I fear I have no choice. I shall, however, ask F[rederic] Harrison's opinion'.[10]

Suspense as to the fate of the manuscript came to an end on 25 November when Smith, Elder's reader, the popular novelist James Payn, informed Gissing that he accepted 'Emily'. Like Mrs Gaussen, Payn was enthusiastic about the story, but he offered a sum which was hardly consonant with his enthusiasm — £50 for all rights. A young writer in straitened circumstances could not afford to haggle, so Gissing had to be content with these paltry terms which allowed the firm of Smith, Elder to make substantial profits on the book's sales for about thirty years. Payn added some sugar to the pill which the young novelist was anyway more than prepared to swallow. It was 'just possible' that, in his capacity as editor, he would run the novel through the *Cornhill Magazine*, in which case Gissing would receive another £50. Gissing's style, he added hyperbolically, was better than anything since George Eliot. At a meeting of publisher's reader and author on 8 December 1885 it was settled that they would try to catch the public by publishing the book anonymously, but a final decision about serialization in the *Cornhill* could only be made in two months' time — a delay which was eventually to affect the fate of the story, for *Demos*, Gissing's current novel from November 1885 onwards, relegated 'Emily' to the back of both author's and publisher's minds. From Smith, Elder's point of view, there was a most fortunate coincidence between the subject of *Demos* and the socialist demonstrations which punctuated the autumn and winter of 1885-1886. Publishing *Demos*, which was promptly accepted by Payn even before the third volume was written, was far more urgent than printing for the readers of the *Cornhill* the tragic story of a governess called Emily Hood. It was *Demos* which was issued anonymously and with all possible celerity in March 1886 and 'Emily', after being retitled *A Life's Morning*, achieved publication only after *Demos, Isabel Clarendon* and *Thyrza*.

For some two years, 'Emily' dropped out of Gissing's correspondence until, abruptly, in early November 1887, Payn wrote announcing that a better title must be found for the forthcoming serialization. Gissing suggested 'Her Will and Her Way', then, as this had been used previously, 'The Morning of Her Life', and ultimately the title under which the novel came to be known. It was apparently at this stage, and not in 1885, that Payn made an extraordinary request which has earned him in Gissing criticism a reputation for being a pretentious ass and a harmful one at that. He made it a condition for publication that Gissing should resuscitate his heroine and lead her to the altar. As there was but one witness, his old college friend and fellow-novelist Morley Roberts, of Gissing's reactions (which are echoed nowhere in his letters to his relatives), it is imperative to quote him: 'I think nothing on earth, or in some hell for men of letters, could have made [Gissing] more angry and wretched. If there was one thing that he clung to during the whole of his working time, it was sincerity, and sincerity in literary work implies an absolute freedom from alien and extrinsic influence. I can well remember what he said to me about [Payn's] suggestion. He abused him and the publishers; the public, England, the world, and the very universe. He almost burst into tears as he explained to me what he had been obliged to do for the sake of the great fifty pounds he was to get for the book ... I do not suppose he ever put anything on paper in his life which cost him such acute mental suffering as the last three chapters of this book which were written to [James Payn's] barbaric order'.[11] How long it took Gissing to reshuffle the ending of his story is unknown as his diary in its final form begins only a couple of months after Payn's *diktat* and his correspondence is mute on the subject — doubtless, as Roberts implies, mute with anger and indignation. At least four distinct hints at what the original ending was to be — the death by heart failure of Emily on the eve of marrying Wilfrid Athel — are still to be found in the last two chapters he left untouched (XXII and XXIII), on pp. 307, 311, 318 and 319.

A recently discovered letter from Gissing to Payn, dated 25 November 1887, shows Gissing at work in the early stages of proof-reading:

> Dear Mr. Payn,
>
> The phrase is an affected one; I ought to have altered it, as I have now done. I was given to such things just at that time.
>
> This is not, I trust, a revise, for I see that a ludicrous misprint just above stands uncorrected.
>
> I will certainly avoid alteration save when there is

something really painful. It is not likely there will be many such instances when the story gets well going.

I thank you for your good opinion of my style in general.

Yours very truly,

George Gissing[12]

He still would have liked the story to appear anonymously, but not in this either was his will allowed to prevail. His publishers could not be reasonably expected to repeat barely two years later the stratagem they had used for *Demos*. By 22 November he had read the first batch of proofs and concluded that on the whole the novel read better than he expected.[13] As the printers proceeded his opinion went through many ups and downs. He thundered against the serial method — a vile way of publishing, he said — but admitted that it was as a rule twice as profitable as publication in volume form. In the *Cornhill*, it amounted to a full year's advertisement. He vowed nonetheless that he would do his best to resist serialization henceforth and would not allow any story he valued particularly to appear in that fashion. On 18 February 1888 he wrote to Ellen: 'The *Cornhill* story is disgusting me; I fear it gets poorer and poorer; I can only hope that it will very soon be forgotten'.[14] This was a reflection of his current depressed mood for, when five weeks later he commented again on the narrative after reviewing his gusto for work he confessed to the same correspondent that now he had read the proofs of *A Life's Morning* to the end of the August number, he began to see that it was by no means contemptible. Again he blamed the method of publication and expressed his confidence that his artistic instincts had not deserted him.[15] Anyhow there were signs that serialization was good publicity for him: for instance he received a letter from one W. C. Sowerby, of Derby, who said he recognized Wakefield in the book, and another from a Miss E. I. Scott, who was 'finishing her education' in Paris and begged for his autograph and advice! The Wakefield press mentioned the novel to its readers.

When the book was issued in volume form Gissing declared himself glad to be in Italy, at a safe distance from the newsrooms where he could have come across notices in newspapers and magazines. He did his best to discourage comments from his friends and relatives, writing to Eduard Bertz: 'If I saw a *single* review, I might as well at once go back to London; my pleasure here would be at an end'.[16] To his great surprise, the novel, which he had written for publication in two volumes, appeared in three, a reaction we should interpret as evidence that only the proofs of the serial version were read by him. Obviously Smith, Elder dealt with him in a cavalier manner. So did one or two reviewers, but on the whole the story was given a friendly reception, and the *Whitehall Review* called it his masterpiece.[17] Most critics praised the character drawing, the conversational parts, the plot and even the *dénouement* which was so hateful to the author. Clearly the protagonist Wilfrid Athel pleased less than Beatrice Redwing, whose aura of noble renunciation appealed to the taste of the average sentimentalist, and even less than Emily Hood, 'a heroine of a thousand' according to the *Graphic*, but an unattractive person by the *Guardian*'s dictum. The only recurrent criticism concerned the style which, in the opinion of half a dozen critics was somewhat pedantic or affected in places or lacking in 'the happy brevity which even the amateur should know is the soul of other things besides wit'.[18] Had Gissing read the *Pall Mall Gazette* review he would have wondered whether Meredith had held its writer's hand since the author of *A Life's Morning* was advised to confine himself to studies of the working-class, 'to that class of life which he knows so intimately, and has described with such skill and fidelity in *Demos* and *Workers in the Dawn*'. Sweetest of all judgments would have been to him that of the *Manchester Guardian* which placed him in the company to which he naturally belongs: 'Mr Gissing reminds us partly of George Eliot and partly of Mr Henry James, but with this difference that he never sneers.'

II

Thematically *A Life's Morning* might be defined as Gissing's contribution to the (by the mid-eighties) well-worn subject of the governess within the equally well-worn framework of the contrasted civilizations of North and South. It is also a novel which looks upon life from the opposite angles of realism and aestheticism and depicts the human condition as heavily determined by circumstances, a flexible term with connotations interior and exterior to man. More obviously it is a psychological drama coloured by the idealism of the period, but nonetheless a highly personal work of art in which the author stands confessed on every page, even though the happy ending tells us more about James Payn's notion of what a novel should be than about Gissing's.

It would be risky to assert that he had in mind Elizabeth Gaskell's

North and South as much as Charlotte Brontë's *Jane Eyre* when he
decided to write this book. The provisional title, 'Emily', indicates
that he saw the story primarily as that of a girl who, handicapped by
her social origins, physical frailty and fate, fails to achieve self-
fulfilment, but it is nevertheless certain that he thought from the
start of placing Emily's life and her divided loyalties against a double
background, the industrial north and the rural south, with markedly
cultural associations in each case. He had probably read Mrs
Gaskell's novel but like all the literature that was thematically fairly
close to his own favourite subjects, this tale about the condition of
England in the mid-1850s could not move him because it was lacking
in the spirit which *he* would have put into it. Despite Clara Collet's
efforts to interest him in his mid-Victorian predecessor in social
fiction, he hardly responded. The North here is not Manchester, as
it was to be in *Born in Exile*, but his native place, Wakefield.
Emphasis is not laid mainly on the merits and demerits of Yorkshire
and Surrey, of the new manufacturing world and the old rural world.
The two contrasted backgrounds are seen in perspective; they never
matter more than or as much as, Emily Hood and Wilfrid Athel, but
we have no chance of forgetting the influence of environment.

It is hardly surprising that the story offended some people in
Wakefield when it appeared in 1000. It described Dunfield and
nearby localities in the tone of a young man who has an axe to grind.
Things and people are represented gloomily: ugliness, pollution,
narrow-mindedness, commercialism, lack of culture, unpleasant
human relationships are repeatedly denounced, in particular at the
beginning of Chapter IV and in Chapter VII. One would like to
believe that Gissing exaggerated, but various testimonies are extant,
photographic or reminiscential, which attest to the veracity of his
picture. *Old Wakefield in Photographs*, a pictorial record compiled
by Harold Speak and Jean Forrester in 1972, certainly does not give
the lie to the physical descriptions to be found in the novel. No local
historian is known to have contested Gissing's statement in Chapter
VII that 'if any Dunfield schoolboy exhibited faculties of a kind
uncommon in the town, he was despatched to begin life on a more
promising scene; those who remained, who became the new
generation of business men, of town councillors, of independent
electors, were such as could not by any possibility have made a living
elsewhere. Those elders who knew Dunfield best could not point to
a single youth of fair endowments who looked forward to remaining

in his native place.' George himself, together with his brothers, had been sent away to a boarding-school in Cheshire at his father's death, and he gives us to understand in his story that whatever true education Emily had received was not given her locally. If her pupil, Jessie Cartwright, must be viewed as representative, then the Dunfield young ladies were a pretty unattractive lot. Emily, like so many protagonists of Gissing's novels, is born in exile, and this exile in *A Life's Morning*, as in the better known case of Godwin Peak, is not only social and intellectual, but also geographical. The material defilement of nineteenth-century Wakefield prompted Gissing to react as an intellectual who was familiar with the works of Matthew Arnold, John Ruskin and Walter Pater. When walking about with her father in Dunfield (Chapter V), Emily 'tried to believe that this [the common just outside the town] at length was really the country; there were no houses in view; meadows lay on either hand, the leafage was thick. But it was not mere prejudice which saw in every object a struggle with hard conditions, a degeneration into coarseness, a blight.' In a short story with a Wakefield setting written a few years before, 'The Quarry on the Heath' (which he turned to some account in his novel, seeing that it had not been printed), he had tried his hand at an even gloomier picture.[19] In both narratives material discomfort is associated with mental constriction of a spiritual nature. Emily's leanings towards asceticism proceed from her northern heritage, as does the same strain in Beatrice Redwing, whose uncle, the liberal M.P. Baxendale, is also a major Dunfield figure.

The dichotomy Yorkshire-Surrey is first suggested with some irony as early as Chapter III, entitled 'Lyrical', that is when Surrey is at its most vernal. In a novel which was to end tragically, it was in order that we should be offered a glimpse of Paradise before lapsing into Purgatory. 'To compare The Firs with that plain little dwelling on the skirts of a Yorkshire manufacturing town which she called her home, was to understand that inestimable advantage of those born into the material refinement which wealth can command, of those who breathe from childhood the atmosphere of liberal enjoyment, who walk from the first on clean ways, with minds disengaged from anxiety of casual soilure, who know not even by domestic story the trammels of sordid preoccupation.' Surrey is all that Yorkshire is not. It is evocative of untainted nature, spaciousness, leisureliness, culture and spiritual freedom. Mr Athel dabbles in egyptology, a

past-oriented occupation, while James Hood patiently and ponder-
ously studies electricity, with (to Gissing) its exclusively material
and future-looking connotations, in his spare time. And Surrey, in
the person of the protagonist, is as it were prolonged by Italy, the
homeland of his deceased mother, which under the author's pen
signified a land of artists and sunshine. The Athels live on the
interest of their invested wealth, the Hoods are continually obsessed
with the struggle for life. Of course, the arcadianism of Surrey stems
from pleasant summertime experiences with the Frederic Harrisons
in the early 1880s, experiences about which Gissing wrote
rapturously to his relatives, but without much effect on any of them,
George's ideas being almost systematically distrusted by the elder
Mrs Gissing and her daughters. As recently as 24 August 1885 he had
remarked to Ellen after a visit to the Harrisons: 'The more I see of
Surrey the more convinced I am that it is the ideal of English rustic
scenery.'[20] He had by then written only the first chapter of his book
and saw the home counties in a Meredithian light, a consequence of
his late contacts with the novelist in his capacity as manuscript
reader for Chapman & Hall. Gissing once declared *The Ordeal of
Richard Feverel* to be one of his favourite novels and signs of his
admiration crop up in *A Life's Morning* (in *Isabel Clarendon* as well),
especially in Chapter III. The wood-scene (p 19) would seem to
come straight from Meredith's story and there are brief moments
when Mr Athel and Mrs Rossall remind one of Sir Austin Feverel
and Lady Blandish. No difficult or ugly master-and-man relationship
is discernible in Surrey. Indeed human labour has vanished
altogether from this arcadian environment. We have to go north if
we are to see a mill-owner of the type we associate with the industrial
novels of the mid-century. Dagworthy, the villain, is the man, and in
his study of him as an employer, Gissing somewhat unexpectedly
moves to the left of the political kaleidoscope. Mrs Gaskell, in *North
and South* and in her earlier tale *Mary Barton*, was sitting on the
fence. Gissing found such a position uncomfortable. 'The employer
of labour is not as a rule troubled with a lively imagination,' he
observed unsparingly in Chapter XIII, 'a pity, for it would surely
gratify him to feel in its fulness at times his power of life and death.'
And in a tone which anticipates some of the gloomier passages in *The
Nether World* he wrote despondently of the ageing Hood couple in
Chapter V: 'Time had robbed them of youth, and the injustice of
the world's order had starved love to less than a shadow of itself, to a

mere habit of common suffering. Tender memories were buried in the grave of children whom the resources of ever so modest a fortune would have kept alive; the present was a mere struggle to support existence, choking the impulses of affection'. The pendulum of Gissing's wavering political sympathies was most unstable in the mid-eighties: it went right in *Isabel Clarendon*, left in *A Life's Morning*, right again in *Demos* and left again in *Thyrza*. Mrs Baxendale, in the present novel, obviously bathes in the sunshine of the author's approval.

No such passion appears in the treatment of the other major theme, that of the governess. Emily Hood works in that capacity in five chapters only out of twenty-six, but *A Life's Morning*, although overlooked by students of the governess, a favourite character in Victorian fiction, unquestionably belongs to the well-established tradition. 'What is the position of a governess?' asked an anonymous writer in the *English Woman's Journal* in November 1860. 'She has none. While engaged in a family ... she is infinitely less considered than the servants; she has no companionship whatsoever; very frequently, not a syllable is addressed to her from week's end to week's end by the members of the family as if she were in disgrace ... The servants have their hall and their social pleasures; the governess is condemned to solitude'.[21] In this description we do not quite recognize the governess in charge of Pattie and Minnie Rossall at The Firs, not so much because we scarcely see her teaching as because Gissing is only marginally interested in a literary tradition which goes at least as far back as the novels of Jane Austen. He was familiar with the governesses in the latter works as he was with Becky Sharp, Jane Eyre, Agnes Grey and, perhaps also, Lady Isabel Vane in Mrs Henry Wood's best-selling story, *East Lynne*, but he did not set out to devote his whole novel to a study of the governess as a social type. True, like all governesses, Emily finds her position in the household of her employers comparatively ambiguous and uncomfortable, her wages are not very satisfactory and her tenure is uncertain, but her capacities are acknowledged, her personality is appreciated, and at no moment does the narrator represent her as a victim of her employers. Surely she does not belong to any of the six categories of governesses identified by Katharine West in her survey published in 1949[22]: the Downtrodden, the Valued Friend, the Strict Instructress (or Dragon), the Self-Seeking Adventuress, the Villainess and the Snob-Exhibit. Emily is not a stock character, she is a product of her social environment and of Gissing's exalted idealism. Still there is no doubt that, as a literary beginner (since, let it be repeated, he had published only two books when he wrote the story of Emily Hood), he was trying to capitalise on the popularity of the governess with Victorian readers. Patricia Thomson tells us that 'in 1851 there were no fewer than 24,770 governesses in England, and in point of pathos even distressed needlewomen had to yield place to indigent governesses. An allusion to a governess in a novel was as sure to arouse a stock, emotional response in the minds of the readers as a reference to death. Everyone was familiar with her conventional attributes. She was bound to be a lady — preferably the daughter of a clergyman, she was always impoverished, unprotected and, by virtue of her circumstances, reasonably intelligent and submissive. But though she appeared on the scene in this ready-made gown, there was nothing to prevent the novelist embellishing it to his taste, adding a flounce of coquettishness here or a slashing of deceitfulness there'.[1]

Gissing adapted this pattern to his requirements. He did not make Emily a glamorous creature, a self-seeker or even a romantic sentimentalist. He is but mildly and temporarily preoccupied with the attitudes of her employers after Wilfrid Athel has declared his love to her and informed of it his father and aunt. The tragedy does not originate from that quarter, and we are in no doubt as to Wilfrid's determination to ignore whatever objections his relatives are only too apt to raise on account of social differences between the lovers. The tragedy results from the misbehaviour of the heroine's father, also from Emily's remorse at having done nothing to prevent the catastrophe and from her conviction that her parent's theft and suicide make her for ever unsuitable as a potential wife to such an upper-class young man as Wilfrid Athel. There are no petty persecutions here, like those endured by Agnes Grey, no resentful indignation against social injustice, no mood of rebellious independence like that embodied by Jane Eyre either. Emily Hood's sufferings largely derive from her noble conception of personal dignity, from her masochistic taste for self-sacrifice. She is not rejected by her lover, with whom his relatives' principles carry little weight; her banishment is self-inflicted. Besides, by the time it is enacted, she has ceased to be seen by the reader primarily as a governess. Spirit, soul, mind she has in plenty, nor has she in this field anything to envy Wilfrid. But where Gissing follows tradition is when he chooses to make Emily a victim. Between the covers of a book, the governess was condemned to be pitied, and James Payn proved that he was well aware of the emotional appeal of the theme, of its marketable value, when he decided to serialize the story in the *Cornhill*. By demanding a happy ending he showed his venal, low-brow anxiety to offer its audience as many of the bright aspects of the subject as possible, endangering thereby the literary value of the book.

Seen in the light of Gissing's attitude to his heroine the story appears to be distinctly late Victorian. Few were, earlier in the century, the novelists who were prepared to approve of a match between a governess and a socially superior young man. Emily Brontë, Wilkie Collins and Trollope were among them, however, so that Gissing is in excellent company. But one should also be aware that by the eighties, indeed at least one decade earlier, persecution of the governess in fiction had become unusual. Patronage was thought to be more rewarding — in coin of the realm, be it understood. Yet only a critic unaware of Gissing's artistic integrity could accuse him of having debased his own standards in this novel. The traditional parental reaction is plainly expressed by Wilfrid's father in Chapter IV ('A Conflict of Opinions'): '"I mean, Wilf, that I am not yet in the frame of mind to regard the children's governess as my daughter-in-law. Miss Hood may be all you say; I would not willingly be anything but scrupulously just. The fact remains that this is not the alliance which it became you to make. It is, in a very pronounced sense, marrying beneath you. It is not easy for me to reconcile myself to that"'. So the sociological value of the story remains unaffected. Besides, if justice is to be done to the author's intentions, the whole image of governessing must be seen in the light of his aestheticism in the mid-eighties.

At no time did he respond more fully to the doctrine of art for art's sake than when he was busy planning and writing *A Life's Morning*. The book is fraught with the cult of beauty as he had found it successively in Ruskin and Walter Pater. His correspondence and papers show that he devoted much time to studying *Modern Painters* in 1884 — he turned to Ruskin's five volumes again later and it is to this second spell of study that the notes in his *Commonplace Book* correspond — and that Pater's *Renaissance* and *Marius the Epicurean* were also books in which he positively delighted. His commonplace book of quotations, *Extracts from my Reading*, contains a number of favourite quotations from both authors. Gissing was perhaps mainly grateful to Ruskin for drawing public attention to the problems of English industrialized society, but he would not follow him in his denunciation of the 'pestilent art of the Renaissance' as arising from an immoral society. If Ruskin's insistence on a direct relation between moral and artistic values left him indifferent, his attacks on the industrialism of the day with its consequences on the physiognomy of England and on the mental attitudes of its inhabitants earned his full approval. Gissing certainly had in mind, while composing his novel, Ruskin's assault on the deforming mechanism, and the squalid misery of modern cities. Where he could not follow Ruskin (art and morality could not cohabit without art being choked to death, he thought), Pater pointed to a path that was altogether free of the dross of ethical prejudice. On 7 October 1885 we find him quoting this passage from *Marius* to his sister Margaret, who was then struggling miserably to get private lessons: 'He was acquiring what is ever the true function of all higher education to teach — a system, or art, namely, of so relieving the ideal or poetic traits, the elements of distinction, in our every-day life — of so exclusively living in them — that the unadorned remainder of it, the mere drift and *débris* of life, becomes as though it were not.'[24] This might serve as an epigraph to *A Life's Morning*.

To make one's life a work of art, to see life around one as a work of art, to be an artist in life — such is the ideal Gissing lends to Emily — and to Wilfrid. 'The task before her,' he wrote in Chapter III, 'a task of which in these days she was growing more and more conscious, was to construct an existence every moment of which should serve an all-pervading harmony.' Love of nature, worship of beauty, thirst for knowledge are items of the aesthetic programme to which both Wilfrid and Emily subscribe. 'My despair,' exclaims Wilfrid after being invalided from Balliol, 'is the universality of my interests.' In Emily, we are warned by the narrator, idealism would not ally itself with compromise. Here we have an echo of Pater's own austerity and power of discrimination, not of Wilde's extravagant enactments of the new aesthetic sensibility. What Emily is aiming at is a form of purified ecstasy that can only bloom when removed from the matter-of-fact world and its solidified pattern of thought and behaviour. Pater's view is that the quest of beauty is the finest occupation one can find for oneself during the 'indefinite reprieve' from death which we call life. The comparison between Emily's two homes in Chapter III emphasises her hedonist response to the comforts of existence at The Firs: 'Thus it was with a sense of well-being that she stepped on rich carpets, let her eyes wander over the light and dark of rooms where wealth had done the bidding of taste, watched the neat and silent ministering of servants. These things to her meant priceless opportunity, the facilitating of self-culture.' Emily reads Dante, she rises at early hours so as to have the garden to herself in all its freshness, the pursuit of beauty becomes with her a religion, a source of spiritual delight. The passage describing her outing in the early morning before Wilfrid joins her expresses Gissing's Paterian discipleship at its apex, and it is significant that after borrowing from religious imagery he allows us to glimpse at the reverse of aestheticism, that is asceticism, into which she seeks refuge as soon as fate turns inimical. There is no equivalent of this strain in Wilfrid, no 'darker strain' that Gissing readily associated with a certain Northern female mentality which he had observed at close quarters within his own family, and which he was later to analyse at greater length in such novels as *The Emancipated* and *Born in Exile*. Fortunately she does not yield to whatever religious impulses may lie latent in her, even though Gissing, in the middle of the story, goes on to use religious metaphors, referring for instance on p. 174 to her state of mind, which 'had something of the martyr's joy'.

Both the aesthetic and ascetic strains are also noticeable in Beatrice Redwing, and she, too, proves capable of that self-sacrifice which harmonized so well with the ethos of the period. But in her case asceticism has a religious colouring uncongenial to the author. She is not altogether free from the taint of idealisation so typical of Gissing until after he met and *lived with* Gabrielle Fleury, but she has at least a number of shortcomings which are made palpable to Wilfrid and the reader, notably a marked aptness for jealousy and peevishness, and these shortcomings consolidate her humanity. Her aestheticism finds its sole expression in singing, a form approved of by the narrator, who nonetheless levels some shafts at her eclectic reconciliation of religious piety, bodily exercise and artistic leanings. Short of the 'vulgarities of hysterical pietism,' she evinces spiritual proclivities with which Gissing has no patience. Mrs Rossall is even less spared as she cannot plead the excuse of prime youth. The satire of sabbatarianism in Chapter XII and of revivalist meetings in Chapter XIV shows the limits of his tolerance; it surfaces again in such minor novels as *The Emancipated* and *Denzil Quarrier*, where it accords better with the general atmosphere of the narratives.

If the treatment of aestheticism in *A Life's Morning* circumscribes the typicality of the story as a Gissing story, there are many aspects of it which should serve as a warning to anyone tempted to regard it as minor *because* uncharacteristic. In it are incorporated some of the novelist's deepest beliefs derived from painful personal experience. At the root of the tragedy we find poverty and the evils it is fraught with. If the heroine's father, James Hood, were not a poor clerk whose humdrum life is sorely beset with harrowing money difficulties, he would not be led to commit suicide and his daughter would experience no psychological crisis at a moment when fate places happiness within her reach. The robbery of the ten-pound note put as a bait in a ledger by Dagworthy may of course be seen as a melodramatic device from which springs the whole action less the last three chapters; if so, actual life must be melodramatic to an unsuspected extent. But is it not safer to view the incident as an illustration of Samuel Johnson's statement, quoted by Gissing in *Henry Ryecroft*, that 'poverty is so great an evil, and pregnant with so much temptation, so much misery, that I cannot but earnestly enjoin you to avoid it'?[25] Further, even though the story's setting is far removed from the London slums with which Gissing's novels of the period are associated, the basic theme remains the same — the power of money. Grafted onto this is the notion of fate (the word itself recurs with insistent frequency in the novel), of circumstances. Emily, like her weak, unfortunate father, and a theory of unheroic Gissing heroes, is a victim of circumstances in the full, dramatic sense that this phrase of course does not have in the short story of that name. The sequence of events which trigger off the catastrophe may seem ludicrous enough now that hats no longer are indispensable tokens of respectability, but, given the social conventions of the period, it is all but too plausible, and no commentator has ever made light of it. Lastly, in the wake of the notion of fate comes that of alienation, the Gissing subject *par excellence*.

So the significance of *A Life's Morning* among his works comes out radiantly. The book deserves our full attention with all the more urgency as it was itself, and remains, a victim of circumstances, or as Morley Roberts put it punningly, of 'Payn and poverty'. It is one of the most distressing incidents in English literature that an incompetent publisher's reader should have been allowed to spoil the conclusion of a story written with so much intellectual fervour. May the original ending emerge some day in a sale-room and the novel's integrity be at long last restored. One's notion of justice would welcome such an event.

Notes

1 'George Gissing', *Nation* (New York), 17 January 1907, pp. 53-55. Reprinted in *Gissing: The Critical Heritage*, ed. Pierre Coustillas and Colin Partridge, London and Boston: Routledge & Kegan Paul, 1972, pp. 519-28.

2 *A Guide to the Best Fiction in English*, London: Routledge & Sons, 1913, pp. 116-18.

3 Letter to Algernon of 5 October 1883, *George Gissing on Fiction*, ed. Jacob and Cynthia Korg, London: Enitharmon Press, 1978, pp. 23-25.

4 Letter of 2 August 1885, Berg Coll. Published in part in *Letters of George Gissing to His Family*, ed. Algernon and Ellen Gissing, London: Constable, 1927, pp. 160-61.

5 Letter dated Saturday [15 August 1885], Yale.

6 Letter in the Berg Coll., published in part in *Letters of George Gissing to His Family*, pp. 167-68

7 Letter to Ellen of 9 October 1885. Original in private collection. Published in part in *Letters of George Gissing to His Family*, pp. 171-72.

8 Letter to Algernon of 10 October 1885, Carl H. Pforzheimer Library. Published in part in *Letters of George Gissing to His Family*, p. 170.

9 31 October 1885, *Letters of George Gissing to His Family*, p. 172.

10 Letter of 4 November 1885, Berg Coll. Published in part in *Letters of George Gissing to His Family*, pp. 172-73.

11 *The Private Life of Henry Maitland*, London: Eveleigh Nash, 1912, pp. 91-92. See also Roberts's introduction to the Nash & Grayson edition of *A Life's Morning* (1927). At Gissing's death, some doubt was cast on the reality of Gissing's revision of the novel's ending at the request of James Payn. An obituarist in the *Outlook* ('George Gissing', 2 January 1904, pp. 649-50) alluded to the tampering 'with the original MS. of its ending in order to please a public alleged to require prettiness even from him.' A month later ('George Gissing', 30 January 1904, p. 19) the same writer retracted after writing to Smith, Elder, who declared that they had 'no record of having advised Mr Gissing to reconstruct the ending of *A Life's Morning*' and to Algernon Gissing who replied: 'Though living with my brother at the time he wrote the book in question [1885] I cannot recall any remark of his on the point you wish to settle.' Despite appearances these testimonies have little weight when compared with Morley Roberts's words. Algernon Gissing was not

living with his brother when Payn made his extraordinary demand. As Payn died in 1898 and George Smith, the head of the firm, in 1901, it is hardly surprising that no one could confirm the statement originally made by the *Outlook* obituarist.

12 Pierre Coustillas, 'Thomas Seccombe Writes the Gissing Entry in the D.N.B.,' *Gissing Newsletter*, October 1977, pp. 1-18, and January 1978, pp. 18-34.

13 Letter to Katie (Algernon Gissing's wife), 22 November 1887, Yale.

14 Berg Coll.

15 Letter of 25 March 1888, Berg Coll.

16 Letter of 6 December 1888, Yale. Published in *The Letters of George Gissing to Eduard Bertz*, ed. Arthur C. Young, London: Constable, 1961, p. 21.

17 For references to reviews of the book, see the Bibliography.

18 'Literature of the Day,' *Daily Telegraph*, 25 December 1888, p. 7.

19 *George Gissing: Essays and Fiction*, ed. Pierre Coustillas, Baltimore and London. The Johns Hopkins Press, 1970, pp. 204-26. The relationship between the short story, probably written in 1881, and the novel is discussed in the introduction to this volume.

20 Berg Coll. *Letters of George Gissing to His Family*, p. 167.

21 As quoted by Patricia Hollis in *Women in Public: The Women's Movement 1850-1900*, London: George Allen & Unwin, 1979, p. 90.

22 Chapter of Governesses: A Study of the Governess in English Fiction 1800-1949, London: Cohen & West, 1949, p. 10.

23 Patricia Thomson, *The Victorian Heroine: A Changing Ideal 1837-1873*, Oxford University Press, 1956, p. 39.

24 Berg Coll.

25 Spring V.

A LIFE'S MORNING

A LIFE'S MORNING

BY

GEORGE GISSING

AUTHOR OF 'DEMOS' 'THYRZA' ETC.

A NEW EDITION

LONDON
SMITH, ELDER, & CO., 15 WATERLOO PLACE
1890

CONTENTS.

———◦◦◦———

A LIFE'S MORNING.

CHAPTER I.

AN UNDERGRADUATE AT LEISURE.

WILFRID ATHEL went down invalided a few days after the beginning of Trinity term. The event was not unanticipated. At Christmas it had been clear enough that he was overtaxing himself; his father remarked on the fact with anxiety, and urged moderation, his own peculiar virtue. Wilfrid, whose battle with circumstances was all before him, declined to believe that the body was anything but the very humble servant of the will. So the body took its revenge.

He had been delicate in childhood, and the stage of hardy naturalism which interposes itself between tender juvenility and the birth of self-consciousness did not in his case last long enough to establish his frame in the vigour to which it was tending. There was nothing sickly about him; it was only an excess of nervous vitality that would not allow body to keep pace with mind. He was a boy to be, intellectually, held in leash, said the doctors. But that was easier said than done. What system of sedatives could one apply to a youngster whose imagination wrought him to a fever during a simple walk by the seashore, who if books were forcibly withheld consoled himself with the composition of five-act tragedies, interspersed with lyrics to which he supplied original strains? Mr. Athel conceived a theory that such exuberance of emotionality might be counterbalanced by studies of a strictly positive nature; a tutor was engaged to ground young Wilfrid in mathematics and the physical sciences. The result was that the tutor's enthusiasm for these pursuits communicated

itself after a brief repugnance to the versatile pupil; instincts
of mastery became as vivid in the study of Euclid and the
chemical elements as formerly in the humaner paths of learning; the plan had failed. In the upshot Wilfrid was sent to
school; if that did not develop the animal in him, nothing
would.

He was not quite three-and-twenty when the break-down
removed him from Oxford. Going to Balliol with a scholar-
ship, he had from the first been marked for great things, at
all events by the measure of the schools. Removal from the
system of home education had in truth seemed to answer in
some degree the ends aimed at; the lad took his fair share of
cricket and football, and kept clear of nervous crises. At the
same time he made extraordinary progress with his books.
He acquired with extreme facility, and his ambition never
allowed him to find content in a second place; conquest became his habit; he grew to deem it the order of nature that
Wilfrid Athel's name should come first in the list. Hence a
reputation to support. During his early terms at Balliol he
fagged as hard as the mere dullard whose dear life depended
upon a first class and a subsequent tutorship. What he
would make of himself in the end was uncertain; university
distinctions would probably be of small moment to him as
soon as they were achieved, for already he spent the greater
portion of his strength in lines of study quite apart from the
curriculum, and fate had blessed him with exemption from
sordid cares. He led in a set devoted to what were called advanced ideas; without flattering himself that he was on the
way to solve the problem of the universe, he had satisfaction
in reviewing the milestones which removed him from the unconscious man, and already clutched at a measure of positive
wisdom in the suspicion that he might shortly have to lay
aside his school-books and recommence his education under
other teachers. As yet he was whole-hearted in the pursuit
of learning. The intellectual audacity which was wont to be
the key-note of his conversation did not, as his detractors held,
indicate mere bumptiousness and defect of self-measurement;
it was simply the florid redundancy of a young mind which
glories in its strength, and plays at victory in anticipation.
It was true that he could not brook the semblance of inferiority; if it were only five minutes' chat in the Quad, he
must come off with a phrase or an epigram; so those duller
heads who called Athel affected were not wholly without their

justification. Those who shrugged their shoulders with the
remark that he was overdoing it, and would not last out to
the end of the race, enjoyed a more indisputable triumph.
One evening, when Athel was taking the brilliant lead in an
argument on 'Fate, free-will, foreknowledge absolute,' his
brain began to whirl, tobacco-smoke seemed to have dulled
all the lights before his eyes, and he fell from his chair in a
fainting-fit.

He needed nothing but rest; that, however, was imperative. Mr. Athel brought him to London, and the family
went down at once to their house in Surrey. Wilfrid was an
only son and an only child. His father had been a widower
for nearly ten years; for the last three his house had been
directed by a widowed sister, Mrs. Rossall, who had twin girls.
Mr. Athel found it no particular hardship to get away from
town and pursue his work at The Firs, a delightful house in
the midst of Surrey's fairest scenery, nor would Mrs. Rossall
allow that the surrender of high season cost her any effort.
This lady had just completed her thirty-second year; her girls
were in their tenth. She was comely and knew it, but a con-
stitutional indolence had preserved her from becoming a
woman of fashion, and had nurtured in her a reflective mood
which, if it led to an unusual originality of thought, at all
events contributed to an appearance of culture. At the time
of her husband's death she was at the point where graceful
inactivity so often degenerates into slovenliness. Mrs. Rossall's
homekeeping tendencies and the growing childhood of her
twins tended to persuade her that her youth was gone; even
the new spring fashions stirred her to but languid interest,
and her music, in which she had some attainments, was all
but laid aside. With widowhood began a new phase of her
life. Her mourning was unaffected; it led her to pietism;
she spent her days in religious observance, and her nights in
the study of the gravest literature. She would have entered
the Roman Church but for her brother's interposition. The
end of this third year of discipline was bringing about another
change, perhaps less obvious to herself than to those who
marked her course with interest, as several people did. Her
reading became less ascetic, she passed to George Herbert
and the 'Christian Year,' and by way of the decoration of
altars proceeded to thought for her personal adornment. A
certain journal of society which she had long ago abandoned
began to show itself occasionally in her rooms, though only

as yet by oversight left to view. She spoke with her brother on the subject of certain invitations, long neglected, and did not seem displeased when he went beyond her own motion to propose the issuing of cards for a definite evening. Then came Wilfrid's break-down. There was really no need, said Mr. Athel, that she should transfer herself immediately to the country, just when everybody was well settled in town. But Mrs. Rossall preferred to go; she was not sure that the juncture had not some connection with her own spiritual life. And she maintained, on the whole, a seemly cheerfulness.

Mr. Athel was an Egyptologist of some distinction. Though not in person or manner suggestive of romantic antecedents, he had yet come by this taste in a way which bordered on romance. Travelling in Southern Europe at about the age which Wilfrid had now reached, he had the good fortune to rescue from drowning an Italian gentleman then on a tour in Greece. The Italian had a fair daughter, who was travelling with him, and her, after an acquaintance of a few weeks, Athel demanded by way of recompense. Her father was an enthusiastic student of Egyptian antiquities; the Englishman plied at one and the same time his wooing and the study of hieroglyphics, with marked success in both directions. The Mr. Athel who at that time represented parental authority, or at all events claimed filial deference, was anything but pleased with the step his son had taken; he was a highly respectable dealer in grain, and, after the manner of highly respectable men of commerce, would have had his eldest son espouse some countrywoman yet more respectable. It was his opinion that the lad had been entrapped by an adventurous foreigner. Philip Athel, who had a will of his own, wedded his Italian maiden, brought her to England, and fought down prejudices. A year or two later he was at work in Egypt, where he remained for some twelve months; his studies progressed. Subsequently he published certain papers which were recognised as valuable. Wilfrid found the amusement of his childhood in his father's pursuit; he began to decipher hieratic not much later than he learned to read English. Scarabs were his sacred playthings, and by the time of his going to school he was able to write letters home in a demotic which would not perhaps have satisfied Champollion or Brugsch, but yet was sufficiently marvellous to his schoolfellows and gratifying to his father.

For the rest, Philip Athel was a typical English gentleman. He enjoyed out-of-door sports as keenly as he did the

pursuit of his study; he had scarcely known a day's illness in
his life, owing, he maintained, to the wisdom with which he
arranged his day. Three hours of study was, he held, as
much as any prudent man would allow himself. He was
always in excellent spirits, ever ready to be of service to a
friend, lived with much moderation on victuals of the best
quality procurable, took his autumnal holiday abroad in a
gentlemanly manner. With something of Liberatio Radicalism in his political views, he combined a stout respect for
British social institutions; affecting to be above vulgar prejudices, he was in reality much prepossessed in favour of
hereditary position, and as time went on did occasionally half
wish that the love he had bestowed on his Italian wife had
been given to some English lady of 'good' family. He was
liberal, frank, amiably autocratic in his home, apt to be
peppery with inferiors who missed the line of perfect respect,
candid and reasonable with equals or superiors. For his boy
he reserved a store of manly affection, seldom expressing
itself save in bluff fashion; his sister he patronised with
much kindness, though he despised her judgment. One had
now and then a feeling that his material circumstances aided
greatly in making him the genial man he was, that with beef
and claret of inferior quality he might not have been altogether so easy to get along with. But that again was an
illustration of the English character.

We find the family assembling for breakfast at The Firs
one delightful morning at the end of July. The windows of
the room were thrown open, and there streamed in with the
sunlight fresh and delicious odours, tonics alike of mind and
body. From the Scotch firs whence the dwelling took its
name came a scent which mingled with wafted breath from
the remoter heather, and the creepers about the house front,
the lovely bloom and leafage skirting the lawn, contributed
to the atmosphere of health and joy. It was nine o'clock.
The urn was on the gleaming table, the bell was sounding,
Mr. Athel stepped in straight from the lawn, fresh after his
ten minutes' walk about the garden. Wilfrid Athel appeared
at the same moment; he was dark-complexioned and had
black, glossy hair; his cheeks were hollower than they should
have been, but he had not the aspect of an invalid. Mrs.
Rossall glided into the room behind him, fresh, fair, unde-
monstrative. Then came the twins, by name Patty and
Minnie, delicate, with promise of their mother's English style

of beauty; it was very hard to distinguish them, their uncle had honestly given up the pretence long ago, and occasionally remonstrated with his sister on the absurdity of dressing them exactly alike. The last to enter the room was the governess, Miss Emily Hood.

Mr. Athel, having pronounced a grace, mentioned that he thought of running up to town; did anybody wish to give him a commission? Mrs. Rossall looked thoughtful, and said she would make a note of two or three things.

'I haven't much faith in that porridge regimen, Wilf,' remarked the master of the house, as he helped himself to chicken and tongue. 'We are not Highlanders. It's dangerous to make diet too much a matter of theory. Your example is infectious; first the twins; now Miss Hood. Edith, do you propose to become a pervert to porridge?'

'I have no taste for it,' replied his sister, who had become absent-minded.

'There's a certain dishonesty about it, moreover,' Mr. Athel pursued. 'Porridge should be eaten with salt. Milk *and* sugar—didn't I hear a suggestion of golden syrup, more honestly called treacle, yesterday? These things constitute evasion, self-deception at the least. In your case, Miss Hood, the regimen is clearly fruitful of ill results.'

'Of what kind, Mr. Athel?'

'Obviously it leads to diminution of appetite. You were in the habit of eating a satisfactory breakfast; at present some two ounces of that farinaceous mess——'

'My dear Philip!' interposed Mrs. Rossall, still absently.

'I hold that I am within my rights,' asserted her brother. 'If Miss Hood goes down into Yorkshire in a state of emaciation——'

Wilfrid and the twins showed amusement.

'To begin with,' pursued Mr. Athel, 'I hold that sweet food the first thing in the morning is a mistake; the appetite is checked in an artificial way, and impaired. Even coffee——'

'You would recommend a return to flagons of ale?' suggested Wilfrid.

'I am not sure that it wasn't better dietetically.'

Mrs. Rossall had taken an egg, but, after fruitlessly chipping at the shell throughout this conversation, put down her spoon and appeared to abandon the effort to commence her meal. Presently she broke silence, speaking with some diffidence.

'I really think I will go to town with you, Philip,' she said. 'I want some things you can't very well get me, and then I ought to go and see the Redwings. I might persuade Beatrice to come to us for a day or two.'

'Do so by all means. You're quite sure,' he added with a smile, 'that I couldn't save you the trouble of the journey? I have no objection to visiting the Redwings.'

'I think it will be better if I go myself,' replied Mrs. Rossall, with a far-off look. 'I might call on one or two other people.'

Having decided this point, she found herself able to crack the egg. The anticipation of her day in London made her quite gay throughout the meal.

The carriage was at the door by ten o'clock, to drive to Dealing, the nearest station, some four miles away. The twins had gone upstairs with Miss Hood to their lessons, and Wilfrid was sauntering about the hall. His father paused by him on the way to the carriage.

'What do you propose to do with yourself, Wilf?' he asked.

'Ride, I think.'

'Do. Go over to Hilstead and lunch there. Capital lunch they give you at the inn; the last time I was there they cooked me one of the best chops I ever ate. Oberon wants exercise; make a day of it.'

'Very well.'

'You're not looking quite so well, I'm afraid,' remarked his father, with genuine solicitude in his tone. 'Haven't been reading, have you?'

'No.'

'No impudence, mind, I must stop that porridge regimen; it doesn't suit you. Ready, Edith?' he shouted heartily at the foot of the stairs.

Mrs. Rossall came down, buttoning her gloves.

'If I were you, Wilf,' she said, 'I'd go off somewhere for the day. The twins will only worry you.'

Wilfrid laughed.

'I am going to eat unexampled chops at the "Waggoner" in Hilstead,' he replied.

'That's right. Good-bye, my dear boy. I wish you'd get fatter.'

'Pooh, I'm all right.'

The landau rolled away. Wilfrid still loitered in the hall,

a singular look of doubt on his face. In a room above one of
the twins was having a music lesson ; a certain finger-exercise
was being drummed with persistent endeavour at accuracy.

'How can she bear that morning after morning?' the
young man murmured to himself.

He took his straw hat and went round to the stables.
Oberon was being groomed. Wilfrid patted the horse's sleek
neck, and talked a little with the man. At length he made
up his mind to go and prepare for riding ; Oberon would be
ready for him in a few minutes.

In the porch Patty ran to meet him.

'Truant!' Wilfrid exclaimed. 'Have I caught you in the
act of escape?'

'I was going to look for you,' said the child, putting her
arm through his and swinging upon him. 'We want to know
if you'll be back for lunch.'

'Who wants to know?'

'I and Minnie and Miss Hood.'

'Oh, you are Patty, then, are you?'

This was an old form of joke. The child shook her dark
curls with a half-annoyed gesture, but still swung on her
cousin as he moved into the house. Wilfrid passed his arm
about her playfully.

'Can't you make up your mind, Wilf?' she asked.

'Oh yes, my mind is quite made up,' he replied, with a
laugh.

'And won't you tell me?'

'Tell you? Ah, about lunch. No, I shall not be back.'

'You won't? Oh, I am sorry.'

'Why are you sorry, indistinguishable little maiden?' he
asked, drawing out one of her curls between his fingers, and
letting it spring back again into its circling beauty.

'We thought it would be so nice, we four at lunch.'

'I am warned to avoid you. The tone of conversation
would try my weak head ; I am not capable yet of intellectual
effort.'

The little girl looked at him with puzzled eyes.

'Well, it can't be helped,' she said. 'I must go back to
my lessons.'

She ran off, and Wilfrid went up to his dressing-room.
When he came down, Oberon was pawing the gravel before
the door. He mounted and rode away.

His spirits, which at first seemed to suffer some depression, took vigour once more from the air of the downs. He put Oberon at a leap or two, then let the breeze sing in his ears as he was borne at a gallop over the summer land, golden with sunlight. In spite of his still worn look, health was manifest in the upright vigour of his form, and in his eyes gleamed the untroubled joy of existence. Hope just now was strong within him, a hope defined and pointing to an end attainable; he knew that henceforth the many bounding and voiceful streams of his life would unite in one strong flow onward to a region of orient glory which shone before him as the bourne hitherto but dimly imagined. On, Oberon, on! No speed that would not lag behind the fore flight of a heart's desire. Let the stretch of green shadowing woodland sweep by like a dream; let the fair, sweet meadow-sides smile for a moment and vanish; let the dark hill-summits rise and sink. It is the time of youth and hope, of boundless faith in the world's promises, of breathless pursuit.

Hilstead was gained long before lunch could be thought of. Wilfrid rode on, and circled back towards the hostelry famous for chops about the hour of noon. He put up his horse, and strayed about the village till his meal was ready; after he had eaten it he smoked a cigar among hollyhocks and sunflowers When impatience possessed him. He looked at his watch several times, annoyed to find that so little of the day was spent. When he at last set forth again, it was to ride at walking pace in the direction of home. He reached a junction of roads, and waited there for several minutes, unable to decide upon his course. He ended by throwing the reins on Oberon's neck.

'Go which way you will,' he said aloud.

Oberon paced forward to the homeward route.

'So be it. On, then! An hour will bring us to The Firs.'

The house was all but reached, when Wilfrid caught a glimpse of a straw hat moving into a heath-clad hollow a hundred yards from the road. He pressed on. At the gate stood a gardener.

'James,' he cried, leaping down, 'take the horse to the stable, will you?'

And, instead of going up to the house, he walked back in the direction he had come till he reached the hollow in which the straw hat had disappeared. Miss Hood sat on the ground, reading. She was about to rise, but Wilfrid begged her not to move, and threw himself into a reclining posture.

'I saw you as I rode past,' he said, in a friendly way. 'I suppose the twins are straying?'

'They are at Greenhaws,' was the reply, 'Mrs. Winter called for them immediately after lunch. She will bring them back early in the evening.'

'Ah!'

He plucked sprigs of heather. Miss Hood turned to her book.

'I've had a magnificent ride,' Wilfrid began again. 'Surely there is no country in England so glorious as this. Don't you enjoy it?'

'Very much.'

'I have never seen the Yorkshire moors. The scenery, of course, is of a much wilder kind?'

'I have not seen them myself,' said the governess.

'I thought you might have taken your holidays sometimes in that direction.'

'No. We used to go to a seaside place in Lincolnshire called Cleethorpes. I suppose you never heard of it?'

'I think not.'

Wilfrid continued to pluck heather, and let his eyes catch a glimpse of her face now and then. Miss Hood was a year younger than himself, and had well outgrown girlishness. She was of very slight build, looked indeed rather frail; but her face, though lacking colour, had the firmness of health. It was very broad at the forehead, and tapered down into narrowness; the eyes seemed set at an unusual distance from each other, though the nose was thin and of perfect form, its profile making but a slight angle away from the line of the brows. Her lips were large, but finely curved; the chin was prominent, the throat long. She had warm brown hair.

Few would at first sight have called her face beautiful, but none could deny the beauty of her hands. Ungloved at present, they lay on the open pages of the book, unsurpassable for delicate loveliness. When he did not venture to look higher, Wilfrid let his eyes feed on the turn of the wrist, the faint blue lines and sinuous muscles, the pencilling about the finger-joints, the delicate white and pink nails.

Miss Hood was habitually silent when in the company of others than the children. When she replied to a question it was without timidity, but in few, well-chosen words. Yet her manner did not lack cheerfulness; she impressed no one as being unhappy, and alone with the twins she was often

gay enough. She was self-possessed, and had the manners of
a lady, though in her position this was rather to be observed
in what she refrained from doing than in what she did.
Wilfrid had, on first meeting her, remarked to himself that it
must imply a certain force of individuality to vary so distinctly from the commonplace even under the disadvantage of
complete self-suppression ; he had now come to understand
better the way in which that individuality betrayed itself.

'Shall you go to Cleethorpes this year?' was his next
question.

'I think not. I shall most likely pass the holidays at
home,'

'And study electricity?'

In a former conversation she had surprised him by some
unexpected knowledge of the principles of electricity, and
explained the acquirement by telling him that this subject
was her father's favourite study. Wilfrid put the question
now with a smile.

'Yes, very likely,' she replied, smiling also, but faintly
'It gives my father pleasure when I do so.'

'You have not a keen interest in the subject yourself?'

'I try to have.'

Her voice was of singular quality; if she raised it the
effect was not agreeable, owing possibly to its lack of strength,
but in low tones, such as she employed at present, it fell on
the ear with a peculiar sweetness, a natural melody in its
modulation.

'The way in which you speak of your father interests me,'
said Wilfrid, leaning his chin upon his hand, and gazing at
her freely. 'You seem so united with him in sympathy.'

She did not turn her eyes to him, but her face gathered
brightness.

'In sympathy, yes,' she replied, speaking now with more
readiness. Our tastes often differ, but we are always at one
in feeling. We have been companions ever since I can remember.'

'Is your mother living?'

'Yes.'

Something in the tone of the brief affirmative kept Wilfrid
from further questioning.

'I wonder,' he said, 'what you think of the relations
existing between myself and my father. We are excellent
friends, don't you think? Strange—one doesn't think much

about such things till some occasion brings them forward. Whether there is deep sympathy between us, I couldn't say. Certainly there are many subjects on which I should not dream of speaking to him unless necessity arose ; partly, I suppose, that is male reserve, and partly English reserve. If novels are to be trusted, French parents and children speak together with much more freedom ; on the whole that must be better.'

She made no remark.

' My father,' he continued, ' is eminently a man of sense ; if I reflect on my boyhood, I see how admirable his treatment of me has always been. I fancy I must have been at one time rather hard to manage ; I know I was very passionate and stubbornly self-willed. Yet he neither let me have my own way nor angered me by his opposition. In fact, he made me respect him. Now that we stand on equal terms, I dare say he has something of the same feeling towards myself. And so it comes that we are excellent friends.'

She listened with a scarcely perceptible smile.

' Perhaps this seems to you a curiously dispassionate way of treating such a subject,' Wilfrid added, with a laugh. ' It illustrates what I meant in saying I doubted whether there was deep sympathy between us. Your own feeling for your father is clearly one of devotedness. You would think no sacrifice of your own wishes too great if he asked it of you.'

' I cannot imagine any sacrifice, which my father could ask, that I should refuse.'

She spoke with some difficulty, as if she wished to escape the subject.

' Perhaps that is a virtue that your sex helps to explain,' said Wilfrid, musingly.

' You do not know,' he added, when a bee had hummed between them for half a minute, ' how constant my regret is that my mother did not live till I was old enough to make a friend of her. You know that she was an Italian ? There was a sympathy taken out of my life. I believe I have more of the Italian nature than the English, and I know my mother's presence would be priceless to me now that I could talk with her. What unsatisfactory creatures we are as children, so imperfect, so deficient ! It is worse with boys than with girls. Compare, for instance, the twins with boys of ten. What coarse, awkward, unruly lumps of boisterousness youngsters mostly are at that age ! I dislike boys, and

more than ever when I remember myself at that stage.
What an insensible, ungrateful, brainless, and heartless brat
I was ! '

' You must be wrong in one respect,' she returned, watching a large butterfly. ' You could not have been brainless.'

' Oh, the foundation of tolerable wits was there, no doubt;
but it is just that undeveloped state that irritates me. Suppose I were now ten years old, and that glorious butterfly
before me ; should I not leap at it and stick a pin through it
—young savage ? Precisely what a Hottentot boy would do,
except that he would be free from the apish folly of pretending
a scientific interest, not really existing. I rejoice to have
lived out of my boyhood ; I would not go through it again for
anything short of a thousand years of subsequent maturity.'

She just glanced at him, a light of laughter in her eyes.
She was abandoning herself to the pleasure of hearing him
speak.

' That picture of my mother,' he pursued, dropping his
voice again, ' does not do her justice. Even at twelve years
old—(she died when I was twelve)—I could not help seeing
and knowing how beautiful she was. I have thought of her
of late more than I ever did ; sometimes I suffer a passion of
grief that one so beautiful and lovable has gone and left a
mere dumb picture. I suppose even my memory of her will
grow fainter and fainter, founded as it is on imperfect understanding, dim appreciation. She used to read Italian to me
—first the Italian, then the English—and I thought it, as
often as not, a bore to have to listen to her ! Thank Heaven,
I have the book she used, and can now go over the pieces,
and try to recall her voice.'

The butterfly was gone, but the bee still hummed about
them. The hot afternoon air was unstirred by any breeze.

' How glad I am,' Wilfrid exclaimed when he had brooded
for a few moments, ' that I happened to see you as I rode
past ! I should have wandered restlessly about the house in
vain, seeking for some one to talk to. And you listen so
patiently. It is pleasant to be here and talk so freely of things
I have always had to keep in my own mind. Look, do look
at that bastion of cloud over the sycamore ! What glorious
gradation of tints ! What a snowy crown ! '

' That is a pretty spray,' he added, holding to her one that
he had plucked.

She looked at it ; then, as he still held it out, took it from him. The exquisite fingers touched his own redder and coarser ones.

'Have you friends in Dunfield?' he asked.

'Friends?'

'Any real friend, I mean—any girl who gives you real companionship?'

'Scarcely that.'

'How shall you spend your time when you are not deep in electrics? What do you mean to read these holidays?'

'Chiefly German, I think. I have only just begun to read it.'

'And I can't read it at all. Now and then I make a shot at the meaning of a note in a German edition of some classical author, every time fretting at my ignorance. But there is so endlessly much to do, and a day is so short.'

'Isn't it hateful,' he broke forth, 'this enforced idleness of mine? To think that weeks and weeks go by and I remain just where I was, when the loss of an hour used to seem to me an irreparable misfortune. I have such an appetite for knowledge, surely the unhappiest gift a man can be endowed with; it leads to nothing but frustration. Perhaps the appetite weakens as one grows in years; perhaps the sphere of one's keener interests contracts; I hope it may be so. At times I cannot work—I mean, I could not—for a sense of the vastness of the field before me. I should like you to see my rooms at Balliol. Shelves have long since refused to take another volume; floor, tables, chairs, every spot is heaped. And there they lie; hosts I have scarcely looked into, many I shall never have time to take up to the end of my days.'

'You have the satisfaction of being able to give your whole time to study.'

'There is precisely the source of dissatisfaction! My whole time, and that wholly insufficient. I have a friend, a man I envy intensely; he has taken up the subject of Celtic literature; gives himself to it with single-heartedness, cares for nothing that does not connect itself therewith; will pursue it throughout his life; will know more of it than any man living. My despair is the universality of my interests. I can think of no branch of study to which I could not surrender myself with enthusiasm; of course I shall never master one. My subject is the history of humanity; I would know everything that man has done or thought or felt. I cannot separate lines of study. Philology is a passion with me, but how shall I part the history of speech from the history of thought? The etymology of any single word will hold me for hours; to follow it up I must traverse centuries of human culture. They tell me I have a faculty for philosophy, in the narrow sense of the word; alas! that narrow sense implies an exhaustive knowledge of speculation in the past and of every result of science born in our own time. Think of the sunny spaces in the world's history, in each of which one could linger for ever! Athens at her fairest, Rome at her grandest, the glorious savagery of Merovingian courts, the kingdom of Frederick II, the Moors in Spain, the magic of Renaissance Italy—to become a citizen of any one age means a lifetime of endeavour. It is easy to fill one's head with names and years, but that only sharpens my hunger. Then there is the world of art; I would know every subtlest melody of verse in every tongue, enjoy with perfectly instructed taste every form that man has carved or painted. I fear to enter museums and galleries; I am distracted by the numberless desires that seize upon me, depressed by the hopelessness of satisfying them. I cannot even enjoy music from the mere feeling that I do not enjoy it enough, that I have not had time to study it, that I shall never get at its secret. . . . And when is one to live? I cannot lose myself in other men's activity and enjoyments. I must have a life of my own, outside the walls of a library. It would be easy to give up all ambition of knowledge, to forget all the joy and sorrow that has been and passed into nothingness; to know only the eternity of a present hour. Might one not learn more in one instant of unreflecting happiness than by toiling on to a mummied age, only to know in the end the despair of never having lived?

He again raised his eyes to her face. It was fixed in a cold, absent gaze; her lips hardened into severity, the pose of her head impressive, noble. Athel regarded her for several moments; she was revealing to him more of her inner self than he had yet divined.

'What are your thoughts?' he asked quietly.

She smiled, recovering her wonted passiveness.

'Have you not often much the same troubles?'

'They are only for the mind which is strong enough to meet and overcome them,' she replied.

'But look, my mind has given way already! I am imbecile. For ever I shall be on the point of a break-down, and

each successive one will bring me nearer to some final catastrophe—perhaps the lunatic asylum—who knows ?'

' I should think,' she said gravely, ' that you suggested a
truth. Very likely your mind will contract its range and
cease to aim at the impossible.'

' But tell me, have you not yourself already attained that
wisdom ? Why should you make pretences of feebleness which
does not mark you ? You have a mind as active as my own ;
I know that perfectly well. What is your secret of contentment ? Won't you help me in this miserable plight ? '

' No, Mr. Athel, I have none but very ordinary powers of
mind, and perhaps it is my recognition of that which keeps
me contented. There is indeed one principle of guidance
which I have worked out for myself——'

' Ah ! And that ?'

' It will not enlighten you, for it is only the choice of a
natural and easy course, seeing that difficult ones are closed.
The literature of learning is out of my reach, so I limit myself to the literature of beauty, and in this I try to keep to
the best.'

' You are right, you are right ! To know the masterpieces
of literature, pure literature, poetry in its widest sense ; that
is the wise choice. Think ; we feed ourselves with the second-
hand wisdom of paltry philosophisers and critics, and Shakespeare waits outside the door with the bread of life. From
Homer—— Alas ! you do not read Greek ?'

She shook her head.

' And you work at German ! In Heaven's name change
your language forthwith ! Why should you not know Greek ?
You *must* know Greek ! I will give you books, I will advise
you, show you the essentials to begin with. There are still a
few days before you go into Yorkshire ; you can work during
the holidays on lines I shall set you ; you can write and tell
me your——'

He paused, for her face had lost its smile, and wore again
that coldly respectful look which she seldom put off save in
her privacy with the children. For the last quarter of an
hour he had marked in her quite another aspect ; the secret
meanings of her face had half uttered themselves in eye and
lip. His last words seemed to recall her to the world of fact.
She made a slight movement and closed the book on her
lap.

' Greek is more than I can undertake, Mr. Athel,' she

said in a quietly decided tone. 'I must be content with translations.'

'Translations! You would not say that so calmly if you knew what you were renouncing. Everything, everything in literature, I would give up to save my Greek. You will learn it, I know you will; some day I shall hear you read the hexameters as beautifully as you read English poetry to the girls. Will you not begin if I beg you to?'

The elbow on which he rested moved a few inches nearer to her. He saw the pearly shadows waver upon her throat, and her lips tremble into rigidity.

'My time in the holidays will be very limited,' she said. 'I have undertaken to give some help to a friend who is preparing to become a teacher, and '—she tried to smile—'I don't think I must do more work whilst at home than is really necessary.'

'No, that is true,' Wilfrid assented unwillingly. 'Never mind, there is plenty of time. Greek will be overcome, you will see. When we are all back in town and the days are dull, then I shall succeed in persuading you.'

She looked about her as if with thought of quitting her place. Her companion was drawn into himself; he stroked mechanically with his finger-tips the fronds of bracken near him.

'I suppose I shall go up again in October,' he began. 'I wish there were no necessity for it.'

'But surely it is your one desire?' the other replied in genuine surprise.

'Not to return to Oxford. A few months ago it would have been, but this crisis in my life has changed me. I don't think I shall adapt myself again to those conditions. I want to work in a freer way. I had a positive zeal even for examinations; now that seems tame—well, boyish. I believe I have outgrown that stage; I feel a reluctance to go back to school. I suppose I must take my degree, and so on, but it will all be against the grain.'

'Your feeling will most likely alter when you have thoroughly recovered your health.'

'No, I don't think it will. Practically my health is all right. You don't,' he added with a smile, 'regard me as an irresponsible person, whose feeble remarks are to be received with kind allowance?'

'No, I did not mean that.'

He gazed at her, and his face showed a growing trouble.

'You do not take too seriously what I said just now about the weakness of my mind? It would be horrible if you thought I had worked myself into a state of amiable imbecility, and was incapable henceforth of acting, thinking, or speaking with a sound intellect. Tell me, say in plain words that is not your way of interpreting me.'

He had become very much in earnest. Raising himself to a position in which he rested on one hand, he looked straight into her face.

'Why don't you reply? Why don't you speak?'

'Because, Mr. Athel, it is surely needless to say that I have no such thought.'

'No, it is not needless; and even now you speak in a way which troubles me. Do not look away from me. What has my aunt told you about me?'

She turned her face to him. Her self-command was so complete that not a throb of her leaping heart betrayed itself in vein or muscle. She even met his eyes with a placid gaze which he felt as a new aspect of her countenance.

'Mrs. Rossall has never spoken to me of your health,' she said.

'But my father's jokes; he has a way of humorous exaggeration. You of course understand that; you don't take seriously all he says?'

'I think I can distinguish between jest and earnest.'

'For all that, you speak of the recovery of my health as if I were still far from the wholly rational stand-point. So far from my being mentally unsound, this rest has been a growing-time with me. Before, I did nothing but heap my memory with knowledge of books; now I have had leisure to gather knowledge of a deeper kind. I was a one-sided academical monster; it needed this new sense to make me human. The old college life is no longer my ideal; I doubt if it will be possible. At any rate, I shall hurry over the rest of my course as speedily as may be, that I may begin really to live. You must credit what I am saying; I want you to give me distinct assurance that you do so. If I have the least doubt, it will trouble my mind in earnest.'

Miss Hood rose to her feet in that graceful effortless way of which girls have the secret.

'You attribute a meaning to my words that I never thought of,' she said, again in the distant respectful manner.

Wilfrid also rose.

'And you give me credit for understanding myself, for being as much master of my mind as I am of my actions?'

'Surely I do, Mr. Athel.'

'You are going to the house? It is nearly five o'clock; your conscience tells you that a civilised being must drink tea. I think I shall walk over to Greenhaws; I may as well save Mrs. Winter the trouble of bringing back the children.'

He hesitated before moving away.

'How little that cloud has changed its form! I should like to stay here and watch it till sunset. In a week I suppose I shall be looking at some such cloud over Mont Blanc. And you, in Dunfield.'

'No, there we have only mill-smoke.'

She smiled, and passed from the hollow to the road.

CHAPTER II.

BEATRICE AND WITH

MIDWAY in breakfast next morning, at a moment when Mrs. Rossall was describing certain originalities of drawing-room decoration observed on the previous day at a house in town, the half-open door admitted a young lady who had time to glance round the assembled family before her presence was observed. In appearance she was very interesting. The tints of her fine complexion were warmed by exercise in the morning air, and her dark eyes brightened by pleasurable excitement; she carried her hat in her hand, and seemed to have been walking bare-headed, for there were signs of wind-play in her abundant black hair. But neither face nor attire suggested rusticity: the former was handsome, spirited, with a hint of uncommon things in its changeful radiance; the latter was the result of perfect taste choosing at will among the season's costumes. At her throat were fastened two blossoms of wild rose, with the dew still on them, and the hand which held her lace-trimmed sunshade carried also a spray of meadow-sweet.

Mr. Athel, looking up from the end of the table, was the first to perceive her.

'*Guardami ben : ben son, ben son Beatrice !*' he exclaimed, rising and moving from his place. ' But how in the world has she got here ? '

' Beatrice ! ' cried Mrs. Rossall, following the general direction of eyes. ' Here already ! But you surely haven't come from town this morning ? '

' But indeed I have,' was the reply, in a joyous voice, whose full, rich quality took the ear captive. ' Will you let me sit down just as I am ? Patty, here's a rose for you, and, Minnie, another for you.' She took them from her dress. ' How do you do, Mr. Wilfrid ? '

The governess was mentioned to her by name ; Beatrice looked at her steadfastly for a moment.

' But how have you got here ? ' inquired Mrs. Rossall. ' You must have left London at an unheard-of hour ; and how have you come from Dealing ? '

' Clearly she has walked,' said Mr. Athel. ' Don't you see the spoils of her progress ? '

' Oh yes, I have walked,' replied the girl. ' I suppose I'm in a dreadful state ; towards the end I almost ran. I was so afraid lest I should miss breakfast, and you can't imagine how hungry I am. Is that oatmeal porridge you are eating, Mr. Wilfrid ? Oh, do let me have some ; how delicious it will be ! '

' Nonsense, Beatrice,' interposed Mrs. Rossall. ' Let Mr. Athel give you some of that pâté, or will you have——'

' I've been a vegetarian for a month,' was the reply.

' You don't mean it ? '

' Most strictly. No—eggs are not permitted ; only the feebler school allows them. You can't think how much better I have been in body and mind since I adopted the new diet.'

' But whatever train did you start by ? ' pressed Mrs. Rossall.

' Half-past six. I never can sleep these short summer nights. I was up about five o'clock, and just as I was going to read I saw the railway time-table. I looked for the first train and determined to come by it. I wrote a short note to let mother know what had become of me, then in a minute or two I got my things packed, and last of all stole out of the house to find a cab. Luckily, a policeman was just passing the door ; he found one for me in no time. Not a soul was up, so I dragged the trunk out on to the landing, and then made the cabman creep upstairs like a burglar to fetch it.

Of course he thought I was running away; he enjoyed the joke wonderfully; you should have seen his smile when I paid him at the station. Perhaps you'll let them fetch my luggage before lunch?'

'But won't your mother be alarmed?' asked Mrs. Rossall.

'Why should she? She knows I am very capable of taking care of myself. I wouldn't have missed this walk for anything. I only lost my way once, and then, luckily, a farmer came driving along: he told me I had half a mile more. I trebled his distance, which made it about right.'

'It's a good four miles from the station,' remarked Mr. Athel.

'Is It? If I hadn't been so hungry I shouldn't have minded as much again. You're not angry with me, Mrs. Rossall, for coming before I was expected?'

A curious note of irresponsible childishness came out now and then in her talk, as in this last question; it was the more noticeable for the air of maturity and self-possession which on the whole characterised her. She continued to talk with much vivacity, making at the same time a hearty meal. Her place at the table was between Wilfrid and Patty; on the opposite side sat Miss Hood and Minnie. As often as her eyes fell upon the governess's face, they rested there for a moment, searchingly, as if with endeavour to recall some memory.

'Who is responsible for your vegetarianism?' Wilfrid asked. 'Is Mr. Cresset preaching the doctrine?'

'No, Mr. Cresset is not preaching the doctrine,' was the reply, in a tone which evidently contained reference to previous dissensions.

'Surely there is nothing offensive in the suggestion?' remarked the young man mildly.

'Yes, there is something offensive. Your references to Mr. Cresset are always offensive.'

'You do me injustice. Aunt, I take you to witness, didn't I praise ungrudgingly a sermon of his we heard last Christmas?'

'I remember quite well,' said Beatrice; 'you regarded it as extraordinary that anything good could come from that source. Mr. Athel, I take you to witness, wasn't that his tone?'

'Patty,' interposed Mrs. Rossall, 'do change your place and sit between those two; they never can be next each other without quarrelling.'

Breakfast drew out to unusual length. Miss Redwing was full of the season's news, and Mrs. Rossall's reviving interest in such vanities scarcely affected concealment. Mr. Athel, too, though he supported a jesting tone, clearly enjoyed listening to the girl's vivacious comments on the world which amuses itself. Wilfrid talked less than usual.

He and his father strolled together into the garden an hour later, and found Beatrice reclining in a hammock which had recently been suspended in a convenient spot. She had one hand beneath her head, the other held a large fan, with which she warded off stray flakes of sunlight falling between the leaves.

'Isn't this exquisite?' she cried. 'Let no one hint to me of stirring before lunch-time. I am going to enjoy absolute laziness.'

'I thought you would have preferred a gallop over the downs,' said Mr. Athel.

'Oh, we'll have that this afternoon; you may talk of it now, and I shall relish it in anticipation. Or, better still, sit down and tell us old stories about Egypt, and let us forget the age we live in.'

'What is amiss with the age?' inquired Mr. Athel, who stood smoking a cigar and was in his wonted state of satisfaction with himself and the universe.

'Everything is amiss. If you had been with me yesterday in a street I was visiting, not a quarter of a mile from home—— But I'm going to forget all that now. How deliciously warm it is here in the shade! I must have a hammock in our garden at Cowes.'

'When do you go back?' Mr. Athel asked.

'In about a fortnight. It has done mother no end of good; don't you think she looks remarkably well, Mrs. Rossall? I'm afraid she finds it a little dull though.'

When his father had returned to the house, Wilfrid sat on the grass and rested his head against the arm of the low garden chair in which Mrs. Rossall was reclining. The sound of a grass-cutter alone mingled with the light rustling of the trees. It was one of those perfect summer mornings when the sun's rays, though streaming from a cloudless sky, are tempered by a gentle haze in the upper regions of the air, when the zenith has a tinge of violet and on the horizon broods a reddish mist. From this part of the garden only a glimpse of the house was visible; an upper window with white cur-rains, cool, peaceful. All else on every side was verdure and bloom.

'Is it possible,' Beatrice asked, when there had been silence for a few moments, 'that I can have met Miss Hood anywhere before to-day? Her face is strangely familiar to me.'

'She has never been in London before she came to us,' said Mrs. Rossall.

'But you have relatives in Dunfield, I think?' remarked Wilfrid.

'To be sure,' said his aunt; 'she comes from Dunfield, in Yorkshire. Do you think you can have met her there?'

'Ah, that explains it,' Beatrice cried eagerly, 'I knew I had seen her, and I know now where it was. She gave lessons to my uncle's children. I saw her when I was staying there the last time, three—no, four years ago. I can't recall her by her name, but her face, oh, I remember it as clearly as possible.'

'What a memory you have, Beatrice!' said Mrs. Rossall.

'I never forget a face that strikes me.'

'In what way did Miss Hood's face strike you?' Wilfrid asked, as if in idle curiosity, and with some of the banter which always marked his tone to Beatrice.

'You would like some deep, metaphysical reason, but I am not advanced enough for that. I don't suppose I thought much about her at the time, but the face has stayed in my mind. But how old is she?'

'Two-and-twenty,' said Mrs. Rossall, smiling.

'A year older than myself; my impression was that she was more than that. I think I only saw her once; she was with us at lunch one day. We spoke of her shyness, I remember; she scarcely said a word all the time.'

'Yes, she is very shy,' assented Mrs. Rossall.

'That's a mistake, I think, aunt,' said Wilfrid; 'shyness is quite a different thing from reticence.'

'Reticent, then,' conceded the lady, with a smile to Beatrice. 'At all events, she is very quiet and agreeable and well-bred. It is such a good thing to have a governess who really seems well-bred; it does make it so much easier to treat her with consideration.'

'Do the children like her?' Beatrice asked.

'Very much indeed. And it's wonderful how she controls them; they are scatter-brained little creatures.'

'Will she go abroad with you?'

'Oh, no, I don't think that necessary.'

Wilfrid presently left the two to their gossip. The conversation naturally turned to him.

'How is his health?' Beatrice asked.

'He seems quite recovered. I don't think there was ever anything to occasion much alarm, but his father got frightened. I expect we shall bring him back from Switzerland as well as ever he was.'

'What ever has he done with himself the last two months?' mused the girl.

'Well, it has been rather hard to keep him occupied away from books. He has been riding a good deal, and smoking a good deal.'

'And talking a good deal?'

'Well, yes, Wilf is fond of talking,' admitted Mrs. Rossall, 'but I don't think he's anything like as positive as he was. He does now and then admit that other people may have an opinion which is worth entertaining. Celia Dawlish was with us a fortnight ago; she declared him vastly improved.'

'She told him so?'

'No, that was in private to me.'

'But I think Celia and he always got on well together,' said Beatrice in an idly meditative tone, moving the edge of her fan backwards and forwards a few inches above her face.

A few minutes later, after a silence, she said—

'Do you know what I am thinking?'

'What?' asked Mrs. Rossall, with an air of interest.

'That if I were to close my eyes and keep quiet I should very soon be fast asleep.'

The other laughed at the unexpected reply.

'Then why not do so, dear? It's warm enough; you couldn't take any harm.'

'I suppose the walk has tired me.'

'But if you had no sleep last night? How is it you can't sleep, I wonder? Is it the same when you are at Cowes?'

'No, only in London. Something troubles me; I feel that I have neglected duties. I hear voices, as distinct as yours now, reproving me for my idle, frivolous life.'

'Nonsense! I am sure you are neither idle nor frivolous. Do doze off, if you can, dear; I'll go and get something to read.'

' You won't be angry with me ? ' the girl asked, in the tone of an affectionate weary child.

' I shall if you use ceremony with me.'

Beatrice sighed, folded her hands upon the fan, and closed her lids. When Mrs. Rossall returned from the house with a magazine and a light shawl, the occupant of the hammock was already sound asleep. She threw the shawl with womanly skill and gentleness over the shapely body. When she had resumed her seat, she caught a glimpse of Wilfrid at a little distance ; her beckoned summons brought him near.

' Look,' she whispered, pointing to the hammock. ' When did you see a prettier picture ? '

The young man gazed with a free smile, the expression of critical appreciativeness. The girl's beauty stirred in him no mood but that. She slept with complete calm of feature ; the half-lights that came through the foliage made an exquisite pallor on her face, contrasting with the dark masses of her hair. Her bosom rose and fell in the softest sighing ; her pure throat was like marble, and her just parted lips seemed to need a protector from the bees. . . .

While she sleeps, let us learn a little more of her history. Some five-and-twenty years previously, Alfred Redwing was a lecturer on Greek and Latin at a small college in the North of England, making shift to live on a beggarly stipend. Handsome, pleasing, not quite thirty, he was well received in such semblance of society as his town offered, and, in spite of his defects as a suitor, he won for his wife a certain Miss Baxendale, the daughter of a well-to-do manufacturer. She brought him at once a few hundreds a year, and he pursued his college work in improved spirits. His wife had two brothers ; one had early gone to America, the other was thriving as a man of business in the town of Dunfield. With Laurence Baxendale, who dated his very occasional letters from various parts of the United States, the family might be said to have parted for good ; before leaving England he had got on ill terms with his father and brother, and it was only a persistent affection for his sister that caused him to give any sign of himself year after year. When this sister had been Mrs. Redwing for about two years, she one day received an intimation from solicitors that Laurence was dead and had left her the whole of a very considerable fortune, the product, mainly, of dealings in lumber. Mr. and Mrs. Redwing in fact found themselves possessed of nearly fourteen thousand a year, pro·

ceeding from most orderly investments. This would naturally involve a change in their mode of life. In the first place they paid a visit to America ; then they settled in London, where, about the same time, their only child, Beatrice was born. A month after the child's coming into the world, the father withdrew from it—into a private lunatic asylum. He had not been himself from the day when he heard of the fortune that had come to him ; such an access of blessedness was not provided for in the constitution of his mind. Probably few men of his imaginative temperament and hard antecedents could have borne the change without some little unsettling of mental balance ; we are framed to endure any amount of ill, but have to take our chance in the improbable event of vast joy befalling us. Poor Redwing conceived a suspicion that his wife desired to murder him ; one night as she was following him into their bedroom, he suddenly turned round, caught hold of her with violence, and flung her to the ground, demanding the knife which he protested he had seen gleam in her hand. It was no longer safe to live with him ; he was put under restraint, and never again knew freedom. In less than a year he died, a moping maniac.

Mrs. Redwing was an invalid thenceforth ; probably it was only the existence of her child that saved her life. An affection of the heart in course of time declared itself, but, though her existence was believed to hang on a thread, she lived on and on, lived to see Beatrice grow to womanhood. She kept a small house in London, but spent the greater part of the year at home or foreign health-resorts. Her relatives had supposed that she would return to her own country, but Mrs. Redwing had tastes which lacked gratification in a provincial manufacturing town. Without having achieved much positive culture, she had received from her husband an impulse towards the development of certain higher possibilities in her nature, and she liked the society of mentally active people. The state of her health alone withheld her from a second marriage ; she was not a very patient invalid, and suffered keenly in the sense of missing the happiness which life had offered her. In the matter of her daughter's education she exercised much care. Doctrinal religion had a strong hold upon her, and it was her solicitude that Beatrice should walk from the first in the ways of Anglican salvation. She dreaded the ' spirit of the age.' With a better judgment in pure literature than falls to the lot of most women—or men either—she yet

oanished from her abode, wherever it might be anything that
remotely savoured of intellectual emancipation; her æsthetic
leanings she deemed the great temptation of her life, for she
frankly owned to her friends that many things powerfully attracted her, which her conscience bade her shun as dangerous.
Her generosity made her a shining light in the world which
busies itself in the dispensing or receiving of ecclesiastical
charity. The clerical element was very strong in the circle
that surrounded her. At the same time her worldly tastes
did not go altogether ungratified. She was very fond of
music, and her unlimited powers in the provision of first-rate
musical entertainment brought to her house acquaintances of
a kind that would not otherwise have been found there. The
theatre she tabooed, regarding this severity as an acceptable
sacrifice, and not troubling to reflect what share her ill-health
had in rendering it a fairly easy one. In brief, she was a
woman of a genial nature, whose inconsistencies were largely
due to her inability to outgrow early conditions.

Beatrice inherited her mother's mental restrictions, but
was endowed with a subtlety of nature, which, aided by her
circumstances, made her yet more a being of inconsistencies
and contradictions. In religion it was not enough for her to
conform; zeal drove her into the extremest forms of ritualistic
observance. Nor did even for her personal salvation suffice;
the logic of a compassionate nature led her on to various forms
of missionary activity; she haunted vile localities, ministering
alike to soul and body. At the same time she relished keenly
the delights of the masquerading sphere, where her wealth
and her beauty made her doubly welcome. From praying by
the bedside of a costermonger's wife, she would speed away to
shine among the brightest in phantasmagoric drawing-rooms;
her mother could seldom accompany her, but there was
always some one ready to chaperon Beatrice Redwing. Once
in the world from which thought is banished, she seemed as
thoughtless as any. Her spiritual convictions put no veto
even upon dancing. Yet her mood at such times was not the
entire self-abandonment of the girl who is born but to waltz.
In spite of the sanction of custom, she could not wholly
suppress her virginal instincts, and, however unconsciously,
something in her nature held itself aloof. She led a life of in-
decision. Combining in herself such contradictory elements,
she was unable to make close friendships. Her intimacy with
Mrs. Rossall, which dated from her late childhood, was not

the perfect accord which may subsist between women of very different characters, yet here she gave and received more sympathy than elsewhere. It was her frequent saying that she came to Mrs. Rossall's house when she wanted to rest. Here she could be herself, could pass without interval from pietistic argument to chatter about her neighbours, could indulge in impulses of confession as with no one else, could put off the strain of existence which was the result of her conflicting impulses. But it was only during a portion of the year that she could have Mrs. Rossall's society ; at other times, though no one suspected it, she suffered much from loneliness. With her mother she was in accord on the subjects of religion and music, but even natural affection, blending with these sympathies, could not bring about complete unity ; in her home there was the same lack that she experienced in the outer world. For all her versatility, she was not in appearance emotional ; no one seemed less likely to be overcome by passion. Her enthusiasms fell short of the last note of sincerity. Perhaps it was on this account that she produced no strong impression, in spite of her beauty. Her personality suffered on acquaintance from defect of charm. Was it a half-consciousness of this that led her now and then into the curious affectation of childishness already remarked ? Did she feel unable to rely for pleasing upon those genuine possessions which for some reason could never advantageously display themselves ? . . . .

For more than an hour she slept. At her waking she found Minnie standing by her side.

' Are your lessons over ? ' she asked, passing at once into full consciousness, without sign of having slept.

The child replied that they were.

' Where is Miss Hood ? '

' In the summer-house.'

Beatrice rose, and they walked towards the summer-house together. It was in a corner of the garden, hidden among acacias and laurels, a circular hut in the ordinary style. Patty and the governess were seated within. Beatrice entered, and took a seat with them.

' Is your memory as good as my own, Miss Hood ? ' she said pleasantly. ' Do you remember our meeting four years ago ? '

The other regarded her with quiet surprise, and said she had no recollection of the meeting.

'Not at Mr. Baxendale's, my uncle's, one day that you lunched with us when I was staying there?'

Miss Hood had wholly forgotten the circumstance. It served, however, for the commencement of a conversation, which went on till Mrs. Rossall, finding the hammock deserted, was guided by the sound of voices to where the two girls and the children sat.

In the afternoon there was a setting forth into the country. Mr. Athel drove his sister and the children; Wilfrid and Beatrice accompanied them on horseback. The course to be pursued having been determined, the riders were not at pains to keep the carriage always within sight.

'Why did Miss Hood decline to come?' Mr. Athel inquired, shortly after they had started.

'She gave no reason,' Mrs. Rossall replied. 'It was her choice to stay at home.'

'Of course you asked her in a proper way?'

'Why, Philip, of course I did.'

'Miss Hood never alters her mind,' remarked Patty.

'Never,' exclaimed the other twin with decision.

'An admirable characteristic,' commented their uncle, 'provided her decision is right to begin with.'

Beatrice had just led off at a gallop; Wilfrid necessarily followed her. When the pace slackened, they began to talk of indifferent things. On the crest of a hill, whence the carriage could be seen far away on the white road, the girl reined in, and, turning to her companion, asked abruptly—

'What is your opinion of Miss Hood?'

'Why do you ask such a question?'

'Because I should like to know. She interests me, and you must have had opportunities enough lately of studying her character.'

'Why does she interest you?'

'I can't say. I thought you might help me to discover the reason. You have often said that you liked women of strongly marked character.'

'How do you conclude that she is one?'

'I feel it; we were talking together before lunch. I don't think I like her; I don't think she has principles.'

Wilfrid laughed.

'Principles! The word is vague. You mean, no doubt, that she doesn't seem to have commonplace prejudices.'

'That's just what I wanted you to say.'

She let her horse move on. The young man followed, his eyes gazing absently before him, a smile fixed upon his lips.

Beatrice looked over her shoulder.

'Does she read the same kind of books that you do?'

'Unfortunately I read no books at all.'

She paused again to let him get to her side.

'What a pity it can't continue!'

'What?'

'Your inability to read.'

'That is the kindest remark I have heard for a long time!' exclaimed Wilfrid with a good-natured laugh.

'Very likely it is, though you don't mean it. When you read, you only poison your mind. It is your reading that has made you what you are, without faith, without feeling. You dissect everything, you calculate motives cynically, you have learnt to despise everyone who believes what you refuse to, you make your own intellect the centre of the world. You are dangerous.'

'What a character! To whom am I dangerous?'

'To anyone whom it pleases you to tempt, in whom you find the beginnings of disbelief.'

'In brief, I have no principles?'

'Of course you have none.'

'In other words, I am selfish?'

'Intensely so.'

It was hard to discover whether she were in earnest. Wilfrid examined her for a moment, and concluded that she must be. Her eyes were gleaming with no mock seriousness, and there was even a slight quiver about her lips. In all their exchanges of banter he had never known her look and speak quite as she did now. As he regarded her there came a flush to her cheek. She turned her head away and rode on.

'And what moves you to visit me with this castigation at present, Miss Redwing?' he asked, still maintaining his jesting tone.

'I don't know,' she answered carelessly. 'I felt all at once able to say what I thought.'

'Then you do really think all this?'

'Assuredly I do.'

He kept silence a little.

'And you can't see,' he began, rather more seriously, 'that you are deplorably lacking in the charity which surely should be among *your* principles?'

There are some things to which charity must not be extended.'

'Let us say, then, discretion, insight.' He spoke yet more earnestly. 'You judge me, and, in truth, you know as little of me as anyone could. The attitude of your mind prevents you from understanding me in the least; it prevents you from understanding any human being. You are consumed with prejudice, and prejudice of the narrowest, most hopeless kind. Am I too severe?'

'Not more so than you have often been. Many a time you have told me how you despised me.'

He was silent, then spoke impulsively.

'Well, perhaps the word is not too strong; though it is not your very self that I despise, but the ignorance and bigotry which possess you. It is a pity; I believe you might be a woman of quite a different kind.'

'Of pronounced character?'

'Precisely. You are neither one thing nor another. You have told me what you think of me; shall I be equally frank and speak as if you were a college friend? For at all events we are friends.'

'I am not sure of that.'

'Oh, but I am; and we shall be friends none the worse for ingenuousness on both sides. Look at the position in which you stand. One moment you are a woman of the world, the next you run frantic with religious zeal, another turn and you are almost an artist, at your piano; when you are tired of all these you become, or try to become, a sort of *ingénue*. In the name of consistency, be one thing or another. You are quite mistaken in thinking that I despise religious enthusiasm in itself. Become a veritable Beatrice, and I will venerate you infinitely. Give up everything to work in London always, and you shall have my warmest admiration. But you are not sincere.'

'I am sincere!' she broke in, with more passion than he had ever imagined her capable of uttering.

'I cannot call it sincerity. It is impossible that you should be sincere; you live in the latter end of the nineteenth century; the conditions of your birth and education forbid sincerity of this kind.'

'I am sincere,' she repeated, but in a low voice, without looking at him.

'On the other hand,' he proceeded, 'surrender yourself

entirely to the life of society, and I will still respect you.
You are a beautiful woman; you might be inexpressibly
charming. Frankly recognise your capabilities, and cultivate
your charm. Make a study of your loveliness; make it your
end to be a queen in drawing-rooms.'

'You insult me.'

'I can't see that I do. There is nothing contemptible in
such an aim; nothing is contemptible that is thorough. Or
you have the third course. Pursue music with seriousness.
Become a real artist; a public singer, let us say. No
amateur nonsense; recognise that you have a superb voice,
and that by dint of labour you may attain artistic excellence.
You talk of getting up concerts in low parts of London, of
humanising ruffians by the influence of music. Pshaw!
humanise humanity at large by devotion to an artistic ideal;
the other aim is paltry, imbecile, charlatan.'

He tried to see her face; she rode on, holding it averted.

'Follow any one of these courses, and you will make of
yourself a true woman. By trying to be a bit of everything
you become insignificant. Napoleon the Great was a curse
to mankind, but one thinks more of him than of Napoleon
the Little, who wasn't quite sure whether to be a curse or a
blessing. There is a self in every one of us; the end of our
life is to discern it, bring it out, make it actual. You don't
yet know your own self; you have not the courage to look
into your heart and mind; you keep over your eyes the
bandage of dogmas in which you only half believe. Your
insincerity blights the natural qualities of your intellect.
You have so long tried to persuade yourself of the evil of
every way of thinking save ecclesiastical dogmatism, that you
cannot judge fairly even those to whom you are most friendly.
Cannot you see that the world has outgrown the possibility
of one universal religion? For good or for evil, each of us
must find a religion in himself, and you have no right whatever to condemn before you have understood.'

'You cannot say that you have any religion,' she said,
facing him. He saw to his astonishment that there had been
tears in her eyes.

'You cannot say that I have none. The radical fault of
your uninstructed way of looking at things is that you
imagine mankind and the world to be matters of such simple
explanation. You learn by heart a few maxims, half a dozen
phrases, and there is your key to every mystery. That is the

child's state of mind. You have never studied, you have never thought. Your self-confidence is ludicrous; you and such as you do not hesitate to judge offhand men who have spent a long life in the passionate pursuit of wisdom. You have no reverence. It is the fault you attribute to me, but wrongly; if you had ever brought an open mind to our conversations, you would have understood that my reverence even for your ideal is not a wit less than your own; it is only that I see it in another light. You say that I have no religion : what if I have not ? Are one's final conclusions to be achieved in a year or two of early manhood ? I have my inner voices, and I try to understand them. Often enough they are ambiguous, contradictory; I live in hope that their bidding will become clearer. I search for meanings, try to understand myself, strive after knowledge.'

'You might as well have been born a pagan. One voice has spoken; its bidding is the sufficient and only guide.'

'Say rather that so it seems to you. Your inheritance of conviction is not mine; your mode of reasoning and my own have nothing in common. We inhabit different worlds.'

Beatrice let her eyes turn slowly to his face. The smile with which he met her found no reflection on her counten- ance; her look was that of one who realises a fatality.

'Shall we join them ?' she asked in a moment, nodding towards the far-off carriage which was about to hide itself among trees.

Wilfrid mused instead of answering. She began to ride on.

'Stay one minute,' he said. 'I have been anything but courteous in my way of speaking to you, but it was better to put off idle forms, was it not ?'

'You; I shall know henceforth what you think of me.'

'Not from this one conversation, if you mean that.'

'Well, it does not matter.'

'Perhaps not. Difference of opinion has fortunately little to do with old-standing kindness.'

'I am not sure that you are right, at all events when it has expressed itself in words of contempt.'

It was not resentment that her voice conveyed, but some thing which Wilfrid found it harder to bear. Her drooped eyelids and subdued tone indicated a humble pride, which the protest of her beauty made pathetic.

'We will never speak of such things again,' he said

D

gently. 'Let me have your forgiveness. When we join them down there, they will laugh at us and say we have been quarrelling as usual ; in future I think we mustn't quarrel, we are both of us getting too old for the amusement. When you sing to us to-night, I shall remember how foolish I was even to pretend contempt.'

'You will be thinking,' she said, 'that I am a mere amateur.'

'If I do, I shall be an ungrateful wretch—and an insensible one, to boot.'

She rode down the hill without replying.

CHAPTER III.

LYRICAL.

MISS HOOD did not, of course, dine with the family. Though, as Mrs. Rossall said, it was a distinct advantage to have in the house a governess whom one could in many respects treat as an equal, yet there was naturally a limit, in this as in all other matters. We have not yet, either in fact or in sentiment, quite outgrown the social stage in which personal hiring sets on the hired a stigma of servitude. Mrs. Rossall was not unaware that, in all that concerned intellectual refinement, her governess was considerably superior to herself, and in personal refinement not less a lady ; but the fact of quarterly payments, spite of all this, inevitably indicated a place below the salt. Mr. Athel, though, as we have seen, anxious to indulge himself in humane regard whenever social regulations permitted, was the last man to suffer in his household serious innovations upon traditional propriety.

So Miss Hood—Emily, as she was called by the little group of people away in Yorkshire, to whom she was other than a governess ; Emily, as we will permit ourselves to call her henceforth—always had the meal of tea with the children. After that the evening was her own, save that the twins kept her company until their hour of bedtime. The school-room was also her sitting-room. After half-past eight in the evening she had it to herself, and there she passed many an hour of quiet content, playing softly on the piano, reading, dreaming. In the matter of books she was well off ; Mr.

Athel and his sister had subscriptions at several London libraries, and of these the governess was invited to make free use. It was some restraint upon her that her choice of reading always passed under Mrs. Rossall's eyes, but not so much after the first few weeks. The widow was by this time well advanced in the resumption of purely mundane literature, and the really liberal tone which prevailed in the house removed apprehension in the pursuit of modern studies. For it was rather an ideal towards which she was working than an attainment in fact, that eclecticism of which she spoke to Wilfrid Athel. The monthly library lists which came under her eyes offered many a sore temptation. She was true on the whole to her system; she did not read at random, and never read frivolously; but a taste strongly directed to the best in literature will find much in the work of our day especially its criticism, which is indispensable as guidance, or attractive by its savour. This was not Emily's first access, fortunately, to the streams of contemporary thought; already she had enjoyed and largely used opportunities of the most various reading. She was able now to choose with discretion, and in a great degree to make her study serve directly the scheme of culture which she had devised for herself.

Few governesses had so pleasant a life. Mrs. Rossall, supported by her brother's views, imposed on her children a minimum of brain-work. Bodily health was after all the first thing, especially in the case of girls. A couple of hours' school in the morning, one hour given to preparation of lessons after tea—this for the present was deemed quite enough. ' Your companionship throughout the day will always be forming their minds,' Mrs. Rossall said in one of her earliest conversations with Emily; it was pleasantly put, and truer than it would have been in the case of many instructresses. The twins were not remarkably fond of their lessons, but in Emily's hands they became docile and anxious to please. She had the art of winning their affection without losing control over them; had Mrs. Rossall's rather languid habits of mind allowed her to give attention to the subject, she would have been struck with the singular combination of tenderness and reverence which the two entertained towards their teacher. Little laxities of behaviour and phrase upon which their mother's presence would be no check, they did not venture to allow themselves when with Emily; her only reproof was a steady gaze, eloquent of gentleness, but it proved quite sufficient. The twins were in truth submitting to the force of character. They felt it without understanding what it meant; one other person in the house experienced the same influence, but in his case it led to reflection.

Wilfrid was at Balliol when Miss Hood first arrived; he saw her for the first time when he came to town after his collapse. All hastened away to The Firs together. Wilfrid suffered no positive illness; he shared in the amusements of the family, and, with the exception of a good deal of pishing and pshawing at the restraints put upon him, had the appearance of one taking an ordinary holiday. There was undeniable truth in Beatrice Redwing's allusion to his much talking; without social intercourse he would soon have become ill in earnest; association with intelligent—all the better if argumentative—people was an indispensable condition of his existence. In his later school, and early college, days this tendency to give free utterance to his thoughts made him not altogether the most delightful of companions to such as were older than himself; his undeniable cleverness and the stores of knowledge he had already acquired needed somewhat more of the restraint of tact than his character at that time supplied. People occasionally called him a prig; now and then he received what the vernacular of youth terms ' a sitting upon.' The saving feature of his condition was that he allowed himself to be sat upon gracefully; a snub well administered to him was sure of its full artistic, and did not fail in its moral, effect: there was no vulgar insolence in the young fellow. What he received he could acknowledge that he deserved. A term or two at Balliol put this right; in mingling with some that were his equals, and one or two who were his superiors, he learned prudence in the regulation of his speech.

For a brie. time he perhaps talked not quite so much. When his ' set ' was formed, the currents of argument and rhetoric had once more free course, but they were beginning to flow less turbidly. His nature, as we know, was not merely vehement; he had the instincts of a philosophical inquirer, and his intellect speedily outgrew the stage of callowness. When he came down for his first ' long ' the change in him was so marked that it astonished all who met him; that he appeared wholly unconscious of the ripening he had undergone only made his development more impressive. He had gone away a boy, and returned a man.

He talked no less than ever, but in a markedly improved tone. He was graver, more seemly in the buoyant outbreaks in which he still occasionally indulged. One reason of his rapid maturing no doubt lay in the fact that he was already working too hard; his sprightliness was in a measure subdued by wear of tissue. His father was shrewd enough to suspect something of this, but it was difficult to interfere in any way. A month in Switzerland seemed to set things right. On the present more serious occasion, it had been deemed better not to set forth on a journey forthwith; perfect repose at the house in Surrey was all that was advised in the first instance. But it was clear that Wilfrid must have some one to talk with. A succession of visits from such friends as were available was speedily arranged. By the end of the first week, Wilfrid had accommodated himself to his circumstances. His fretting at the regulations imposed for his health almost ceased. At first this change was viewed with suspicion, especially when he became more absorbed in reflectiveness, and seemed to have less taste for conversation. However, he was perfectly cheerful; there were no further symptoms to excite alarm. Nor did the brooding period last very long. The only permanent change was that he ceased to grumble at his hard lot, and appeared to find his position very tolerable.

'It is the physical reaction,' observed Mr. Athel to his sister. 'The body is indulging itself; recovery of health absorbs his energies.'

Opportunities for anything like sustained converse with Miss Hood, Wilfrid found very few and far between; only once before the long talk in the hollow had he been able to gratify his curiosity—perhaps already some other feeling—in a dialogue of any intimacy. In a situation such as this, delicacy prescribed a very rigid discretion; Emily, moreover, was not facile of approach. Throughout the day she was scarcely away from the children; of course he could and did often exchange words with her in the presence of the twins, but he felt himself held at a distance by a tact which was perfect; without undue reserve, without a shadow of unrefined manoeuvring, Emily limited their intercourse in precisely the way that Mr. Athel or Mrs. Rossall would have deemed becoming. Then there were almost always guests at the house. With prudent regard to the character of these visitors, Mrs. Rossall chose opportunities for inviting the governess to the drawing-room during the evening, but Emily was not wholly at her ease under such conditions, and Wilfrid was withheld by only half-conscious motives from talking with her at these times. He shrank from subjecting himself to examination whilst encouraging her to speak on the subjects he would naturally choose; he felt, too, that she desired him not to address her, though this perception came to him in subtle ways of which he could render to himself no account. For all this, their acquaintance, nay their intimacy, grew. If ever eyes habitually expressed a self-respecting frankness, if ever any were incapable of ignoble artifice, they were Emily's; yet as time went on Wilfrid began to long for the casual meeting with her glance for the mere reason that he felt it as an exchange of words between her and himself. Thus it was that, when at length the first real conversation came, it seemed the sequel of many others, seemed so to both of them. They had divined each other; speech did but put the seal of confirmation on knowledge gained by mutual sympathy.

It may be presumed that neither Mr. Athel nor Mrs. Rossall was altogether regardless of possibilities suggested by the abiding beneath the same roof of an impetuous young man, forced into idleness, and a girl who was above the average in mental endowments, whilst, on the whole, she might be considered interesting in appearance. They exchanged no remark on the subject; it was scarcely likely they should; but during the first few weeks both were observant. Their observations were reassuring to them. And indeed they had not anticipated trouble, for the simple reason that both believed Wilfrid's affections to tend already in a marked direction, and one of which they altogether approved. That he would some day take for his wife Beatrice Redwing was a conclusion upon which father and aunt had settled their minds; the conclusion was reasonable enough, and well supported by such evidence as the case admitted. Mr. Athel had at an earlier period entertained certain misgivings as to the desirability of such a marriage; misgivings which had reference to the disastrous story of the Redwing household; the conception of hereditary tendencies has become a strong force in our time, and pronounced madness in a parent cannot as easily be disregarded as it once was. But the advantages of the alliance were so considerable, its likelihood so indisputable, that prudence had scarcely fair play; besides, Beatrice had reached her twenty-first year without any sign of mental trouble, and seemed as sound a girl as could anywhere be discovered. The habitual sword-crossing between her and Wilfrid was naturally regarded as their mode of growing endeared to each other; their intellectual variances could not, by a sober gentleman of eight-and-forty and by a young widow whose interest in the world was reviving, be regarded as a bar to matrimony. 'Family,' Beatrice would not bring, but she was certain to inherit very large fortune, which, after all, means more than family nowadays. On the whole it was a capital thing for Wilfrid that marriage would be entered upon in so smooth a way. Mr. Athel was not forgetful of his own course in that matter; he understood his father's attitude as he could not when resisting it, and was much disposed to concede that there might have been two opinions as to his own proceeding five-and-twenty years ago. But for Beatrice, the young man's matrimonial future would have been to his father a subject of constant apprehension; as it was, the situation lost much of its natural hazard.

In Emily there was nothing that suggested sentimentality; rather one would have thought her deficient in sensibility, judging from the tone of her conversation. She did not freely express admiration, even in the form of assent to what was said by others. To interpret her reticence as shyness was a misunderstanding, or a misuse of words, natural in the case of an inexact observer like Mrs. Rossall. Four years ago, when Beatrice met her in Dunfield, her want of self-confidence was pronounced enough; she had at that time never quitted her provincial home, and was in the anomalous position of one who is intellectually outgrowing very restricted social circumstances. The Baxendales were not wrong in discussing her as shy. But that phase of her life was now left far behind. Her extreme moderation was deliberate; it was her concession to the fate which made her a governess. Courtesy and kindliness might lead those whose bread she ate to endeavour occasionally to remove all show of social distinction; neither her temperament nor her sense of comeliness in behaviour would allow her to shrink from such advances, but she could not lose sight of the unreality of the situations to which they led. Self-respect is conditioned by the influence of circumstance on character; in Emily it expressed itself as a subtle sensitiveness to grades of sympathy. She could not shut her eyes to the actuality of things; sincerity was the foundation of her being, and delicate appreciation of its degrees in others regulated her speech and demeanour with an exactitude inappreciable by those who take life in a rough and ready way. When engaged in her work of teaching, she was at ease ; alone in the room which had been set apart for her, she lived in the freedom of her instincts ; but in Mrs. Rossall's drawing-room she could only act a part, and all such divergence from reality was pain. It was not that she resented her subordination, for she was almost devoid of social ambitions and knew nothing of vulgar envy ; still less did it come of reasoned revolt against the artificial ordering of precedences ; Emily's thoughts did not tend that way. She could do perfect justice to the amiable qualities of those who were set above her ; she knew no bitterness in the food which she duly earned ; but, by no one's fault, there was a vein of untruth in the life she had to lead. To remind herself that such untruth was common to all lives, was an outcome of the conditions of society, did not help her to disregard it ; nature had endowed her with a stern idealism which would not ally itself with compromise. She was an artist in life. The task before her, a task of which in these days she was growing more and more conscious, was to construct an existence every moment of which should serve an all-pervading harmony. The recent birth within her of a new feeling was giving direction and vigour to the forces of her being ; it had not as yet declared itself as a personal desire ; it wrought only as an impassioned motive in the sphere of her intellectual aspirations. She held herself more persistently apart from conventional intercourse ; she wished it had been possible to keep wholly to herself in the hours when her services were not demanded. Mr. Athel, who liked to express himself to young people with a sort of paternal geniality, rallied her one day on her excessive study, and bade her be warned by a notorious example. This had the effect of making her desist from reading in the presence of other people.

She had known much happiness during these two months at The Firs, happiness of a kind to dwell in the memory and be a resource in darker days. Though mere personal ease was little the subject of her thoughts, she prized for its effect upon her mind the air of graceful leisure, of urbane repose, which pervaded the house. To compare The Firs with that plain little dwelling on the skirts of a Yorkshire manufacturing town which she called her home, was to understand the inestimable advantage of those born into the material refine-

ment which wealth can command, of those who breathe from
childhood the atmosphere of liberal enjoyment, who walk from
the first on clean ways, with minds disengaged from anxiety
of casual soilure, who know not even by domestic story the
trammels of sordid preoccupation. Thus it was with a sense
of well-being that she stepped on rich carpets, let her eyes
wander over the light and dark of rooms where wealth had
done the bidding of taste, watched the neat and silent ministering of servants. These things to her meant priceless
opportunity, the facilitating of self-culture. Even the little
room in which she sat by herself of evenings was daintily
furnished, when weary with reading, it eased and delighted
her merely to gaze at the soft colours of the wall-paper, the
vases with their growing flowers, the well-chosen pictures, the
graceful shape of a chair ; she nursed her appreciation of these
joys, resisted the ingress of familiarity, sought daily for novel
aspects of things become intimately known. She rose at early
hours that she might have the garden to herself in all its
freshness ; she loved to look from her window into the calm
depth of the summer midnight. In this way she brought into
consciousness the craving of her soul, made the pursuit of
beauty a religion, grow to welcome the perception of new
meaning in beautiful things with a spiritual delight. This
was the secret of her life, which she guarded so jealously,
which she feared even by chance to betray in the phrasings of
common intercourse. Wilfrid had divined it, and it was the
secret influence of this sympathy that had led her to such
unwonted frankness in their latest conversation.

Mrs. Rossall had spoken to her of Beatrice Redwing's
delightful singing, and had asked her to come to the drawing-
room during the evening ; having declined the afternoon's
drive, Emily did not feel able to neglect this other invitation
The day had become sultry towards its close ; when she joined
the company about nine o'clock, she found Beatrice with Mrs.
Rossall sitting in the dusk by the open French windows, Mr.
Athel in a chair just outside, and Wilfrid standing by him,
the latter pair smoking. The sky beyond the line of dark
greenery was still warm with after-glow of sunset.

Emily quietly sought a chair near Mrs. Rossall, from whom
she received a kind look. Mr. Athel was relating a story of
his early wanderings in Egypt, with a leisurely gusto, an
effective minuteness of picturing, the result of frequent repetition. At the points of significance he would pause for a

moment or two and puff life into his cigar. His anecdotes were seldom remarkable, but they derived interest from the enjoyment with which he told them; they impressed one with a sense of mental satisfaction, of physical robustness held in reserve, of life content among the good things of the world.

'Shall we have lights?' Mrs. Rossall asked, when the story at length came to an end.

'Play us something first,' said Beatrice. 'This end of twilight is so pleasant.'

Mrs. Rossall went to the piano, upon which still fell a glimmer from another window, and filled the room with harmony suiting the hour. Wilfrid had come in and seated himself on a couch in a dark corner; his father paced up and down the grass. Emily watched the first faint gleam of stars in the upper air.

Then lamps and candles were brought in. Beatrice was seen to be dressed in dark blue, her hair richly attired, a jewelled cross below her throat, her bosom and arms radiant in bare loveliness. Emily, at the moment that she regarded her, found herself also observed. Her own dress was of warm grey, perfectly simple, with a little lace at the neck and wrists. Beatrice averted her eyes quickly, and made some laughing remark to Mr. Athel.

'I know you always object to sing without some musical preparation,' said Mrs. Rossall, as she took a seat by the girl's side. 'I wonder whether we ought to close the windows; are you afraid of the air?'

'Oh, leave them open!' Beatrice replied. 'It is so close.'

Her cheeks had a higher colour than usual; she lay back in the chair with face turned upwards, her eyes dreaming.

'You are tired, I am afraid,' Mrs. Rossall said, 'in spite of your sleep in the hammock. The first day in the country always tires me dreadfully.'

'Yes, I suppose I am, a little,' murmured Beatrice.

'Not too tired, I hope, to sing,' said Wilfrid, coming from his couch in the corner to a nearer seat. His way of speaking was not wholly natural; like his attitude, it had something constrained; he seemed to be discharging a duty.

'Observe the selfishness of youth,' remarked Mr. Athel.

'Age, I dare say, has its selfishness too in the present instance,' was Mrs. Rossall's rejoinder.

'To whom does that refer?' questioned her brother, jocosely.

Beatrice turned her head suddenly towards Emily.

'Shall I sing, Miss Hood?' she asked, with a touch of her *ingénue* manner, though the playfulness of her words rang strangely.

'It will give me much pleasure to hear you,' was the sober reply, coming after an instant of embarrassment.

Beatrice rose. Her movement across the room had a union of conscious stateliness and virgin grace which became her style of beauty; it was in itself the introduction to fine music. Mrs. Rossall went to accompany. Choice was made of a solo from an oratorio; Beatrice never sang trivialities of the day, a noteworthy variance from her habits in other things. In a little while, Wilfrid stirred to enable himself to see Emily's face; it showed deep feeling. And indeed it was impossible to hear that voice and remain unmoved; its sweetness, its force, its skill were alike admirable. Beatrice conversing was quite other than Beatrice when she sang; music was her mode of self-utterance; from the first sustained note it was felt that a difficulty of expression had been overcome, and that she was saying things which at other times she could not, disclosing motives which as a rule the complexities of her character covered and concealed, which were not clear to her own consciousness till the divine impulse gave them form. It was no shallow nature that could pour forth this flood of harmony. The mere gift of a splendid voice, wrought to whatever degree of perfection, would not invest with this rare power. In technical qualities she might have much still to learn, but the passionate poetry of her notes was what no training could have developed, and it would never evince itself with more impressiveness than to-night.

It seemed frivolous to speak thanks. Wilfrid gazed out into the dark of the garden, Emily kept her eyes bent downward. She heard the rustle of Beatrice's dress near her. Mr. Athel began to speak of the piece; the sound of Beatrice's voice replying caused Emily at length to look up, and she met the dark eyes, still large with the joy of song. Her own gaze had a beautiful solemnity, a devout admiration, of which it was impossible to doubt the genuineness; Beatrice, observing it, smiled very slightly before turning away again.

A quarter of an hour after, Emily withdrew, Mrs. Rossall played a little, and talk of an idle kind followed. Wilfrid was not disposed to take his usual part in conversation, and his casual remarks were scarcely ever addressed to

Beatrice. Presently Mrs. Rossall wished to refer to the
' Spectator,' which contained a criticism of a new pianist of
whom there was much talk just then.

' Have you had it, Wilf ? ' Mr. Athel asked, after turning
over a heap of papers in vain.

' Oh, the " Spectator," ' Wilfrid replied, rousing himself
from absentness. ' Yes, I had it in the summer-house just
before dinner; I believe I left it there. Shall I fetch it ? '

' It would serve you right if I said yes,' admonished Mrs.
Rossall. 'In the first place you had no business to be
reading it——'

' I will go,' Wilfrid said, rising with an effort.

' No, no; it will do to-morrow.'

' May as well get it now,' he said indifferently, and went
out by the window.

That part of the garden through which he walked lay in
the shadow of the house; the sky was full of moonlight, but
the moon itself was still low. A pathway between laurels led
to the summer-house. Just short of the little building, he
passed the edge of shade, and, before entering, turned to view
the bright crescent as it hung just above the house-roof.
Gazing at the forms of silvered cloud floating on blue depths,
he heard a movement immediately behind him; he turned,
to behold Emily standing in the doorway. The moon's rays
shone full upon her; a light shawl which seemed to have
covered her head had slipped down to her shoulders, and one
end was held in a hand passed over her breast. There was
something in the attitude which strikingly became her; her
slight figure looked both graceful and dignified. The marble
hue of her face, thus gleamed upon, added to the statuesque
effect; her eyes had a startled look, their lids drooped as
Wilfrid regarded her.

' You have been sitting here since you left us ? ' he asked,
in a voice attuned to the night's hush.

' I was tempted to come out; the night is so beautiful.'

' It is.'

He uttered the assent mechanically; his eyes, like hers,
had fallen, but he raised them again to her face. It seemed
to him in this moment the perfect type of spiritual beauty;
the brow so broad and pure, the eyes far-seeing in their
maidenly reserve, the lips full, firm, of infinite refinement
and sweetness. He felt abashed before her, as he had never
done. They had stood thus but a moment or two, yet it

seemed long to both. Emily stepped from the wooden threshold on to the grass.

'Somebody wants the "Spectator,"' he said hurriedly. 'I believe I left it here.'

'Yes, it is on the table.'

With a perfectly natural impulse, she quickly re-entered the house, to reach the paper she had seen only a minute ago. Without reflection, heart-beats stifling his thought, he stepped after her. The shadow made her turn rapidly; a shimmer of silver light through the lattice-work still touched her features ; her lips were parted as if in fear.

'Emily!'

He did not know that he had spoken. The name upon his tongue, a name he had said low to himself often to-day and yesterday, was born of the throe which made fire-currents of his veins, the passion which at the instant seized imperiously upon his being. She could not see his face, and hers to him was a half-veiled glory, yet each knew the wild gaze, the all but terror, in the other's eyes, that anguish which indicates a supreme moment in life, a turning-point of fate.

She had no voice. Wilfrid's words at length made way impetuously.

'I thought I could wait longer, and try in the meanwhile to win your kind thoughts for me ; but I dare not part from you for so long, leaving it a mere chance that you will come back. I must say to you what it means, the hope of seeing you again. All the other desires of my life are lost in that. You are my true self, for which I shall seek in vain whilst I am away from you. Can you give me anything—a promise of kind thought—a hope—to live upon till I see you?'

'I cannot come back.'

But for the intense stillness he could not have caught the words ; they were sighed rather than spoken.

'Because I have said this?—Emily!'

He saw the white shape of her hand resting upon the table, and held it in his own, that exquisite hand which he had so often longed to touch ; how cold it was! yet how soft, living! She made no effort to draw it away.

'I cannot say now what I wish to,' he spoke hurriedly. 'I must see you to-morrow—you will not refuse? I *must* see you! You are often out very early ; I shall be at the hollow, where we talked yesterday, early, at seven o'clock—you will come? If the morning is not fine, then the day after. Emily, you will meet me?'

'I will meet you.'

He touched her fingers with his lips, took the paper, and hastened back to the house. His absence had not seemed long: it was only of five minutes. Reaching the open windows, he did not enter at once, but stood there and called to those within to come and admire the night; he felt his face hot and flushed.

'What is there remarkable about the night?' asked Mr. Athel, sauntering forwards.

'Come and look at this glorious moon, Miss Redwing,' Wilfrid exclaimed, once more with the natural friendliness of his habitual tone to her.

'It seems to have put you into excellent spirits,' remarked Mrs. Rossall, as, followed by Beatrice, she approached the window. 'Have you found the "Spectator?" that's the point.'

Wilfrid continued speaking in a raised voice, for it was just possible, he thought, that Emily might come this way round to enter, and he wished her to be apprised of their presence. All went back into the room after a few moments, and, as the air had grown cooler, the windows were closed. As Wilfrid seated himself in a dusky part of the room, he noticed that Beatrice was regarding him steadily. She had not spoken since his return, and did not do so till she presently rose to say good-night. To Wilfrid she used no form of words, merely giving him her hand; that other had been so cold, how hot this was!

She laughed as she turned from him.

'What is the source of amusement?' inquired Mr. Athel, who was standing by with his hands upon his hips.

'Indeed I don't know,' returned Beatrice, laughing again slightly. 'I sometimes laugh without cause.'

Emily had passed upstairs and gone to her bedroom but a moment before, treading with quick soundless steps. When Wilfrid left her in the summer-house, she stood unmoving, and only after a minute or two changed her attitude by putting her palms against her face, as if in the gloom she found too much light. It was a sensation of shame which came upon her, a tremor of maidenhood in re-living, swift instant by instant, all that had just passed. Had she in any way aided in bringing about that confession? Had she done anything, made a motion, uttered a tone, which broke away the barrier between herself and him? When she could recover self-consciousness, disembarrass herself of the phantom moments which would not fleet with the rest of time, it was scarcely joy which she read in her heart; apprehension, dismay, lack of courage to look forward beyond this night, these oppressed her. Then, close upon the haunting reality of his voice, his touch, came inability to believe what had happened. Had a transient dreamful slumber crept upon her as she sat here alone? So quickly had the world suffered re-creation, so magical the whelming of old days in a new order, so complete the change in herself. One word she knew which had power from eternity to do these things, and that word neither he nor she had uttered. But there was no need, when the night spoke it in every beat of time.

Fearful of being seen, she at length ventured to return to the house. Moonlight streamed full upon her bed; it would have irked her as yet to take off her clothes, she lay in the radiance, which seemed to touch her with warm influences, and let her eyes rest upon the source of light. Then at length joy came and throned in her heart, joy that would mate with no anxious thought, no tremulous brooding. This was *her* night! Whom might be other happy beings in the world to whom it was also the beginning of new life, but in her night was its consecration, hers the supremacy of blessedness. Let the morrow wait on the hour of waking, if indeed sleep would ever come; this moment, the sacred *now*, was all that she could comprehend.

She undressed at length, and even slept, fitfully, always to start into wakefulness with a sense of something to be thought upon, to be realised to be done. The weariness of excitement perturbed her joy; the meeting which was to take place in a few hours became a nervous preoccupation. The moonlight had died away; the cold light of dawn began to make objects in the room distinct. Was it good to have consented so readily to meet him? Nay, but no choice had been left her; his eagerness would take no refusal; and it was impossible for things to remain as they were, without calmer talk between them. It was her resource to remember his energetic will, his force of character; the happiness of passively submitting to what he might dictate; sure of his scrupulous honour, his high ideal. Could she indeed have borne to go into exile from his presence, without a hope that this the noblest and most aspiring life that had ever approached her might be something more than a star to worship? If wealth comes, we wonder how we drew breath in poverty; yet we lived, and should have lived on. Let the gods be thanked, whom it pleases to clothe the soul with joy which is superfluous to bare existence! Might she not now hallow herself to be a true priestess of beauty? Would not life be vivid with new powers and possibilities? Even as that heaven was robing itself in glory of sunrise, with warmth and hue which strengthened her again to overcome anxieties. Was he waking? Was he impatient for the hour of his meeting with her? She would stand face to face with him in the full sunlight this time, but with what deep humility! Should she be able to find words? She had scarcely spoken to him, ever, as yet, and now there was more to say than hours of solitude would leave time for. She knew not whether to bid the sun linger or speed.

There was nothing unusual in her rising and going forth early, though perhaps she had never issued from the house quite so early as this morning; it was not yet six o'clock when she gently closed the garden-gate behind her, and walked along the road which led on to the common. The sun had already warmed the world, and the sheen of earth and heaven was at its brightest; the wind sweeping from the downs was like the breath of creation, giving life to forms of faultless beauty. Emily's heart lacked no morning hymn; every sense revelled in that pure joy which is the poetry of praise. She wished it had been near the hour of meeting, yet again was glad to have time to prepare herself. Walking, she drank in the loveliness about her, marked the forms of trees, the light and shade of heavy leafage, the blendings of colour by the roadside, the grace of remote distances; all these things she was making part of herself, that in memory they might be a joy for ever. It is the art of life to take each moment of mental joy, of spiritual openness, as though it would never be repeated, to cling to it as a pearl of great price, to exhaust its possibilities of sensation. At the best, such moments will be few amid the fateful succession of common cares, of lassitudes, of disillusions. Emily had gone deep enough in thought already to understand this; in her rapture there was no want of discerning consciousness. If this morning were to be unique in her life, she would have gained from it all that it had to give. Those subtle fears, spiritual misgivings, which lurked behind her perceptions would again have their day, for it was only by striving that she had attained her present modes of thought; her nature concealed a darker strain, an instinct of asceticism, which had now and again predominated, especially in the period of her transition to womanhood, when the material conditions of her life were sad and of little hope. It was no spirit of unreflective joy that now dwelt within her, but the more human happiness extorted from powers which only yield to striving. Hitherto her life's morning had been but cold and grey; she had trained herself to expect no breaking forth of gleams from the sober sky. This sudden splendour might be transitory.

But who was that already standing by the hollow? Was it likely that he would be later than she at the place of meeting? Emily stood with a shock of life at the gates of her heart. She tried to keep her eyes raised to his as she approached slowly, he with more speed. Would she not after all find voice for the things she had to say?

Wilfrid came to her with bare head, and took her hand; no more than took her hand, for he was in awe of the solemn beauty of her countenance.

' You thought I should keep you waiting?' he asked in a low voice trembling with joy. ' I have watched the sun rise.'

' The door had not been opened——'

' My window is not high above the ground, he answered, with an uncertain laugh.

They walked side by side over the heather, towards the beginning of a wood, young fir trees mingling with gorse and bracken. Beyond was the dense foliage of older growths. He had again taken one of her hands, and so led her on.

' Emily !'

She was able to look into his face for a moment, but the moving of her lips gave no sound.

' I could not sleep,' he went on, ' so I read of you till dawn in the Knightes Tale. It is a name I have always loved, sweet, musical, but of deep meaning. Will you not let me hear you speak, Emily?'

She uttered a few timid words, then they passed on in silence till the wood was all about them.

' May I tell you the plan which I have made in the night?' he said, as they stood on a spot of smooth turf, netted with sunlight. ' You leave us in two days. Before we start for London, I shall speak with my father, and tell him what has come about. You remember what I was saying about him the day before yesterday; perhaps it was with a half-thought of this—so daring I was, you see! I have no fear of his kindness, his good sense. At the same time, it is right you should know that my independence is assured; my grandfather left me far more than enough for mere needs. By the summer of next year I shall be free of Oxford. I care little now for such honours as those; you have honoured me more than any other voice has power to do. But my father would be disappointed if I did not go on to the end, and do something of what is expected. Now you must tell me freely: is there absolute necessity for your maintaining yourself in the meanwhile, for your leaving home?'

'There is,' she replied.

'Then will you continue to teach the children as usual?' She was touched with apprehension.

'Gladly I would do so—but is it possible? Would you conceal from Mrs. Rossall——'

Wilfrid mused.

'I meant to. But your instincts are truer than mine; say what you think. I believe my father would countenance it, for it involves no real deceit.'

'If you wish it,' Emily said, after a silence, in a low voice.

'Of my aunt,' pursued Wilfrid, 'I have just this degree of doubt. She might make difficulties; her ways of thinking differ often from ours. Yet it is far better that you should continue to live with us. I myself shall scarcely ever be at home; it will not be as if I dwelt under the roof; I will make my visits as short as possible, not to trouble you. I could not let you go to the house of other people—you to lack consideration, perhaps to meet unkindness! Rather than that, you shall stay in your own home, or I will not return to Oxford at all.'

Emily stood in anxious thought. He drew a step nearer to her; seemed about to draw nearer still, but checked himself as she looked up.

'I fear we must not do that,' she said. 'Mrs. Rossall would not forgive me.'

Woman's judgment of woman, and worth much more than Wilfrid's rough and ready scheming.

Wilfrid smiled.

'Then she also shall know,' he exclaimed. 'She shall take my view of this; I will not be gainsaid. What is there in the plan that common sense can object to ? Your position is not that of a servant ; you are from the first our friend ; you honour us by the aid you give, efficient as few could make it. Yes, there shall be no concealment ; far better so.'

' You have no fear of the views they will take ? '

' None ! ' he said, with characteristic decision. ' If they are unreasonable, absurd, our course is plain enough. You will be my wife when I ask you to, Emily ? '

She faltered, and held her hand to him.

' Is it worth while to go back to Oxford ? ' he mused, caressing the fingers he had kissed.

Oh, you ; you must,' Emily urged, with a sort of fear in her sudden courage. ' You must not disappoint them, your father, your friends.

' My fair wise one ! ' he murmured, gazing rapturously at her. ' Oh, Emily, think what our life will be ! Shall we not drain the world of its wisdom, youth of its delight ! Hand in hand, one heart, one brain—what shall escape us ? It was you I needed to give completeness to my thought and desire.'

The old dream, the eternal fancy. This one, this and no other, chosen from out the myriads of human souls. Individuality the servant of passion ; mysteries read undoubtingly with the eye of longing. Read perhaps so truly ; who knows ?

She came nearer, imperceptibly, her raised face aglow like the morning.

' Wilfrid—you believe—you know that I love you ? '

The last word breathed out in the touching of lips with lips. What could he reply, save those old, simple words of tenderness, that small vocabulary of love, common to child and man ? The goddess that made herself woman for his sake—see, did he not hold her clasped to him ! But she was mute again. The birds sang so loudly round about them, uttered their hearts so easily, but Emily could only speak through silence. And afterwards she knew there was so much she should have said. What matter ? One cannot find tongue upon the threshold of the holy of holies.

CHAPTER IV.

A CONFLICT OF OPINIONS.

BEATRICE REDWING'S visit only extended over the second day, and during that there was little, if any, separate conversation between her and Wilfrid. The change in her from the free gaiety and restfulness of the morning of her arrival could not escape notice, though she affected a continuance of the bright mood. Mr. Athel and his sister both observed her real pre-occupation, as if of trouble, and mentally attributed it to something that had passed during the afternoon's ride. Mrs. Rossall did not look for confidences. Beatrice would gossip freely enough of trivial experiences, or of the details of faith and ritual, but the innermost veil of her heart was never raised; all her friends felt that, though they could not easily have explained in what way they became conscious of this reserve, she seemed so thoroughly open, not to say so shallow. She left The Firs to return to town, and thence in a week or two went to Cowes, a favourite abode of her mother's.

The next day, Emily also left, journeying to London on her way to the north. Wilfrid and she had no second meeting; their parting was formal, in the family circle. Mr. Athel displayed even more than his usual urbanity; Mrs. Rossall was genuinely gracious; the twins made many promises to write from Switzerland. Emily was self-possessed, but Wilfrid read in her face that she was going through an ordeal. He felt the folly of his first proposal, that she should play a part before Mrs. Rossall through the winter months. He decided, moreover, that no time should be lost in making the necessary disclosure to his father. Naturally it would be an anxious time with Emily till she had news from him. She had asked him to direct letters to the Dunfield post office, not to her home; it was better so for the present.

Wilfrid, though anything but weakly nervous, was impatient of suspense, and, in face of a situation like the present, suffered from the excitability of an imaginative temperament. He had by no means yet outgrown the mood which, when he was a boy, made the anticipation of any delight a physical illness. In an essentially feeble nature this extreme sensibility

is fatal to sane achievement; in Wilfrid it merely enforced
the vigour of his will. As a child he used to exclaim that
he *could* not wait; at present he was apt to say that he would
not. He did not, in very truth, anticipate difficulties with his
father, his conviction of the latter's reasonableness being
strongly supported by immense confidence in his own powers
of putting a case incontrovertibly. As he had said to Emily,
he could scarcely allow that deep affection for his father dwelt
within him, nor did the nature of the case permit him to feel
exactly reverent; these stronger emotions were reserved for
the memory of the parent who was long dead. He thought
of his father with warm friendliness, that temper which is
consistent with clear perception of faults and foibles, which
makes of them, indeed, an occasion for the added kindliness
of indulgence, and which, on the other hand, leaves perfect
freedom in judgment and action. We know that it is for the
most part a misfortune to be the son of a really great man,
and for the reason that nature, so indifferent to the individual,
makes the well-being of each generation mainly consist in
early predominance over the generation which gave it birth.
Wilfrid suffered no much exceptional hardship. At three-and-
twenty he felt himself essentially his father's superior. He
would not have exposed the fact thus crudely, for he was susceptible to the comely order of things. The fact was a fact,
and nature, not he, was responsible for it. That, and the
circumstance of his material independence, would necessarily
keep the ensuing interview well within the limits of urbane
comedy. The young man smiled already at the suggested
comparison with his father's own choice in matrimony.
Wilfrid had never had the details of that story avowedly
represented to him, but it was inevitable that he should have
learnt enough to enable him to reconstruct them with tolerable accuracy.

Emily was gone long before the hour of luncheon. After
that meal, Mr. Athel lit a cigar and went to a favourite seat
in the garden. Mrs. Rossall was going with the twins to make
a farewell call on neighbouring friends. As soon as the carriage had left the house, Wilfrid sought his father, who was
unbending himself with a review.

'I thought you would have gone with your aunt,' Mr.
Athel remarked, after a glance to see who was approaching
him.

'I had an object in remaining behind,' Wilfrid returned,

composedly, seating himself on a camp-stool which he had brought out. 'I wished to talk over with you a matter of some importance.'

'Oh?'

Mr. Athel stroked his chin, and smiled a little. It occurred to him at once that something relative to Beatrice was about to be disclosed.

'What is it?' he added, throwing one leg over the other, and letting the review lie open on his lap.

'It concerns Miss Hood,' pursued the other, assuming the same attitude, save that he had nothing to lean back against. 'A day or two ago I asked her to engage herself to me, and she consented.'

Perhaps this was the simplest way of putting it. Wilfrid could not utter the words with complete calmness; his hands had begun to tremble a little, and his temples were hot. By an effort he kept his eyes steadily fixed on his father's face, and what he saw there did not supply encouragement to proceed in the genial tone with which he had begun. Mr. Athel frowned, not angrily, but as if not quite able to grasp what had been told him. He had cast his eyes down.

There was silence for a moment.

'I have chosen the earliest moment for telling you of this,' Wilfrid continued, rather hurriedly. 'It was of course better to leave it till Miss Hood had gone.'

On the father's face displeasure had succeeded to mere astonishment

'You could have told me few things that I should be so sorry to hear,' were his first words, delivered in an undertone and with grave precision.

'Surely that does not express your better thought,' said Wilfrid, to whom a hint of opposition at once gave the firmness he had lacked.

'It expresses my very natural thought. In the first place, it is not pleasant to know that clandestine proceedings of this kind have been going on under my roof. I have no wish to say anything disrespectful of Miss Hood, but I am disposed to think that she has mistaken her vocation; such talents for dissimulation would surely have pointed to——'

Mr. Athel had two ways of expressing displeasure. Where ceremony was wholly unnecessary, he gave vent to his feelings in an outburst of hearty English wrath, not coarsely, for his instincts were invariably those of a gentleman, but in the cultivated autocratic tone; an offending groom, for instance, did not care to incur reproof a second time. Where this mode of utterance was out of place, he was apt to have recourse to a somewhat too elaborate irony, to involve himself in phrases which ultimately led to awkward hesitations, with the effect that he grew more heated by embarrassment. Had he been allowed to proceed, he would at present have illustrated this failing, for he had begun with extreme deliberation, smoothing the open pages with his right hand, rounding his words, reddening a little in the face. But Wilfrid interposed.

'I must not let you speak or think of Miss Hood so mistakenly,' he said firmly, but without unbecoming self-assertion. 'She could not possibly have behaved with more reserve to me than she did until, three days ago, I myself gave a new colour to our relations. The outward propriety which you admit has been perfectly genuine; if there is any blame in the matter— and how can there be any?—it rests solely upon me. I dare say you remember my going out to fetch the "Spectator," after Miss Redwing had been singing to us. By chance I met Miss Hood in the garden. I was led to say something to her which made a longer interview inevitable; she consented to meet me on the common before breakfast the following morning. These are the only two occasions which can be called clandestine. If she has disguised herself since then, how could she have behaved otherwise? Disguise is too strong a word; she has merely kept silence. I need not inquire whether you fully believe what I say.'

'What you say, I believe, as a matter of course,' replied Mr. Athel, who had drummed with his fingers as he listened impatiently. 'It can scarcely alter my view of the position of things. Had you come to me before offering yourself to this young lady, and done me the honour of asking my advice, I should in all probability have had a rather strong opinion to express; as it is, I don't see that there is anything left to be said.'

'What would your opinion have been?' Wilfrid asked.

'Simply that for an idle fancy, the unfortunate result of unoccupied days, you were about to take a step which would assuredly lead to regret at least, very probably to more active repentance. In fact, I should have warned you not to spoil your life in its commencement.'

'I think, father, that you would have spoken with too little knowledge of the case. You can scarcely know Miss

Hood as I do. I have studied her since we came here, and with—well, with these results.'

Mr. Athel looked up with grave sadness.

'Wilf, this is a deeply unfortunate thing, my boy. I grieve over it more than I can tell you. I am terribly disappointed. Your position and your hopes pointed to very different things. You have surprised me, too; I thought your mind was already made up, in quite a different quarter.'

'You refer to Miss Redwing?'

'Naturally.'

'You have, indeed, been mistaken. It was impossible that I should think of her as a wife. I must have sympathy, intellectual and moral. With her I have none. We cannot talk without flagrant differences—differences of a serious, a radical nature. Be assured that such a thought as this never occurred to Miss Redwing herself; her very last conversation with me forbids any such idea.'

Mr. Athel still drummed on the book, seemingly paying little heed to the speaker.

'You find sympathy in Miss Hood?' he asked suddenly, with a touch of sarcasm.

'The deepest. Her intellectual tendencies are the same as my own; she has a mind which it refreshes and delights me to discover. Of course that is not all, but it is all I need speak of. I know that I have chosen well and rightly.'

'I won't be so old-fashioned,' remarked Mr. Athel, still with subdued sarcasm, 'as to hint that some thought of me might have entered into your choosing' (did he consciously repeat his own father's words of five-and-twenty years back, or was it but destiny making him play his part in the human comedy?) 'and, in point of fact' (perhaps the parallel touched him at this point), 'you are old enough to judge the affair on its own merits. My wonder is that your judgment has not been sounder. Has it occurred to you that a young lady in Miss Hood's position would find it at all events somewhat difficult to be unbiassed in her assent to what you proposed?'

'Nothing has occurred to me,' replied Wilfrid, more shortly than hitherto, 'which could cast a shadow of suspicion on her perfect truth. I beg that you will not suggest these things. Some day you will judge her with better knowledge.'

'I am not sure of that,' was the rejoinder, almost irritably uttered.

'What do you mean by that, father?' Wilfrid asked in a lower tone.

'I mean, Wilf, that I am not yet in the frame of mind to regard the children's governess as my daughter-in-law. Miss Hood may be all you say; I would not willingly be anything but scrupulously just. The fact remains that this is not the alliance which it became you to make. It is, in a very pronounced sense, marrying beneath you. It is not easy for me to reconcile myself to that.'

It was Wilfrid's turn to keep silence. What became of his plans? They were hardly in a way to be carried out as he had conceived them. A graver uneasiness was possessing him. Resolve would only grow by opposition, but there was more of pain in announcing an independent course than he had foreseen.

'What are your practical proposals?' his father inquired, his mollified tone the result of observing that he had made a certain impression, for he was distinctly one of the men who are to be overcome by yielding.

'I had a proposal to make, but as with a man than it is hardly worth while to speak of it. I shall have to reflect.'

'Let me hear what you were going to say. There's no harm in that, at all events.'

'My idea was, that, with your consent and my aunt's, Miss Hood should return just as if nothing had happened, and continue to teach the twins till next summer, when I should have done with Oxford. There appears to me to be nothing irrational or unseemly in such a plan. If she were our cook or housemaid, there might be reasonable objections. As it is, it would hardly involve a change even in your tone to her, seeing that you are in the habit of treating her as a lady, and with a certain degree of familiar kindness. I confess I had anticipated no difficulties. We are not a household of bigoted Conservatives; it is hard for me to imagine you taking any line but that of an enlightened man who judges all things from the standpoint of liberal reflection. I suppose my own scorn of prejudices is largely due to your influence. It is not easy to realise our being in conflict on any matter involving calm reasonableness.'

In another this would have been a shrewd speech. Wilfrid was incapable of conscious artifice of this kind; this appeal, the very strongest he could have made to his father, was urged in all sincerity, and derived its force from that very fact. He possessed not a little of the persuasive genius which goes to make an orator—hereafter to serve him in fields as yet undreamed of—and natural endowment guided his feeling in the way of most impressive utterance. Mr. Athel smiled in spite of himself.

'And what about your aunt?' he asked. 'Pray remember that it is only by chance that Miss Hood lives under my roof. Do you imagine your aunt equally unprejudiced?'

Mr. Athel was, characteristically, rather fond of sideglancings at feminine weaknesses. An opportunity of the kind was wont to mellow his mood.

'To be quite open in the matter,' Wilfrid replied, 'I will own that my first idea was to take you alone into my confidence; to ask you to say nothing to Aunt Edith. Miss Hood felt that that would be impossible, and I see that she was right. It would involve deceit which it is not in her nature to practise.'

'You and Miss Hood have discussed us freely,' observed the father, with a return to his irony.

'I don't reply to that,' said Wilfrid, quietly. 'I think you must give me credit for the usual measure of self-respect; and Miss Hood does not fall short of it.'

The look which Mr. Athel cast at his son had in it something of pride. He would not trust himself to speak immediately.

'I don't say,' he began presently, with balancing of phrase, 'that your plan is not on the face of it consistent and reasonable. Putting aside for the moment the wretchedly unsatisfactory circumstances which originate it, I suppose it is the plan which naturally suggests itself. But, of course, in practice it is out of the question.'

'You feel sure that aunt would not entertain it?'

'I do. And I don't see how I could recommend her to do so.'

Wilfrid reflected.

'In that case,' he said, 'I have only one alternative. I must give up my intention of returning to Oxford, and marry before the end of the year.'

The words had to his own ears a somewhat explosive sound. They were uttered, however, and he was glad of it.

A purpose thus formulated he would not swerve from. Of that his father too was well aware.

Mr. Athel rose from his seat, held the rolled-up magazine in both hands behind his back, and took a turn across a few yards of lawn. Wilfrid sat still, leaning forward, watching his father's shadow. The shadow approached him.

'Wilf, is there no via media? Cannot Miss Hood remain at home for a while? Are you going to throw up your career, and lay in a stock of repentance for the rest of your life?'

'I don't think you quite understand me, father. I contemplate no action which could possibly be injured even by my immediate marriage. If you mean University honours— I care nothing about them. I would go through the routine just for the sake of completeness; it is her strong wish that I should. But my future, most happily, does not depend on success of that kind. I shall live the life of a student, my end will be self-culture. And Miss Hood is unfortunately not able to remain at home. I say unfortunately, but I should have regarded it as preferable that she should continue in her position with us. You and aunt Edith would come to know her, and the air of a home like ours would, I believe, suit her better than that of her own. There is nothing in her work that might not be performed by any lady.'

'What do you know of her people?'

'Nothing, except that her father has scientific interests. It is plain enough, though, that they cannot be without refinement. No doubt they are poor; we hardly consider that a crime.'

He rose, as if he considered the interview at an end.

'Look here,' said Mr. Athel, with a little bluffness, the result of a difficulty in making concessions; 'if Miss Hood returned to us, as you propose, should you consider it a point of honour to go on with your work at Balliol as if nothing had happened, and to abstain from communication with her of a kind which would make things awkward?'

'Both, undoubtedly. I could very well arrange to keep away from home entirely in the interval.'

'Well, I think we have talked enough for the present. I have no kind of sympathy with your position, pray understand that. I think you have made about as bad a mistake as you could have done. All the same, I will speak of this with your aunt——'

'I think you had better not do that,' interrupted Wilfrid, 'I mean with any view of persuading her. I am afraid I can't very well bring myself to compromises which involve a confession of childish error. It is better I should go my own way.'

'Well, well, of course, if you take the strictly independent attitude——'

Mr. Athel took another turn on the lawn, his brows bent. It was the first time that there had ever been an approach to serious difference between himself and his son. The paternal instinct was strong in him, and it was inevitable that he should be touched by sympathetic admiration of his past self as revived in Wilfrid's firm and dignified bearing. He approached the latter again.

'Come to me in the study about ten to-night, will you?' he said.

It was the end of the discussion for the present.

Shortly after dinner, when coffee had been brought to the drawing-room, Wilfrid wandered out to the summer-house. Emily would be home by this time. He thought of her . . . .

'The deuce of it is,' exclaimed Mr. Athel, conversing with his sister, 'that it's so hard to find valid objections. If he had proposed to marry a barmaid, one's course would be clear, but as it is——'

Mrs. Rossall had listened in silence to a matter-of-fact disclosure of Wilfrid's proceedings. In the commencement her attention had marked itself by a slight elevation of the brows; at the end she was cold and rather disdainful. Observation of her face had the result of confirming her brother in the apologetic tone. He was annoyed at perceiving that Edith would justify his prediction.

'I am sorry to hear it, of course,' were her first words, 'but I suppose Wilfrid will act as he chooses.'

'Well, but this isn't all,' pursued Mr. Athel, laying aside an affectation of half-humorous indulgence which he had assumed. 'He has urged upon me an extraordinary proposal. His idea is that Miss Hood might continue to hold her position here until he has taken his degree.'

'I am not surprised. You of course told him that such a thing was out of the question?'

'I said that *you* would probably consider it so.'

'But surely—— Do you hold a different view?'

'Really, I hold no views at all. I am not sure that I have got the right focus yet. I know that the plans of a lifetime are upset; I can't get much beyond that at present.'

Mrs. Rossall was deeply troubled. She sat with her eyes drooped, her lower lip drawn in.

'Do you refer to any plan in particular?' she asked next.

'Yes, I suppose I do.'

'I am very, very sorry for Beatrice,' she said, in a subdued voice.

'You think it will——'

Mrs. Rossall raised her eyebrows a little, and kept her air of pained musing.

'Well, what is to be done?' resumed her brother, always impatient of mere negatives. 'He has delivered a sort of ultimatum. In the event of this proposal—as to Miss Hood's return—being rejected, he marries at once.'

'And then goes back to Balliol?'

'No, simply abandons his career.'

Mrs. Rossall smiled. It was not in woman's nature to be uninterested by decision such as this.

'Do you despair of influencing him?' she asked.

'Entirely. He will not hear of her taking another place in the interval, and it seems there are difficulties in the way of her remaining at home. Of course I see very well the objections on the surface to her coming back——'

'The objections are not on the surface at all, they are fundamental. You are probably not in a position to see the case as I do. Such a state of things would be ludicrous; we should all be playing parts in a farce. He cannot have made such a proposal to her; she would have shown him at once its absurdity.'

'But the fact of the matter is that she acceded to it,' said Mr. Athel, with a certain triumph over female infallibility.

'Then I think worse of her than I did, that's all.'

'I'm not at all sure that you are right in that,' observed her brother, with an impartial air. 'Pray tell me your serious opinion of Miss Hood. One begins, naturally, with a suspicion that she has not been altogether passive in this affair. What Wilf says is, of course, nothing to the point; he protests that her attitude has been irreproachable.'

'Especially in making assignations for six o'clock in the morning.'

'Well, well, that is merely granting the issue; you are a trifle illogical, Edith.'

'No doubt I am. You, on the other hand, seem to be very much of Wilf's opinion. I am sorry that I can't do as you wish.'

'Well, we shall not gain anything by giving way to irritation. He must be told how matters stand, and judge for himself.'

As Mr. Athel was speaking, Wilfrid entered the room. Impatience had overcome him. He knew of course that a discussion was in progress between his father and his aunt, and calm waiting upon other people's decisions was not in his nature. He came forward and seated himself.

'I gather from your look, aunt,' he began, when the others did not seem disposed to break silence, 'that you take my father's view of what he has been telling you.'

'I am not sure what your father's view is,' was Mrs. Rossall's reply, given very coldly. 'But I certainly think you have proposed what is impossible.'

'Yes, you are right,' rejoined Wilfrid, to the surprise of both. 'The plan was not well considered. Pray think no more of it.'

'What do you substitute?' his father inquired, after another long silence.

'I cannot say.' He paused, then continued with some emotion, 'I would gladly have had your sympathy. Perhaps I fail to see the whole matter in the same light as yourselves, but it seems to me that in the step I have taken there is nothing that should cause lasting difference between us. I involve the family in no kind of disgrace—that, I suppose, you admit?'

Mrs. Rossall made no answer. Mr. Athel moved uneasily upon his chair, coughed, seemed about to speak, but in the end said nothing.

'I am afraid I shall not be able to leave England with you,' continued Wilfrid, rising. 'But that fortunately need cause no change in your plans.'

Mr. Athel was annoyed at his sister's behaviour. He had looked to her for mediation; clearly she would offer nothing of the kind. She was wrapping herself in a cloak of offended dignity; she had withdrawn from the debate.

'Come with me to my room,' he said moving from his chair.

'I think it will be better to have no further discussion,' Wilfrid replied firmly, 'at all events to-night.'

'As you please,' said his father, shortly.

He went from the room, and Wilfrid, without further speech to his aunt, presently followed.

CHAPTER V.

THE SHADOW OF HOME.

THE house which was the end of Emily's journey was situated two miles outside the town of Dunfield, on the high road going southward, just before it enters upon a rising tract of common land known as the Heath. It was one of a row of two-storied dwellings, built of glazed brick, each with a wide projecting window on the right hand of the front door, and with a patch of garden railed in from the road, the row being part of a straggling colony which is called Banbrigg. Immediately opposite these houses stood an ecclesiastical edifice of depressing appearance, stone-built, wholly without ornament, presenting a corner to the highway, a chapel-of-ease for worshippers unable to go as far as Dunfield in the one direction or the village of Pendal in the other. Scattered about were dwelling-houses old and new; the former being cottages of the poorest and dirtiest kind, the latter brick structures of the most unsightly form, evidently aiming at constituting themselves into a thoroughfare, and, in point of fact, already rejoicing in the name of Regent Street. There was a public-house, or rather, as it frankly styled itself in large letters on the window, a dram-shop; and there were two or three places for the sale of very miscellaneous articles, exhibiting the same specimens of discouraging stock throughout the year. At no season, and under no advantage of sky, was Banbrigg a delectable abode. Though within easy touch of country which was not without rural aspects, it was marked too unmistakably with the squalor of a manufacturing district. Its existence impressed one as casual; it was a mere bit of Dunfield got away from the main mass, and having brought its dirt with it. The stretch of road between it and the bridge by which the river was crossed into Dunfield had in its long, hard ugliness something dispiriting. Though hedges bordered it here and there, they were stunted and grimed; though fields were seen on this side and on that, the grass had absorbed too much mill-smoke to exhibit wholesome verdure; it was fed upon by sheep and cows, seemingly turned in to be out of the way till needed for slaughter, and by the sorriest of super-annuated horses. The land was blighted by the curse of what we name—using a word as ugly as the thing it represents—industrialism.

As the cab brought her along this road from Dunfield station, Emily thought of the downs, the woodlands, the fair pastures of Surrey. There was sorrow at her heart, even a vague tormenting fear. It would be hard to find solace in Banbrigg.

Hither her parents had come to live when she was thirteen years old, her home having previously been in another and a larger manufacturing town. Her father was a man marked for ill-fortune: it pursued him from his entrance into the world, and would inevitably—you read it in his face—hunt him into a sad grave. He was the youngest of a large family; his very birth had been an added misery to a household struggling with want. His education was of the slightest; at twelve years of age he was already supporting himself, or, one would say, keeping himself above the point of starvation; and at three-and-twenty—the age when Wilfrid Athel is entering upon life in the joy of freedom—was ludicrously bankrupt, a petty business he had established being sold up for a debt something short of as many pounds as he had years. He drifted into indefinite mercantile clerkships, an existence possibly preferable to that of the fourth circle of Inferno, and then seemed at length to have fallen upon a piece of good luck, such as, according to a maxim of pathetic optimism wherewith he was wont to cheer himself, must come to every man sooner or later—provided he do not die of hunger whilst it is on the way. He married a schoolmistress, one Miss Martin, who was responsible for the teaching of some twelve or fifteen children of tender age, and who, what was more, owned the house in which she kept school. The result was that James Hood once more established himself in business, or rather in several businesses, vague, indescribable, save by those who are unhappy enough to understand such matters—a commission agency, a life insurance agency and a fire insurance ditto, I know not what. Yet the semblance of prosperity was fleeting. As if connection with him meant failure, his wife's school, which she had not abandoned (let us employ negative terms in speaking of this pair), began to fall off; ultimately no school was left. It did in truth appear that Miss Martin had suffered something in becoming Mrs. Hood. At her marriage she was five-and-twenty, fairly good-looking, in temper a trifle exigent perhaps, sanguine, and capable of exertion; she could not claim more than superficial instruction, but taught reading and writing with the usual success which attends teachers of these elements. After the birth of her first child, Emily, her moral nature showed an unaccountable weakening; the origin was no doubt physical, but in story-telling we dwell very much on the surface of things; it is not permitted us to describe human nature too accurately. The exigence of her temper became something generally described by a harsher term; she lost her interest in the work which she had unwillingly entrusted for a time to an assistant; she found the conditions of her life hard. Alas, they grew harder. After Emily, two children were successively born; fate was kind to them, and neither survived infancy. Their mother fell into fretting, into hysteria; some change in her life seemed imperative, and at length she persuaded her husband to quit the town in which they lived, and begin life anew elsewhere. Begin life anew! James Hood was forty years old; he possessed, as the net result of his commercial enterprises, a capital of a hundred and thirty pounds. The house, of course, could be let, and would bring five-and-twenty pounds a year. This it was resolved to do. He had had certain dealings in Dunfield, and in Dunfield he would strike his tent—that is to say, in Banbrigg, whence he walked daily to a little office in the town. Rents were lower in Banbrigg, and it was beyond the range of certain municipal taxings.

Mrs. Hood possessed still her somewhat genteel furniture. One article was a piano, and upon this she taught Emily her notes. It had been a fairly good piano once, but the keys had become very loose. They were looser than ever, now that Emily tried to play on them, on her return from Surrey.

Business did not thrive in Dunfield; yet there was more than ever need that it should, for to neglect Emily's education would be to deal cruelly with the child—she would have nothing else to depend upon in her battle with the world. Poor Emily! A feeble, overgrown child, needing fresh air, which she could not get, needing food of a better kind, just as unattainable. Large-eyed, thin-cheeked Emily; she, too, already in the clutch of the great brute world, the helpless victim of a civilisation which makes its food of those the heart most pities. How well if her last sigh had been drawn in infancy, if she had lain with the little brother and sister in that gaunt, grimy cemetery, under the shadow of mill chimneys! She was reserved for other griefs; for consolations, it is true, but——

Education she did get, by hook or by crook; there was dire pinching to pay for it, and, too well knowing this, the child strove her utmost to use the opportunities offered her. Each morning going into Dunfield, taking with her some sandwiches that were called dinner, walking home again by tea-time, tired, hungry—ah, hungry! No matter the weather, she must walk her couple of miles—it was at least so far to the school. In winter you saw her set forth with her waterproof and umbrella, the too-heavy bag of books on her arm; sometimes the wind and rain beating as if to delay her—they, too, cruel. In summer the hot days tried her perhaps still more; she reached home in the afternoon well-nigh fainting, the books were so heavy. Who would not have felt kindly to her? So gentle she was, so dreadfully shy and timid, her eyes so eager, so full of unconscious pathos. 'Hood's little girl,' said the people on the way who saw her pass daily, and, however completely strangers, they said it with a certain kindness of tone and meaning. A little thing that happened one day— take it as an anecdote. On her way to school she passed some boys who were pelting a most wretched dog, a poor, scraggy beast driven into a corner. Emily, so timid usually she could not raise her eyes before a stranger, stopped, quivering all over, *commanded* them to cease their brutality, divine compassion become a heroism. The boys somehow did her bidding, and walked on together. Emily stayed behind, opened her bag, threw something for the dog to eat. It was half her dinner.

Her mind braced itself. She had a passionate love of learning; all books were food to her. Fortunately there was the library of the Mechanics' Institute; but for that she would have come short of mental sustenance, for her father had never been able to buy more than a dozen volumes, and these all dealt with matters of physical science. The strange things she read, books which came down to her from the shelves with a thickness of dust upon them; histories of

Greece and Rome ('Not much asked for, these,' said the librarian), translations of old classics, the Koran, Mosheim's 'Ecclesiastical History,' works of Swedenborg, all the poetry she could lay hands on, novels not a few. One day she asked for a book on 'Gymnoblastic Hydroids'; the amazing title in the catalogue had filled her with curiosity; she must know the meaning of everything. She was not idle, Emily.

But things in the home were going from bad to worse. When Emily was sixteen, her father scarcely knew where to look for each day's dinner. Something must be done. Activity took a twofold direction. First of all, Emily got work as a teacher in an infant's school. It was at her own motion; she could bear her mother's daily querulousness no longer; she must take some step. She earned a mere trifle; but it was earning, instead of being a source of expense. And in the meantime she worked on for certain examinations which it would benefit her to have passed. The second thing done was that her father abandoned his office, and obtained a place in the counting-house of a worsted-mill, under the firm of Dagworthy and Son. His salary was small, but the blessing of it was its certainty; the precariousness of his existence had all but driven poor Hood mad. There came a season of calm. Emily's sphere of work extended itself; the school only took her mornings, and for the afternoon there was proposed to her the teaching of the little Baxendales. The Baxendales were well-to-do people; the father was, just then, mayor of Dunfield, the mother was related to the member of Parliament for the town. We have had mention of them as connections of Beatrice Redwing.

At nineteen she for the first time left home. Through the Baxendales she obtained the position of governess in a family residing in Liverpool, and remained with them till she went to London, to the Athels. These three years in Liverpool were momentous for her; they led her from girlhood to womanhood, and established her character. Her home was in the house of a prosperous ship-owner, a Lancashire man; outwardly a blustering good-tempered animal, yet with an inner light which showed itself in his love of books and pictures, in his easy walking under the burden of self-acquired riches, in a certain generous freedom which marked his life and thoughts. His forename was Laurence: Emily, in letters to her father, used to call him Lorenzo the Magnificent, a title which became him well enough. In the collection of works of art he was really great; he must have spent appalling sums annually on his picture gallery and the minor ornaments scattered about his house. He had a personal acquaintance, through his pecuniary dealings, with the foremost artists of the day; he liked to proclaim the fact and describe the men. To Emily the constant proximity of these pictures was a priceless advantage; the years she spent among them were equivalent to a university course. Moreover, she enjoyed, as with the Athels later, a free command of books; here began her acquaintance with the most modern literature, which was needful to set her thoughts in order, to throw into right perspective her previous miscellaneous reading, and to mark out her way in the future. Her instinctive craving for intellectual beauty acquired a reflective consistency; she reformed her ideals, found the loveliness of much that in her immaturity had seemed barren, put aside, with gentle firmness, much that had appeared indispensable to her moral life. The meanings which she attached to that word 'moral' largely modified themselves, that they should do so was the note of her progress. Her prayer was for 'beauty in the inward soul,' which, if it grew to be her conviction, was greatly—perhaps wholly— dependent on the perception of external beauty. The development of beauty in the soul would mean a life of ideal purity; all her instincts pointed to such a life; her passionate motives converged on the one end of spiritual chastity.

One ever-present fear she had to strive with in her progress toward serene convictions. The misery of her parents' home haunted her, and by no effort could she expel the superstition that she had only escaped from that for a time, that its claws would surely overtake her and fix themselves again in her flesh. Analysing her own nature, she discerned, or thought she did, a lack of independent vigour; it seemed as if she were too reliant on external circumstances; she dreaded what might follow if their assistance were withdrawn. To be sure she had held her course through the countless discouragements of early years; but that, in looking back, seemed no assurance for the future; her courage, it appeared to her, had been of the unconscious kind, and might fail her when she consciously demanded it. As a child she had once walked in her sleep, had gone forth from the house, and had, before she was awakened, crossed the narrow footing of a canal-lock, a thing her nervousness would not allow her to do at other times. This became to her a figure. The feat she had performed when mere vital instinct guided her, she would have failed in when attempting it with the full understanding of its dangers. Suppose something happened which put an end to her independence—failure of health, some supreme calamity at home—could she hold on in the way of salvation? Was she capable of conscious heroism? Could her soul retain its ideal of beauty if environed by ugliness?

The vice of her age—nay, why call it a vice?—the necessary issue of that intellectual egoism which is the note of our time, found as good illustration in this humble life as in men and women who are the mouthpieces of a civilisation. Preoccupied with problems of her own relation to the world, she could not enjoy without thought in the rear, ever ready to trouble her with suggestions of unreality. Her distresses of conscience were all the more active for being purely human; in her soul dwelt an immense compassion, which, with adequate occasion, might secure to itself such predominance as to dwarf into inefficiency her religion of culture. It was exquisite misery to conceive, as, from inner observation, she so well could, some demand of life which would make her ideals appear the dreams of bygone halcyon days, useless and worse amid the threats of gathering tempest. An essentially human apprehension, be it understood. The vulgarities of hysterical pietism Emily had never known; she did not fear the invasion of such blight as that; the thought of it was noisome to her. Do you recall a kind of trouble that came upon her, during that talk in the hollow, when Wilfrid suggested the case of her being called upon to make some great sacrifice in her father's behalf? It was an instance of the weakness I speak of; the fact of Wilfrid's putting forward such a thought had in that moment linked her to him with precious bonds of sympathy, till she felt as if he had seen into the most secret places of her heart. She dreaded the force of her compassionateness. That dog by the roadside; how the anguish of its eyes had haunted her through the day! It was the revolt of her whole being against the cruelty inherent in life. That evening she could not read the book she had in hand; its phrases seemed to fall into triviality. Yet—she reasoned at a later time—it should not have been so; the haggard gaze of fate should not daunt one; pity is but an element in the soul's ideal of order, it should not usurp a barren sovereignty. It is the miserable contradiction in our lot that the efficiency of the instincts of beauty-worship waits

upon a force of individuality attainable only by a sacrifice of
sensibility. Emily divined this. So it was that she came to
shun the thought of struggle, to seek an abode apart from
turbid conditions of life. She was hard at work building for
her soul its 'lordly pleasure-house,' its Palace of Art. Could
she, poor as she was, dependent, bound by such obvious chains
to the gross earth, hope to abide in her courts and corridors
for ever ? . . .

Friday was the day of her arrival at Banbrigg. On the
Saturday afternoon she hoped to enjoy a walk with her father;
he would reach home from the mill shortly after two o'clock,
and would then have his dinner. Mrs. Hood dined at one,
and could not bring herself to alter the hour for Saturday ; it
was characteristic of her. That there might be no culinary
cares on Sunday morning, she always cooked her joint of
meat on the last day of the week; partaking of it herself at
one o'clock, she cut slices for her husband and kept them
warm, with vegetables, in the oven. This was not selfishness
in theory, however much it may have been so in practice ; it
merely meant that she was unable to introduce variation into
a mechanical order; and, as her husband never dreamed of
complaining, Mrs. Hood could see in the arrangement no
breach of the fitness of things, even though it meant that
poor Hood never sat down to a freshly cooked meal from one
end of the year to the other. To Emily it was simply a
detestable instance of the worst miseries she had to endure at
home. Coming on this first day, it disturbed her much. She
knew the uselessness, the danger, of opposing any traditional
habit, but her appetite at one o'clock was small.

Mrs. Hood did not keep a servant in the house ; she
engaged a charwoman once a week, and did all the work at
other times herself. This was not strictly necessary ; the
expense of such a servant as would have answered purposes
could just have been afforded; again and again Emily had
entreated to be allowed to pay a girl out of her own earnings.
Mrs. Hood steadily refused. No, she had *once* known what it
was to have luxuries about her (that was naturally before her
marriage), but those days were gone by. She thus entailed
upon herself a great deal of labour, at once repugnant to her
tastes and ill-suited to the uncertainty of her health, but all
this was forgotten in the solace of possessing a standing
grievance, one obvious at all moments, to be uttered in a
sigh, to be emphasised by the affectation of cheerfulness.

The love which was Emily's instinct grew chill in the presence of such things.

Saturday was from of old a day of ills. The charwoman was in the house, and Mrs. Hood went about in a fatigued way, coming now and then to the sitting-room, sinking into a chair, letting her head fall back with closed eyes. Emily had, of course, begged to be allowed to give assistance, but her mother declared that there was nothing whatever she could do.

' Shut the door,' she said, ' and then you won't hear the scrubbing so plainly. I can understand that it annoys you ; I used to have the same feeling, but I've accustomed myself. You might play something ; it would keep away your thoughts.

' But I don't want to keep away my thoughts,' exclaimed Emily, with a laugh. ' I want to help you so that you will have done the sooner.'

' No, no, my dear ; you are not used to it. You'll tell me when you'd like something to eat if you get faint,'

' I am not likely to grow faint, mother, if I do nothing.'

' Well, well ; I have a sinking feeling now and then, I thought you might be the same.'

Just when his dinner in the oven had had time to grow crusty, Mr. Hood arrived. He was a rather tall man, of sallow complexion, with greyish hair. The peculiarly melancholy expression of his face was due to the excessive drooping of his eyelids under rounded brows; beneath the eyes were heavy lines ; he generally looked like one who has passed through a night of sleepless grief. He wore a suit of black, which had for several years been his reserve attire, till it grew too seamy for use on Sundays. The whole look of the man was saddening ; to pass him in the street as a stranger was to experience a momentary heaviness of heart. He had very long slender fingers—Emily's matchless hand in a rudimentary form—and it seemed to be a particular solicitude to keep them scrupulously clean ; he frequently examined them, and appeared to have a pleasure in handling things in a dainty way—the pages of a book, for instance. When he smiled it was obviously with effort—a painful smile, for all that an exceedingly gentle one. In his voice there was the same gentleness, a self suppression, as it were ; his way of speaking half explained his want of success in life.

Emily was standing at the window in expectation of his

coming. As soon as he reached the iron gate in front of the house she ran to open the door for him. He did not quicken his step, even stopped to close the gate with deliberate care, but if his face could ever be said to light up, it did so as he bent to the girl's kiss. She took his hat from him, and went to see that his dinner was made ready.

'How fine it is!' he said in his subdued tone, when he came downstairs and stood by the table stroking his newly washed hands. 'Shall we have a walk before tea-time? Mother is too busy, I'm afraid.'

Mrs. Hood came into the room shortly, and seated herself in the usual way.

'Did you bring the cake?' she asked, when her presence had caused silence for a few moments.

'The cake?' he repeated in surprise.

'Didn't I ask you to bring a cake? I suppose my memory is going; I meant to, and thought I mentioned it at breakfast. I shall have nothing for Emily's tea.'

Emily protested that it was needless to get unusual things on her account.

'We must do what we can to make you comfortable, my dear. I can't keep a table like that you are accustomed to, but that I know you don't expect. Which way are you going to walk this afternoon? If you pass a shop you might get a cake, or buns, whichever you like.'

'Well, I thought we might have a turn over the Heath,' said Mr. Hood. 'However, we'll see what we can do.'

A thought of some anxious kind appeared suddenly to strike Mrs. Hood; she leaned forward in her chair, seemed to listen, then started up and out of the room.

Emily sat where she could not see her father eating; it pained, exasperated her to be by him whilst he made such a meal. He ate slowly, with thought of other things; at times his eye wandered to the window, and he regarded the sky in a brooding manner. He satisfied his hunger without pleasure, apparently with indifference.

Shortly after three o'clock the two started for their walk. Not many yards beyond the house the road passed beneath a railway bridge, then over a canal, and at once entered upon the common. The Heath formed the long side of a slowly rising hill; at the foot the road divided itself into two branches, and the dusty tracks climbed at a wide angle with each other. The one which Emily and her father pursued led up to stone quarries, which had been for a long time in working, and, skirting these, to the level ground above them, which was the end of the region of furze and bracken. Here began a spacious tract of grassy common; around it were houses of pleasant appearance, one or two meriting the name of mansion. In one of them dwelt Mr. Richard Dagworthy, the mill-owner, in whose counting-house James Hood earned his living. He alone epresented the firm of Dagworthy and Son; his father had been dead two years, and more recently he had become a widower, his wife leaving him one child still an infant.

At the head of the quarries the two paused to look back upon Dunfield. The view from this point was extensive, and would have been interesting but for the existence of the town itself. It was seen to lie in a broad valley, along which a river flowed; the remoter districts were pleasantly wooded, and only the murkiness in the far sky told that a yet larger centre of industry lurked beyond the horizon. Dunfield offered no prominent features save the chimneys of its factories and its fine church, the spire of which rose high above surrounding buildings; over all hung a canopy of foul vapour, heavy, pestiferous. Take in your fingers a spray from one of the trees even here on the Heath, and its touch left a soil.

'How I wish you could see the views from the hills in Surrey!' Emily exclaimed when they had stood in silence. 'I can imagine nothing more delightful in English scenery. It realises my idea of perfect rural beauty, as I got it from engravings after the landscape painters. Oh, you shall go there with me some day.'

Her father smiled and shook his head a little.

'Perhaps,' he said; and added a favourite phrase of his, 'while there is life there is hope.'

'Of course there is,' rejoined Emily, with gaiety which was unusual in her. 'No smoke; the hills blue against a lovely sky! trees covered to the very roots with greenness; rich old English homes and cottages—oh, you know the kind; your ideal of a cottage—low tiled roofs, latticed windows, moss and lichen and climbing flowers. Farmyards sweet with hay, and gleaming dairies. That country is my home!'

With how rich a poetry it clothed itself in her remembrance, the land of milk and honey, indeed, her heart's home. It was all but impossible to keep the secret of her joy, yet she had resolved to do so, and her purpose held firm.

'I am very glad indeed that you are so happy there,' said
her father, looking at her with that quiet absorption in
another's mood of which he was so capable. 'But it will be
London through the winter. You haven't told me much
about London; but then you were there so short a time.'

'But I saw much. Mrs. Rossall could not have been
kinder; for the first few days it was almost as if I had been
a visitor; I was taken everywhere.'

'I should like to see London before I die,' mused her
father. 'Somehow I have never managed to get so far.'

'Oh, we will see it together some day.'

'There's one thing,' said Mr. Hood, reflectively, 'that I
wish especially to see, and that is Holborn Viaduct. It must
be a wonderful piece of engineering; I remember thinking
it out at the time it was constructed. Of course you have
seen it?'

'I am afraid not. We are very far away from the City.
But I will go and see it on the first opportunity.'

'Do, and send me a full description.'

His thoughts reverted to the views before them.

'After all, this isn't so bad. There's a great advantage in
living so near the Heath. I'm sure the air here is admirable;
don't you smell how fresh it is? And then, one gets fond of
the place one's lived in for years. I believe I should find it
hard to leave Dunfield.'

Emily smiled gently.

'I wonder,' he pursued, 'whether you have the kind of
feeling that came to me just then? It struck me that, suppose anything happened that would enable us to go and live
in another place, there would be a sort of ingratitude, something like a shabby action, in turning one's back on the old
spot. I don't like to feel unkind even to a town.'

The girl glanced at him with meaning eyes. Here was
an instance of the sympathetic relations of which she had
spoken to Wilfrid; in these words was disclosed the origin of
the deepest sensibilities of her own nature.

They pursued their walk, across the common and into a
tree-shaded lane. Emily tried to believe that this at length
was really the country; there were no houses in view, meadows lay on either hand, the leafage was thick. But it was
not mere prejudice which saw in every object a struggle with
hard conditions, a degeneration into coarseness, a blight. The
quality of the earth was probably poor to begin with; the

herbage seemed of gross fibre; one would not risk dipping a finger in the stream which trickled by the roadside, it suggested an impure source. And behold, what creatures are these coming along the lane, where only earth-stained rustics should be met? Two colliers, besmutted wretches, plodding homeward from the 'pit' which is half a mile away. Yes, their presence was in keeping with the essential character of the scene.

'One might have had a harder life,' mused Mr. Hood aloud, when the pitmen were gone by.

'I think there's a fallacy in that,' replied Emily. 'Their life is probably not hard at all. I used to feel that pity, but I have reasoned myself out of it. They are really happy, for they know nothing of their own degradation.'

'By the bye,' said her father presently, 'how is young Mr. Athel, the young fellow who had to come home from college?'

'He is quite well again, I think,' was Emily's reply.

'I suppose, poor fellow, he has a very weak constitution?' Oh no, I think not.'

'What is he studying for? Going into the Church?'

Emily laughed; it was a relief to do so.

'Isn't it strange,' she said, 'how we construct an idea of an unknown person from some circumstance or piece of description? I see exactly what your picture of Mr. Athel is: a feeble and amiable young man, most likely with the shocking voice with which curates sometimes read the lessons——'

She broke off and laughed again.

'Well,' said her father, 'I admit I thought of him a little in that way—I scarcely know why.'

'You could hardly have been further from the truth. Try to imagine the intellectual opposite of such a young man, and you—— That will be far more like Mr. Athel.'

'He isn't conceited? My want of experience has an unfortunate tendency to make me think of young fellows in his position as unbearably vain. It must be so hard to avoid it.

'Perhaps it is, if they have the common misfortune to be born without brains.'

Other subjects engaged their attention.

'When do you take your holiday, father?' Emily asked.

'I think about the middle of this month. It won't be more than a week or ten days.'

'Don't you think you ought to go to Cleethorpes, if only for a day or two?'

To suggest any other place of summer retreat would have been too alarming. Mr. Hood's defect of imagination was illustrated in this matter; he had been somehow led, years ago, to pay a visit to Cleethorpes, and since then that one place represented for him the seaside. Others might be just as accessible and considerably more delightful, but it did not even occur to him to vary. It would have cost him discomfort to do so, the apprehension of entering upon the unknown. The present was the third summer which had passed without his quitting home. Anxiety troubled his countenance as Emily made the proposal.

'Not this year, I think,' he said, as if desirous of passing the subject by.

'Father, what possible objection can there be to my bearing the expense of a week at Cleethorpes? You know how well I can afford it; indeed I should like to go; it is rather unkind of you to refuse.'

This was an old subject of discussion. Since Emily had lived away from home, not only her father, but her mother just as strenuously, had refused to take from her any of the money that she earned. It had been her habit at first indirectly to overcome this resistance by means of substantial presents in holiday time; but she found such serious discomfort occasioned by the practice that most reluctantly she had abandoned it. For the understanding of the Hoods' attitude in this matter, it must be realised how deeply their view of life was coloured by years of incessant preoccupation with pecuniary difficulties. The hideous conception of existence which regards each individual as fighting for his own hand, striving for dear life against every other individual, was ingrained in their minds by the inveterate bitterness of their own experience; when Emily had become a woman, and was gone forth to wrest from the adverse world her own subsistence, her right to what she earned was indefeasible, and affection itself protested against her being mulcted for their advantage. As for the slight additional expense of her presence at home during the holidays, she must not be above paying a visit to her parents; the little inconsistency was amiable enough. Father and mother both held forth to her in the same tone: 'You have the battle of life before you; it is a terrible one, and the world is relentless. Not only is it

your right, but your very duty, to spare every penny you can;
for, if anything happened to prevent your earning money, you
would become a burden upon us—a burden we would gladly
strive to bear, but the thought of which would be very hard
for yourself. If, on the other hand, your mother were left a
widow, think how dreadful it would be if you could give her
no assistance. You are wrong in spending one farthing more
than your absolute needs require; to say you do it in kindness to us is a mere mistake of yours.' The logic was not to
be encountered; it was as irresistible as the social conditions
which gave it birth. Emily had abandoned discussion on
those points; such reasoning cost her sickness of heart. In
practice she obeyed her parents' injunctions, for she herself
was hitherto only too well aware of the fate which might come
upon her in consequence of the most trifling mishap; she
knew that no soul in the world save her parents would think
it a duty to help her, save in the way of bare charity. Naturally her old point of view was now changed; it was this that
led her to revive the discussion with her father, and to speak
in a tone which Mr. Hood heard with some surprise.

'Next year, perhaps, Emily,' he said. 'After Surrey, I
don't think you can really need another change. I am delighted to see how well you look. I, too, am remarkably well,
and I can't help thinking your mother gets stronger. How
do you find her looking?'

'Better than usual, I really think. All the same, it is
clearly impossible for you and her to live on year after year
without any kind of change.'

'Oh, my dear, we don't feel it. It's so different with
older people; a change rather upsets us than otherwise.
You know how nervous your mother gets when she is away
from home.'

Their walk brought them round again to the top of the
Heath. Mr. Hood looked at his watch, and found that it was
time to be moving homewards. Tea was punctually at five.
Mrs. Hood would take it ill if they were late, especially on
Saturday.

As they walked across the smooth part of the upper common, looking at the houses around, they saw coming towards
them a gentleman followed by three dogs. He was dressed
in a light tweed suit, and brandished a walking-stick, as if
animal spirits possessed him strongly.

'Why, here comes Mr. Dagworthy,' remarked Mr. Hood,

in a low tone, though the other was still at a considerable distance. 'He generally goes off somewhere on Saturday afternoon. What a man he is for dogs! I believe he keeps twenty or thirty at the house there.'

Emily evinced just a little self-consciousness. It was possible that Mr. Dagworthy would stop to speak, for she had become, in a measure, acquainted with him in the preceding spring. She was at home then for a few weeks before her departure for London, and the Baxendales, who had always shown her much kindness, invited her to an evening party, at which Dagworthy was present. He had chatted with her on that occasion.

Yes, he was going to speak. He was a man of five-and-thirty, robust, rather florid, with eyes which it was not disagreeable to meet, though they gazed with embarrassing persistency, and a mouth which he would have done well to leave under the natural shelter of a moustache; it was at once hard and sensual. The clean-shaving of his face gave his appearance a youthfulness to which his tone of speech did not correspond.

'How do you do, Miss Hood? Come once more into our part of the world, then? You have been in London, I hear.'

It was the tone of a man long accustomed to have his own way in life, and not overmuch troubled with delicacies of feeling. His address could not be called disrespectful, but the smile which accompanied it expressed a sort of good-natured patronage, perhaps inevitable in such a man when speaking to his clerk's daughter. The presence of the clerk himself very little concerned him. He kept his eyes steadily on the girl's face, examining her with complete frankness. His utterance was that of an educated man, but it had something of the Yorkshire accent, a broadness which would have distressed the ear in a drawing-room.

Emily replied that she had been in London; it did not seem necessary to enter into details.

'Pleasant afternoon, isn't it? Makes one want to get away to the moors. I suppose you will be off somewhere soon with your family, Mr. Hood?'

He would not have employed the formal prefix to his clerk's name but for Emily's presence; the father knew that, and felt grateful.

'Not this year, I think, sir,' he replied, with perfect cheerfulness.

Of the three dogs that accompanied Dagworthy, one was a handsome collie. This animal came snuffing at Emily's hand, and involuntarily, glad perhaps to have a pretence for averting her face, she caressed the silky ears.

'Fine head, isn't it, Miss Hood?' said Dagworthy at once, causing her to remove her hand quickly. 'Ay, but I've a finer collie than that. Just walk in with me, will you?' he added, after a scarcely perceptible pause. 'I always like to show off my dogs. You're in no hurry, I suppose? Just come and have a look at the kennels.'

Emily was deeply annoyed, both because such a visit was in itself distasteful to her, and on account of the irritation which she knew the delay would cause her mother. She did not for a moment expect her father to refuse; his position would not allow him to do so. Mr. Hood, in fact, murmured thanks, after a mere half glance at his daughter, and the three walked together to Dagworthy's house, the entrance to which was not fifty yards from where they were standing.

The dwelling was neither large nor handsome, but it stood in a fine garden and had an air of solid well-being. As soon as they had passed the gates, they were met by a middle-aged woman carrying a child of two years old, an infant of wonderfully hearty appearance. At the sight of its father it chuckled and crowed. Dagworthy took it from the woman's arms, and began a game which looked not a little dangerous; with surprising strength and skill, he tossed it up some feet into the air, caught it as it descended, tossed it up again. The child shrieked with delight, for all that the swift descent positively stopped its breath, and made a hiatus in the screaming.

'Theer, that's abaht enough, Mr. Richard,' said the woman, in broad dialect, when the child had gone up half a dozen times; she was nervous, and kept holding out her arms involuntarily. 'Ah doan't ovver much fancy that kind o' laakin. What's more, he's allus reight dahn fratchy after a burn o' that. Coom nah, he'll niwer want you to stop. Do a' done nah, Mr. Richard.'

'Here you are then; take him in, and tell them I want some tea; say I have friends with me.'

The child was carried away, roaring obstreperously, and Dagworthy, laughing at the vocal power displayed, led the way round to the back of the house. Here had been constructed elaborate kennels; several dogs were pacing in freedom about the clean yard, and many more were chained up. Much information was imparted to the visitors concerning the more notable animals; some had taken prizes at shows, others were warranted to do so, one or two had been purchased at fancy prices. Mr. Hood now and then put a question, as in duty bound to do; Emily restricted her speech to the absolutely necessary replies.

Dagworthy conducted them into the house. It appeared to be furnished in a solid, old-fashioned way, and the ornaments, though few, were such as might better have been dispensed with. Old Dagworthy had come to live here some five-and-twenty years previously, having before that occupied a small house in conjunction with his mill. He had been one of the 'worthies' of Dunfield, and in his time did a good deal of useful work for the town. Personally, he was anything but amiable, being devoid of education and refinement, and priding himself on his spirit of independence, which exhibited itself in mere boorishness. Though anything but miserly, he had, where his interests were concerned, an extraordinary cunning and pertinacity; he was universally regarded as one of the shrewdest men of business in that part of Yorkshire, and report credited him with any number of remarkable meannesses. It was popularly said that 'owd Dick Dagworthy' would shrink from no dirty trick to turn a sixpence, but was as likely as not to give it away as soon as he had got it. His son had doubtless advanced the character of the stock, and, putting aside the breeding of dogs, possessed many tastes of which the old man had no notion; none the less, he was credited with not a little of his father's spirit in business. In practical affairs he was shrewd and active; he never—as poor Hood might have testified—paid a man in his employ a penny more than there was need, and fell far short of the departed Dagworthy's generosity; to be at his mercy in a pecuniary transaction was to expect and to receive none. For all that, there was something in the man which hinted at qualities beneath the surface; a glance, a tone, now and then, which seemed on the point of revealing a hidden humanity.

When he chose, he could be courteous; he was so at present, as he requested Emily and her father to seat themselves in a large homely room which looked out upon the garden. The woman who had carried the child reappeared and poured out cups of tea. When she had left the room—

'I must ask you to excuse the roughness of my establishment, Miss Hood,' he said. 'I have to make shift for the present with Mrs. Jenkins. She isn't as refined as she might be, but she's been with us here for more than twelve years, and I should be sorry to replace her with any other servant.'

Pieces of bread and butter of somewhat undue solidity were offered. Emily declined anything but the cup of tea. She was very ill at ease, though she succeeded in suppressing any manifestation of it; Dagworthy kept his gaze on her constantly.

'Now I know you didn't care very much about the dogs,' he said to her presently. 'I think I've got something here that will be rather more in your line.'

He brought from a corner of the room a large portfolio, set it upon a chair in front of Emily, and exposed its contents. These were a number of fine photographs of continental cathedrals and churches.

'I bought these when I took my run through France and Germany last year,' he explained. 'I've something of a turn for architecture, I believe; at all events, I know I like a fine building, and I like to find out all I can about it.'

He went through the collection, with remarks which proved that he had certainly attained a rudimentary knowledge of the subject, and that his appreciation was often keen when his technical understanding might be at fault.

'The worst of it is,' he said, at one point, with a modesty which was a new feature in his conversation, 'I can't pronounce the names properly. Now, how do you read that, Miss Hood? To be sure; I know it when I hear it. Have you ever been in France?'

The negative reply came.

'You'd like to see the old-fashioned streets in which some of these churches stand.'

As soon as it was possible to do so, Emily looked meaningly at her father, and he, just as anxious to be on his way homeward, rose for leave-taking. Dagworthy offered no opposition; he went with them to the gates, and shook hands with both, then stood gazing after them as they walked across the common.

'Well, I never knew young Dagworthy anything like that before,' said Mr. Hood, when they were at some distance from the gate. 'I couldn't believe it when he asked us to go into the house.'

'I'm afraid mother will be very uneasy,' was Emily's reply.

'Yes, my dear, I'm afraid she will; let's walk sharply. But he was really uncommonly pleasant; I shall think a good deal better of him than I have done.'

This was the only aspect of the afternoon's adventure which presented itself to Mr. Hood. Emily was divided between relief at having got away from that persistent gaze and apprehension of what might meet them on their arrival at home. The latter feeling was only too well justified. Mrs. Hood sat in the kitchen, the window darkened. When speech was at length elicited from her, it appeared that a headache to which she was subject had come on in its severest form. Emily was at once active with remedies, not that any of those that she urged were likely to avail themselves, but because she was well aware that the more solicitude she showed the sooner her mother would resume her ordinary state. Mrs. Hood begged to be left to herself; let them have their tea and leave her in the kitchen, she was best there, out of people's way; it would soon be bedtime, the evening was practically gone. In the course of half an hour she was at length prevailed upon to come into the sitting-room, and even to taste a cup of tea. At first she had paid no attention to the reasons alleged for the unpunctuality; little by little she began to ask questions on her own account, petulantly but with growing interest. Still, the headache was not laid aside, and all spent a very dolorous evening.

In the relation these things have their humorous side; Emily may be excused if she was slow to appreciate it. She knew very well that the crisis meant for her father several days of misery, and perhaps in her youthful energy she was disposed to make too little allowance for her mother, whose life had been so full of hardship, and who even now was suffering from cares and anxieties the worst of which her daughter was not allowed to perceive. After the girl's early departure to her bedroom the other two sat talking drearily; after one of her headaches Mrs. Hood always dwelt in conversation on the most wretched features of her life, with despairing forecast. Poor woman, there was little of a brighter kind to occupy her thoughts. Two occasions of grave anxiety were at present troubling her, and, though he spoke of them less, her husband in no less a degree. It had just been announced to them that at the ensuing Christmas their rent would be raised, and at the same time the tenant who had for years occupied the house which they owned in the town of Barnhill had given notice of departure. There was a certain grotesqueness in the fact of James Hood being a proprietor of real estate. Twice an attempt had been made to sell the house in question, but no purchaser could be found; the building was in poor repair, was constantly entailing expense to the landlord, and, in the event of its becoming unoccupied, would doubtless wait long for another tenant. This event had some about, or would in a couple of months, and the loss of that five-and-twenty pounds a year would make the difficulty of existence yet more desperate. Once more an attempt at sale must be made, in itself involving outlays which, however petty, could ill be borne; and to sell, even if it could be done, meant a serious loss of income.

'What did it mean, do you think?' Mrs. Hood asked, recurring to the subject of Dagworthy and his astonishing behaviour. She put the question dispiritedly, not venturing to hope for a solution that would help her to a more cheerful frame of mind.

Hood scarcely dared to utter the words which came into his mind.

'You remember that they met at the Baxendales'——'

'How did Emily behave?' the mother next inquired.

'She was very quiet. I don't think she liked it. We must bear in mind the kind of society she is used to. Young Dagworthy won't seem of much account to her, I fancy.'

'But he has had a good education, hasn't he?'

'Pretty good, I suppose. He confessed to us, though, that he couldn't pronounce French words.'

'It's quite certain,' said Mrs. Hood, 'he wouldn't have invited you in if you had been alone.'

'Certain enough,' was the reply, in a tone wholly disinterested. 'But it must have been just a fancy, a whim. Things of that kind don't happen nowadays.'

'Not to us, at all events,' murmured the other dejectedly.

'Well, there must come what will,' she added, leaning her head back once more, and losing interest in the subject. 'I hope nothing and expect nothing.'

Alas, these two sitting together in the dull little room, speaking in disjointed phrases of despondency, exchanging no look, no word of mutual kindness, had they not once loved each other, with the love of youth and hope? Had it not once been enough to sit through long evenings and catch with eagerness each other's lightest word? Time had robbed them of youth,

and the injustice of the world's order had starved love to less
than a shadow of itself, to a mere habit of common suffering.
Tender memories were buried in the grave of children whom
the resources of ever so modest a fortune would have kept
alive; the present was a mere struggle to support existence,
choking the impulses of affection. One would not murmur at
the kindly order of life, whereby passion gives place to gentle
habitudes, and the fiery soul of youth tames itself to comely
gravity; but that love and joy, the delights of eager sense and
of hallowed aspiration, should be smothered in the foul dust
of a brute combat for bread, that the stinted energies of early
years should change themselves to the blasted hopes of failing
manhood in a world made ill by human perverseness, this is
not easily—it may be, not well—borne with patience. Put
money in thy purse; and again, put money in thy purse;
for, as the world is ordered, to lack current coin is to lack the
privileges of humanity, and indigence is the death of the soul.

CHAPTER VI.

A VISITOR BY EXPRESS.

It had been arranged that Emily should receive news from
Wilfrid by the first post on Monday morning. Her father
left home at half-past eight, and Emily, a little ashamed at so
deceiving him, went into the town at the same time on pretence of a desire to share his walk. Taking leave of him as
soon as the mill was in sight, she walked towards the post-
office. At this early hour there was no one before the counter:
she overcame her nervousness and asked for letters. That
which she expected was given to her, and at the same time a
telegram.

The sight of the telegram agitated her. Drawing aside,
she opened it at once. Wilfrid had despatched it the previous
night from London. 'I shall be in Dunfield at one o'clock
to-morrow. Please leave a note for me at the post-office,
appointing any place of meeting at any time you like. I
shall find the place from your description.'

The letter, as she could perceive by feeling it, was long;
there was no necessity to open it until she reached home.
But the note she must write at once. In agitation which
would scarcely allow her to reflect, she left the office and

sought a small shop where she could procure note-paper. On her way she devised a plan for meeting. In the shop where she made her purchase, she was permitted also to write the note. Having stamped the envelope, she returned to the post-office, and, to make sure that no delay might disappoint Wilfrid, gave the letter into the hands of a clerk, who promised, with a smile, that it should at once be put into the right place. Emily found the smile hard to bear, but fortunately she was unknown.

Then she set forth homewards. Such news as this, that she would see and speak with Wilfrid in a few hours, set self-command at defiance. Between joy at the thought that even now he was nearing her, and fear of the events which might have led him to such a step, she was swayed in a tumult of emotion. She longed to open the letter, yet felt she could not do so in the public roads. She tried to think whether any ill chance could possibly interpose to prevent her being at the place of meeting; none was to be anticipated, unless, what was very unlikely, her mother should propose to join her afternoon walk. But what could his coming mean? She feared that she understood too well,

Often she had to check the over-haste of her pace, and the way seemed terribly long, but at length she was at home and close shut in her bedroom. The letter did not aid her to account for his coming; it had been written late on Friday night, but made absolutely no reference to what had passed between Wilfrid and his relations. It was a long and passionate poem of his love, concerned not with outward facts, but with states of feeling. Only at the end he had added a post-script, saying that he should write again on Monday.

It was difficult to live through the morning. She felt that she must be busy with her hands, and, her mother's objections notwithstanding, set herself resolutely to active house-work. Her anxious feelings in this way toned themselves to mere cheerfulness. She listened with unfailing patience to the lengthily described details of domestic annoyances of which Mrs. Hood's conversation chiefly consisted, and did her best to infuse into her replies a tone of hopefulness, which might animate without betraying too much. The hours passed over, and at length it was time to set forth. Mrs. Hood showed no desire to leave home. Emily, though foreseeing that she might again be late for tea, did not venture to hint at such a possibility, but started as if for a short walk.

Not much more than a mile from Banbrigg, in a direction away alike from the Heath and from Dunfield, is the village of Pendal, where stand the remains of an ancient castle. Very slight indeed are these relics, one window and some shapeless masses of defaced masonry being alone exposed; but a hill close beside them is supposed to cover more of the fabric, though history tells not how or when the earth was so heaped up. The circle of the moat is still complete, and generally contains water. Pendal Castle Hill, as the locality is called, is approached by a rustic lane leading from the village; it is enclosed like an ordinary meadow, and shadowed here and there with trees. On Sundays and holidays it is a resort much favoured by Dunfieldians; at other times its solitude is but little interfered with. Knowing this, Emily had appointed the spot for the meeting. She had directed Wilfrid to take a train from Dunfield to Pendal, and had described the walk up to the castle hill.

He was not before her this time, and there were endless reasons for fear lest she should wait in vain. She remained standing on the inner side of the stile by which the field was entered, and kept her gaze on the point where the lane turned. A long quarter of an hour passed, then of a sudden the expected form appeared.

There had been no train to Pendal at the right time; he had taken a meal at Dunfield station, and then had found a cab to convey him to the village.

Wilfrid was very calm, only the gleam of his fine eyes showed his delight at holding her hands again. They walked to the side of the hill remote from the road. Wilfrid looked about him, and remarked that the place was interesting. He seemed in no hurry to speak of what had brought him here; they walked hand in hand, like children. 'Emily!'—and then his name in return, with interchange of looks; was it not enough for some minutes?

'There is a fallen trunk,' Wilfrid said, pointing to a remoter spot. 'Shall we sit there?'

'How well it has been managed,' he exclaimed when they had seated themselves. 'You remember the fairy tales in which the old woman bids some one go to a certain place and do such and such a thing and something is sure to happen? "And it befell just as the old woman had said."'

'And I am the old woman. They call her a witch in the stories.'

' A witch, yes ; but so young and beautiful. What delight it was to find your letter, dearest ! What careful directions ! I laughed at your dreadful anxiety to make it quite, quite clear. Won't you take the glove off ? How your hand trembles ; no, I will unbutton it myself.'

He kissed the fingers lightly, and then held them pressed.

' But why have you come all this distance, Wilfrid ? '

' Would it not be enough if I said I had come to see you ? What distance would be too far for that ? '

' But you were to have left England to-day ? '

' So I was, but I shall not go—till you go with me, Emily.'

She looked at him with anxious eyes

' Well, I will tell you all there is to tell. In the first place, my father and my aunt think that the plan of your returning to teach the little girls is not a very good one.'

He spoke with perfect cheerfulness, but firmly, as was his wont. Emily's eyes fell.

' I have felt it myself,' she said.

' And so have I ; so that we are happily all agreed. We talked it all over after you had gone on Friday, and since then I have taken time to make up my mind. I can see that you would be uncomfortable in the house under such conditions ; at the same time it is certainly out of the question that you should go elsewhere ; and so—come to London and let us be married as soon as the arrangements can be made.'

' I don't quite understand, Wilfrid. Do you mean that your father approves this ? '

' They all went off to-day. He knows, no doubt, what my intention is. In a matter like this I must judge for myself.'

She was silent, then asked with apprehension, ' Has it caused trouble ? '

' Of the kind which passes as soon as it has been well talked about,' he answered with a smile ; ' nothing more serious.'

She could not meet his look.

' And you wish not to return to Oxford ? '

' I have done with that. I see now that to go back and play the schoolboy would have been impossible ; all that is over and a new life beginning—you will be in readiness to come up as soon as I send for you ? '

She looked in his face now with pleading.

' It is too hasty, Wilfrid. It was better, far better, that

we should wait till next year. Can it be your father's wish that your marriage should take place in his absence? You know that I have no foolish desires; the more simply everything is done the better it will please me. But I would, I would have it done with your father's goodwill. I foresaw his objections only too well; they are natural, it could not be otherwise; but I hoped that time would help. Let us wait!'

She closed both hands on his, and gazed at him steadily.

'I think you must be guided by me, Emily,' he replied, with his calm self-assertiveness. 'There is no reason why we should wait. My father is a man who very sensibly accepts the accomplished fact. His own marriage, I may tell you, was an affair of decision in the face of superficial objections, and he will only think the better of me for following his example. You say, and I am sure, that you care nothing for the show of a wedding; if you did, I should not be here at this moment. It is only for that that we need postpone the marriage. I will take rooms till I can find a house and have it made ready for us.'

Emily kept silence. She had released his hand. There were signs on her face of severe inward conflict.

'Will you let me go and see your parents?' he asked. 'Shall our marriage take place here? To me it is the same; I would only be ruled by your choice. May I go home with you now?'

'I would say yes if I could make up my mind to a marriage at once,' she answered. 'Dear, let me persuade you.'

'The sound of your words persuades too strongly against their sense, Emily,' he said tenderly. 'I will not put off our marriage a day longer than forms make necessary.'

'Wilfrid, let me say what——'

'I have scraps of superstition in my nature,' he broke in with a half laugh. 'Fate does not often deal so kindly as in giving you to me; I dare not *seem* even to hesitate before the gift. It is a test of the worth that is in us. We meet by chance, and we recognise each other; here is the end for which we might have sought a lifetime; we are not worthy of it if we hold back from paltry considerations. I dare not leave you, Emily; everything points to one result—the rejection of the scheme for your return, my father's free surrender of the decision to myself, the irresistible impulse which has brought me here to you. Did I tell you that I rose in the middle of

the night and went to Charing Cross to telegraph? It would
have done just as well the first thing in the morning, but I
could not rest till the message was sent. I will have no
appearances come between us; there shall be no pause till
you bear my name and have entered my home; after that, let
life do with us what it will.'

Emily drank in the vehement flow of words with delight
and fear. It was this virile eagerness, this force of personality, which had before charmed her thought into passiveness,
and made her senses its subject; but a stronger motive of resistance actuated her now. In her humility she could not
deem the instant gain of herself to be an equivalent to him for
what he would certainly, and what he might perchance, lose.
She feared that he had disguised his father's real displeasure,
and she could not reconcile herself to the abrupt overthrow of
all the purposes Wilfrid had entertained before he knew her.
She strove with all the energy of her own strong character to
withstand him for his good.

'Wilfrid, let it at least be postponed till your father's
return. If his mind is what you say, he will by then have
fully accepted your views. I respect your father. I owe him
consideration; he is prejudiced against me now, and I would
gain his good will. Just because we are perfectly independent
let us have regard for others; better, a thousand times better,
that he should be reconciled to our marriage before it takes
place than perforce afterwards. Is it for my constancy, or
your own, that you fear?'

'I do not doubt your love, and my own is unalterable. I
fear circumstances; but what has fear to do with it; I wish
to make you my own; the empire of my passion is all-sub-
duing. I will not wait! If you refuse me, I have been mistaken; you do not love me.'

'Those are only words,' she answered, a proud smile
lighting the trouble of her countenance. 'You have said
that you do not doubt my love, and in your heart you cannot.
Answer me one question, Wilfrid: have you made little of
your father's opposition, in order to spare me pain? Is it
more serious than you are willing to tell me?'

The temptation was strong to reply with an affirmative.
If she believed his father to be utterly irreconcilable, there
could be no excuse for lingering; yet his nobler self prevailed,
to her no word of falseness.

'I have told you the truth. His opposition is temporary.

When you are my wife he will be to you as to any wife I could have chosen, I am convinced of it.'

'Then more than ever I entreat you to wait, only till his return to England. If you fail then, I will resist no longer. Show him this much respect, dearest; join him abroad now; let him see that you desire his kindness. Is he not disappointed that you mean to break off your career at Oxford? Why should you do that? You promised me—did you not promise me, Wilfrid, that you would go on to the end?'

'I cannot! I have no longer the calmness, no longer the old ambitions,—how trivial they were!'

'And yet there will come a day when you will regret that you left your course unfinished, just because you fell in love with a foolish girl.'

'Do not speak like that, Emily; I hate that way of regarding love! My passion for you is henceforth my life; if it is trifling, so is my whole being, my whole existence. There is no sacrifice possible for me that I should ever regret. Our love is what we choose to make it. Regard it as a foolish pastime, and we are no better than the vulgar crowd—we know how they speak of it. What detestable thoughts your words brought to my mind! Have you not heard men and women, those who have outlived such glimpses of high things as nature ever sent them, making a jest of love in young lives, treating it, from the height of their wisdom forsooth, as a silly dream of boys and girls? If we ever live to speak or think like that, it will indeed be time to have done with the world. Even as I love you now, my heart's darling, I shall love you when years of intimacy are like some happy journey behind us, and on into the very portal of death. Regret! How paltry all will seem that was not of the essence of our love! And who knows how short our time may be? When the end comes, will it be easy to bear, the thought that we lost one day, one moment of union, out of respect for idle prejudices which vanish as soon as they find themselves ineffectual? Will not the longest life be all too short for us?'

'Forgive me the words, dear. Love is no less sacred to me.'

Her senses were playing the traitor; or—which you will —were seconding love's triumph.

'I shall come home with you now,' he said. 'You will let me?'

Why was he not content to win her promise? This proposal, by reminding her most strongly of the inevitable difficulties her marriage would entail, forced her again into
resistance.

'Not now, Wilfrid. I have not said a word of this; I
must prepare them for it.'

'You have not spoken of me?'

'I would not do so till I—till everything was more
certain.'

'Certain!' he cried impatiently. 'Why do you torture
me so, Emily? What uncertainty is there? Everything is
uncertain, if you like to make it so. Is there something in
your mind that I do not understand?'

'You must remember, Wilfrid, that this is a strange, new
thing in my life. It has come to me so suddenly, that even
yet I cannot make it part of my familiar self. It has been
impossible to speak of it to others.'

'Do you think I take it as a matter of course? Is your
love less a magic gift to me? I wake in a terror lest I have
only dreamed of it; but then the very truth comes back, and
shall I make myself miserable with imagining uncertainties,
when there need be none?'

Emily hesitated before speaking again.

'I have told you very little about my home,' she said.
'You know that we are very poor.'

She could not say it as simply as she wished; she was
angry with herself to recognise how nearly her feeling was
one of shame, what a long habit of reason it needed to
expel the unintelligent prejudice which the world bestows at
birth.

'I could almost say I am glad of it,' Wilfrid replied.
'We shall have it in our power, you and I, to help do much.'

'There are many reasons,' she continued, too much
occupied with her thoughts to dwell on what he said, 'why I
should have time to prepare my father and mother. You will
let me write the things which it is not very easy to say.'

'Say what you will, and keep silence on what you will,
Emily. I cannot give so much consequence to these external
things. You and I are living souls, and as such we judge
each other. Shall I fret about the circumstances in which
chance has cased your life? As reasonable if I withdrew my
love from you because one day the colour of your glove did
not please me. Time you need. You shall have it; a week,

ten days. Then I will come myself and fetch you,—or you
shall come to London alone, as you please.'

'Let it be till your father returns.'

'But he will be two months away.'

'You will join him in Switzerland. Your health requires it.'

'My health! Oh, how tired I am of that word! Spare
it me, you at least, Emily. I am well in body and mind;
your love would have raised me if I had lain at the point of
death. I cannot leave England alone; I have made up my
mind that you shall go with me. Have I then no power to
persuade you? You will not indeed refuse?'

He looked at her almost in despair. He had not anticipated more than the natural hesitancy which he would at
once overcome by force of passion. There was something
terrible to him in the disclosure of a quiet force of will equal
to his own. Frustration of desire joined with irritated instincts
of ascendency to agitate him almost beyond endurance.

Emily gazed at him with pleading as passionate as his
own need.

'Do you distrust me?' he asked suddenly, overcome with
an intolerable suspicion. At the same moment he dropped
her hand, and his gaze grew cold.

'Distrust you?' She could not think that she understood him.

'Do you fear to come to London with me?'

'Wilfrid?'

Her bosom heaved with passionate resentment of his
thought.

'Is *that* how you understand my motives?' she asked,
with tremulous, subdued earnestness, fixing upon him a gaze
which he could not meet.

'Yes,' he answered, below his breath, 'in a moment when
love of you has made me mad.'

He turned away, leaning with one hand upon the trunk.
In the silence which followed he appeared to be examining
the shapeless ruins, which, from this point of view, stood out
boldly against the sky.

'When was this castle destroyed?' he asked presently,
in a steady voice.

He received no answer, and turned his eyes to her again.
Emily's face was strung into a hard intensity. He laid his
hand once more upon hers, and spoke with self-control.

'You do not know the strength of a man's love. In that

moment it touched the borders of hate. I know that your mind is incapable of such a suspicion; try to think what it meant to be possessed for an instant by such frenzy.'

'You felt able to hate me?' she said, with a shake in her voice which might have become either a laugh or a sob. 'Then there are things in love that I shall never know.'

'Because your soul is pure as that of the angels they dream of. I could not love you so terribly if you were not that perfection of womanhood to which all being is drawn. Send me to do your bidding; I will have no will but yours.'

How the light of rapture flashed athwart her face! It was hard for her to find words that would not seem too positive, too insubmissive.

'Only till you have lived with your father in the thought of this thing,' she murmured, 'and until I have taught myself to bear my happiness. Are we not one already, dear? Why should you needlessly make your life poorer by the loss—if only for a time—of all the old kindnesses? I think, I know that in a few days your mind will be the same as my own. Do you remember how long it is since we first spoke to each other?'

'Not so many days as make a week,' he answered, smiling.

'Is not that hard to believe? And hard to realise that the new world is still within the old?'

'Sweet, still eyes—give to me some of your wisdom! But you have a terrible way of teaching calmness.'

'You will go straight to the Continent, Wilfrid?'

'Only with one promise.'

'And that?'

'You will bow to my judgment when I return.'

'My fate shall be in your hands.'

They talked still, while the shadows of the ruins moved ever towards them. All the afternoon no footsteps had come near; it was the sight of two strangers which at length bade Emily think of the time. It was after six o'clock.

'Wilfrid, I must go. My absence will seem so strange; what fables I shall have to invent on the way home. Do you know of any train that you can leave by?'

'No; it matters very little; I suppose there is a mail some time to-night? I will go back to Dunfield and take my chance.'

'How tired you will be! Two such journeys in one day.'

' And a draught of the water of life between them. But even now there is something more I ask for.'

' Something more ? '

' One touch of the lips that speak so nobly.'

It was only then that her eyes gleamed for a moment through moisture. But she strengthened herself to face the parting, in spite of a heaviness at the heart like that which she had felt on leaving The Firs. She meant at first to go no further than the stile into the lane, and there Wilfrid held out his hand. She used it to aid herself in stepping over.

' I must go as far as Pendal station,' she said. ' Then you can look at the time-table, and tell me what train you will take.'

They walked the length of the lane almost in silence, glancing at each other once or twice. At the village station, Wilfrid discovered that a good train left Dunfield shortly after nine o'clock. From Pendal to Dunfield there would be a train in a quarter of an hour.

They stood together under the station shed. No other passenger was waiting, and the official had not yet arrived to open the booking-office.

' When shall I hear from you ? ' Emily asked, putting off from instant to instant the good-bye, which grew ever harder to say.

' In less than a week. I shall leave London early to-morrow morning.'

' But it will give you no time for rest.'

' I am not able to rest. Go as often as you can to the castle, that I may think of you as sitting there.'

' I will go very often.'

She could not trust herself to utter more than a few words. As she spoke, the station-master appeared. They moved away to the head of the stairs by which Emily had to leave.

' I shall see your train to-night as it passes Pendal,' she said.

Then there was the clasp of hands, and—good-bye. To Emily the way was dark before her as she hurried on-wards. . . . .

Mrs. Hood had subsided into the calm of bitter resigna-tion. Emily found her in the kitchen, engaged in polishing certain metal articles, an occupation to which she always had recourse when the legitimate work of the day was pretty well over. Years ago, Mrs. Hood had not lacked interest in certain kinds of reading, but the miseries of her life had killed all that; the need of mechanical exertion was constantly upon her, an automatic conscience refused to allow her repose. When she heard Emily entering by the front door, a sickly smile fixed itself upon her lips, and with this she silently greeted the girl.

'It is too bad of me, mother,' Emily said, trying to assume playfulness, which contrasted strangely with an almost haggard weariness on her face. 'You will give me up as hopeless; I will promise, like the children, that it shall never happen again.'

'It is your holiday, my dear' was the reply, as Mrs. Hood went to stir the fire. 'You must amuse yourself in your own way.'

'Of course you have had tea. I really want nothing till supper-time.'

'It was not worth while to make tea for one,' said her mother, with a sigh.

'And you have had none? Then I will make it this minute. When will father be home?'

'It is quite uncertain. He gets more and more irregular.'

'Why should he be kept so beyond the proper time! It is really too bad.'

'My dear, your father is never satisfied with doing his own work; he's always taking somebody else's as well. Of course, they find that out, and they put upon him. I've talked and talked, but it's no use; I suppose it'll go on in the same way to the end.'

Half an hour later Mr. Hood reached home, as usual, worn out. The last half mile of the walk from Dunfield was always a struggle with exhaustion. He had to sit several minutes before he was able to go upstairs to refresh himself with cold water.

'I met Mrs. Cartwright,' he said, when an unexpected cup of tea from Emily's hands had put him into good spirits. 'Jessie got home on Saturday, and wants you to go and see her, Emily. I half promised you would call to-morrow morning.'

'Yes, I will,' said Emily.

'I don't think it's altogether right,' remarked Mrs. Hood, 'that Emily should have to work in her holidays; and I'm sure it's all no use; Jessie Cartwright will never do any good if she has lessons from now to Doomsday.'

'Well, it's very necessary she should,' replied Mr. Hood. 'How ever they live as they do passes my comprehension. There was Mrs. Cartwright taking home fruit and flowers which cost a pretty penny, I'll be bound. And her talk! I thought I should never get away. There's one thing, she never has any but good-natured gossip; I never leave her without feeling that she is one of the best-hearted women I know.'

'I can't say that her daughters take after her,' Mrs. Hood remarked, soothed, as always, by comment upon her acquaintances. 'Amy was here the other afternoon, and all the time she never ceased making fun of those poor Wilkinses; it really was all I could do to keep from telling her she ought to be ashamed of herself. Mary Wilkins, at all events, makes no pretences; she may be plain, but she's a good girl, and stays at home to do what's required of her. As for the Cartwright girls—well, we shall see what'll happen some day. It can't go on, that's quite certain.'

'I don't think there's any real harm in them. They're thoughtless, but then they're very young. They oughtn't to have so much of their own way. What's your opinion of Jessie, Emily? Do you think she'll ever be fit to teach?'

'She might, if she could live apart from her mother and sisters for a time. I think she'll have to come here for her lessons; it's out of the question to do anything at that house.'

It was Mr. Hood's habit to spend his evenings in a little room at the top of the house, which he called his laboratory. It was furnished with a deal table, a couple of chairs, and some shelves. On the table was his apparatus for the study of electricity, mostly the product of his own ingenuity; also a number of retorts, crucibles, test-tubes, and the like, wherewith he experimented chemically. The shelves exhibited bottles and jars, and the dozen or so volumes which made his scientific library. These tastes he had kept up from boyhood; there was something pathetic in the persistency with which he clung to the pretence of serious study, though the physical fatigue which possessed him during his few hours of freedom would in any case have condemned him to mere trifling. Often he came upstairs, lit his lamp, and sat for a couple of hours doing nothing more than play with his instruments, much as a child might; at other times a sudden revival of zeal would declare itself, and he would read and experiment till late in the night, always in fear of the inevitable lecture on his reckless waste of lamp-oil. In the winter time the temperature of this garret was arctic, and fireplace there was none, still he could not intermit his custom of spending at least an hour in what he called scientific study, with the result that he went to bed numbed and shivering. It was but another illustration of possibilities rendered futile by circumstances. It was more than likely that the man might, with fair treatment, have really done something in one or other branch of physics. To Emily, who strove to interest herself in his subjects out of mere love and compassion, he appeared to have gained not a little knowledge of facts and theories. She liked to encourage herself in the faith that his attainments were solid as far as they went, and that they might have been the foundation of good independent work; it helped her to respect her father.

'Will you come up to-night, Emily?' he asked, with the diffidence which he always put into this request.

She assented with apparent cheerfulness, and they climbed the stairs together. The last portion of them was uncarpeted, and their footsteps sounded with hollow echoes under the roof. It was all but dark by this time; Mr. Hood found matches on the table and lit the lamp, which illuminated the bare white washed walls and sloping ceiling with a dreary dimness. There was no carpet on the floor, which creaked as they moved here and there. When her father was on the point of drawing down the blind, Emily interposed.

'Do you mind leaving it up, father?'

'Of course I will,' he assented with a smile. 'But why?'

'The last daylight in the sky is pleasant to look at.'

On the landing below stood an old eight-day clock. So much service had it seen that its voice was grown faint, and the strokes of each hour that it gave forth were whoozed with intervals of several seconds. It was now striking nine, and the succession of long-drawn ghostly notes seemed interminable.

The last daylight—how often our lightest words are omens!—faded out of the sky. Emily kept her eyes upon the windows none the less. She tried to understand what her father was saying sufficiently to put in a word now and then, but her sense of hearing was strained to its utmost for other sounds. There was no traffic in the road below, and the house itself was hushed; the ticking of the old clock, performed with such painful effort that it ever seemed on the point of failing, was the only sign of life outside the garret. At length Emily's ear caught a remote rushing sound; her father's low voice did not overcome it.

'These compounds of nitrogen and oxygen,' he was saying, 'are very interesting. Nitrous oxide, you know, is what they call Laughing Gas. You heat solid nitrate of ammonia, and that makes protoxide of nitrogen and water.'

The words conveyed no sense to her, though she heard them. The rushing sound had become a dull continuous thunder. Her eyes strained into the darkness. Of a sudden the horizon flamed. A train was passing a quarter of a mile away, and the furnace-door of the engine had just been opened to feed the fire, whose strength sped the carriages to far-off London. A streaming cloud of smoke reflected the glare; it was as though some flying dragon vomited crimson fumes. Involuntarily the girl half rose from her seat and pointed.

'What is it?' asked her father, looking round. 'Ah! pretty sight that fire on the smoke. Well, this protoxide of nitrogen, you see——'

CHAPTER VII.

ON THE LEVELS.

NOT the least of many mysteries in the natural history of the Cartwrights was, how they all managed to bestow themselves in the house which they occupied. To be sure, the family— omitting Mr. Cartwright, seldom at home—were all of one sex, which perhaps made the difficulty less insuperable; but the fact remained that Mrs. Cartwright and her five grown-up daughters, together with a maid-servant, lived, moved, and had their being in an abode consisting of six rooms, a cellar, and a lumber closet. A few years ago they had occupied a much more roomy dwelling on the edge of the aristocratic region of Dunfield; though not strictly in St. Luke's—the Belgravia of the town—they of course spoke of it as if it were. A crisis in the fortunes of the family had necessitated a reduction of their establishment; the district in which they now dwelt was humbler, but then it could always be described as 'near North Parade, you know'; North Parade being an equivalent of Mayfair. The uppermost windows commanded a view of the extensive cattle-market, of a long railway viaduct, and of hilly fields beyond.

The five Misses Cartwright did not greatly relish the change; they were disposed even to resist, to hold their ground on the verge of St. Luke's, to tell their father that he must do his duty and still maintain them in that station of life for which they were clearly designed by Providence. But Mr. Cartwright, after many cries of 'Wolf,' found himself veritably at close quarters with the animal, and female argument had to yield to the logic of fact. 'Be thankful,' exclaimed the hard-driven paterfamilias, when his long patience came to an end, 'that we haven't all to go to the Union It 'll come to that yet, mark my word!' And, indeed, few people in Dunfield would have expressed surprise at the actual incidence of this calamity Mr Cartwright was ostensibly a commercial traveller, but obviously he must have joined with this main pursuit many odds and ends of money-making activity, seeing that the family kept out of debt, and still indulged themselves in extravagances which many substantial households would have declared themselves unable to afford. If the town were visited by an opera company, or by some dramatic star going the round of the provinces, the Cartwrights were sure to have prominent seats, and to exhibit themselves in becoming costume. If a bazaar were held, their ready-money was always forthcoming. At flower shows, galas, croquet parties, they challenged comparison with all who were not confessedly of the Dunfield *élite*. They regularly adorned their pew in the parish church, were liberal at offertories, exerted themselves, not without expense, in the Sunday school feast, and the like. How—cried all Dunfield—how in the name of wonder was it done?

We are not concerned to probe the mystery; suffice it that the situation be exhibited as it appeared to the eyes of the world. When the afore-mentioned crisis declared itself, though every one enjoyed the opportunity of exclaiming 'I told you so!' there were few who did not feel really sorry for the Cartwrights, so little of envy mingled with the incessant gossip of which the family were the subject. Mrs. Cartwright was held in more or less affection by every one who knew her. She was a woman of fifty, of substantial frame, florid, and somewhat masculine in manner; a thorough Yorkshire-woman, her tone and demeanour were marked by a frank good-nature which often exaggerated itself into bluffness, and was never consistent with the delicacy of refined taste, but which unmistakably evinced a sound and benevolent disposition. When her sharp temper was stirred—and her daughters gave it abundant exercise—she expressed herself in a racy and vigorous vernacular which there was no opposing; never coarse, never, in the large sense, unwomanly, she made her predominance felt with an emphasis which would fain have been rivalled by many of the mothers of Dunfield. Lavishly indulgent to her girls, she yet kept them thoroughly in hand, and won, if not their tenderness, at all events their affection and respect. The girls themselves were not outwardly charming; Jessie, the youngest but one, had perhaps a certain claim to prettiness, but, like all her sisters, she was of coarse type. Their education had been of the most haphazard kind; their breeding was not a little defective; but a certain tact, common to the family, enabled them to make the very most of themselves, so that they more than passed muster among the middle-class young ladies of the town. As long as they sojourned on the borders of St. Luke's, nothing was farther from the thoughts of any one of them than the idea that they might have to exert themselves to earn their own living; it was only of late that certain emphatic representations on the part of their father had led Mrs. Cartwright to consider which of the girls was good for anything. Amy, the eldest, had rather a weak constitution; it was plain that neither in body nor in mind could she be called upon to exert herself. Eleanor, who came next, had musical faculties; after terrific family debates it was decided that she must give lessons on the piano, and a first pupil was speedily found. Barbara was good for nothing whatever, save to spend money on her personal adornment; considering that she was the plainest of the family— her sisters having repeatedly decided the point—her existence appeared on the whole singularly superfluous. Then came Jessie. Of Jessie her father had repeatedly said that she was the only girl of his who had brains; those brains, if existent, must now be turned to account. But Jessie had long since torn up her school-books into curl-papers, and, as learning accumulated outside her head, it vanished from the interior. When she declared that arithmetic was all but a mystery to her, and that she had forgotten what French she ever knew, there was an unprecedented outbreak of parental wrath: this was the result of all that had been spent on her education! She must get it back as best she could, for, as sure as fate, she should be packed off as a governess. Look at Emily Hood: why, that girl was keeping herself, and, most likely, paying her mother's butcher's bill into the bargain, and her advantages had been fewer than Jessie's. After storms beyond description, Jessie did what her mother called 'buckle to,' but progress was slight. 'You must get Emily Hood to help you when she comes home for her holidays,' was Mrs. Cartwright's hopeful suggestion one night that the girl had fairly broken down and given way to sobs and tears. Emily was written to, and promised aid. The remaining daughter, Geraldine, was held to be too young as yet for responsible undertakings; she was only seventeen, and, besides, there was something rather hopeful going on between her and young Baldwin, the solicitor who had just begun practice in Dunfield. So that, on the whole, Geraldine's lot looked the most promising of all.

In previous years, the family had never failed to betake themselves for three weeks or so to Scarborough, or Whitby, or Bridlington; this year they had for the first time contented themselves with humbler recreation; Mrs. Cartwright and four of the girls managed a week at Ilkley, Jessie was fortunate enough to be invited to stay for a fortnight with friends at the seaside. She was the latest to return. Emily being now at home, there was no longer an excuse for postponing study; books were procured, and Jessie, by way of preparation, endeavoured to fathom the abysses of her ignorance.

We have heard Emily's opinion as to the possibility of studious application in the house of the Cartwrights. Her own visits thither were made as few as possible; she declared that she never came away without a headache. In spite of restricted space, the Cartwrights found it impossible to relinquish the habit of universal hospitality. As if discontented with the narrow proportions of her own family, Mrs. Cartwright was never thoroughly at ease unless she had three or four friends to occupy every available square foot of floor in her diminutive sitting-room, and to squeeze around the table when meals were served. In vain did acquaintances hold apart from a sense of consideration, or time their visits when eating and drinking could scarcely be in question; they were given plainly to understand that their delicacy was an offence, and that, if they stayed away, it would be put down to their pride. It was almost impossible to hit an hour for calling at which the family would be alone; generally, as soon as the

front door opened, the ear of the visitor was assailed with
laughter loud and long, with multitudinous vociferation, Mrs.
Cartwright's rich voice high above all others. The room
itself was a spectacle for men and gods. Not a member of
the family had the most rudimentary instinct of order; no
article, whether of ornament or use, had its recognised station.
Needlework lay in heaps on table, chairs, and floor; you
stretched out your legs too far, and came in contact with a
casual flower-vase, put down to be out of the way; you desired
to open the piano, and had first to remove a tray of wine-
glasses. To listen to the girls' conversation for five minutes
was to understand their surroundings; they were hopelessly
feather-brained, they chattered and gabbled with deafening
persistency. If there was no good in their talk, there could
scarcely be said to be any harm; they lived so completely on
the surface of things that they impressed one as incapable
even of a doubtful thought. One reason why Geraldine was
the only one who had yet definitely attracted a male admirer
might lie in the fact that there was no air of femininity about
the girls, nothing whatever to touch the most susceptible
imagination; a parcel of schoolboys would have been as provocative. And this notwithstanding that they talked incessantly of love-making, of flirtations, of the making and
breaking of matches; it was the very freedom and shallowness
of such gossip that made it wholly unexciting; their mother's
presence put no check on the talk—she, indeed, was very
much like her daughters in choice of subject—and the young
men who frequented the house joined in discussion of sexual
entanglements with a disengaged air which, if it impugned
their delicacy, at all events seemed to testify to practical
innocence.

Those young men! Dunfield was at that time not perhaps
worse off in its supply of marriageable males than other small
provincial towns, but, to judge from the extensive assortment
which passed through the Cartwrights' house, the lot of Dunfield maidens might be held pathetic. They were not especially
ignorant or vulgar, these budding townsmen, simply imbecile.
One could not accuse them of positive faults, for they had no
positive qualities, unless it were here and there a leaning to
physical fatuity. Their interests were concerned with the
pettiest of local occurrences; their favouritisms and animosities
were those of overgrown infants. They played practical jokes
on each other in the open streets; they read the local news-

papers to extract the feeblest of gossip; they had a game which they called politics, and which consisted in badging themselves with blue or yellow, according to the choice of their fathers before them; they affected now and then to haunt bar-parlours and billiard-rooms, and made good resolutions when they had smoked or drunk more than their stomachs would support. If any Dunfield schoolboy exhibited faculties of a kind uncommon in the town, he was despatched to begin life on a more promising scene; those who remained, who became the new generation of business men, of town councillors, of independent electors, were such as could not by any possibility have made a living elsewhere. Those elders who knew Dunfield best could not point to a single youth of fair endowments who looked forward to remaining in his native place.

The tone of Dunfield society was not high.

No wonder that Emily Hood had her doubts as to the result of study taken up by one of the Cartwrights. Still, she held it a duty to give what help she could, knowing how necessary it was that Jessie should, if possible, qualify herself to earn a living. The first thing after breakfast on Tuesday morning she set forth to visit her friends. It was not quite ten o'clock when she reached the house, and she looked forward with some assurance of hope to finding the family alone. Jessie herself opened the door, and Emily, passing at once into the sitting-room, discovered that not only had a visitor arrived before her, but this the very person she would most have desired to avoid. Mr. Richard Dagworthy was seated in conversation with Mrs. Cartwright and her daughters; or rather he had been conversing till Emily's arrival caused a momentary silence. He had called thus early, on his way to the mill, to inquire for Mr. Cartwright's present address, having occasion to communicate with him on business matters.

The room was so small that Emily had a difficulty in reaching Mrs. Cartwright to shake hands with her, owing to Dagworthy's almost blocking the only available way round the table. He stood up and drew back, waiting his turn for greeting; when it came, he assumed the manner of an old friend. A chair was found for Emily, and conversation, or what passed for such, speedily regathered volume. The breakfast things were still on the table, and Miss Geraldine, who was always reluctant to rise of a morning, was engaged upon her meal.

'You see what it's come to, Mr. Dagworthy,' exclaimed
the mother of the family, with her usual lack of reticence.
'Jessie can't or won't learn by herself, so she has to bother
Emily to come and teach her. It's too bad, I call it, just
in her holiday time. She looks as if she wanted to run
about and get colour in her cheeks, don't *you* think so?'

'Well, mother,' cried Jessie, 'you needn't speak as if Emily
was a child in short clothes.'

The other girls laughed.

'I dare say Emily wishes she was,' pursued Mrs. Cartwright. 'When you're little ones, you're all for being grown
up, and when you *are* grown up, then you see how much
better off you were before,—that is, if you've got common
sense. I wish my girls had half as much all put together as
Emily has.'

'I'm sure I don't wish I was a child,' remarked Geraldine,
as she bit her bread-and-butter.

'Of course you don't, Geraldine,' replied Dagworthy, who
was on terms of much familiarity with all the girls. 'If you
were, your mother wouldn't let you come down late to breakfast, would she?'

'I never remember being in time for breakfast since I was
born,' cried the girl.

'I dare say your memory doesn't go far enough back,'
rejoined Dagworthy, with the smile of one who trifled from a
position of superior age and experience.

Mrs. Cartwright laughed with a little embarrassment.
Amy, the eldest girl, was quick with an inquiry whether
Emily had been as yet to the Agricultural Show, the resort at
present of all pleasure-seeking Dunfieldians. Emily replied
that she had not, and to this subject the talk strayed. Mr.
Dagworthy had dogs on exhibition at the show. Barbara
wanted to know how much he would take for a certain animal
which had captivated her; if she had some idea that this
might lead to an offer of the dog as a present, she was doomed
to disappointment, for Dagworthy named his price in the most
matter-of-fact way. But nothing had excited so much interest
in these young ladies as the prize pigs; they were in raptures
at the incredible degree of fatness attained; they delighted to
recall that some of the pigs were fattened to such a point that
rollers had to be placed under their throats to keep their heads
up and prevent them from being choked by the pressure of
their own superabundant flesh. In all this conversation

Dagworthy took his part, but not quite with the same freedom as before Emily's arrival. His eyes turned incessantly in her direction, and once or twice he only just saved himself from absent-mindedness when a remark was addressed to him. It was with obvious reluctance that he at length rose to leave.

'When are you all coming to see me?' he asked, as he stood smoothing his felt hat with the back of his hand. 'I suppose I shall have to give a croquet party, and have some of the young fellows, then you'll come fast enough. Old men like myself you care nothing about.'

'I should think not, indeed,' replied Barbara the plain. 'Why, your hair's going grey. If you didn't shave, you'd have had grey whiskers long ago.'

'When I invite the others,' he returned, laughing, 'you may consider yourself excepted.'

Amid delicate banter of this kind he took his departure. Of course he was instantly the subject of clamorous chatter.

'Will he really give a croquet party?' demanded one, eagerly.

'Not he!' was the reply from another. 'It would cost him too much in tea and cakes.'

'Nonsense!' put in Mrs. Cartwright. 'He doesn't care for society, that's what it is. I believe he's a good deal happier living there by himself than he was when his wife was alive.'

'That isn't very wonderful,' exclaimed Amy. 'A proud, stuck-up thing, she was! Served him right if she made him uncomfortable; he only married her because her people were grand.'

'I don't believe they ever go near him now,' said the mother.

'What did they quarrel about, mother?' asked Jessie. 'I believe he used his wife badly, that's the truth of it.'

'How do you know what the truth of it is?' returned her mother, contemptuously. 'I know very well he did nothing of the kind; whatever his faults are, he's not that sort of man.'

'Well, you must confess, mother, he's downright mean; and you've often enough said Mrs. Dagworthy spent more money than pleased him. I know very well I shouldn't like to be his wife.'

'You wait till he asks you, Jessie,' cried Barbara, with sisterly reproof.

'I don't suppose he's very likely to ask any of you,' said Mrs. Cartwright, with a laugh which was not very hearty. 'Now, Geraldine, *when* are you going to have done your breakfast? Here's ten o'clock, and you seem as if you'd never stop eating. I won't have this irregularity. Now to-morrow morning I'll have the table cleared at nine o'clock, and if you're not down you'll go without breakfast altogether, mind what I say.'

The threat was such an old one that Geraldine honoured it with not the least attention, but helped herself abundantly to marmalade, which she impasted solidly on buttered toast, and consumed with much relish.

'Now you've got Emily here,' pursued Mrs. Cartwright, turning her attack upon Jessie, 'what are you going to do with her? Are you going to have your lessons in this room?'

'I don't know. What do *you* say, Emily?'

Emily was clearly of opinion that lessons under such conditions were likely to be of small profit.

'If it were not so far,' she said, 'I should propose that you came to me every other day; I should think that will be often enough.'

'Why, it's just as far for you to come here,' exclaimed Mrs. Cartwright. 'If you're good enough to teach her—great, lazy thing that she is!—the least she can do is to save you all the trouble she can.'

'I've got an idea,' observed Jessie. 'Why shouldn't we have lessons in the garden?'

'That's just as bad. Emily 'll have the same distance to walk. Don't hear of it, Emily; you make her come to Banbrigg!'

'I don't in the least mind the walk,' Emily said. 'Perhaps we might take it in turns, one lesson in the garden and the next at Banbrigg.'

After ten minutes' vociferous discussion, during which Emily held her peace, this plan was eventually agreed upon.

Jessie ran upstairs to prepare herself to go forth.

'Now don't you let her waste your time, Emily,' said Mrs. Cartwright, in the girl's absence. 'If you see she's doing no good, just give it up. I don't half like the thought of making you drudge in this way in your holidays. I'm sure it's very kind of you to have offered to do it, and it's certain she'll mind you more than she would any one else. She doesn't care a scrap for all I say to her, though she knows well enough it's as much as her father can do to keep things going at all. There never was such bad times in *my* recollection ! How are things in London ? Did you hear much complaint ? '

Emily found it hard to resist a smile at the thought of Mr. Athel or any of those belonging to him indulging in complaints of this nature.

' And what sort of people are they you've got with this time ? ' the other went on to ask. ' Do they treat you well ? '

' Very well indeed.'

It would have been difficult for a stranger, comparing Emily, her tone and bearing, with the members of the Cartwright family, to believe that she came of the same class and had lived through her girlhood under precisely similar conditions. So marked a difference could not but impress even the Cartwrights themselves ; the girls did not behave with entire freedom in her presence, and influences to which they were anything but readily susceptible were apparent in the tone they adopted in addressing her. In spite of themselves, they bowed to a superiority but vaguely understood. Jessie, perhaps, exhibited less of this instinctive reverence than the others, although, in point of fact, her endowments were decidedly above those of her sisters ; the reason being, no doubt, that acknowledged precedence in intellect had fostered in her the worst kind of self-confidence. The girl was intolerably conceited. Emily almost disliked her ; she would have found it a more agreeable task to endeavour to teach any one of the more stupid sisters. It was in the certainty of a couple of hours' moral suffering that she left the house with Jessie.

The garden which was to be the scene of study was ten minutes' walk away from the house. To reach it, they had to pass along a road which traversed the cattle market, a vast area of pens, filled on one day in each week with multitudes of oxen, sheep, and swine. Beyond the market, and in the shadow of the railway viaduct previously referred to, lay three or four acres of ground divided up by hedges into small gardens, leased by people who had an ambition to grow their own potatoes and cabbages, but had no plot attached to their houses. Jessie opened a rough wooden door, made fast by a padlock, and, closing it again behind them, led the way along a narrow path between high hedges, till a second wooden door was reached, which opened into the garden itself. This was laid out with an eye less to beauty than to usefulness. In the centre was a patch of grass, lying between two pear trees ;

the rest of the ground was planted with the various requisites of the kitchen, and in one corner was a well. In the tool house were kept several Windsor chairs; two of these were now brought forth and placed on the grass between the pear trees. But Jessie was not disposed to apply herself on the instant to the books which she had brought in a satchel; her first occupation was to hunt for the ripest gooseberries and currants, and to try her teeth in several pears which she knocked down with the handle of a rake. When at length she seated herself, her tongue began to have its way.

'How I do dislike that Mr. Dagworthy!' she said, with transparent affectation. 'I wonder what he came for this morning. He said he wanted father's address, but I know that was only an excuse. He hasn't been to see us for months. It was like his impudence to ever come at all, after the way he behaved when he married that stuck-up Miss Hanmer.'

'Will you tell me how many of these French exercises you have written?' Emily asked as soon as a pause gave her the opportunity.

'Oh, I don't know,' was the answer; 'about ten, I think. Do you know, I really believe he thinks himself good-looking? And he's as plain as he can be. Don't you think so, Emily?'

'I really have no opinion.'

'It was strange he should come this morning. It was only yesterday I met him over there by the mill,'—Dagworthy's mill stood at one end of the cattle-market,—'and you can't think the impudent way he talked. And, oh, how did he know that you were going to give me lessons?'

'I can't say.'

'Well, he did know, somehow; I was astonished. Perhaps your father told him?'

'That is not very likely.'

'Well, he knew. I wonder who he'll marry next. You may depend upon it he did treat his wife badly; everybody said so. If he were to propose to me, I should answer like that woman did to Henry the Eighth, you know.' She tittered. 'I can't fancy marrying a man who's been married before, could you? I said that to Mrs. Tichborne one day, at Bridlington, and what do you think she answered? Oh, she said, they're the best husbands. Only a good-natured fool marries a second time.'

This was the kind of talk that Emily knew she would have to endure; it was unutterably repugnant to her. She had observed in successive holidays the growth of a spirit in Jessie Cartwright more distinctly offensive than anything which declared itself in her sisters' gabble, however irritating that might be. The girl's mind seemed to have been sullied by some contact, and previous indications disposed Emily to think that this Mrs. Tichborne was very probably a source of evil. She was the wife of an hotel-keeper, the more vulgar for certain affectations of refinement acquired during bar-maidenhood in London, and her intimacy with the Cartwrights was now of long standing. It was Jessie whom she specially affected; with her Jessie had just been spending a fortnight at the seaside. The evil caught from Mrs. Tichborne, or from some one of similar character, did not associate itself very naturally with the silly *naïveté* which marked the girl; she had the air of assuming the objectionable tone as a mark of cleverness. Emily could not trust herself to utter the kind of comment which would naturally have risen to her lips; it would be practically useless, and her relations to Jessie were not such as could engender affectionate zeal in a serious attempt to overcome evil influences. Emily was not of the women whose nature it is to pursue missionary enterprise; instead of calling forth her energies, a situation like the present threw her back upon herself; she sought a retreat from disgust in the sheltered purity of her own heart. Outwardly she became cold; her face expressed that severity which was one side of her character.

'Don't you think it would be better if we made a beginning this morning?' she said, as soon as another pause in the flow of chatter gave her opportunity.

'What a one you are for work!' Jessie protested. 'You seem to take to it naturally, and yet I'm sure it isn't a natural thing. Just think of having to muddle over French grammar at my age! And I know very well it 'll never come to anything. Can you imagine me teaching? I always hated school, and I hate the thought of being a governess. It's different with you; you're right down clever, and you make people take an interest in you. But just think of me! Why I should be thought no more of than a servant. I suppose I should have to make friends with the milkman and the butcher's boy; I don't see who else I should have to talk to. How's a girl to get married if she spends all her time in a nursery teaching children grammar? You don't seem to care whether you're ever married or not, but I do, and it's precious hard to have all my chances taken away.'

This was Jessie's incessant preoccupation; she could not talk for five minutes without returning to it. Herein she only exaggerated her sisters' habits of mind. The girls had begun to talk of ' sweethearts ' and husbands before they were well out of the nursery. In earlier years Emily had only laughed at what she called such foolishness; she could not laugh now. Such ways of thinking and speaking were a profanation of all she held holiest ; words which she whispered in trembling to her heart were vulgarised and defiled by use upon these tinkling tongues ; it was blasphemy against her religion.

Once more she endeavoured to fix the girl's thoughts on the work in hand, and by steady persistence conquered at length some semblance of attention. But an hour proved the utmost limit of Jessie's patience, then her tongue got its way again, and the inevitable subjects were resumed. She talked of the 'gentlemen' whose acquaintance, in a greater or less degree, she had made at the seaside; described their manœuvres to obtain private interviews with her, repeated jokes of their invention, specified her favourites, all at headlong speed of disjointed narrative. Emily sat beneath the infliction, feeling that to go through this on altérnate days for some weeks would be beyond her power. She would not rise and depart, for a gathering warmth within encouraged her to await a moment when speech would come to her aid. It did so at length ; her thought found words almost involuntarily.

'Jessie, I'm afraid we shall not do much good if we always spend our mornings like this ! '

' Oh, but I thought we'd done enough for to-day.'

' Perhaps so, but—— What I want to say is this. Will you, as a kindness to me, forget these subjects when we are together ? I don't mind what else you talk about, but stories of this kind make me fidgety ; I feel as if I should be obliged to get up and run away.'

' Do you really mean it ? You don't like me to talk about gentlemen ? What a queer girl you are, Emily ! Why, you're not settling down to be an old maid at your age, are you ? '

' We'll say so ; perhaps that explains it.'

' Well, that's queer. I can't see, myself, what else there

is to talk about. Grammar's all very well when we're
children, but it seems to me that what a grown-up girl has to
do is to look out for a husband. How you can be satisfied
with books'—the infinite contempt she put into the word!—
'is more than I can make out.'

'But you will do what I ask, as a kindness? I am in earnest; I shall be afraid of seeing you if you can't help talking of
such things.'

Jessie laughed extravagantly; such a state of mind was
to her comical beyond expression.

'You *are* a queer one! Of course I'll do as you wish;
you shan't hear me mention a single gentleman's name, and
I'll tell all the others to be careful whenever you come.'

Emily averted her face: it was saddened with annoyance
at the thought of being discussed in this way by all the Cartwright household.

'You can do that if you like,' she said coldly, 'though it's
no part of my wish. I spoke of the hours when we are together for study.'

'Very well, I won't say anything,' replied the girl, who
was good-natured enough beneath all her vulgarities. 'And
now what shall we do till dinner-time?'

'I must make the best of my way home.'

'Oh, nonsense! Why, you're going to have dinner with
us; of course that was understood.'

Not by Emily, however. It cost a good deal of firmness,
for the Cartwrights one and all would lay hands on you
rather than lose a guest; but Emily made good her escape.
Once well on her way to Banbrigg, she took in great breaths
of free air, as if after a close and unwholesome atmosphere.
She cried mentally for an ounce of civet. There was upon
her, too, that uneasy sense of shame which is apt to possess
a reticent nature when it has been compelled, or tempted, to
some unwonted freedom of speech. Would it not have been
better, she asked herself, to merely avoid the talk she found
so hateful by resolutely advancing other topics? Perhaps
not; it was just possible that her words might bear some
kind of fruit. But she wished heartily that this task of
hopeless teaching had never been proposed to her; it would
trouble her waking every other day, and disturb with a
profitless annoyance the ideal serenity for which she was
striving.

Yet it had one good result; her mother's follies and weaknesses were very easy to bear in comparison, and, when the midday meal was over, she enjoyed with more fulness the peace of her father's room upstairs, where she had arranged a table for her own work. Brilliant sunlight made the bare garret, with its outlook over the fields towards Pendal, a cheerful and homelike retreat. Here, whilst the clock below wheezed and panted after the relentless hours, Emily read hard at German, or, when her mind called for rest, sheltered herself beneath the wing of some poet, who voiced for her the mute hymns of her soul. But the most sacred hour was when her parents had gone to rest, and she sat in her bedroom, writing her secret thoughts for Wilfrid some day to read. She had resolved to keep for him a journal of her inner life from day to day. In this way she might hope to reveal herself more truthfully than spoken words would ever allow ; she feared that never, not even in the confidence of their married life, would her tongue learn to overcome the fear of its own utterances. How little she had told him of herself, of her love ! In Surrey she had been so timid ; she had scarcely done more than allow him to guess her thoughts; and at their last meeting she had been compelled into opposition of his purpose, so that brief time had been left for free exchange of tenderness. But some day she would put this little book of manuscript into his hands, and the shadowy bars between him and her would vanish. She could only write in it late at night, when the still voice within spoke clearly amid the hush. The only sound from the outer world was that of a train now and then speeding by, and that carried her thoughts to Wilfrid, who had journeyed far from her into other countries. Emily loved silence, the nurse of the soul ; the earliest and the latest hours were to her most dear. It had never been to her either an impulse or a joy to realise the existence of the mass of mankind ; she had shrunk, after the first excitement, from the thronged streets of London, passing from them with delight to the quiet country. Others might find their strength in the sense of universal human fellowship ; she would fain live apart, kindly disposed to all, but understanding well that her first duty was to tend the garden of her mind. That it was also her first joy was, by the principles of her religion, justification in pursuing it.

In a few days she obliged her mother to concede to her a share in the work of the house. She had nothing of the common feminine interest in such work for its own value, but it was a pleasure to lessen her mother's toil. There was very little converse between them; for evidently they belonged to different worlds. When Mrs. Hood took her afternoon's repose, it was elsewhere than in the room where Emily sat, and Emily herself did not seek to alter this habit, knowing that she often, quite involuntarily, caused her mother irritation, and that to reduce their intercourse as far as could be without marked estrangement was the best way to make it endurable to both. But the evening hours she invariably devoted to her father; the shortness of the time that she was able to give him was a reason for losing no moment of this communion. She knew that the forecast of the evening's happiness sustained him through the long day, and even so slight a pleasure as that she bestowed in opening the door at his arrival, she would not willingly have suffered him to lose. It did not appear that Mrs. Hood reflected on this exclusive attachment in Emily; it certainly troubled her not at all. This order in the house was of long standing; it had grown to seem as natural as poverty and hopelessness. Emily and her father reasoned as little about their mutual affection; to both it was a priceless part of life, given to them by the same dark powers that destroy and deprive. It behoved them to enjoy it while permitted to do so.

Had she known the recent causes of trouble which weighed upon her parents, Emily would scarcely have been able to still keep her secret from them. The anxiety upon her father's face and her mother's ceaseless complaining were too familiar to suggest anything unusual. She had come home with the resolve to maintain silence, if only because her marriage seemed remote and contingent upon many circumstances; and other reasons had manifested themselves to her even before Wilfrid's visit. At any time she would find a difficulty in speaking upon such a subject with her mother; strange though it may sound, the intimacy between them was not near enough to encourage such a disclosure, with all the explanations it would involve. Nor yet to her father would she willingly speak of what had happened, until it became necessary to do so. Emily's sense of the sanctity of relations such as those between Wilfrid and herself had, through so different a cause, very much the same effects as what we call false shame. The complex motives of virgin modesty had with her become a conscious sustaining power,

I

a faith; of all beautiful things that the mind could conceive, this mystery was the loveliest, and the least capable of being revealed to others, however near, without desecration. Perhaps she had been aided in the nurturing of this ideal by her loneliness; no friend had ever tempted her to confidences; her gravest and purest thoughts had never been imparted to any. Thus she had escaped that blunting of fine perceptions which is the all but inevitable result of endeavouring to express them. Not to speak of mere vulgarity such as Jessie Cartwright exhibited, Emily's instinct shrank from things which usage has, for most people, made matters of course; the public ceremony of marriage, for instance, she deemed a barbarism. As a sacrament, the holiest of all, its celebration should, she felt, be in the strictest privacy; as for its aspect as a legal contract, let that concession to human misery be made with the smallest, not the greatest, violation of religious feeling. Thinking thus, it was natural that she should avail herself of every motive for delay. And in that very wretchedness of her home which her marriage would, she trusted, in a great measure alleviate, she found one of the strongest. The atmosphere of sordid suffering depressed her; it was only by an effort that she shook off the influences which assailed her sadder nature; at times her fears were wrought upon, and it almost exceeded her power to believe in the future Wilfrid had created for her. The change from the beautiful home in Surrey to the sad dreariness of Banbrigg had followed too suddenly upon the revelation of her blessedness. It indisposed her to make known what was so dream-like. For the past became more dreadful viewed from the ground of hope. Emily came to contemplate it as some hideous beast, which, though she seemed to be escaping its reach, might even yet spring upon her. How had she borne that past so lightly? Her fear of all its misery was at moments excessive. Looking at her unhappy parents, she felt that their lot would crush her with pity did she not see the relief approaching. She saw it, yet too often trembled with the most baseless fears. She tried to assure herself that she had acted rightly in resisting Wilfrid's proposal of an immediate marriage, yet she often wished her conscience had not spoken against it. Wilfrid's own words, though merely prompted by his eagerness, ceaselessly came back to her— that it is ill to refuse a kindness offered by fate, so seldom kind. The words were true enough, and their truth answered to that melancholy which, when her will was in abeyance, coloured her views of life.

But here at length was a letter from Wilfrid, a glad, encouraging letter. His father had concluded that he was staying behind in England to be married, and evidently would not have disturbed himself greatly even if such had been the case. All was going well. Nothing of the past should be sacrificed, and the future was their own.

CHAPTER VIII.

A STERNER WOOING.

IT was an unusual thing for the middle of August to find Richard Dagworthy still in Dunfield. Through all the other months of the year he stuck closely to the mill, but the best three weeks of August were his holiday; as a rule he went to Scotland, sometimes in company with a friend, more often alone. In the previous year he had taken a wider flight, and made his first visit to the Continent, but this was not likely to be repeated for some time. He always referred to it as more or less of a feat. The expense, to begin with, was greater than he could readily reconcile himself to, and the indulgence of his curiosity, not inactive, hardly compensated for his lack of ease amid the unfamiliar conditions of foreign travel. Richard represented an intermediate stage of development between the hard-headed operative who conquers wealth, and his descendant who shall know what use to make of it. Therein lay the significance of the man's life.

Its pathos, moreover. Looking at him casually from the outside, one found small suggestion of the pathetic in his hard face and brusque manners; nearer companionship revealed occasional glimpses of a mood out of harmony with the vulgar pursuits and solicitudes which for the most part seemed to absorb him. One caught a hint of loneliness in his existence; his reticences, often very marked in the flow of his unpolished talk, seemed to indicate some disappointment, and a dislike to dwell upon it. In point of fact, his life was rather lonely; his two sisters were married in other towns, and, since the death of his wife, he had held no communications with her relatives. The child was all he had of family, and, though his paternal affections were strong, he was not the man to content his hours of leisure with gambols in a nursery. His dogs were doubtless a great resource, and in a measure made up to him for the lack of domestic interests ; yet there sometimes passed days during which he did not visit the kennels, always a sign to the servants to beware of his temper, which at such seasons was easily roused to fury. The reputation he had in Dunfield for brutality of behaviour dated from his prosecution for violent assault by a groom, whom, in one of his fits of rage, he had all but pounded to a jelly. The incident occurred early in his married life, and was, no doubt, the origin of the very prevalent belief that he had ruled his wife by similar methods. Dunfield society was a little shy of him for some time after, until, indeed, by becoming a widower, he presented himself once more in an interesting light. Though he possibly brought about his wife's death by ill-usage, that did not alter the fact that he had a carriage and pair to offer to the lady whom he might be disposed to make her successor.

His marriage had been of a kind that occasioned general surprise, and, in certain circles, indignation. There had come to live, in one of the smaller houses upon the Heath, a family consisting of a middle-aged lady and her two daughters; their name was Hanmer, and their previous home had been in Hebsworth, the large manufacturing town which is a sort of metropolis to Dunfield and other smaller centres round about. Mr. Hanmer was recently dead; he had been a banker, but suffered grave losses in a period of commercial depression, and left his family poorly off. Various reasons led to his widow's quitting Hebsworth ; Dunfield inquirers naturally got hold of stories more or less to the disgrace of the deceased Mr. Hanmer. The elder of the two daughters Richard Dagworthy married, after an acquaintance of something less than six months. Dunfield threw up its hands in amazement : such a proceeding on young Dagworthy's part was not only shabby to the families which had upon him the claim of old-standing expectancy, but was in itself inexplicable. Miss Hanmer might be good-looking, but Richard (always called 'young' to distinguish him from his father) had surely outgrown such a very infantile reason of choice, when other attractions were, to the Dunfield mind, altogether wanting. The Hanmers were not only poor, but, more shameful still, positively 'stuck up' in their poverty. They came originally from the south of England, forsooth, and spoke in an affected way, pronouncing their vowels absurdly. Well, the consoling reflection was that his wife would soon make him see that she despised him, for if ever there was a thorough Yorkshireman, it was Richard.

Dunfield comments on Mrs. Dagworthy seemed to find some justification in the turn things took. Richard distinctly began to neglect those of his old friends who smacked most of the soil; if they visited his house, his wife received them with an affected graciousness which was so unmistakably 'stuck up' that they were in no hurry to come again, and her behaviour when she returned visits was felt to be so offensive that worthy ladies—already prejudiced—had a difficulty in refraining from a kind of frankness which would have brought about a crisis. The town was perpetually busy with gossip concerning the uncomfortableness of things in the house on the Heath. Old Mr. Dagworthy, it was declared, had roundly bidden his son seek a domicile elsewhere, since joint occupancy of the home had become impossible. Whether such a change was in reality contemplated could never be determined; the old man's death removed the occasion. Mrs. Dagworthy survived him little more than half a year. So there, said Dunfield, was a mistake well done with; and it was disposed to let bygones be bygones.

What was the truth of all this? That Dagworthy married hastily and found his wife uncongenial, and that Mrs. Dagworthy passed the last two years of her life in mourning over a fatal mistake, was all that could be affirmed as fact, and probably the two persons most nearly concerned would have found it difficult to throw more light upon the situation. Outwardly it was as commonplace a story as could be told; even the accession of interest which would have come of Dagworthy's cruelty was due to the imagination of Dunfield gossips. Richard was miserable enough in his home, and frequently bad-tempered, but his wife had nothing worse from him than an angry word now and then. After the first few months of their marriage, the two lived, as far as possible, separate lives; Mrs. Dagworthy spent the days with her mother and sister, Richard at the mill, and the evenings were got through with as little friction as might be between two people neither of whom could speak half a dozen words without irritating or disgusting the other. The interesting feature of the case was the unexpectedness of Dagworthy's

choice. It evinced so much more originality than one looked
for in such a man. It was, indeed, the outcome of ambitions
which were not at all clear to their possessor. Miss Hanmer
had impressed him as no other woman had done, simply
because she had graces and accomplishments of a kind hitherto
unknown to him; Richard felt that for the first time in his
life he was in familiar intercourse with a 'lady.' Her refined
modes of speech, her little personal delicacies, her unconscious
revelation of knowledge which he deemed the result of deep
study, even her pretty and harmless witticisms at the expense
of Dunfield dignitaries, touched his slumbering imagination
with singular force. Miss Hanmer, speedily observing her
power, made the most of it; she was six-and-twenty, and
poverty rendered her position desperate. Dagworthy at first
amused her as a specimen of the wealthy boor, but the evident
delight he found in her society constrained her to admit that
the boor possessed the elements of good taste. The courtship
was of rapid progress, the interests at stake being so simply
defined on either side, and circumstances presenting no kind
of obstacle. The lady accepted him without hesitation, and
triumphed in her good fortune.

Dagworthy conceived that his end was gained; in reality
it was the beginning of his disillusion. It speedily became
clear to him that he did not really care for his wife, that he
had been the victim of some self-deception, which was all the
more exasperating because difficult to be explained. The
danger of brutality on his part really lay in this first discovery
of his mistake; the presence of his father in the house was a
most fortunate circumstance; it necessitated self-control at
a time when it was hardest to maintain. Later, he was too
much altered from the elementary creature he had been to
stand in danger of grossly ill-using his wife. His marriage
developed the man surprisingly; it made him self-conscious
in a degree he could not formerly have conceived. He had
fully believed that this woman was in love with him, and
the belief had flattered him inexpressibly; to become aware
that she regarded him with disgust, only kept under by fear,
was to receive light on many things besides the personal relations between himself and her. If he had not in reality
regarded her at any time with strong feeling, what had made
him so bent on gaining her for his wife? To puzzle this over
—the problem would not quit his mind—was to become dimly
aware of what he had hoped for and what he had missed. It

was not her affection : he felt that the absence of this was not
the worst thing he had to bear. Gradually he came to understand that he had been deceived by artificialities which mocked
the image of something for which he really longed, and that
something was refinement, within and without, a life directed
by other motives and desires than those he had known, a
spirit aiming at things he did not understand, yet which he
would gladly have had explained to him. There followed
resentment of the deceit that had been practised on him ; the
woman had been merely caught by his money, and it followed
that she was contemptible. Instead of a higher, he had wedded
a lower than himself ; she did not care even to exercise the
slight hypocrisy by which she might have kept his admiration ;
the cruelest feature of the wrong he had suffered was that, by
the disclosure of her unworthiness, his wife was teaching him
the real value of that which he had aimed at blindly and so
deplorably failed to gain. Dagworthy had a period almost of
despair ; it was then that, in an access of fury, he committed
the brutality which created so many myths about his domestic
life. To be hauled into the police-court, and to be well aware
what Dunfield was saying about him, was not exactly an agreeable experience, but it had, like his marriage, an educational
value ; he knew that the thrashing administered to the groom
had been a vicarious one, and this actively awakened sense of
a possible inner meaning of things was not without its influence
upon him. It was remarked that he heard the imposition of
his fine with a suppressed laugh. Dunfield, repeating the
story with florid circumstance, of course viewed it as an illustration of his debauched state of mind ; in reality the laugh
came of a perception of the solemn absurdity of the proceedings, and Richard was by so much the nearer to understanding
himself and the world.

His wife's death came as an unhoped-for relief ; he felt like
a man beginning the world anew. He had no leaning to
melancholy, and a prolongation of his domestic troubles would
not have made him less hearty in his outward bearing, but
the progress of time had developed elements in his nature
which were scarcely compatible with a continuance of the life
he had been leading. He had begun to put to himself omin-
ous questions ; such, for instance, as—What necessity was he
under to maintain the appearance of a cheerful domesticity ?
If things got just a trifle more unbearable, why should he not
make for himself somewhere else a new home ? He was, it is

true, startled at his own audacity, and only some strangely powerful concurrence of motives—such as he was yet to know —could in reality have made him reckless. For the other features of his character, those which tended to stability, were still strong enough to oppose passions which had not found the occasion for their full development. He was not exactly avaricious, but pursuit of money was in him an hereditary instinct. By mere force of habit he stuck zealously to his business, and, without thinking much about his wealth, disliked unusual expenditure. His wife had taunted him with meanness, with low money-grubbing; the effect had been to make him all the more tenacious of habits which might have given way before other kinds of reproof. So he had gone on living the ordinary life, to all appearances well contented, in reality troubled from time to time by a reawakening of those desires which he had understood only to have them frustrated. He groped in a dim way after things which, by chance perceived, seemed to have a certain bearing on his life. The discovery in himself of an interest in architecture was an instance; but for his visit to the Continent he might never have been led to think of the subject. Then there was his fondness for the moors and mountains, the lochs and islands, of the north. On the whole, he preferred to travel in Scotland by himself; the scenery appealed to a poetry that was in him, if only he could have brought it into consciousness. Already he had planned for the present August a tour among the Hebrides, and had made it out with his maps and guidebooks, not without careful consideration of expense. Why did he linger beyond the day on which he had decided to set forth?

For several days it had been noticed at the mill that he lacked something of his wonted attention in matters of business. Certainly his occupation about eleven o'clock one morning had little apparent bearing on the concerns of his office; he was standing at the window of his private room, which was on the first floor of the mill, with a large fieldglass at his eyes. The glass was focussed upon the Cartwrights' garden, in which sat Jessie with Emily Hood. They were but a short distance away, and Dagworthy could observe them closely; he had done so, intermittently, for almost an hour, and this was the second morning that he had thus amused himself. Yet, to judge from his face, when he turned away, amusement was hardly his state of mind; his features had a hard-set earnestness, an expression almost savage. And then he walked about the little room, regarding objects absently.

Four days later he was again with his glass at the window; it wanted a few minutes of ten o'clock. Emily Hood had just reached the garden; he saw her enter and begin to pace about the walks, waiting for Jessie's arrival. Dagworthy of a sudden put the glass aside, took his hat, and hastened away from the mill. He walked along the edge of the cattle-market, till he came into the road by which Jessie must approach the garden; he saw her coming, and went on at a brisk pace towards her. The girl was not hurrying, though she would be late; these lessons were beginning to tax her rather too seriously; Emily was so exacting. Already she had made a change in the arrangements, whereby she saved herself the walk to Banbrigg; in the garden, too, it was much easier to find excuses for trifling away time than when she was face to face with Emily at a table. So she came along the road at a very moderate pace, and, on seeing who it was that neared her, put on her pleasantest smile, doubly glad of the meeting; it was always something to try her devices on Richard Dagworthy, and at present the chat would make a delay for which she could urge reasonable excuse.

'The very person I wanted to meet!' Dagworthy exclaimed. 'You've saved me a run all the way up to your house. What are you doing this way? Going to school?'

He pointed to the books she carried.

'Something like it,' replied Jessie, with a wry movement of her lips. 'Why did you want to meet me, though?'

'Because I want you to do something for me—that is, if you will. But, really, where were you going? Perhaps you can't spare time?'

'I was going to the garden,' she said, pointing in that direction. 'I have lessons there with Emily Hood. Beastly shame that I should have to do lessons, isn't it? I feel too old for that; I've got other things to think about.

She put her head on one side, and rustled the pages of a French grammar, at last throwing a glance at Richard from the corners of her eyes.

'But do you expect Miss Hood to come soon?' Dagworthy asked, playing his part very well, in spite of a nervousness which possessed him.

'No doubt she's in the garden already. I've given her a

key, so that if she gets there first—— But what do you want me to do?'

'Why, I was going to ask you to walk to the station and meet the ten thirty-five train from Hebsworth. Your father will get in by it, I expect, and I want him to come and see me at once at the mill.'

'All right,' Jessie exclaimed with eagerness, 'I'll go. Just let me run and tell Emily——'

Dagworthy was consulting his watch.

'You've only bare time to get to the station, walking as quickly as you can? Which is your garden? Let me go and tell her you are not coming.'

'Will you? The second door round the corner there. You'll have to apologise properly—I hope you know how to.'

This was Jessie's maidenly playfulness; she held out her hand, with many graces, to take leave.

'If he doesn't come,' said Dagworthy, 'will you just walk over to the mill to let me know?'

'I don't know that I shall; I don't think it would be proper.'

'Ho, ho! I like that! But you'll have to be off, or you'll never get there in time.'

She ran away, rejoicing in her escape from the lesson. Of course she looked back several times; the first glance showed her Dagworthy still gazing after her, at the second she saw that he was walking towards the garden.

He pushed open the wooden door, and passed between the hedges; the next door stood open, and he already saw Emily; she had seated herself under one of the pear trees, and was reading. As soon as his eyes discovered her he paused; his hands clasped themselves nervously behind him. Then he proceeded more slowly. As soon as he stepped within the garden, Emily heard his approach, and turned her head with a smile, expectant of Jessie. At the sight of Dagworthy the smile vanished instantly, she became noticeably pale, and at length rose with a startled motion.

Dagworthy drew near to her; when close enough to hold out his hand, he could no longer keep his eyes upon her face; they fell, and his visage showed an embarrassment which, even in her confusion—her all but dread—Emily noticed as a strange thing. She was struggling to command herself, to overcome by reason the fear which always attacked her in this man's presence. She felt it as a relief to be spared the steady gaze which, on former meetings, he had never removed from her.

'You are surprised to see me here?' he began, taking hold of the chair which Emily had risen from and swaying it backwards and forwards. Even his voice was more subdued than she had ever known it. 'I have come to apologise to you for sending Miss Cartwright to meet her father at the station. I met her by chance just out there in the road, and as I wanted a messenger very badly I took advantage of her good-nature. But she wouldn't go unless I promised to come here and explain her absence.'

'Thank you,' Emily replied, as naturally as she could. 'Will she still come back for her lesson, do you think?'

'I'm afraid not; she said I had better ask you to excuse her this morning.'

Emily gathered up two or three books which lay on the other chair.

'You find her rather troublesome to teach, I should be afraid,' Dagworthy pursued, watching her every moment. 'Jessie isn't much for study, is she?'

'Perhaps she is a little absent now and then,' replied Emily, saying the first thing that occurred to her.

She had collected her books and was about to fasten a strap round them

'Do let me do that for you,' said Dagworthy, and he forestalled her assent, which she would probably not have given, by taking the books from her hands. He put up his foot on the chair, as if for the convenience of doing the strapping on his knee, but before he had finished it he spoke again.

'You are fond of teaching, I suppose?'

'Yes, I like it.'

She stood in expectant waiting, her hands held together before her, her head just bent. The attitude was grace itself. Dagworthy raised his eyes slowly from her feet to her face.

'But you wouldn't care to go on with it always?'

'I—I don't think about it,' she replied, nervousness again seizing her. There was a new look in his eyes, a vehemence, a fervour, which she dared not meet after the first glance. He would not finish the strapping of the books, and she could not bid him do so. Had she obeyed her instinct, she would have hastened away, heedless of anything but the desire to quit his presence.

'How long will your holidays be?' he asked, letting the books fall to the chair, as if by accident.

'Till the end of September, I think.'

'So long? I'm glad to hear that. You will come again some day to my house with your father, won't you?'

The words trembled upon his lips; it was not like his own voice, he could not control it.

'Thank you, Mr. Dagworthy,' she replied.

He bent to the books again, and this time succeeded in binding them together. As he fastened the buckle, drops of perspiration fell from his forehead.

Emily thanked him, and held forth her hand for the books. He took it in his own.

'Miss Hood——'

She drew her hand away, almost by force, and retreated a step; his face terrified her.

'I sent Jessie off on purpose,' he continued. 'I knew you were here, and wanted to speak to you alone. Since I met you that day on the Heath, I have had no rest—I've wanted so to see you again. The other morning at the Cartwrights' it was almost more than I could do to go away. I don't know what's come to me; I can't put you out of my thoughts for one minute; I can't give my attention to business, to anything. I meant to have gone away before now, but I've put it off, day after day; once or twice I've all but come to your house, to ask to see you——'

He spoke in a hurried, breathless way, almost with violence; passion was forcing the words from him, in spite of a shame which kept his face on fire. There was something boyish in the simplicity of his phrases; he seemed to be making a confession that was compelled by fear, and at length his speech lost itself in incoherence. He stood with his eyes fixed on the ground; perspiration covered his face.

'Mr. Dagworthy——'

Emily tried to break the intolerable silence. Her strength was answering now to the demand upon it; his utter abashment before her could not but help her to calmness. But the sound of her first word gave him voice again.

'Let me speak first,' he broke forth, now looking full at her. 'That's nothing of what I wanted to say; it sounds as if I wasn't man enough to know my own mind. I know it well enough, and I must say all I have to say, whilst you're here to listen to me. After all, you're only a girl; but if you'd come here straight from heaven, I couldn't find it harder to speak to you.'

'Mr. Dagworthy, don't speak like this—don't say more—I beg you not to! I cannot listen as you would wish me to.'

'You can't listen? But you don't know what I have to say still,' he urged, with hasty entreaty, his voice softer. 'I'm asking nothing yet; I only want you to know how you've made me feel towards you. No feeling will ever come to you like this that's come to me, but I want you to know of it, to try and understand what it means—to try and think of me. I don't ask for yes or no, it wouldn't be reasonable; you haven't had to think of me in this way. But God knows how I shall live without you; it would be the cruelest word woman ever said if you refused even to give me a hope.'

'I cannot—do hear me—it is not in my power to give you hope.'

'Oh, you say that because you think you must, because I have come to you so suddenly; I have offended you by talking in this way when we scarcely know each other even as friends, and you have to keep me at a distance; I see it on your face. Do you think there is a danger that I should be less respectful to you than I ought? That's because you don't understand me. I've spoken in rough, hasty words, because to be near you takes all sense from me. Look, I'm quieter now. What I ought to have said at first is this. You're prejudiced against me; you've heard all sorts of tales; I know well enough what people say about me—well, I want you to know me better. We'll leave all other feelings aside. We'll say I just wish you to think of me in a just way, a friendly way, nothing more. It's impossible for you to do more than that at first. No doubt even your father has told you that I have a hasty temper, which leads me to say and do things I'm soon sorry for. It's true enough, but that doesn't prove that I am a brute, and that I can't mend myself. You've heard things laid to my charge that are false—about my doings in my own home—you know what I mean. Get to know me better, and some day I'll tell you the whole truth. Now it's only this I ask of you—be just to me. You're not a woman like these in Dunfield who talk and talk behind one's back; though I have seen so little of you, don't I know the difference between you and them? I'm ignorant enough, compared with you, but I can feel what it is that puts you above all other women. It must be that that makes me mad to gain a kind word from you. One word—that you'll try to think of me ; and I'll live on that as long as I can.'

The mere utterances help little to an understanding of the terrible force of entreaty he put into this speech. His face, his hands, the posture of his body, all joined in pleading. He had cast off all shamefacedness, and spoke as if his life depended on the answer she would return ; the very lack of refinement in his tone, in his pronunciation of certain words, made his appeal the more pathetic. With the quickness of jealousy, he had guessed at the meaning there might lie in Emily's reluctance to hear him, but he dared not entertain the thought ; it was his passionate instinct to plead it down. Whatever it might be that she had in mind, she must first hear him. As he spoke, he watched her features with the eagerness of desire, of fear ; to do so was but to inflame his passion. It was an extraordinary struggle between the force of violent appetite and the constraint of love in the higher sense. How the former had been excited, it would be hard to explain. Wilfrid Athel had submitted to the same influence. Her beauty was of the kind which, leaving the ordinary man untouched, addressed itself with the strangest potency to an especially vehement nature here and there. Her mind, uttering itself in the simplest phrases, laid a spell upon certain other minds set apart and chosen. She could not speak but the soul of this rude mill-owner was exalted beyond his own intelligence.

Forced to wait the end of his speech, Emily stood with her head bowed in sadness. Fear had passed ; she recognised the heart-breaking sincerity of his words, and compassionated him. When he became silent, she could not readily reply. He was speaking again, below his breath.

'You are thinking ? I know how you can't help regarding me. Try only to feel for me.'

'There is only one way in which I can answer you,' she said ; ' I owe it to you to hide nothing. I feel deeply the sincerity of all you have said, and be sure, Mr. Dagworthy, that I will never think of you unjustly or unkindly. But I can promise nothing more ; I have already given my love.'

Her voice faltered before the last word, the word she would never lightly utter. But it must be spoken now ; no paraphrase would confirm her earnestness sufficiently.

Still keeping her eyes on the ground, she knew that he had started.

'You have promised to marry some one ? ' he asked, as if it were necessary to have the fact affirmed in the plainest words before he could accept it.

She hoped that silence might be her answer.

'Have you ? Do you mean that ? '

' I have.'

She saw that he was turning away from her, and with an effort she looked at him. She wished she had not; his anguish expressed itself like an evil passion; his teeth were set with a cruel savageness. It was worse when he caught her look and tried to smile.

'Then I suppose that's—that's the end,' he said, as if he would make an effort to joke upon it, though his voice all but failed in speaking the few words.

He walked a little apart, then approached her again.

'You don't say this just to put me off ? ' he asked, with a roughness which was rather the effect of his attempt to keep down emotion than intentional.

'I have told you the truth,' Emily replied firmly.

'Do other people know it ? Do the Cartwrights ? '

'You are the only one to whom I have spoken of it.'

'Except your father and mother, you mean ? '

'They do not know.'

Though so troubled, she was yet able to ask herself whether his delicacy was sufficiently developed to enjoin silence. The man had made such strange revelation of himself, she felt unable to predict his course. No refinement in him would now have surprised her; but neither would any outbreak of boorishness. He seemed capable of both. His next question augured ill.

'Of course it is not any one in Dunfield ? '

'It is not.'

Jealousy was torturing him. He was quite conscious that he should have refrained from a single question, yet he could no more keep these back than he could the utterance of his passion.

'Will you——'

He hesitated.

'May I leave you, Mr. Dagworthy ? ' Emily asked, seeing that he was not likely to quit her. She moved to take the books from the chair.

'One minute more.—Will you tell me who it is?—I am a brute to ask you, but—if you—— Good God! How shall I bear this?'

He turned his back upon her; she saw him quiver. It was her impulse to walk from the garden, but she feared to pass him.

He faced her again. Yes, the man could suffer.

'Will you tell me who it is?' he groaned rather than spoke. 'You don't believe that I should speak of it? But I feel I could bear it better; I should know for certain it was no use hoping.'

Emily could not answer.

'It is some one in London?'

'Yes, Mr. Dagworthy, I cannot tell you more than that. Please do not ask more.'

'I won't. Of course your opinion of me is worse than ever. That doesn't matter much.—If you could kill as easily as you can drive a man mad, I would ask you to still have pity on me.—I'm forgetting: you want me to go first, so that you can lock up the garden.—Good-bye!'

He did not offer his hand, but cast one look at her, a look Emily never forgot, and walked quickly away.

Emily could not start at once homewards. When it was certain that Dagworthy had left the garden, she seated herself; she had need of rest and of solitude to calm her thoughts. Her sensation was that of having escaped a danger, the dread of which thrilled in her. Though fear had been allayed for an interval, it regained its hold upon her towards the end of the dialogue; the passion she had witnessed was so rude, so undisciplined, it seemed to expose elementary forces, which, if need be, would set every constraint at defiance. It was no exaggeration to say that she did not feel safe in the man's presence. The possibility of such a feeling had made itself known to her even during the visit to his house; to find herself suddenly the object of his almost frenzied desire was to realise how justly her instinct had spoken. This was not love, as she understood it, but a terrible possession which might find assuagement in inflicting some fearful harm upon what it affected to hold dear. The Love of Emily's worship was a spirit of passionate benignity, of ecstatic calm, holy in renunciations, pure unutterably in supreme attainment. Her knowledge of life was insufficient to allow her to deal justly with love as exhibited in Dagworthy; its gross side was too offensively prominent; her experience gave her no power of rightly appreciating this struggle of the divine flame in a dense element. Living, and having ever lived, amid idealisms, she was too subjective in her interpretation of phenomena so new to her. It would have been easier for her to judge impartially had she witnessed this passion directed towards another; addressed to her, in the position she occupied, any phase of wooing would have been painful; vehemence was nothing less than abhorrent. Wholly ignorant of Dagworthy's inner life, and misled with regard to the mere facts of his outward behaviour, it was impossible that she should discern the most deeply significant features of the love he expressed so ill, impossible for her to understand that what would be brutality in another man was in him the working of the very means of grace, could circumstances have favoured their action. One tribute her instinct paid to the good which hid itself under so rude a guise ; as she pondered over her fear, analysing it as scrupulously as she always did those feelings which she felt it behoved her to understand once for all, she half discovered in it an element which only severe self-judgment would allow; it seemed to her that the fear was, in an infinitesimal degree, of herself, that, under other conditions, she might have known what it was to respond to the love thus offered her. For she neither scorned nor loathed the man, notwithstanding her abhorrence of his passion as devoted to herself. She wished him well; she even found herself thinking over those women in Dunfield whom she knew, if perchance one of them might seem fitted to make his happiness. None the less, it was terrible to reflect that she must live, perhaps for a long time, so near to him, ever exposed to the risk of chance meetings, if not to the danger of a surprise such as to-day's ; for she could not assure herself that he would hold her answer final. One precaution she must certainly take; henceforth she would never come to the garden save in Jessie's company. She wondered how Dagworthy had known of her presence here, and it occurred to her to doubt of Jessie; could the latter have aided in bringing about this interview ? Dagworthy, confessing his own manœuvre, would naturally conceal any conscious part in it that Jessie might have taken.

Her spirits suffered depression as she communed thus with herself; all the drearier aspects of her present life were emphasised ; she longed, longed with aching of the heart for the day which should set her free for ever from these fears

and sorrows. Another secret would henceforth trouble her.
Would that it might remain a secret! If Jessie indeed knew
of this morning's events, there was small likelihood that it
would remain unknown to others; then the whole truth must
be revealed. Would it not be better to anticipate any such
discovery, to tell her father this very day what had happened
and why it was so painful to her? Yet to speak of Dagworthy
might make her father uneasy in his position at the mill—would
inevitably do so. Therein lay a new dread. Was Dagworthy
capable of taking revenge upon her father? Oh surely, surely
not!—The words passed her lips involuntarily. She would
not, she could not, believe so ill of him; had he not implored
her to do him justice? . . . .

When Mr. Hood returned from business on the following
day, he brought news that Dagworthy had at last gone for
his holiday. It was time, he said; Dagworthy was not looking himself; at the mill they had been in mortal fear of one
of his outbreaks.

'Did he speak harshly to you, father?' Emily was driven
to ask, with very slight emphasis on the 'you.'

'Fortunately,' was the reply, with the sad abortive laugh
which was Mr. Hood's nearest approach to mirth, 'fortunately
he left me alone, and spoke neither well nor ill. He didn't
look angry, I thought, so much as put out about something.'

Emily was relieved from one fear at least, and felt grateful
to Dagworthy. Moreover, by observation, she had concluded
that Jessie could not possibly be aware of what had taken
place in the garden. And now Dagworthy was likely to be
away for three weeks. Her heart was lighter again.

CHAPTER IX.

CIRCUMSTANCE.

DAGWORTHY was absent not quite a fortnight, and he returned
looking anything but the better for his holiday. The wholesome colour of his cheeks had changed almost to sallowness;
those who met him in Dunfield looked at him with surprise
and asked what illness he had been suffering. At the mill,
they did not welcome his re-appearance; his temper was
worse than it had been since the ever-memorable week which

witnessed his prosecution for assault and battery. At home, the servants did their best to keep out of his way, warned by Mrs. Jenkins. She, good woman, had been rash enough to bring the child into the dining-room whilst Dagworthy was refreshing himself with a biscuit and a glass of wine upon his arrival; in a minute or two she retreated in high wrath.

' Let him dom me, if he loikes,' she went away exclaiming; ' ah'm ovver auld to care much abaht such fond tantrums ; but when he gets agaate o' dommin his awn barn, it fair maaks my teeth dither ageean. The lad's aht on his 'eead.'

That was seven o'clock in the evening. He dined an hour later, and when it was dark left the house. Between then and midnight he was constantly in and out, and Mrs. Jenkins, who was kept up by her fears that ' t' master ' was seriously unwell, made at length another attempt to face him. She knocked at the door of the sitting-room, having heard him enter a minute or two before; no answer was vouchsafed, so she made bold to open the door. Dagworthy was sitting with his head upon the table, his arms stretched out ; he appeared to be asleep.

' Mr. Richard ! ' she said softly. ' Mr. Richard ! '

He looked up. ' Well ? What is it ? '

' Yo' scahr'd me ; ah thowt summat 'ad come to yo'. What's wrong wi' yo', Mr. Richard ? You look as if you could hardly ho'd your heead up.'

To her surprise he spoke quite calmly.

' Yes, I've got a bit of a headache. Get me some hot water, will you ? I'll have some brandy and go to bed.'

She began to advise other remedies, but Dagworthy speedily checked her.

' Get me some hot water, I tell you, and go to bed yourself. What are you doing up at this hour ? '

He went to business at the usual time next morning, and it seemed as if the worst had blown over ; at home he was sullen, but not violent.

The third day after his return, on entering his office at the mill, he found Hood taking down one of a row of old ledgers which stood there upon a shelf.

' What are you doing ? ' he asked abruptly, at the same time turning his back upon the clerk.

Hood explained that he was under the necessity of searching through the accounts for several years, to throw light upon a certain transaction which was giving trouble.

' All right,' was the reply, as Dagworthy took his keys out to open his desk.

A quarter of an hour later, he entered the room where Hood was busy over the ledger. A second clerk was seated there, and him Dagworthy summoned to the office, where he had need of him. Presently Hood came to replace the ledger he had examined, and took away the succeeding volume. A few minutes later Dagworthy said to the clerk who sat with him—

' I shall have to go away for an hour or so. I'm expecting a telegram from Legge Brothers; if it doesn't come before twelve o'clock, you or Hood must go to Hebsworth. It had better be Hood; you finish what you're at. If there's no telegram, he must take the twelve-thirteen, and give this note here to Mr. Andrew Legge; there'll be an answer. Mind you see to this.'

At the moment when Dagworthy's tread sounded on the stairs, Mr. Hood was on the point of making a singular discovery. In turning a page of the ledger, he came upon an envelope, old and yellow, which had evidently been shut up in the book for several years ; it was without address and unsealed. He was going to lay it aside, when his fingers told him that it contained something ; the enclosure proved to be a ten-pound note, also old and patched together in the manner of notes that have been sent half at a time.

' Now I wonder how that got left there ? ' Hood mused. ' There's been rare searching for that, I'll be bound. Here's something to put our friend into a better temper.'

He turned the note over once or twice, tried in vain to decipher a scribbled endorsement, then restored it to the envelope. With the letter in his hand, he went to the office.

' Mr. Dagworthy out ? ' he asked of his fellow-clerk on looking round.

The clerk was a facetious youth. He rose from his seat, seized a ruler, and began a species of sword-play about Hood's head, keeping up a grotesque dance the while. Hood bore it with his wonted patience, smiling faintly.

' Mr. Dagworthy out ? ' he repeated, as soon as he was free from apprehension of a chance crack on the crown.

' He is, my boy. And what's more, there's a chance of your having a spree in Hebsworth. Go down on your knees and pray that no telegram from Foot Brothers—I mean, Legge—arrives during the next five-and-twenty minutes.'

' Why ? '

' If not, you're to takee this notee to Brother Andrew Leggee,—comprenez ? The boss was going to send me, but he altered his mind, worse luck.'

' Twelve-thirteen ? ' asked Hood.

' Yes. And now if you're in the mind, I'll box you for half a dollar—what say ? '

He squared himself in pugilistic attitude, and found amusement in delivering terrific blows which just stopped short of Hood's prominent features. The latter beat a retreat.

Twelve o'clock struck, and no telegram had arrived; neither had Dagworthy returned to the mill. Hood was indisposed to leave the envelope to be given by other hands; he might as well have the advantage of such pleasure as the discovery would no doubt excite. So he put it safely in his pocket-book, and hastened to catch the train, taking with him the paper of sandwiches which represented his dinner. These he would eat on the way to Hebsworth.

It was a journey of ten miles, lying at first over green fields, with a colliery vomiting blackness here and there, then through a region of blight and squalor, finally over acres of smoke-fouled streets, amid the roar of machinery; a journey that would have crushed the heart in one fresh from the breath of heaven on sunny pastures. It was a slow train, and there were half a dozen stoppages. Hood began to eat his sandwiches at a point where the train was delayed for a few minutes by an adverse signal; a coal-pit was close by, and the smoke from the chimney blew in at the carriage windows, giving a special flavour to the bread and meat. There was a drunken soldier in the same compartment, who was being baited by a couple of cattle-drovers with racy vernacular not to be rendered by the pen. Hood munched his smoky sandwich, and with his sad eyes watched the great wheel of the colliery revolve, and the trucks rise and descend. The train moved on again. The banter between the other three passengers was taking an angry turn; to escape the foul language as far as possible, Hood kept his head at the window. Of a sudden the drunken soldier was pushed against him, and before he could raise his hands, his hat had flown off on the breeze.

He turned round with angry remonstrance. The soldier had fallen back on to the seat, and was grinning inanely; the drovers were enjoying the joke beyond measure

'Theer, lad!' one of them cried. 'Tha's doon it nah! Tha'll a' to buy him a new 'at for his 'eead, soon as we get i'to Hebs'orth.'

' 'Appen he's got no brass,' suggested the other, guffawing.

It was the case ; the soldier had a copper or two at most. The drovers of course held themselves free of responsibility. Hood felt in his own pocket ; but he was well aware that a shilling and three-halfpence was all he carried with him— save the bank-note in his pocket-book. Yet it was impossible to go through Hebsworth with uncovered head, or to present himself hatless at the office of Legge Brothers. Already the train was slackening speed to enter the station. Would any hatter trust him, on his representing whence he came ? He feared not. Not the least part of his trouble was the thought of having to buy a new hat at all ; such an expense was ill to be borne just now. Of course—he said to himself, with dreary fatalism—a mishap is sure to come at the worst time. It was the experience of his life.

Hood was a shy man ; it was misery to have attention drawn to himself as it naturally would be as soon as he stepped out on to the platform. But there was no help ; with a last angry look at the drunken soldier, he nerved himself to face the ordeal. As he walked hurriedly out of the crowd, the cry ' Cab, sir ? ' fell upon his ears. Impossible to say how he brought himself to such a pitch of recklessness, but in a moment he was seated in a hansom, having bidden the driver take him to the nearest hatter's. The agony of em-barrassment has driven shy men to strange audacities, but who ever dared more than this ? *He would be compelled to change the note !*

Whatever might be the cause, whether it was the sudden sense of refuge from observation, or the long unknown pleasure of riding in a cab, as he sped along the streets he grew almost merry; at length he positively laughed at the adventure which had befallen him. It mattered nothing whether he gave Dag-worthy the money in a note or in change, and, on being told the story, his employer might even feel disposed to pay for the hat. He *would* pay for the hat! By the time the cab drew up, Hood had convinced himself of this. He was in better spirits than he had been for many a day.

' Can you change me a ten-pound note ? ' were his first words to the hatter. ' If you can't, I must go elsewhere ; I have nothing smaller.'

The salesman hesitated.

' You want a silk hat ? '

' Yes, but not an expensive one.'

A pen was brought, and Hood was requested to endorse the note. What security—under the circumstances—such a proceeding could give, the hatter best knew; he appeared satisfied, and counted out his sovereigns. Hood paid the cabman, and walked off briskly towards the office of Legge Brothers.

He stopped in the middle of the pavement as if a shot had struck him. Supposing Dagworthy had no recollection of a ten-pound note having been lost, nor of any note having been lost; and supposing it occurred to him that he, Hood, had in reality found a larger sum, had invented the story of the lost hat, and was returning a portion only of his discovery, to gain the credit of honesty ? Such an idea could only possess the brain of a man whose life had been a struggle amid the chicaneries and despicabilities of commerce; who knew that a man's word was never trusted where there could enter the slightest suspicion of an advantage to himself in lying; whose daily terror had been lest some error, some luckless chance, should put him within the nets of criminality. It is the deepest curse of such a life as his that it directs the imagination in channels of meanness, and preoccupies the thought with sordid fears. What would it avail him, in the present instance, to call the shopman to witness? The note, ten to one, would be paid away, and here also a man's word was worth nothing. But Dagworthy might merely think such an accusation: ay, that would be the worst. To lie henceforth under suspicion of dishonesty: that meant, to lose his place before long, on some pretence.

And he felt that, in spite of absolute sincerity, he could not stand before Dagworthy and tell his tale with the face and voice of an honest man,—felt it with a horrible certainty. In a man of Hood's character, this state of mind was perfectly natural. Not only was he weakly constructed, but his incessant ill-fortune had done him that last wrong which social hardship can inflict upon the individual, it had undermined his self-respect. Having been so often treated like a dog, he had come to expect such treatment, and, what was worse, but feebly to resent it. He had lost the conscious dignity of manhood ; nay, had perhaps never possessed it, for his battle had begun at so early an age. The sense that he was wretchedly poor, and the knowledge that poverty is the mother of degradation, made him at any moment a self-convicted criminal ; accused, however wrongly, it was inevitable that his face should be against him. To go to Dagworthy with sovereigns in his hand, and this story upon his lips, would be to invite suspicion by every strongest sign of guilt.

I am representing the poor fellow's thoughts and feelings. Whether or not Dagworthy would really entertain such a suspicion is quite another matter. For the first time in his life, Hood had used for his own purposes money which did not belong to him ; he did it under the pressure of circumstances, and had not time to reflect till the act was irrevocable. Then this horror came upon him. Forgetting his errand, he drew aside into a quieter street, and struggled with his anguish. Do you laugh at him for his imbecility ? Try first to understand him.

But his business must be performed; with trembling limbs he hurried onwards, and at length reached the office of Legge Brothers. The member of the firm to whom the note which he bore was addressed had but a few minutes ago left the place ; he would return within an hour. How could the time be spent ? He began to wander aimlessly about the streets. In passing a spot where scaffolding was erected before new buildings, the wish entered his mind that something might fall and crush him. He thought of such an end as a blessed relief.

A hand was laid upon his shoulder, and at the touch his heart leaped as though it would burst his side. He turned and, with starting eyes, glared at the man before him, a perfect stranger, he thought.

'Is it ? Or isn't it ? Hood, or his ghost ? '

The man who spoke was of the shabbiest appearance, wearing an almost napless high hat, a coloured linen shirt which should have been at the laundress's, no neck-tie, a frock-coat with only one button, low shoes terribly down at heel ; for all that, the most jovial-looking man, red-nosed, laughing. At length Hood was capable of recognising him.

'Cheeseman ! Well, who on earth would have expected to meet you ! '

' I've followed you half along the street ; couldn't be sure. Afraid I startled you at last, old friend.'

They had known each other as young men, and it was now ten years at least since they had met. They were companions in ill-hap, the difference between them being that Cheeseman bore the buffets of the world with imperturbable good humour; but then he had neither wife nor child, kith nor kin. He had tried his luck in all parts of England and in several other countries; casual wards had known him, and he had gained a supper by fiddling in the streets. Many a beginning had he made, but none led to anything; he seemed, in truth, to enjoy a haphazard existence. If Cheeseman had possessed literary skill, the story of his life from his own hand would have been invaluable; it is a misfortune that the men who are richest in 'material' are those who would never dream of using it.

They were passing a public-house; Cheeseman caught his friend by the arm and, in spite of resistance, drew him in.

'Two threes of gin hot,' was his order. 'The old drink, Hood, my boy; the drink that has saved me from despair a thousand times. How many times have you and I kept up each other's pecker over a three of gin ! You don't look well ; you've wanted old Cheeseman to cheer you up. Things bad ? Why, damn it, of course things are bad ; when were they anything else with you and me, eh ? Your wife, how is she ? Remember me to her, will you ? She never took to me, but never mind that. And the little girl? How's the little girl ? Alive and well, please God ? '

'Rather more than a little girl now,' returned Hood. 'And doing well, I'm glad to say. She's a governess; has an excellent place in London.'

'You don't say so ? I never was so glad to hear anything in my life ! Ah, but Hood, you're leaving me behind, old friend ; with the little girl doing so well you can't call your-self a poor devil ; you can't, upon my soul ! I ought to have married ; yes, I should ha' married long ago ; it 'ud a' been the making of me. It's the sole speculation, I do believe, that I haven't tried. Ah, but I've got something before me now ! What say you to a patent fire-escape that any man can carry round his waist ? Upon my soul, I've got it ! I'm going to London about it as soon as I can get my fare ; and that I shall have to-morrow, please God.'

'What brings you to Hebsworth ? '

'I don't care much to talk about it in a public place,' replied Cheeseman, with caution which contrasted comically with his loud tone hitherto. 'Only a little matter, but—— Well, we'll say nothing about it; I may communicate with you some day. And you ? Do you live here ? '

Hood gave an account of his position. Under the influence of the glass of spirits, and of the real pleasure it gave him to see one of the very few men he had ever called friend, he had cast aside his cares for the moment. They went forth presently from the bar, and, after a few paces, Cheeseman took his friend by the coat collar and drew him aside, as if to impart a matter of consequence.

'Two threes of gin!' he said, with a roll of the eye which gave his face a singularly humorous expression. 'That's sixpence. A tanner, Hood, was the last coin I possessed. It was to have purchased dinner, a beefsteak pudding, with cabbage and potatoes; but what o' that? When you and I meet, we drink to old times; there's no getting out of that.'

Hood laughed, for once in a really natural way. His usual abstemiousness made the gin potent.

'Why,' he said, 'I confess to feeling hungry myself; I've only had a sandwich. Come along; we'll have dinner together.'

'You mean it, old friend?' cried the other, with irrepressible delight.

'Of course I mean it. You don't think I'll let you spend your last coin, and send you off dinnerless? Things are bad, but not quite as bad as that. I'm as hungry as a hunter; where is there an eating-house?'

They found one at a little distance.

'It must be beefsteak pudding, Hood,' whispered Cheeseman, as they entered. 'I've set my heart on that. Whatever else you like, but a beefsteak pudding to start with.'

The article was procurable, smoking, juicy. Cheeseman made an incision, then laid down his knife and gloated over his plate.

'Hood,' he said, with much solemnity, 'you've done me many a kindness, old friend, but this caps all. I'm bound to you for life and death. I should have wandered about these streets a starving man.'

The other laughed still; he had a fit of laughter on him; he had not laughed so since he was young.

'Stout-and-mild is my drink, Hood,' remarked Cheeseman, suggestively. 'It has body, and I need the support.'

They each had a pint, served in the native pewter. When Cheeseman had taken a deep draught he leaned forward across the table.

'Hood, I don't forget it ; never you believe that I forget it, however appearances may be against me ? '

'Forget what ?—give me the mustard, as soon as you can spare it ; ha, ha ! '

'That ten-pound note ! '

Hood dropped his knife and fork.

'What on earth's up ? You look just like you did when I clapped you o' the shoulder. Your nerves are out of order, old friend.'

'Why, so they are. I know now what you mean ; I couldn't for the life of me think what you were talking about.'

'Don't think I forget it,' pursued the other, after a mouth-ful.

'It's twelve years last Easter since you lent me that ten-pound note, and it's been on my conscience ever since. But I shall repay it ; never you fear but I'll repay it. Did I men-tion a fire-escape that any man can wear round his waist ? Hush ! wait a month or two. Let me make a note of your address whilst I think of it. This pudding's hot, but it's a fault on the right side, and time 'll mend it. You wouldn't mind, I daresay, being my agent for Dunfield—for the fire-escape, you know ? I'll communicate with you, don't fear.'

A hot meal in the middle of the day was a luxury long unknown to Hood. Now and again the thought of what he was doing flashed across him, but mere bodily solace made his conscience dull. As the meal proceeded he even began to justify himself. Was he never to know an hour's enjoy-ment ? Was his life to be unbroken hardship ? What if he had borrowed a few shillings without leave ; somehow diffi-culties would be got over ; why, at the very worst, Emily would gladly lend him a pound. He began to talk of Emily, to praise her, to wax warm in the recounting of her goodness, her affection. What man living had so clever and so loving a daughter !

'It's what I said, Hood,' put in Cheeseman, with a shake of the head. ' You've left me behind. You've got into smooth water. The old partnership of ill-luck is broken up. Well, well ! I ought to have married. It's been my one mistake in life.'

'Why, it's none too late yet,' cried Hood, merrily.

'None too late ! Powers defend us ! What have I got to marry on ? '

' But the fire-escape ? '

' Yes, yes, to be sure ; the fire-escape ! Well, we'll see ; wait till things are set going. Perhaps you're right ; perhaps it isn't too late. And, Hood——'

' Well ? '

' You couldn't manage one single half-crown piece, could you ? To be sure there's always an archway to be found, when night comes on, but I can't pretend to like it. I always try to manage a bed at least once a week—no, no, not if there's the least difficulty. Times are hard, I know. I'd rather say not another word about it.'

' Nonsense ; take the half-crown and have done with it. Why, you've cheered me up many a half-crownsworth ; I feel better than I did. Don't I look it ? I feel as if I'd some warmth in my body. What say you, Cheeseman ? *One* half-pint more ? '

' Come, come, old friend ; that's speaking feelingly. You shouldn't try me in that way, you know. I shouldn't like to suggest a pint, with a scrap of cheese. Eh ? No, no ; follow your own counsel, boy ; half a pint be it.'

But the suggestion was accepted. Then at length it occurred to Hood that time must be wearing away ; he spoke of the obligation he was under to finish his business and return to Dunfield as soon as possible. Cheeseman declared himself the last man to stand in the way of business. They left the eating-house and walked together part of the way to the office of Legge Brothers.

' Old friend, I'm grateful to you,' said Cheeseman, when at length they parted. ' I've got your address, and you shall hear from me ; I've a notion it won't be so long before we meet again. In any case it's another day to look back upon ; I little thought of it when I spent twopence-halfpenny on my breakfast this morning and left sixpence for dinner. It's a rum world, eh, Hood ? Good-bye, and God bless you ! '

Hood hurried on to the office, received his reply, and proceeded to the station. He had more than half an hour to wait for a train. He took a seat in the waiting-room, and began to examine the money in his pocket, to ascertain exactly the sum he would have to replace. The deficit amounted to a little less than eighteen shillings. After all, it was very unlikely that Dagworthy would offer to bear the expense of the lost hat. Say that a pound had to be restored.

He was in the comfortable mood, following upon unusual

indulgence of the appetite, in which the mind handles in a free and easy way the thoughts it is wont to entertain with unquestionable gravity; when it has, as it were, a slippery hold on the facts of life, and constructs a subjective world of genial accommodations. A pound to restore; on the other hand, nine pounds in pocket. The sight of the sovereigns was working upon his imagination, already touched to a warmer life than was its habit. Nine pounds would go a long way towards solving the financial difficulties of the year; it would considerably more than replace the lacking rent of the house in Barnhill; would replace it, and pay as well the increased rent of the house at Banbrigg for twelve months to come. Looked at in this way, the money became a great temptation.

His wife—how explain to her such a windfall? For it was of course impossible to use it secretly. There was a way, seemingly of fate's providing. If only he could bring himself to the lie direct and shameless.

After all, a lie that would injure no mortal. As far as Dagworthy was concerned, the money had long since become the property of nobody; Dagworthy did not even know that this sum existed; if ever missed, it must have been put out of mind long ago. And very possibly it had never belonged to Dagworthy; some cashier or other clerk might just as well have lost it. Hood played with these speculations. He did not put to himself the plain alternative: Shall I keep the money, or shall I give it up? He merely let a series of reflections pass over his mind, as he lay back on the cushioned seat, experiencing an agreeable drowsiness. At the moment of finding the note, he would have handed it over to his employer without a thought; it would perhaps not even have occurred to him to regret that it was not his own. But during the last three hours a singular chain of circumstances had led to this result: it was just as possible as not that Hood would keep the coins in his pocket and say nothing about them.

It was time to go to the train. Almost with the first moving of the carriages he fell into a doze. A sense of mental uneasiness roused him now and then, but only for a few moments together; he slumbered on till Dunfield was reached.

At the entrance to the mill he was in fierce conflict with himself. As is usually the case in like circumstances, the

sleepy journey had resulted in bodily uneasiness ; he had a
slight headache, was thirsty, felt indisposed to return to work.
When he had all but crossed the threshold, he turned sharply
back, and entered a little public-house a few yards away ; an
extraordinary thing for him to do, but he felt that a small
glass of spirits would help him to quieter nerves, or at all
events would sustain his unusual exhilaration till the interview with Dagworthy was over. At the very door of the
office he had not decided whether it should be silence or
restitution.

'That you, Hood ? ' Dagworthy asked, looking up from
a letter he was writing. 'Been rather a long time, haven't
you ? '

The tone was unusually indulgent. Hood felt an accession of confidence ; he explained naturally the cause of his
delay.

'All right,' was the reply, as Dagworthy took the note
which his correspondent had sent.

Hood was in his own room, and—the money was still in
his pocket. . . .

He did not set out to walk home with his usual cheerfulness that evening. His headache had grown worse, and he
wished, wished at every step he took, that the lie he had to
tell to his wife was over and done with. There was no repentance of the decision which, it seemed on looking back, he had
arrived at involuntarily. The coin which made his pocket
heavy meant joy to those at home, and, if he got it wrong-
fully, the wrong was so dubious, so shadowy, that it vanished
in comparison with the good that would be done. It was not
—he said to himself—as if he had committed a theft to dis-
sipate the proceeds, like that young fellow who ran away from
the Dunfield and County Bank some months ago, and was
caught in London with disreputable associates. Here was a
ten-pound note lying, one might say, by the very roadside,
and it would save a family from privation. Abstractly, it was
wrong ; yes, it was wrong ; but would abstract right feed him
and pay his rent for the year to come ? Hood had reached
this stage in his self-examination ; he strengthened himself
by protest against the order of things. His headache nursed
the tendency to an active discontent, to which, as a rule, his
temperament did not lend itself.

But there remained the telling of the lie. How he wished
that Emily were not at home ! To lie before Emily, that was

the hardest part of his self-imposed task. He could not respect his wife, but before Emily, since her earliest companionship with him, he had watched his words scrupulously; as a little girl she had so impressed him with the purity of her heart that his love for her had been the nearest approach he ever knew to the spirit of worship; and since her attainment of mental and moral independence, his reverence for her had not been unmixed with awe. When her eyes met his, he felt the presence of a nature indefinitely nobler than his own; not seldom he marvelled in his dim way that such a one called him father. Could he ever after this day approach her with the old confidence? Nay, he feared her. His belief in her insight was almost a superstition. Would she not read the falsehood upon his face?

Strange state of mind; at one and the same time he wished that he had thought of Emily sooner, and was glad that he had not. That weight in his pocket was after all a joyous one, and to have been conscious of Emily as he now was, might—would—have made him by so much a poorer man.

She, as usual, was at the door to meet him, her face even gladder than its wont, for this morning there had been at the post-office a letter from Switzerland. How she loved that old name of Helvetia, printed on the stamps! Wilfrid wrote with ever fuller assurance that his father's mind was growing well-disposed, and Emily knew that he would not tell her other than the honest truth. For Wilfrid's scrupulous honesty she would have vouched as—for her father's.

'You look dreadfully worn out,' she said, as Hood bent his head in entering.

'I am, dear. I have been to Hebsworth, among other things.'

'Then I hope you had dinner there?'

He laughed.

'I should think I had!'

It was one of Mrs. Hood's bad days; she refused to leave the kitchen. Emily had tried to cheer her during the afternoon, but in vain. There had been a misunderstanding with the next-door neighbour, that lady having expressed herself rather decidedly with regard to an incursion made into her premises by the Hoods' cat.

'She speaks to me as if I was a mere working-woman,' Mrs. Hood exclaimed, when Emily endeavoured to soothe her. 'Well, and what else am I, indeed? There was a time when no one would have ventured to speak so.'

'Mother, how can you be troubled by what such a woman says?'

'Yes, I know I am in the wrong, Emily; you always make me see that.'

So Emily had retreated to the upper room, and Mrs. Hood, resenting neglect more even than contradiction, was resolved to sit in the kitchen till bedtime.

Hood was glad when he heard of this.

'If you'll pour out my tea, Emily,' he said in an under-tone, 'I'll go and speak to mother for a few moments. I have news that will please her.'

He went into the kitchen and, in silence, began to count sovereigns down upon the table, just behind his wife, who sat over some sewing and had not yet spoken. At the ring of each coin his heart throbbed painfully. He fully realised, for the first time, what he had done.

At the ring of the fifth sovereign Mrs. Hood turned her head.

'What's that?' she asked snappishly.

He went on counting till the nine were displayed.

'What is it?' she repeated. 'Why do you fidget me so?'

'You'd never guess,' Hood answered, laughing hoarsely. 'I had to go to Hebsworth to-day, and who ever do you think I met there? Why, old Cheeseman.'

He paused.

'And he—no, I'll never believe he paid his debt!' said his wife, with bitter congratulation. For years the name of Cheeseman had been gall upon her tongue; even now she had not entirely ceased to allude to him, when she wished to throw especial force of sarcasm into a reminiscence of her earlier days. A woman's powers in the direction of en-venomed memory are terrible.

'You have said it,' was Hood's reply under his breath. 'It was providential. What did I do, but go and lose my hat out of the window of the train—had it knocked off by a drunken fellow, in fact. But for this money I should have gone about Hebsworth bareheaded, and come home so, too.'

'A new hat! There's a pretty penny gone! Well, it's too much to hope that any good luck should come without bad at the same time.'

'Well, now you won't fret so much about the rent, Jane?'

He laid his hand upon her shoulder. It was a movement of tenderness such as had not come to him for years ; he felt the need of sympathy ; he could have begged her to give him a kind look. But she had resumed her sewing ; her fingers were not quite steady, that was all.

He left the money on the table and went to Emily in the sitting-room. She was sitting at the table waiting for him with her kindly eyes.

'And what has the wise woman been doing all day ? ' he asked, trying in vain to overcome that terrible fluttering at his side which caught his breath and made him feel weak.

They talked for some minutes, then footsteps were heard approaching from the kitchen. Mrs. Hood entered with her sewing—she always took the very coarsest for such days as this—and sat at a little distance from the table. As the con-versation had nothing to do with Cheeseman's debt, she grew impatient.

'Have you told Emily ? ' she asked.

'No, I haven't. You shall do that.'

Hood tried to eat the while ; the morsels became like sawdust in his mouth, and all but choked him. He tried to laugh ; the silence which followed his effort was ghastly to him.

'You see, it never does to believe too ill of a man,' he said, when he found Emily's look upon him.

Mrs. Hood grew more at her ease, and, to his relief, began to talk freely. Emily tortured him by observing that he had no appetite. He excused himself by telling of his dinner in Hebsworth, and, as soon as possible, left the table. He went upstairs and hoped to find solitude for a time in the garret.

Emily joined him, however, before long. At her entrance he caught up the first bottle his hand fell upon, and seemed to be examining it.

'What is that?' Emily asked, noticing his intentness, which in reality had no meaning.

'This? Oh, cyanide of potassium. I was looking—no, it's nothing. Will you read me something for half an hour, Emily?'

By this means he would avoid talking, and he knew that the girl was always delighted by the request. She generally read poetry of a kind she thought might touch him, longing to establish more of intellectual sympathy between him and herself. So she did to-night. Hood scarcely followed after the first line; he became lost in feverish brooding. When she laid the volume down, he looked up and held out his hand to her. She, at all events, would not disregard his caress; indeed, Emily took the hand and kissed it.

Then began one of the more intimate conversations which sometimes took place between them. Emily was driven now and then to endeavour to make clear to him her inner life, to speak of her ideals, her intellectual convictions. He listened always with an air of deep humility, very touching in a parent before a child. Her meaning was often dark to his sight, but he strove hard to comprehend, and every word she uttered had for him a gospel sanction. To-night his thoughts strayed; her voice was nothing but the reproach of his own soul; the high or tender words were but an emphasis of condemnation, reiterated, pitiless. She was speaking thus out of her noble heart to him—him, the miserable hypocrite; he pretended to listen and to approve. His being was a loathed burden.

If she had spoken thus last night, surely her voice would have dwelt with him through the hour of temptation. Oh, could it not be morning again, and the day yet to live? The clock below wheezed out nine strokes as if in answer.

CHAPTER X.

AT THE SWORD'S POINT.

DAGWORTHY in these days could scarcely be deemed a man, with humanity's plenitude of interacting motives, of contrasting impulses, of varying affections. He was become one passion, a personified appetite. He went through his routine, at the mill and elsewhere, in a mechanical way; all the time his instincts and habits subjugated themselves to the frenzy which chafed at the centres of his life. In his face you saw the monomaniac. His eyes were bloodshot; his lips had a parched yellowness of tone; his skin seemed dry and burning. Through the day he talked, gave orders, wrote letters, and, by mere force of lifelong habit, much in his usual way; at night he wandered about the Heath, now at a great pace, driven by his passions, now loitering, stumbling. Between dark and dawn he was fifty times in front of the Hoods' house; he watched the extinguishing of the lights in window after window, and, when all were gone, made away with curses on his lips, only to return an hour later, to torture himself with conjecture which room might be Emily's. His sufferings were unutterable. What devil—he groaned—had sent upon him this torment? He wished he were as in former days, when the indifference he felt towards his wife's undeniable beauty had, as it seemed, involved all womankind. In those times he could not have conceived a madness such as this. How had it arisen? Was it a physical illness? Was it madness in truth, or the beginning of it? Why had it not taken him four months ago, when he met this girl at the Baxendales'? But he remembered that even then she had attracted him strangely; he had quitted the others to talk to her. He must have been prepared to conceive this frantic passion on coming together with her again.

Love alone, so felt and so frustrated, would have been bad enough; it was the added pang of jealousy that made it a fierce agony. It was well that the man she had chosen was not within his reach; his mood was that of a murderer. The very heat and vigour of his physical frame, the native violence of his temper, disposed him to brute fury, if an instinct such as this once became acute; and the imaginative energy which lurked in him, a sort of undeveloped genius, was another source of suffering beyond that which ordinary men endure. He was a fine creature in these hours, colossal, tragic; it needed this experience to bring out all there was of great and exceptional in his character. He was not of those who can quit the scene of their fruitless misery and find forgetfulness at a distance. Every searing stroke drove him more desperately in pursuit of his end. He was further from abandoning it, now that he knew another stood in his way, than he would have been if Emily had merely rejected him. He would not yield her to another man; he swore to himself that he would not, let it cost him and her what it might.

He had seen her again, with his glass, from the windows of the mill, had scarcely moved his eyes from her for an hour. A hope came to him that she might by chance walk at evening on the Heath, but he was disappointed; Emily, indeed, had long shunned walks in that direction. He had no other means of meeting her, yet he anguished for a moment's glimpse of her face.

To-day he knew a cruel assuagement of his torture. He had returned from his short absence with a resolve to risk an attempt which was only not entirely base by virtue of the passion which inspired it, and it appeared to him that his stratagem had succeeded. Scruples he had indeed known, but not at all of the weight they would have possessed for most men, and this not only because of his reckless determination to win by any means; his birth and breeding enabled him to accept meanness as almost a virtue in many of the relations and transactions of life. The trickery and low cunning of the mercantile world was in his blood; it would come out when great occasion saw use for it, even in the service of love. He believed it was leading him to success. Certainly the first result that he aimed at was assured, and he could not imagine a subsequent obstacle. He would not have admitted that he was wronging the man whom he made his tool; if honesty failed under temptation it was honesty's own look-out. Ten to one he himself would have fallen into such a trap, in similar circumstances; he was quite free from pharisaical prejudice; had he not reckoned on mere human nature in devising his plan? Nor would the result be cruel, for he had it in his power to repay a hundredfold all temporary pain. There were no limits to the kindness he was capable of, when once he had Emily for his wife; she and hers should be overwhelmed with the fruits of his devotion. It was to no gross or commonplace future that the mill-owner looked forward. There were things in him of which he was beginning to be conscious, which would lead him he could not yet see whither. Dunfield was no home for Emily; he knew it, and felt that he, too, would henceforth have need of a larger circle of life. He was rich enough, and by transferring his business to other hands he could become yet richer, gaining freedom at the same time. No disappointment would be in store for him as in his former marriage; looking back on that he saw now how boyish he had been, how easily duped. There was not even the excuse of love.

He held her gained. What choice would she have, with the alternative to be put before her? It was strange that, in spite of what should have been sympathetic intelligence, he made a slight account of that love which, as she told him, she had already bestowed. In fact, he refused to dwell upon the thought of it ; it would have maddened him in earnest. Who could say ? It was very possible she had told him a falsehood; it was quite allowable in any woman, to escape from a difficult position. In his heart he did not believe this, knowing her better, though his practical knowledge of her was so slight ; but it was one of the devices by which he mitigated his suffering now and then. If the engagement existed, it was probably one of those which contemplated years of waiting, otherwise why should she have kept silence about it at home ? In any case he held her ; how could she escape him ? He did not fear appeals to his compassion ; against such assaults he was well armed. Emily pleading at his feet would not be a picture likely to induce him to relax his purpose. She could not take to flight, the very terms of his control restrained her. There might be flaws in his case, legally speaking, but the Hoods were in no position to profit by these, seeing that, in order to do so, they must begin by facing ruin. Emily was assuredly his.

To-day was Friday. He knew, from talk with the Cartwrights, that Jessie's lessons were on alternate days, and as he had seen the two in the garden this morning, there would be no lesson on the morrow. It was not easy to devise a plot for a private interview with Emily, yet he must see her to-morrow, and of course alone. A few words with her would suffice. To call upon her at the house would be only his last resource. He felt assured that she had not spoken to her parents of the scene in the garden ; several reasons supported this belief, especially the reflection that Emily would desire to spare her father the anxieties of a difficult position. Taking this for granted, his relations with her must still be kept secret in order to avoid risking his impunity in the tactics he counted upon. His hope was that she would leave the house alone in the course of the morning.

It has been mentioned that a railway bridge crossed the road a short distance beyond the Hoods' house. On the embankment beyond this bridge, twenty or thirty yards from the road, was a cluster of small trees and shrubs, railed in from the grass which elsewhere grew upon the slope, and from the field at its foot. Here, just hidden behind a hawthorn bush and a climbing bramble, Dagworthy placed himself shortly before eight o'clock on Saturday morning, having approached the spot by a long circuit of trespass ; from this position he had a complete view of the house he wished to watch. He came thus early because he thought it possible that Emily accompanied her father on his morning's walk into Dunfield; in which case he would follow at a distance, and find his opportunity as the girl returned. There had been rain in the night, and his passage through the bushes covered him with moisture; the thick grass, too, in which he stood, was so wet that before long his feet grew damp and cold. He was little mindful of bodily discomfort; never moving his eyes for a moment from the door which would give Emily to his view, he knew nothing but the impatience which made it incredible that his watch could keep pace with time; he seemed to have been waiting for hours when yet it was only half-past eight. But at length the door opened. He strained his sight across the distance, but with no reward. Hood left the house alone, and walked off quickly in the direction of Dunfield.

He must wait. It might happen that Emily would not quit home at all during the early part of the day, but he must wait on the chance. He dreaded lest rain should fall, which would naturally keep her within doors, but by nine o'clock the sky had cleared, and he saw the leaves above him drying in the sunlight. Inactivity was at all times intolerable to him; to stand thus for hours was an exercise of impatient patience which only his relentless passion made possible; his body yielded to a sort of numbness, whilst the suffering expectancy of his mind only grew keener. He durst not avert his eyes from the door for an instant; his sight ached and dazzled. Still he waited.

At eleven o'clock Emily came forth. A savage delight seized him as he watched her cross the patch of garden. At the gate she hesitated a moment, then took the way neither to the Heath nor to Dunfield, but crossed to the lane which led to Pendal. From his hiding-place Dagworthy could follow her so far, and with ecstasy he told himself that she must be going to the Castle Hill. She carried a book in her hand.

At length he moved. His limbs had stiffened; it was with difficulty that he climbed to the top of the embankment. Thence he could see the whole track of the lane, which went, indeed, almost parallel with the railway line. He walked in the same direction, keeping at some distance behind Emily. Before reaching the village of Pendal, he had to cross a field, and enter the lane itself. There was now the danger that the girl might look back. But she did not. She was reading as she walked, and continued to do so the whole way to the stile which led into the Castle Hill. But now it mattered little if she turned her head.

He let her pass the stile, and himself paused before following. He was agitated; that which he was about to do seemed harder than he had imagined; he had a horrible fear lest his resolution might fail at the last moment. The brute in him for an instant almost slept. The woman in the field yonder was not only the object of his vehement desire; all the nobler possibilities of his nature united to worship her, as the highest and holiest he knew. In his heart was a subtle temptation, the voice of very love bidding him cast himself at her feet and sue but for the grace of so much human kindness as would make life without her endurable. He remembered the self-abasement which had come upon him when he tried to tell her of his love; the offering had seemed so gross, so unworthy to be brought before her. Would it not be the same now? He dreaded her power to protect herself, the secret might of purity which made him shrink at her steady gaze. But he had gone through much in the last fortnight; the brute forces had grown strong by habit of self-assertion. He looked up, and the fact that Emily had gone from his sight stung him into pursuit.

She was sitting where she had sat with Wilfrid, on the fallen tree; the book lay at her side, and she was giving herself to memory. Treading on the grass, he did not attract her attention till he almost stood before her; then she looked at him, and at once rose. He expected signs of apprehension or embarrassment, but she seemed calm. She had accustomed herself to think of him, and could no longer be taken by surprise. She was self-possessed, too, in the strength of the thoughts which he had disturbed.

He fed his eyes upon her, and kept so long silent that Emily's cheek coloured, and she half turned away. Then he spoke abruptly, yet with humility, which the consciousness of his purpose could not overcome.

'You know that I have been away since I saw you last. I tried to put you out of my mind. I couldn't do it, and I am driven back to you.'

'I hoped we should not meet again like this, Mr. Dagworthy,' Emily replied, in a low voice, but firmly. She felt that her self-respect was to be tested to the uttermost, but she was better able to control herself than at the last interview. The sense of being passionately sought cannot but

enhance a woman's dignity in her own eyes, and Emily was
not without perception of the features in Dagworthy's character which made him anything but a lover to be contemned.
She dreaded him, and could not turn away as from one who
tormented her out of mere ill-breeding.

'I cannot ask you to pardon me,' he returned, 'for however often you asked me to leave you, I should pay no heed.
I am here because I can't help myself; I mean what I say—
I can't, I can't help it! Since you told me there was no hope,
I seem to have been in hell. These are not words to use to
you—I know it. It isn't that I don't respect you, but because
I must speak what I feel. Look—I am worn out with suffering; I feel as if it would take but a little more to kill me,
strong man as I am. You don't think I find a pleasure in
coming and facing that look you have? I don't know that I
ever saw the man I couldn't meet, but before you I feel—
I can't put it into words, but I feel I should like to hide my
face. Still, I have come, I have followed you here. It's more
than I can do to give you up.'

At the last words he half sobbed. Her fear of him would
not allow Emily to feel deep distress, but she was awed by
the terrible evidence of what he endured. She could not at
once find words for reply.

'Will you sit down?' he said. 'I will stand here, but I
have more to say to you before I go.'

'Why should you say more?' Emily urged. 'Can you
not think how very painful it is to hear you speak in this way?
What purpose can it serve to speak to me when I may not
listen?'

'You must listen. I can't be sent away as you would
another man; no other on earth can love you as I do, no one.
No one would do for you all that I would do. My love gives
me a claim upon you. It is you that have brought me to this
state; a woman owes a man something who is driven mad by
her. I have a right to be here and to say all I feel.'

He was struggling with a dread of the words he had come
to utter; a wild hope sprang in him that he might yet win her
in other ways; he used language recklessly, half believing that
his arguments would seem of force. His passion was in the
death-grapple with reason and humanity.

'If your regard for me is so strong,' Emily replied, 'should
you not shrink from causing me pain? And indeed you have
no such right as you claim. Have I in any way sought to win

your affection? Is it manly to press upon me a suit which you know it is out of my power to favour? You say you respect me; your words are not consistent with respect. I owe you nothing, Mr. Dagworthy, and it is certainly my right to demand that you will cease to distress and trouble me.'

He stood with his eyes on the ground.

'That is all you have to say?' he asked, almost sullenly.

'What more can I say? Surely you should not have compelled me to say even so much. I appeal to your kindness, to your sense of what is due from a man to a woman, to let me leave you now, and to make no further attempt to see me. If you refuse, you take advantage of my powerlessness. I am sure you are not capable of that.'

'Yes, I am capable of more than you think,' he replied, the words coming between his teeth. His evil demon, not himself, was speaking; in finding utterance at length it made him deadly pale, and brought a cold sweat to his brow. 'When you think afterwards of what I say now, remember that it was love of you that made me desperate. A chance you little dream of has put power into my hands, and I am going to use it. I care for nothing on this earth but to make you my wife—and I can do so.'

Terror weighed upon her heart. His tone was that of a man who would stick at nothing, and his words would bear no futile meaning. Her thoughts were at once of her father; through him alone could he have power over her. She waited, sick with agonised anticipation, for what would follow.

'Your father——'

The gulf between purpose and execution once passed, he had become cruel; human nature has often enough exemplified the law in prominent instances. As he pronounced the words, he eyed her deliberately, and, before proceeding, paused just long enough to see the anguish flutter in her breast.

'Your father has been guilty of dishonesty; he has taken money from the mill. Any day that I choose I can convict him.'

She half closed her eyes and shook, as if under a blow. Then the blood rushed to her face, and, to his astonishment, she uttered a strange laugh.

'*That* is your power over me!' she exclaimed, with all the scorn her voice could express. 'Now I know that you are

indeed capable of shameful things.   You think I shall believe
that of my father ? '

Dagworthy knew what it was to feel despicable. He would,
in this moment, have relinquished all his hope to be able to
retract those words. He was like a beaten dog before her ;
and the excess of his degradation made him brutal.

' Believe it or not, as you choose. All I have to say is
that your father put into his pocket yesterday morning a ten-
pound note of mine, which he found in a ledger he took out
of my room. He had to go to Hebsworth on business, and
there he changed the note to buy himself a new hat ; I have
a witness of it. When he came back he of course had nothing
to say about the money ; in fact, he had stolen it.'

She heard, and there came into her mind the story of
Cheeseman's debt. That was of ten pounds. The purchase
her father had been obliged to make, of that also she had
heard. Last night, and again this morning, her mother had
incessantly marvelled at this money having been at length
returned ; it was an incredible thing, she had said; only the
sight of the coins could convince her of its truth. Emily's
mind worked over the details of the previous evening with
terrible rapidity and insight. To her directly her father had
spoken not a word of the repayment ; he had bidden her keep
in another room while he informed her mother of it ; he had
shown disinclination to return to the subject when, later, they
all sat together. ' Well, here it is,' he had said, ' and we'll talk
no more about it.' She heard those words exactly as they were
spoken, and she knew their tone was not natural ; even at
the time that had struck her, but her thought had not dwelt
upon it.

She almost forgot Dagworthy's presence ; he and his threats
were of small account in this shaking of the depths of her
nature.   She was awakened by his voice.

' Do you think I am lying to you for my own purposes ? '

' I cannot say,' she answered, with unnatural calm.   ' It is
more likely than that what you say is true.'

He, by now, had attained a self-control which would not
desert him.   So far in crime, there was no turning back ; he
could even enjoy the anticipation of each new move in the
game, certain of winning. He could be cruel now for cruelty's
sake ; it was a form of fruition.

' Well,' he said, ' it is your own concern whether you
believe me or not. If you wish for evidence, you shall have

it, the completest. What I have to say is this. From now till Monday morning your father is free. Whether I have him arrested then or not depends upon yourself. If you consent to become my wife as soon as it is possible for us to be married, neither you nor he will ever hear another word of the matter. What's more, I will at once put him in a position of comfort. If you refuse, there will be a policeman ready to arrest him as soon as he comes to the mill; if he tries to escape, a warrant will be issued. In any case he will be ruined.'

Then, after a pause—

' So you have till to-morrow night to make up your mind. You can either send me a note or come and see me; I shall be at home whenever you come.'

Emily stood in silence.

' I hope you quite understand what I mean,' Dagworthy continued, as if discussing an ordinary matter of business. ' No one will ever dream that your father has done anything to be ashamed of. After all, it is not so impossible that you should marry me for my own sake ; '—he said it with bitterness. ' People will see nothing to wonder at. Fortunately, no one knows of that—of what you told me. Your father and mother will be easy for the rest of their lives, and without a suspicion that there has been anything but what appears on the surface. I needn't say how things are likely to look in the other event.'

Still she stood silent.

' I don't expect an answer now——'

Emily shook her head.

'But,' he continued, ' you mustn't leave it after to-morrow night. It will be too late.'

She began to move away from him. With a step or two he followed her ; she turned, with a passionate movement of repulsion, terror, and hate transfiguring her countenance, made for the expression of all sweet and tender and noble things.

Dagworthy checked himself, turned about, and walked quickly from the place.

CHAPTER XI.

EMILY'S DECISION.

EMILY reached home a few minutes before dinner-time. Her mother came to her from the back of the house, where things were in Saturday tumult, speaking with a voice of fretful satisfaction.

'I'd just given you up, and was wondering whether to let the meat spoil or begin dinner alone.'

'I am sorry to be late, mother.'

'No, you're not late, my dear,' the mother admitted. 'It's only that you're a little uncertain, and when one o'clock draws on I can never be quite sure of you, if you're out. I must say I like punctuality, though I dare say it's an old-fashioned kind of thing. Which would you like, potatoes baked or boiled? I've got both, as I always think the baked keep better for your father.'

'Whichever you have yourself, mother.'

'Now, child, do make a choice! As if you couldn't say which you would prefer.'

'Boiled.'

'There now, you say that because you think there won't be enough of the others. I know very well you always like the baked, when I have them. Don't you, now, Emily?'

'Mother, which you like! What *does* it matter?'

'Well, my dear, I'm sure I only wanted to please you,' said Mrs. Hood, in her tone of patience under injury. 'I can't see why you should be angry with me. If I could give you more choice I would. No doubt you're used to having potatoes done in all sorts of superior ways, but unfortunately I wasn't brought up as a cook——'

The strange look with which Emily was regarding her brought her to a pause; her voice dropped.

'Mother dear,' said the girl, in a low and shaken tone, 'I am neither foolish nor unkind; do try to believe that. Something is troubling me. To-day let your choice be mine.'

Mrs. Hood moved away, and served the dinner in silence.

'What is your trouble, my dear?' she asked presently. 'Can't you tell me?'

Emily shook her head. Her mother relapsed into thoughtfulness, and they finished their meal with little conversation. Mrs. Hood was just rising from the table, when there was a sound of some one opening the gate before the house; she looked to the window, and at once uttered an exclamation of astonishment.

' Well! If that isn't—— ! He hasn't altered a bit all these years ! '

' Who is it, mother ? ' Emily asked nervously.

' Why, my dear, it's that man Cheeseman ! The very idea of his coming here ! Now, mark my words, he's come to ask for that money back again, or for some of it, at all events. It was just showing off, pretending to pay it back; exactly like him ! But if your father's foolish enough to do anything of the kind—— There, he's knocking. I hoped never to see his face again as long as I lived; how ever he can have the impudence to come ! I suppose I must let him in; but I'm sure I shan't offer him any dinner.'

Emily had risen from her chair, and was trembling with excitement.

' Oh yes, mother,' she cried, with a joy which astonished Mrs. Hood, ' we must behave kindly to him. He paid father the money; we must remember that.'

' Well, you'll see if I'm not right. But I can't keep him standing at the door. Do untie this apron, Emily ; I'm so nervous, I can't get at the knot. See, now, if he hasn't come for the money back again.'

' Never mind ; he paid it ! He paid it ! '

' I can't understand you, child. What is there to be so pleased about ? '

' Mother, do go to the door. Or shall I ? '

The girl was overcome with a sudden light in utter darkness. She grasped at her mother's explanation of the visitor's arrival ; unable, in her ardour, to calculate probabilities, to review details. Dagworthy had been guilty of a base falsehood ; the man approached who could assure her of it. It was a plot, deeply planned. In some manner Dagworthy had learned what had happened to her father in Hebsworth, and had risked everything on the terror he could inspire in her. The coming of her father's friend was salvation.

She found herself clasping his hand warmly.

' Well, Miss Hood,' Cheeseman came in exclaiming, ' you may perhaps have half a recollection of me, when you're told

who I am, but I'm quite sure I shouldn't have known you.
Your good father was telling me about you yesterday; rare
and proud he was to speak of you, too, and not without reason,
I see. Mrs. Hood, you've no need to complain of your fortune. Times have been hard, no doubt, but they've brought
you a blessing. If I had a young lady such as this to look
at me and call me father—well, well, it won't do to think
of it.'

In spite of her determination, Mrs. Hood was mollified
into an offer of dinner. Mr. Cheeseman affected to refuse,
but at a word from Emily he allowed himself to be persuaded.
The two sat with him, and listened to his talk of bygone days.
Emily's face was flushed; she kept her eyes on Cheeseman
as if his arrival were that of a long-hoped-for friend. The
visitor abounded in compliments to mother and daughter
alike. He ate, the while, with extreme heartiness, and at
length drew from the table in the most effusive mood.

'Mrs. Hood,' he said, leaning forward, 'I owe you an
apology, many apologies. You and your good husband in
times long past did me a service of a very substantial kind.
You thought I had forgotten it—yes, you couldn't help but
think it——'

'Oh, we won't talk about that, Mr. Cheeseman,' interposed
Mrs. Hood, not without a suggestion in her tone that she had
indeed entertained the thought attributed to her.

'Ah, but I can't help speaking of it,' said Cheeseman,
feelingly. 'Miss Hood, you probably don't know what I refer
to; you were a very little lady in those days. They were
hard times with me; indeed, I've never known anything else.
I was saying to your good father yesterday that he could no
longer talk of his ill-luck. Many a day he and I have encouraged each other to face fortune, but that's all over for
him; he's got his foot on firm ground, thank heaven! I'm
still catching at straws, you see; I dare say it's a good deal
my own fault; and then I never had a good wife to look after
me, and a daughter growing up to teach me prudence. Well
but, Miss Hood, I was saying that your father did me a great
service; he lent me what was a large sum for him in those
days——'

'Not a little one even in these, Mr. Cheeseman,' remarked
Mrs. Hood.

'Well, well, but in those times it was a thing few men in
his position would have done. He lent me a ten-pound note,

Miss Hood, and it's right you should know it. Years have gone by, years, and any one would think I'd kept out of the way to avoid paying the money back. I assure you, Mrs. Hood, and to you, Miss Hood, I give my solemn word of honour, that I've never from that day to this had more money than would just keep me in bread and cheese and such poor clothing as this you see on me. Why, even yesterday, as no doubt your good father has told you, I had but a sixpenny-piece in the world, but one coin of sixpence. Ah, you may well look sad, my good young lady. Please God, you'll never know what that means. But one sixpence had I, and but for my old friend I should have been hard driven to find a place of rest last night. Now do I look and speak like an un-grateful man? Mrs. Hood, I've come here this day because I felt in duty bound to call on you, being so near. I didn't know your address, till that meeting by chance yesterday. When my old friend left me, I got restless; I felt I must see you all again before I went south, as I hope to do—to-morrow, perhaps. I felt I must clear myself from the charge of in-gratitude; I couldn't live easy under it. It was too much like a piece of dishonesty, and that I've never yet been guilty of, for all I've gone through, and, please God, never shall. My old friend Hood and I, in days even before he had the happi-ness to meet you, Mrs. Hood, we used to say to each other— Let luck do its worst, we'll live and die honest men. And, thank heaven, we've kept our word; for an honester man than James Hood doesn't walk the earth, and no one ever yet brought a true charge of dishonesty against Alfred Cheese-man.'

He looked from mother to daughter. The former sat in helpless astonishment, gazing about her; Emily had hardened her face.

'You find it a sad tale,' Cheeseman proceeded. 'Why, so it is, dear ladies. If ever I had owned a ten-pound note, over and above the price of a loaf of bread and a night's lodging, it should have been put aside with the name of James Hood written on the back of it, and somehow I'd have found him out. And I say the same thing now. Don't think, Mrs. Hood, that I'm pleading my poverty as a way of asking you to forgive the debt. The debt shall be paid; be assured of that. If I can only get to London, there's a prospect before me; I have a project which I explained to my old friend yesterday. You shall have the money, and, what's more, you shall have interest—four per cent. per annum. Oh yes, you shall. Only let me somehow get to London.'

The gate sounded again.

'Emily,' exclaimed Mrs. Hood, 'there's your father!'

She was pale, and the hand with which she pointed could not steady itself.

'Mother,' said the girl, just above her breath, 'go! He is coming in!'

Mrs. Hood rose and left the room. Cheeseman could not but observe that some strange agitation possessed them both. Possibly he explained it by the light of his own conscience. He sat, smiling at Emily rather uneasily. Then, seeing that there was likely to be a delay before Hood entered, he bent forward to speak confidentially.

'Miss Hood, I see it in your face, you're as kind and warm-hearted as your father is, and that's saying much. You won't think hardly of a poor fellow who oftener misses a dinner than gets one? Every word I've said to you's as true as the light of heaven. And my only chance is to get to London. I've made an invention, and I feel sure I know a man who will buy it of me. It took my last farthing to get here from Hebsworth. You don't think hardly of me? I don't drink, on my word I don't; it's sheer hard luck. Ah, if I had a home like this! It 'ud be like living in the garden of Eden. Well, well!'

The door opened, and Hood came in, followed by his wife. He was laughing, laughing loudly; the voice was so unlike his that this alone would have caused Emily to gaze at him in astonishment.

'So you've looked us up!' he exclaimed, holding out his hand. 'Why, you couldn't have done better; I was sorry afterwards I hadn't asked you. My wife tells me you've had dinner; you won't mind sitting by whilst I eat? And what do you think of Emily, eh? Grown a little since you saw her last—ha, ha! So you've made up your mind to go to London? Emily had dinner? Why, of course you have; I was forgetting. Baked potatoes! Remember my old weakness for them baked, Cheeseman? We used to buy 'em in the street at night, halfpenny apiece, eh? Old man with one arm, remember? We used to hear him coming when he was half a mile off; what a voice! And the man who sold peas; remember him? "All 'ot! All 'ot!" We were lads then, eh, Cheeseman? Emily, just a mouthful, with butter? Let me tempt you. No?—What train did you come by?'

He talked ceaselessly. There was a spot of red in the midst of each of his sallow cheeks, and his eyes gleamed with excitement. On leaving the mill a sudden thirst had come upon him, and he had quenched it with a glass of spirits at the first public-house he passed. Perhaps that had some part in his elation.

Emily almost immediately withdrew and went up to her bedroom. Here she sat alone for more than an hour, in fear lest her mother should come to the door. Then she heard the gate open, and, looking from the window, saw her father and his friend pass into the road and walk away together, the former still talking in an excited way. A minute or two later came the knock which she dreaded. She opened the door, and her mother entered.

'Emily, did you ever know your father so strange?' Mrs. Hood asked, in a tone of genuine alarm. She had sunk upon a chair, and looked to the girl as if overcome with physical weakness. 'What can it all mean? When I asked him why he had told that story about the money, he only laughed —said it was a joke, and he'd explain it all before long. *I* can't think where the money came from! And now he's gone to pay that man's fare to London, and no doubt to lend him more money too.'

Emily made no reply. She stood near the window, and looked out at the clouds which were breaking after a brief shower.

'Wherever the money may have come from,' pursued her mother, 'it's cruel that it should go in this way. We never wanted it worse than we do now. It's my belief he's borrowed it himself; a nice thing to borrow for one's own needs, and then throw it away on such a good-for-nothing as that.'

Emily turned and put a question quietly.

'Are you in more than usual need of money?'

'Well, my dear, you know I always try to say as little about such things as I can, but now your father's been and borrowed—as of course he must have done—there's no choice but to tell you. The house at Barnhill's going to be empty at the end of the quarter, and our rent here's going to be raised, and, all things coming together, we've had a good deal to make us anxious. It's just like your father—wanting to make me believe that things are better than they really are; it always was his way, and what's the good of it I never could see. Of course he means it well, but he'd far better have been open about it, and have told me what he was going to do.'

Emily was shaken with agitation.

'Mother!' she exclaimed, 'why have you both insisted on keeping silence before me about your difficulties? There was no kindness in it; you have done me the cruelest wrong. Had I not money in plenty beyond what I needed? What if the future be uncertain? Has not the present its claims, and can your needs be separated from mine? Because you have succeeded in keeping me apart from the troubles of your life, you—you and father—have thought you had done a praiseworthy thing. Is it not bad enough that one human being should be indifferent to the wants of another, just because they call each other strangers? Was it right to bring such a hateful spirit of independence into a home, between parents and child? If the world is base and unjust, is not that a reason the more why we should draw ever more closely to each other, and be to each other all that our power allows? Independent! Because I earned money and could support myself, you have told me I must be independent, and leave you the same. That is the lesson that life has taught you. It is well to have understanding for lessons of a deeper kind.'

'Well, my child,' protested the mother, to whom the general tenor of such reasoning was well-nigh as dark as its special application, 'we have always felt we were doing our duty to you. At your age it is only right you should have your money for yourself; who knows when you may want it? I don't think you should be angry with us, just because we've felt we'd rather put up with a little hardship now and then than have you feel some day we'd been a burden on you. I haven't complained, and I'm not complaining now. I'm sorry I came to speak to you about such a thing. It seems as if you could never take a thing as I mean it. It's like the potatoes at dinner; I meant to do you a kindness by giving you the choice, and you flew out as if you hadn't patience with me.'

Emily kept her eyes upon the window.

'How you can say,' went on Mrs. Hood, 'that we've been cruel to you and done you a wrong—— I know we've very different ways of looking at most things, but where we've wronged you is more than I can understand.'

' You have taken from me,' replied Emily, without moving her eyes, ' the power to help you. I might have done much, now I can do nothing ; and your loss is mine.'

' No, indeed, it isn't, and shan't be, Emily. Your father and I have always said that one thing, that you shouldn't suffer by us. What did your father always say years ago ? " Emily," he said, " shall have a good education, however we stint ourselves ; then, when she grows up, she'll always be able to keep herself from want, and our poverty won't matter to her." And in that, at all events, he was right, and it's come about as he said. No, Emily, we're not going to be a burden to you, so don't fear it.'

' Mother, will you let me be by myself a little ? I will come down to you presently.'

' Aren't you well, my dear ?' the mother asked, with a mixture of offended reserve and anxiety occasioned by the girl's voice and aspect.

' I have a headache. I will rest till tea-time.'

Mrs. Hood had for a long time been unused to tend Emily with motherly offices ; like her husband, she was not seldom impressed with awe of this nature so apart from her own. That feeling possessed her now ; before Emily's last words she moved away in silence and closed the door behind her gently.

The irony of fate, coming out so bitterly in all that her mother had said, was like a cold hand on Emily's heart. She sat again in the chair from which she had risen, and let her head lie back. Her vitality was at a low ebb ; the movement of indignation against the cruelty which was wrecking her life had passed and left behind it a weary indifference. Happily she need not think yet. There were still some hours of respite before her ; there was the night to give her strength. The daylight was a burden ; it must be borne with what patience she could summon. But she longed for the time of sacred silence.

To a spirit capable of high exaltations, the hour of lassitude is a foretaste of the impotence of death. To see a purpose in the cold light of intellectual conviction, and to lack the inspiring fervour which can glorify a struggle with the obstacles nature will interpose, is to realise intensely the rugged baldness of life stripped of illusion, life as we shall see it when the end approaches and the only voice that convinces tell us that all is vanity. It is the mood known by the artist when, viewing the work complete within his mind, his heart lacks its joy and his hand is cold to execute. Self-consciousness makes of life itself a work of art. There are the blessed moments when ardour rises in pursuit of the ideal, when it is supreme bliss to strive and overcome; and there are the times of aching languor, when the conception is still clear in every line, but the soul asks wearily—To what end? In Emily it was reaction after the eagerness of her sudden unreasoning hope. Body and mind suffered beneath a burden of dull misery. Motives seemed weak; effort was weary and unprofitable; life unutterably mean. It could scarcely be called suffering, to feel thus.

She was roused by voices below, and, immediately after, her mother came to her door again.

'Isn't it vexatious?' Mrs. Hood whispered. 'Here are Jessie and Geraldine. I'm obliged to ask them to stay tea. Do you feel well enough to come down?'

Emily went down at once, almost with a sense of relief, and presented herself to the girls very much in her usual way.

'Now, I know very well you don't want us,' said Jessie, with her sprightly frankness. 'We shouldn't have thought of coming if it hadn't been that we met Mr. Hood just this side of the bridge, and he forced us to come on; he said it wouldn't be very long before he was back himself. But of course we shan't stay tea, so it's no use——'

'Oh, of course not,' put in Geraldine. 'We know Mrs. Hood's always far too busy on a Saturday afternoon. *I* didn't want to come; I told Jessie it would be far better to put it off till to-morrow——'

'All the same,' resumed her sister, 'she wanted to see you very much. She's got something to tell you. Now you may as well get it out and done with, Jerry; you needn't expect I'm going to help you.'

The two giggled together.

'What is it,' inquired Mrs. Hood. 'I daresay I could guess if I tried very hard. Couldn't you, Emily?'

'Now then, Jerry, for the awful news,' urged her sister.

'No, *you'll* have to tell, Jessie,' said the other, giggling and blushing.

'Well, I suppose one of us must. She's been and engaged herself to Mr. Baldwin. Of course we all knew——'

'Now, Jessie, you knew nothing of the kind!'

'Didn't I, though! Oughtn't she to be ashamed of herself, at her age, Mrs. Hood! I know what Emily's opinion is; she's simply disgusted. Look at her, and see if she isn't.'

The gabble of the two girls was worthy of the occasion; their tongues went like mill-clappers. Whilst her mother busied herself in preparing tea, Emily sat and listened; fortunately there was little need for her to talk. To herself she seemed to be suffering a kind of trance, without detriment to her consciousness. The chattering and grimacing girls appeared before her as grotesque unrealities, puppets animated in some marvellous way, and set to caricature humanity. She tried to realise that one of them was a woman like herself, who had just consented to be a man's wife; but it was impossible to her to regard this as anything but an aping of things which at other times had a solemn meaning. She found herself gazing at Geraldine as one does at some singular piece of mechanism with a frivolous purpose. And it was not only the individuals that impressed her thus; these two represented life and the world. She had strange, cynical thoughts, imaginings which revolted her pure mind even whilst it entertained them. No endeavour would shake off this ghastly clairvoyance. She was picturing the scene of Geraldine's acceptance of the offer of marriage; then her thoughts passed on to the early days of wedded life. She rose, shuddering, and moved about the room; she talked to drive those images from her brain. It did but transfer the sense of unreality to her own being. Where was she, and what doing? Had she not dreamed that a hideous choice had been set before her, a choice from which there was no escape, and which, whatever the alternative she accepted, would blast her life? But that was something grave, earnest, and what place was there for either earnestness or gravity in a world where Geraldine represented womanhood wooed and about to be wedded? There was but one way of stopping the gabble which was driving her frantic; she threw open the piano and began to play, to play the first music that came into her mind. It was a passage from the Moonlight Sonata. A few moments, and the ghosts were laid. The girls still whispered together, but above their voices the pure stream of music flowed with gracious oblivion. When Emily ceased, it was with an inward fervour of gratitude to the master and the instrument. To know that, was to have caught once more the point of view from which life had meaning. Now let them chatter and mop and mow; the echo of that music still lived around.

Hood had not returned when they sat down to tea. Jessie began to ask questions about the strange-looking man they had met in company with him, but Mrs. Hood turned the conversation.

' I suppose you'll be coming with the same tale next, Jessie,' she said, with reference to Geraldine.

' Me, Mrs. Hood ? No, indeed; I haven't had lessons from Emily for nothing. It's all very well for empty-headed chits like Jerry here, but I've got serious things to attend to. I'm like Emily, she and I are never going to be married.'

' Emily never going to be married ? ' exclaimed Mrs. Hood, half seriously. ' Ah, you mustn't believe all Emily tells you.'

' Oh, she hasn't told me that herself, but I'm quite sure she would be offended if any one thought her capable of such frivolity.'

' Emily will keep it to herself till the wedding-day,' said Geraldine, with a mocking shake of the head. ' She isn't one to go telling her secrets.'

At this point Hood made his appearance. His wife paid no heed to him as he entered; Emily glanced at him furtively. He had the look of a man who has predetermined an attitude of easy good-humour, nor had the parting with Cheeseman failed to prove an occasion for fresh recourse to that fiery adjuvant which of a sudden was become indispensable to him. Want of taste for liquor and lifelong habit of abstemiousness had hitherto kept Hood the soberest of men; he could not remember to have felt the warm solace of a draught taken for solace' sake since the days when Cheeseman had been wont to insist upon the glass of gin at their meetings, and then it had never gone beyond the single glass, for he felt that his head was weak, and dreaded temptation. Four-and-twenty hours had wrought such a change in him, that already to enter a public-house seemed a familiar act, and he calculated upon the courage to be begotten of a smoking tumbler. Previously the mere outlay would have made him miserable, but the command of unearned coin was affecting him as it is wont to affect poor men. The new aid given to Cheeseman left a few shillings out of the second broken sovereign. Let the two pounds—he said to himself—be regarded as gone; eight remained untouched. For the odd shillings, let them serve odd expenses. So when he had purchased Cheeseman's ticket to King's Cross, he was free with small change at the station bar. At the last moment it occurred to him that he might save himself a walk by going in the train as far as Pendal. So it was here that the final parting had taken place.

He seated himself with his legs across a chair, and began to talk to Geraldine of the interesting news which Jessie had just whispered to him when they met on the road. The character of his remarks was not quite what it would have been a day or two ago ; he joked with more freedom than was his custom. Studiously he avoided the eyes of his wife and daughter. He declined to sit up to the table, but drank a cup of tea with his hands resting on the back of a chair.

The Cartwright sisters were anxious to use the evening for a visit to certain other friends ; shortly after six o'clock they took their departure. While Emily and Mrs. Hood were seeing them away at the door, Hood went upstairs to his laboratory.

' Emily, come here,' Mrs. Hood said, with anxious earnestness, leading the way back into the sitting-room. And, when the door was closed——

' My dear, what *is* the matter with him ? Don't you notice his strangeness ? '

' Yes, mother, I do.'

' Can he have—— It's a thing he never does ! You know what I mean ? That Cheeseman has been taking him to a public-house ; I am sure of it.'

Emily had had no such thought. To her a squalid horror clung about the suggestion. To picture her father in such circumstances was to realise a fresh fall into degradation, no doubt the inevitable consequence of that she already knew of. There was a painful stricture at her heart ; a cry of despair all but found utterance.

Her father's voice was calling from the stair-head— ' Emily ! ' She darted to the door in momentary terror and replied.

' Will you come up ? ' Hood said ; ' I want you.'

She ascended to the garret. Hood was standing with his back to the little window, so that his face was shadowed. Emily moved to the table, and, with her hands resting upon it, her eyes bent, stood waiting.

' Emily,' he began, still with a remnant of artificial

pleasantry, though his voice was not entirely under control, 'I want to explain that money-matter to you. It doesn't look well; I am a good deal ashamed of myself; if I was a boy I should deserve a whipping for telling a fib, shouldn't I ?'

It was impossible to make reply to such words.

'The truth is this,' he went on more nervously; 'we've been in a little difficulty, your mother and I, that we didn't see any good in troubling you about. In fact, there's a raising of rent, and one or two other little things. When I was in Hebsworth yesterday I had an opportunity of borrowing ten pounds, and I thought it better to do so. Then I met Cheeseman, and it was his mention of the debt put into my head the stupid thought of trying to spare your mother anxiety. Of course, such tricks never succeed; I might have known it. But there, that's the truth of the matter, and I'm easier now —now I've told it.'

Her heart bled for him, so dreadful to her ears was the choking of his voice upon the last words. At the same time she was hot with anguish of shame. He stood before her a wretched culprit, hiding his guilt with lie upon lie; he, her father, whom she had reverenced so, had compassionated so, whom she loved despairingly. She could not raise her head; she could not speak. She longed to spring to him and hold him in her arms, but other thoughts paralysed the impulse. Had there lain nothing in the background, had his falsehood, his weakness, been all, she could have comforted and strengthened him with pure pity and love. But the consciousness of what was before her killed her power to stead him in his misery. She could not speak out her very thought, and to palter with solemn words was impossible. Hypocrisy from her to him at this moment—hypocrisy, however coloured with sincere feeling, would have sunk her in her own eyes beyond redemption.

'Let us speak no more of it, father,' she replied without raising her head.

He was sober enough now, and in her voice, her attitude, he read his hopeless condemnation. Between him and this high-hearted woman had come that which would never be removed; before her he was shamed to eternity. Never again could he speak with her of truth, of justice, of noble aims; the words would mock him. Never again could he take her kiss upon his lips without shrinking. Her way henceforth lay ever further from his own. What part had she in a life become so

base ? What place had she under a roof dishonoured ? **If**
some day she wedded, his existence would be to her a secret
shame. For—worst thought of all—it was whispered to his
conscience that she did not credit even what he now told her.
He seemed to himself to have betrayed the second untruth by
his way of speaking it. In the silence which followed upon
her words he heard promptings of despair. How could he
live in her presence from day to day, not daring to meet her
eyes? He looked back upon the years behind him, and they
seemed to overflow with peaceful happiness. Irretrievable, his
yielding and his shame ; irrecoverable, the conscious rectitude
bartered so cheaply. He saw now that his life had held vast
blessings, and they were for ever lost.

Emily was speaking.

' Do you wish to stay here this evening, father ? '

' No,' he answered hastily, ' I only called you up for—for
that.'

Her heart reproached her with cruelty, but what remained
save to leave him to himself? They could not face each
other, could not exchange a natural word.

' Emily ! '

She turned at the door. He had called her, but did not
continue to speak.

' Yes, father ? '

' It's only for to-night. You'll—you'll sit with me again
as usual ? '

' Oh, I hope so ! '

A rush of tears had its way as she closed the door, something so deeply pathetic had there been in that appeal. It
was the first time that her misery had found this outlet ;
unable to calm herself at once, she turned aside into her bedroom. Tears did not come to her readily ; indeed, it was years
since she had shed them ; the fit shook her with physical
suffering. The weeping would not stay itself, and to force her
sobs into silence was almost beyond her power. She flung
herself desperately by the bedside, throwing out her arms in
the effort to free her chest from its anguishing constraint.

In an hour she went down. Her mother was sitting
miserably in the kitchen, and Emily, dreading to have to talk
again, kept apart in the parlour. When it began to dusk,
Hood descended, and supper was prepared for in the usual way.
There was small pretence of conversation, and, as soon as
possible, Emily bade her parents good-night. It was long

before she heard them go to their room; they whispered together in passing her door.

And now the solemn hours shed about her guardian silence, and she could listen to the voice of her soul. It was incredible that the morning of the day which was not yet dead had witnessed that scene between her and Dagworthy on the Castle Hill; long spaces of featureless misery seem to stretch between. Perforce she had overborne reflection; one torment coming upon another had occupied her with mere endurance; it was as though a ruthless hand tore from her shred after shred of the fair garment in which she had joyed to clothe herself, while a voice mockingly bade her be in congruence with the sordid shows of the world around. For a moment, whilst Beethoven sang to her, she knew the light of faith; but the dull mist crept up again and thickened. Weeping had not eased her bosom; she had only become more conscious of the load of tears surcharging it. Now she lay upon her bed in the darkness, hushing idle echoes of day, waiting upon the spirit that ever yet had comforted and guided her.

What, divested of all horror due to imagination, was the threat to which her life lay subject? Dagworthy had it in his power to ruin her father, to blast his remaining years with a desolation to which the life-long struggle with poverty would be the mere pleasantry of fate. She could no longer entertain a doubt of the guilt the first suggestion of which excited her scornful laughter, and she knew it to be more than probable that her father had yielded to temptation purposely put in his way. She was not unconscious of the power of reprisal which so gross a plot put into her hands, though it was true that the secrecy Dagworthy had maintained in his intercourse with her left but her bare assertion for evidence against him. Yet the thought was profitless. Suppose he did not venture to prosecute on the charge of theft, none the less could he work the ruin he menaced; mere dismissal from his employment, with mention of the cause to this and the other person, was all that was needed to render the wretched clerk an outcast, hopeless of future means of livelihood, for ever disgraced in the eyes of all who knew him. She felt the cruelty of which this man, whose passions she had so frenzied, was readily capable. She believed he would not spare her an item of suffering which it was in his power to inflict. She knew that appeal to him was worse than useless, for it was only too clear that for her to approach him was to inflame his resolution.   Her instinctive fear of him was terribly justified.

With her alone, then, it lay to save her parents from the most dreadful fate that could befal them, from infamy, from destitution, from despair.   For, even if her father escaped imprisonment, it would be impossible for him to live on in Dunfield, and how, at his age, was a new life to be begun? And it was idle to expect that the last degradation would be spared him ; his disgrace would involve her ; Dagworthy's jealousy would not neglect such a means of striking at her engagement.   And Wilfrid must needs know ; to Emily not even the possibility of hiding such a thing from him suggested itself.   Could she become his wife with that stigma upon her, bringing as dowry her beggared parents for him to support?

Did it mean that ?   Was this the thought that she had dreaded to face throughout the day ?   Was it not only her father whose ruin was involved, and must she too bid farewell to hope?

She let those ghastly eyes stare from the darkness into her own, and tried to exhaust their horror.   It overtaxed her courage ; with a smothered cry of fear she sprang upright, and her shaking hands struck a flame to bring light into the room.   Not once, but again and again, did the chill of terror pass through her whole frame.   She caught a passing glimpse of her image in the glass, and was fascinated into regarding it closely.   'You, who stand there in the pitiless night '—thus did thought speak within her—' you, poor human thing, with the death-white face and eyes staring in all but distraction, is this the very end of the rapturous dream which has lulled you whilst destiny wrought your woe ?   Is it even now too late to struggle ?   Is this the wild sorrow of farewell to love, the beginning of an anguish which shall torture your soul to death ?   Have you lost *him* ? '   For moments it was as though life fought with the last and invincible enemy.   On the spot where she had been standing she sank powerless to her knees, clinging to the nearest object, her head falling back.

The clock outside her door struck one ; how long the dull vibration seemed to endure.   She was conscious of it, though lying with all but palsied faculties.   It was the first of the divisions which marked her long vigil ; the hours succeeded each other quickly ; between voice and voice there seemed to pass but a single wave of surging thought.   But each new warning of coming day found her nearer the calm of resolve.

Look at this girl, and try to know her. Emily knew but one article of religion, and that bade her preserve, if need be, at the cost of life, the purity of her soul. This was the supreme law of her being. The pieties of kindred were as strong in her as in any heart that ever beat, but respect for them could not constrain her to a course which opposed that higher injunction. Growing with her growth, nourished by the substance which developed her intellectual force, a sense of all that was involved in her womanhood had come to be the guiding principle of her existence. Imagine the great artist Nature bent upon the creation of a soul which should hold in subtlest perfection of consciousness every element essential to the successive ideals of maiden, wife, mother, and the soul of this girl is pictured. Her religion of beauty was the symbolic expression of instincts wholly chaste ; her body was to her a temple which preserved a sacred flame, and she could not conceive existence if once the shrine had suffered desecration. We are apt to attribute to women indiscriminately at least the outlines of this consciousness ; for the vast majority it confuses itself with the prescriptions of a traditional dogma, if not with the mere prejudice of social usage. For Emily no external dogma existed, and the tenor of her life had aided her in attaining independence of ignoble dictation. Her views were often strangely at variance with those of the social tribunal which sits in judgment on virtue and vice. To her, for instance, the woman who sells herself with ecclesiastical sanction differed only in degree of impurity from her whose track is under the street-lamps. She was not censorious, she was not self-righteous ; she spoke to no one of the convictions that ruled her, and to herself held them a mystery of holiness, a revelation of high things vouchsafed she knew not whence nor how. Suppose her to have been heart-free at this juncture of her fate, think you she would have found it a whit less impossible to save her father by becoming Dagworthy's wife. There was in her thought but one parallel to this dire choice which lay before her : it was the means offered to Isabel of rescuing her brother Claudio. That passion of purity which fired Isabel's speech was the breath of Emily's life. She knew well that many, and women too, would spare no condemnation of what they would call her heartless selfishness ; she knew that the paltriest considerations of worldly estate are deemed sufficient to exact from a woman the sacrifice now demanded of her. That was no law to Emily. The moral sense which her own nature had developed must here alone control her. Purity, as she understood it—the immaculate beauty of the soul—was her religion: if other women would die rather than deny the object of their worship, to her the ideal of chastity was worth no less perfect a zeal. Far removed from the world which theorises, she presented in her character a solution of the difficulties entertained by those who doubtingly seek a substitute for the old religious sanctions. Her motives had the simplicity of elemental faith; they were indeed but the primary instincts of womanhood exalted to a rare perfection and reflected in a consciousness of exceeding lucidity.

The awakening of love in such a nature as this was, as it were, the admission to a supreme sacrament. Here was the final sanction of the creed that had grown from within. In the plighting of her troth to Wilfrid Athel, Emily had, as she herself saw it, performed the most solemn and sacred act of her life; instead of being a mere preliminary to a holy observance which should in truth unite them, it made that later formality all but trivial. It was the aspiration of her devoutest hours that this interchange of loving promise might keep its binding sanctity for ever, that no touch of mutability might come upon her heart till the last coldness stayed its beating. A second love appeared to her self-contradicted; to transfer to another those thoughts which had wedded her soul to Wilfrid's would not merely be sin, it was an impossibility. Did he ever cease to cherish her—a thought at which she smiled in her proud confidence—that could in nothing affect her love for him, which was not otherwise to be expressed than as the sum of her consciousness. . . . .

The pale light of dawn began to glimmer through the window-blind. Emily gave it full admission, and looked out at the morning sky; faintest blue was growing between streaks of cold grey. Her eyes ached from the fixedness of intense thought; the sweet broad brow was marble, the disorder of her hair spoke of self-abandonment in anguish. She had no thought of seeking rest; very far from her was sleep and the blessedness of oblivion. She felt as though sleep would never come again.

But she knew what lay before her; doubt was gone, and there only remained fear to shake her heart. A day and a night had to be lived through before she could know her fate, so long must she suffer things not to be uttered. A day and a

night, and then, perchance—nay, certainly—the vanguard of
a vast army of pain-stricken hours. There was no passion
now in her thought of Wilfrid; her love had become the
sternness of resolve which dreads itself. An hour ago her
heart had been pierced with self-pity in thinking that she
should suffer thus so far away from him, without the possibility of his aid, her suffering undreamt by him. Now, in her
reviving strength, she had something of the martyr's joy. If
the worst came, if she had spoken to him her last word of
tenderness, the more reason that her soul should keep un-
sullied the image of that bliss which was the crown of life.
His and his only, his in the rapture of ideal love, his whilst
her tongue could speak, her heart conceive, his name.

CHAPTER XII.

THE FINAL INTERVIEW.

On six days of the week, Mrs. Hood, to do her justice, made
no show of piety to the powers whose ordering of life her
tongue incessantly accused ; if her mode of Sabbatical observance was bitter, the explanation was to be sought in the
mere force of habit dating from childhood, and had, indeed,
a pathetic significance to one sufficiently disengaged from the
sphere of her acerbity to be able to judge fairly such mani-
festations of character. A rigid veto upon all things secular,
a preoccupied severity of visage, a way of speaking which
suggested difficult tolerance of injury, an ostentation of discomfort in bodily inactivity—these were but traditions of
happier times ; to keep her Sunday thus was to remind herself of days when the outward functions of respectability
did in truth correspond to self-respect; and it is probable
that often enough, poor woman, the bitterness was not only
on her face. As a young girl in her mother's home she had
learnt that the Christian Sabbath was to be distinguished by
absence of joy, and as she sat through these interminable
afternoons, on her lap a sour little book which she did not
read, the easy-chair abandoned for one which hurt her back,
the very cat not allowed to enter the room lest it should
gambol, here on the verge of years which touch the head
with grey, her life must have seemed to her a weary pilgrim-

age to a goal of discontent. How far away was girlish laughter, how far the blossoming of hope which should attain no fruitage, and, alas, how far the warm season of the heart, the woman's heart that loved and trusted, that joyed in a new-born babe, and thought not of the day when the babe, in growing to womanhood, should have journeyed such lengths upon a road where the mother might not follow.

Neither Hood nor his daughter went to church; the former generally spent the morning in his garret, the latter helped herself against the depression which the consciousness of the day engendered by playing music which respect would have compelled her to refrain from had her mother been present. The music was occasionally heard by an acquaintance who for some reason happened to be abroad in church time, and Mrs. Hood was duly informed of the sad things done in her absence, but she had the good sense to forbid herself interference with Emily's mode of spending the Sunday. She could not understand it, but her husband's indifference to religion had taught her to endure, and, in truth, her own zeal, as I have said, was not of active colour. Discussion on such subjects there had never been. Her daughter, she had learnt to concede, was strangely other than herself; Emily was old enough to have regard for her own hereafter.

Breakfast on Sunday was an hour later than on other days, and was always a very silent meal. On the day which we have now reached it was perhaps more silent than usual. Hood had a newspaper before him on the table; his wife wore the wonted Sabbath absentness, suggestive of a fear lest she should be late for church; Emily made a show of eating, but the same diminutive slice of bread-and-butter lasted her to the end of the meal. She was suffering from a slight feverishness, and her eyes, unclosed throughout the night, were heavy with a pressure which was not of conscious fatigue. Having helped in clearing the table and ordering the kitchen, she was going upstairs when her mother spoke to her for the first time.

'I see you've still got your headache,' Mrs. Hood said, with plaintiveness which was not condolence.

'I shall go out a little, before dinner-time,' was the reply.

Her mother dismally admitted the wisdom of the proposal, and Emily went to her room. Before long the bell of the chapel-of-ease opposite began its summoning, a single querulous bell, jerked with irregular rapidity. The bells of Pendal church sent forth a more kindly bidding, but their music was marred by the harsh clanging so near at hand. Emily heard and did not hear. When she had done housemaid's office in her room, she sat propping her hot brows, waiting for her mother's descent in readiness for church. At the sound of the opening and closing bedroom door, she rose and accompanied her mother to the parlour. Mrs. Hood was in her usual nervous hurry, giving a survey to each room before departure, uttering a hasty word or two, then away with constricted features.

The girl ascended again, and, as soon as the chapel bell had ceased its last notes of ill-tempered iteration, began to attire herself hastily for walking. When ready, she unlocked a drawer and took from it an envelope, of heavy contents, which lay ready to her hand. Then she paused for a moment and listened. Above there was a light footfall, passing constantly hither and thither. Leaving the room with caution, she passed downstairs noiselessly and quitted the house by the back door, whence by a circuit she gained the road. Her walk was towards the Heath. As soon as she entered upon it, she proceeded rapidly—so rapidly, indeed, that before long she had to check herself and take breath. No sun shone, and the air was very still and warm; to her it seemed oppressive. Over Dunfield hung a vast pile of purple cloud, against which the wreaths of mill smoke, slighter than on week-days, lay with a dead whiteness. The Heath was solitary; a rabbit now and then started from a brake, and here and there grazed sheep. Emily had her eyes upon the ground, save when she looked rapidly ahead to measure the upward distance she had still to toil over.

On reaching the quarry, she stayed her feet. The speed at which she had come, and an agitation which was increasing, made breathing so difficult that she turned a few paces aside, and sat down upon a rough block of stone, long since quarried and left unused. Just before her was a small patch of marshy ground, long grass growing about a little pool. A rook had alighted on the margin, and was pecking about. Presently it rose on its heavy wings; she watched it flap athwart the dun sky. Then her eye fell on a little yellow flower near her feet, a flower she did not know. She plucked and examined it, then let it drop carelessly from her hand.

The air was growing brown; a storm threatened. She looked about her with a hasty fear, then resumed her walk to the upper part of the Heath. Reaching the smooth sward, she made straight across it for Dagworthy's house.

Crossing the garden, she was just at the front door, when it was opened, and by Dagworthy himself. His eyes fell before her.

'Will you come this way?' he said, indistinctly.

He led into the large sitting-room where he had previously entertained Emily and her father. As soon as he had closed the door, he took eager steps towards her.

'You have come,' he said. 'Something told me you would come this morning. I've watched at the window for you.'

The assurance of victory had softened him. His voice was like that of one who greets a loving mistress. His gaze clung to her.

'I have come to bring you this!' Emily replied, putting upon the table the heavy envelope. 'It is the money we owe you.'

Dagworthy laughed, but his eyes were gathering trouble.

'You owe me nothing,' he said, affecting easiness.

'How do you mean that?' Emily gave him a direct look. Her manner had now nothing of fear, nor even the diffidence with which she had formerly addressed him. She spoke with a certain remoteness, as if her business with him were formal. The lines of her mouth were hard; her heavy lids only half raised themselves.

'I mean that you owe nothing of this kind,' he answered, rather confusedly. His confidence was less marked; her look overcame his.

'Not ten pounds?'

'Well, *you* don't.' He added, 'Whose is this money?'

'It is my own; I have earned it.'

'Does your father know you are paying it?'

'He does not. I was not likely to speak to him of what you told me. There is the debt, Mr. Dagworthy; we have paid it, and now I will leave you.'

He examined her. Even yet he could not be sure that he understood. In admitting her, he had taken it for granted that she could come with but one purpose. It was but the confirmation of the certain hope in which he had lived through the night. Was the girl a simpleton? Had she got it into her head that repayment in this way discharged his hold upon her father? It was possible; women are so ludicrously ignorant of affairs. He smiled, though darkly.

' Why have you brought this money ? ' he asked.

She was already moving nearer to the door. He put himself in her way.

' What good do you imagine this is ? '

' None, perhaps. I pay it because I wish to.'

' And—is it your notion that this puts your father straight ? Do you think this is a way out of his difficulty ? '

' I have not thought that. But it was only to restore the money that I came.'

There was silence.

' Have you forgotten,' he asked, half wonderingly, half with quiet menace, ' what I said to you yesterday ? '

' You see my answer,' said Emily, pointing hastily to the table. ' I owe you that, but I can give you nothing more.' Her voice quivered, as she continued, ' What you said to me yesterday was said without thought, or only with evil thoughts. Since then you have had hours of reflection. It is not in your power—it would be in the power of no man who is not utterly base and wicked—to repeat such words this morning. Mr. Dagworthy, I believe in the affection you have professed for me ; feeling that, you are incapable of dastardly cruelty. I will not believe your tongue against yourself. In a moment of self-forgetfulness you spoke words which you will regret through your life, for they were inhuman, and were spoken to a defenceless girl. After hearing them, I cannot beg your mercy for my father ; but you know that misfortune which strikes him falls also upon me. You have done me the greatest wrong that man can do to woman ; you owe me what reparation is in your power.'

She had not thought to speak thus. Since daylight dawned her heart had felt too numb, too dead; barely to tell him that she had no answer to his words was the purpose with which she had set out. The moment prompted her utterance, and words came without reflection. It was a noble speech, and nobly delivered ; the voice was uncertain at times, but it betrayed no weakness of resolve, no dread of what might follow. The last sentences were spoken with a dignity which rebuked rather than supplicated. Dagworthy's head bowed as he listened.

He came nearer.

' Do you think me,' he asked, under his breath, ' a mere ignorant lout, who has to be shamed before he knows what's manly and what isn't ? Do you think because I'm a manufacturer, and the son of one, that I've no thought or feeling above my trade ? I know as well as you can tell me, though you speak with words I couldn't command, that I'm doing a mean and a vile thing—there ; hear me say it, Emily Hood. But it's not a cruel thing. I want to compel you to do what, in a few years, you'll be glad of. I want you to accept love such as no other man can give you, and with it the command of pretty well everything you can wish for. I want to be a slave at your feet, with no other work in life than finding out your desires and satisfying them. You're not to be tempted with money, and I don't try to ; but I value the money because it will give me power to show my love. And mind what I say ; ask yourself if it isn't true. If you hadn't been engaged already, you'd have listened to me ; I feel that power in myself ; I know I should have made you care for me by loving you as desperately as I do. I wouldn't have let you refuse me—you hear, Emily ? Emily ! Emily ! Emily !—it does me good to call you by your name—I haven't done so before to-day, have I, Emily ? Not a cruel thing, because I offer you more than any man living can, more of that for which you care most, the life a highly educated woman can appreciate. You shall travel where you will ; you shall buy books and pictures, and all else to your heart's content ; and, after all, you shall love me. That's a bold word, but I tell you I feel the power in me to win your love. I'm not hateful to you, even now ; you can't really despise me, for you know that whatever I do is for no mean purpose. There is no woman living like you, and to make you my wife I am prepared to do anything, however vile it seems. Some day you'll forgive it all, because some day you'll love me ! '

It was speaking as he had never yet done. He assumed that his end was won, and something of the triumph of passion endued his words with a joyous fervour. Very possibly there was truth in much that he said, for he spoke with the intense conviction which fulfils prophecies. But the only effect was to force Emily back upon her cold defiance.

' I am in your house, Mr. Dagworthy,' she said, ' and you can compel me to hear whatever you choose to say. But I have no other answer than that you know. I wish to leave you.'

His flushed eagerness could not at once adapt itself to another tone.

' No, you don't wish to leave me. You want to see that

I am a man of my word, that I mean what I say, and am not afraid to stick to it. Emily, you don't leave me till you have promised to be my wife. You're a noble girl. You wouldn't be frightened into yielding. And it isn't that way I want to have you. You're more now in my eyes than ever. It shall be love for love. Emily, you will marry me ? '

What resources of passion the man was exhibiting ! By forethought he could have devised no word of these speeches which he uttered with such vigour ; it was not he who spoke, but the very Love God within him. He asked the last question with a voice subdued in tenderness ; his eyes had a softer fire.

Emily gave her answer.

' I would not marry you, though you stood to kill me if I refused.'

No bravado, no unmeasured vehemence of tone, but spoken as it would have been had the very weapon of death gleamed in his hand.

He knew that this was final.

' So you are willing that your father shall be put into the dock at the police-court to-morrow morning ? '

' If you can do that, it must be so.'

' If I *can* ? You know very well I have the power to, and you ought to know by now that I stick at nothing. Go home and think about it.'

' It is useless. I have thought. If you think still to make me yield by this fear, it is better that you should act at once. I will tell you : If I were free, if I had the power to give myself to you in marriage, it would make your threat of no more avail. I love my father ; to you I cannot say more than that ; but though I would give my life to save his from ruin, I could not give—my father would not wish me, oh never !—my woman's honour. You will find it hard to understand me, for you seem not to know the meaning of such words.'

She closed with stern bitterness, compelled to it by the tone of his last bidding. A glorious beauty flashed in her face. Alas, Wilfrid Athel would never know the pride of seeing thus the woman he knew so noble. But Wilfrid was in her heart ; his soul allied itself with hers and gave her double strength. Dagworthy had wrought for her that which in the night's conflict she could not bring about by her own force ; knowing, in the face of utter despair, the whole depth of the love with which she held to her father, she could yet speak his doom with calmness, with clear intelligence that the sacrifice she was asked to make was disproportionate to the disaster threatened.

He answered with cold decision.

' It's you who don't know me. I've nothing more to say to you ; you are at liberty to go. To-morrow your father will be before the magistrates.'

Emily moved to the door. The sound of the words had blanched her lips. She felt that, if she would keep hold upon her bodily strength, she must breathe the outer air.

' Look here, I say,' he exclaimed, stepping to the table. ' Take the money. I've nothing to do with that.'

She made a motion with her hand, but hastened still and escaped. Once in the garden she all but ran, thinking she heard his footsteps in pursuit, and smitten with that sudden terror which comes sometimes when a danger is escaped. But she had gained the Heath, and it was certain now that he had not tried to overtake her, a glance back showed her that no one was in sight. She walked rapidly on, though her heart seemed about to burst, walked without pausing till she had reached the quarry. Here she sat on the same stone as before. She was in dread of fainting ; the anguish of her leaping blood was intolerable ; she had neither sight nor hearing. But the crisis of suffering passed ; she let her head fall forward and buried it upon her lap.

Perhaps for ten minutes she remained thus, then a great crash from the near heavens caused her to look up. It was raining, had rained since she sat there, though she had not known it. In the little pool before her great drops splashed and made a miniature tempest. The yellow flower she had plucked lay close by, and was beaten by the rain. It lightened vividly, and there followed heavier thunder than before.

She wished to shed tears—tears were choking her, but would not rise and shed themselves ; she could only sob, aloud, hysterically. The words ' Father ' and ' Wilfrid ' broke from her lips several times. Was there red-hot metal poured upon her forehead ?

It cost her a great effort to rise and walk homewards. The rain streamed down, but she could no longer hasten. Still she reached the house before her mother's return from church, and she was glad of that.

CHAPTER XIII.

THE CUTTING OF THE KNOT.

FOR the final failure of his plot Dagworthy was in no wise prepared. He had anticipated prolonged scenes, passionate pleadings, appeals to his better nature, and to his shame; but that his threat should prove ineffectual was not among his fears. Illustrating a well-known tendency of human nature, his reckless egoism based its confidence on the presumed existence of heroic self-devotion in his victim. Starting from a knowledge of the close affection between Emily and her father, the logic of desire had abundant arguments to prove that the girl must and could act in but one way. Dagworthy's was not an original mind; the self-immolation of daughters (not of sons) on their parents' behalf is among vulgar conceptions of the befitting, and it is more than probable that the mill-owner was half-consciously supported by precedents drawn from his readings in popular fiction. His imagination, as is commonly the case, was only strong in the direction of his wishes; neglecting Emily's avowed attachment to an accepted lover—whose shadowiness made him difficult to realise even as an obstacle—he dwelt persistently on the thought of Hood's position, and found it impossible to imagine a refusal on Emily's part to avert from her father the direst of calamities. That other motive, the strength of which in Emily was independent of her plighted troth, was not within the range of his conceptions; that a woman should face martyrdom rather than marry without love was a contingency alien to his experience and to the philosophy wherewith nature had endowed him. In spite of the attributes of nobleness which so impressed him in the object of his love, Dagworthy could give no credit to the utterance of such a feeling. Whilst Emily spoke, he was for the moment overcome by a vision of vague glories; reflecting on her words, he interpreted them as merely emphasising her determination to wed one only. Their effect was to give new food to his jealousy.

That solace of men's unconscious pessimism, the faith, pathetically clung to, that in frustration of desire is the soul's health, is but too apt to prove itself fallacious just where its efficiency would show most glorious. Is there not lurking somewhere in your mind, notwithstanding the protests of your realistic intelligence, more than half a hope that Richard Dagworthy will emerge radiant from the gulf into which his passions have plunged him? For the credit of human nature! But what if human nature oft establishes its credit by the failures over which we shake our heads? Of many ways to the resting-place of souls, the way of affliction is but one; cling, if it please you, to the assurance that this is the treading of the elect, instinct will justify itself in many to whom the denial of a supreme need has been the closing of the upward path. Midway in his life, when slow development waited but occasion to establish the possibilities of a passionate character, Dagworthy underwent the trial destined to determine the future course of his life. One hesitates to impute it to him as a fault that he was not of the elect. A mere uneducated Englishman, hitherto balancing always between the calls from above and from below, with one miserable delusion and its consequent bitterness ever active in his memory, he could make no distinction between the objects which with vehemence he desired and the spiritual advantage which he felt the attainment would bring to him; and for the simple reason that in his case no such distinction existed. Even as the childhood of civilisation knows virtue only in the form of a concrete deity, so to Dagworthy the higher life of which he was capable took shape as a mortal woman, and to possess her was to fulfil his being. With the certainty that she was beyond his reach came failure of the vital forces which promised so much. A pity; for it flatters us poor mortals to discern instances of the soul's independence of the body. I would it had been otherwise with Dagworthy; I have but to relate the facts. It was no dark angel that had whispered to him through the hours of his waiting for Emily's surrender. High aims, pure ambitions, were stronger in him than they ever had been; stronger than they ever would be again. It was when Emily left him with those proud words of defiance that the veritable demon took stand at his ear. The leaping, fruitful sap of his being turned itself to gall. He sat with a brow of blackness; cruel projects worked in his brain.

Not only had he lost her, but his loss was another's gain. The pricking of jealousy, for a while suspended, again became maddening. He had heard her say that she would die rather than be his wife; judge, then, what must be her love of the man she had chosen. His desire now was to do her injury, and his fiercest torment was the thought that he dared not fulfil the menace with which he had hoped to overwhelm her. If he prosecuted Hood, all the circumstances of the case would inevitably come out; Emily had friends in Dunfield, and if her father's guilt were once disclosed, there would be no reason for her concealment of what had happened; facts like these put forward in mitigation of punishment would supply the town with a fearful subject of comment—nay, was he safe from the clutch of the law? Of these things he had not troubled to think, so assured was he that the mere threat would suffice. From his present point of view it was easy enough to see that the plot had been a wretched piece of bungling; in failing of its end it became the project of a simpleton. Had the girl herself been cool enough to see this? Did she defy him in knowledge of the weakness of his position? Probably not; in that case she would have spoken differently; she had granted, and clearly with sincerity, his power to do what he threatened. And then the fact remained that he could injure Hood irremediably by means short of criminal proceedings. Emily—his reasoning was accurate enough—had not been careful to distinguish between modes of injury, where each meant ruin.

What he dared to do, he would. He was acquainted with the wretched story of struggle which had ended in Hood's taking refuge, as a clerk with a mean salary, from the extremities of destitution. To dismiss the man after private accusation would be to render his prospects worse than ever, for it was easy to whisper here and there the grounds of dismissal. Emily's mouth would be closed by the necessity of keeping secret her father's dishonesty. But this revenge fell short of his appetite for cruelty; it would strike the girl herself only indirectly. And it was possible that her future husband might have it in his power to give her parents aid. Yet he persuaded himself that the case was otherwise; Emily's secrecy had impressed him with the belief that the match she contemplated was anything but a brilliant one. Could he devise no graver hurt? Through the Sunday afternoon and the night which followed, he pondered ceaselessly on means of evil, delighted to flesh his fangs even in imagination. Many a vile plan dwelt with him which he knew he durst not put into practice. Monday morning came and found him no further than the crime which had first suggested itself. Fevered with eagerness to accomplish that at least, he left home earlier than usual. It might be that the day would bring fresh counsel.

To Emily the hours following upon her visit to the house on the Heath had brought unnatural quietness. Physical suffering troubled her, but the energies of her mind were for the time expended; the aching of her brow involved thought in sluggishness. She did not shun her parents, and even talked with them in a listless way; solitude would have been irksome to her just now. For once she felt glad of her mother's way of spending Sunday; to sit inactive was all that she desired. It was understood that her head distressed her.

In the afternoon, and again in the evening, the single bell of the chapel clanged for worshippers. Mrs. Hood was not in the habit of attending service more than once in the day; she sat on her uneasy chair, at times appearing to read, more often gazing out of the windows. The road had more traffic than on week-days, for it was the recreation of a certain class of Dunfieldians to drive out in parties to the Heath, either hiring a vehicle or using their own trade-carts. It would have been a consolation to observe that in the latter case the quadruped employed benefited by its owner's regard for his own interests; possibly an acute spectator might have discerned gradations of inhumanity. To the casual eye there showed but a succession of over-laden animals urged to the utmost speed; the national predilection exhibiting itself crudely in this locality. Towards nightfall the pleasure-seekers returned, driving with the heightened energy attributable to Bacchic inspiration, singing, shouting, exchanging racy banter with pedestrians. So the hours dragged wearily on, wheezed out, one after one, by the clock on the stairs. Hood was at no time fertile in topics of conversation; to-day he maintained almost unbroken silence. Tea was prepared, partaken of, removed; supper, three hours later. The day closed with rain and a rising wind.

Emily heard it about the house as she lay through hours of sleeplessness. At first a light slumber had come to her; it was broken by the clock striking eleven. Probably she was roused at the first stroke, for, failing to count, the number seemed to her so interminable that she started up and made to herself fretful complaint. Pain was weakening her self-control; she found herself crying in a weary, desolate way, and could not stop her tears for a long time. The gusts of wind went by her windows and bore their voices away on to

the common, wailing and sobbing in the far distance; rain
spattered the windows at times. When her tears ceased,
Emily hid her face in the pillow and moaned; often she
uttered Wilfrid's name. To-day she should by agreement
have written to him, but to do so had been impossible. He
would be uneasy at her silence. Oh, how could she ever write
to him again? What might happen to-morrow? At the
thought, she held her breath and lay in silence.

She rose in time for breakfast, but at the last moment could
not bring herself to go down to the meal. To face her father
was impossible. Her mother came to the door, and Emily
answered her that she would lie for an hour or two longer,
being still unwell. During the half-hour that followed she sat
listening intently to every sound in the house. Hood, having
breakfasted, came upstairs and entered his room; when, a
few minutes later, he came out, his steps made a pause at her
threshold. Her heart beat in sickening fear; she could not
have found voice to reply to him had he spoken. But he did
not do so, and went downstairs. She heard him open the
front door, and sprang to the window to catch a glimpse of
him. At the gate he turned and looked up to her window;
his face was sorrowful. Emily held back that he might not
see her; when it was too late she could not understand this
movement, and longed to wave him a good-bye. She threw
up the sash; her father did not turn again.

We follow him. Not very long after his arrival at the
mill, Dagworthy himself appeared. Hood's evil conscience
led him to regard with apprehension every unusual event.
Dagworthy's unwonted earliness was still troubling his mind,
when a messenger summoned him to the private room.
There was nothing extraordinary in this, but Hood, as he
crossed the passage, shook with fear; before knocking and
pushing open the door, he dashed drops from his forehead
with his hand. Dagworthy was alone, sitting at the desk.

'Shut the door,' he said, without turning his eyes from a
letter he was reading.

The clerk obeyed, and stood for a full minute before anything more was addressed to him. He knew that the worst
had come.

Dagworthy faced half round.

'One day early last week,' he began, averting his eyes
after a single glance, 'I was looking over one of these ledgers'
—he pointed to the shelf—'and left an envelope to mark a

place. I forgot about it, and now that I look, the envelope has gone. It contained a bank-note. Of course you came across it in the course of your work.'

It was rather an assertion than a question. Whilst he was speaking, the courage of despair had taken hold upon his hearer. Like the terrible flash of memory which is said to strike the brain of a drowning man, there smote on Hood's mind a vision of the home he had just quitted, of all it had been and all it might still be to him. This was his life, and he must save it, by whatever means. He knew nothing but that necessity; all else of consciousness was vague swimming horror.

'No, sir,' was his reply, given with perfect firmness, 'I found no envelope.'

Dagworthy's coarse lips formed a smile, hard and cruel. He faced his clerk.

'Oh, you didn't?'

'In which ledger did you leave it, sir?' Hood asked, the dryness of his throat rendering speech more difficult as he proceeded. Still, his eye was fixed steadily on Dagworthy's face; it was life at stake. 'I have not had them all.'

'I don't remember which it was,' replied the other, 'and it doesn't much matter, since I happen to know the note. I dare say you remember buying a new hat in Hebsworth last Friday?'

The love of inflicting pain for its own sake, an element of human nature only overgrown by civilisation, was showing itself strongly in Dagworthy. He was prolonging this scene. On his way to the mill he had felt that the task would be rather disagreeable; but we cannot nurture baseness with impunity, and, face to face with a man under torture, he enjoyed the spectacle as he scarcely would have done a little while ago. Perhaps the feeling that his first blow at Emily was actually struck gave him satisfaction, which he dwelt upon.

Hood made no reply to the question. He would not admit to himself that this was the end, but he had no voice.

'You hear me?' Dagworthy reminded him.

'Yes. I bought a hat.'

'And you paid for it with the note I have lost. I happen to know it.'

There was silence.

'Well, you understand that under ordinary circumstances you would be at once given in charge.' Dagworthy spoke almost cheerfully. 'If I don't do that it's out of consideration for your age and your family. But as you are not to be trusted, of course I can't continue to employ you.'

A wild hope sprang in Hood's eyes, and the rush of grati-tude at his heart compelled him to speak.

'Oh, Mr. Dagworthy, you are generous! You have always treated me with kindness; and this is how I repay you. It was base; I deserve no mercy. The temptation—' he grew incoherent; 'I have been driven hard by want of money. I know that is no excuse. I had no intention at first of taking the money; I came here to give it you; I should have done so without a thought of dishonesty, but you happened to be away. In going to Hebsworth I lost my hat, and I had not enough money of my own to buy another; I had to change the note—that was the temptation—I will return it.—But for this work here, I might by now have been in the workhouse. Try, sir, to forgive my baseness; I cannot forgive myself.'

Dagworthy turned his face away.

'Well,' he said, with a wave of the hand, 'all that's too late.'

'Sir,' Hood pursued, spurred by foresight of penury per-haps as much as by dread of having to explain his dismissal at home, for penury had been his relentless foe through life; 'Sir, is it in vain to ask you to give me another chance? I am not a dishonest man; never before has such a temptation come to me, and surely never would again. Will you—I entreat you to think what it means—at my age—my wife—— I ought to be content with thanking you for having spared me—how few would have done that! Let me continue to serve you—a lower salary—if it be ever so little—till I have regained your confidence——'

Dagworthy was drumming with his fingers on the desk. Not for an instant did he falter in his purpose, but it gave him pleasure to be thus prayed to. The employer of labour is not as a rule troubled with a lively imagination; a pity, for it would surely gratify him to feel in its fulness at times his power of life and death. Native defect and force of habit render it a matter of course that a small population should eat or starve at his pleasure; possibly his resolution in seasons of strike is now and then attributable to awakening of insight and pleasure in prolonging his rôle of hunger-god. Dagworthy appreciated his victim's despair all the more that it made present to him the wretchedness that would fall on Emily.

Think not that the man was unashamed. With difficulty he could bring himself to meet Hood's look. But self-contempt may well consist with perseverance in gratification of ignoble instincts.

When Hood ceased, there came this reply.

' I shall not grant what you ask, simply because it is against my principles. I let you off, for it would do me no good to punish you, and certainly, as regards yourself, the lesson will be enough. But I can't keep you in my employ, so we'll talk no more about it. You were going to take your holiday from the end of this week, I think ? Very well, let it be supposed that you begin to-day instead, and in a day or two write me a note giving up your place.'

This was not yielding on Dagworthy's part; it merely occurred to him as a way of protecting himself if there should be future need.

Hood was standing with bent head ; he seemed unable either to speak or to depart.

' You may go,' Dagworthy said.

' Sir,—I may refer to you ? ' asked the wretched man, roused by the bidding.

' No, I think not,' was the calm reply. ' Unless, of course, you are willing that I should state the plain facts of the case ? '

Hood staggered from the room. . . . .

When Emily came down in the course of the morning, her appearance was such that her mother uttered an exclamation of alarm.

' Why, child, you are like a ghost ! Why didn't you stay in bed ? I was just coming up to you, hoping you'd been asleep. I must go for Dr. Evans at once.'

Emily resisted.

' But I certainly shall, say what you like. No headache would make you look like that. And you're as feverish as you can be. Go up to bed again ; you hardly look, though, as if you could climb the stairs. I'll put on my things and go round.'

It was only by affecting anger that Emily could overcome her mother's purpose. She did indeed feel ill, but to submit to treatment was impossible whilst this day lasted. Far worse than her bodily fever was the mental anguish which would not allow her to remain in one place for more than a few minutes at a time, and did not suffer the pretence of occupation. How would it come about? Was her father at this moment in the hands of the police? How would the first news come to Banbrigg, and when? The sound of every vehicle on the road was an approaching terror; she was constantly at the window to watch the people who came near. It had seemed to her that she realised what this trial would be, yet her anticipations had fallen far below the experience of these fearful hours. At instants, she all but repented what she had done, and asked herself if there was not even now a chance of somehow saving her father. The face which he had raised to the window as he left home smote her heart. Not a word of kindness had she spoken to him since Friday night. Oh, what inconceivable cruelty had possessed her, that she let him go this morning without even having touched his hand! Could her mind endure this? Was she not now and then near to delirium? Once she went to the window, and, to her horror, could see nothing; a blue and red mist hovered before her eyes. It left her, but other symptoms of physical distress grew from hour to hour, and she dreaded lest strength to endure might wholly forsake her before night came. She tried to picture her father returning as usual; human pity might have spoken even in Dagworthy's heart; or if not so, then he might have been induced to forbear by a hope of winning her gratitude. Very agony made her feel almost capable of rewarding such mercy. For Wilfrid seemed now very far away, and her love had fallen to the background; it was not the supreme motive of her being as hitherto. Would she suffer thus for Wilfrid? The question forced itself upon her, and for reply she shuddered; such bonds seemed artificial compared with those which linked her to her father, the love which was coeval with her life. All feeling is so relative to circumstances, and what makes so stable as the cement of habit?

In the early hours of the afternoon a lull of utter weariness relieved her; she lay upon the couch and all but slept; it was something between sleep and loss of consciousness following on excessive pain. She awoke to find the doctor bending over her; Mrs. Hood had become so alarmed that she had despatched a neighbour secretly on the errand. Emily was passive, and by her way of speaking half disguised the worst features of her state. Nevertheless, the order was given that she should go to bed. She promised to obey.

' As soon as father comes,' she said, when alone again with her mother. ' It cannot be long till his time.'

She would not yield beyond this. But the hour of return came, and her father delayed. Then was every minute an eternity. No longer able to keep her reclining position, she stood again by the window, and her eyes lost their vision from straining upon one spot, that at which Hood would first appear. She leaned her head upon the window-sill, and let her ears take their turn of watching ; the first touch of a hand at the gate would reach her. But there came none.

Can hours thus be lived through ? Ah, which of us to whom time has not been a torment of hell ? Is there no nether Circle, where dread anticipation eternally prolongs itself, eternally varied with hope in vain for ever ?

Mrs. Hood had abandoned her useless protests ; she came and sat by the girl.

' I've no doubt he's gone to the Walkers',' she kept saying, naming acquaintances with whom Hood occasionally spent an evening. Then, ' And why need you wait for him, my dear ? Can't he go up and see you as soon as he gets in ? '

' Mother,' Emily said at last, ' will you go to the Walkers' and ask ? It is not really very far. Will you go ? '

' But, my child, it will take me at least an hour to walk there and back ! I should only miss him on the way. Are you afraid of something ? '

' Yes, I am. I believe something has happened to him.'

' Those are your fancies. You are very poorly ; it is cruel to me to refuse to go to bed.'

' Will you go, mother ?—If you do not, I must ; ill or not, I must go.'

She started to her feet. Her mother gazed at her in fear, —believing it the beginning of delirium.

' Emily, my dear child,' she pleaded, laying her hand on the girl's arm, ' won't you come upstairs,—to please me, dear ? '

' Mother, if you will go, I promise to lie here quietly till you return.'

' But it is impossible to leave you alone in the house. Look, now, it is nine o'clock ; in half an hour, an hour at most, your father will be back. Why, you know how often he stays late when he gets talking.'

Emily was silent for a few minutes. Then she said—

' Will you ask Mrs. Hopkins to send her servant ? '

' But think—the trouble it will be giving.'

' Will you do it ? I wish it. Will you go and ask her !
I will give the girl money.'

' If you are so determined, of course I will ask her. But
I'm sure——'

At length she left the room, to go out of the house by the
back-door and call at the neighbours'. Scarcely was she
away, when Emily darted upstairs, and in an instant was
down again, with her hat and a cloak ; another moment, and
she was out in the road. She did not forget the terror her
mother would suffer, on finding her gone ; but endurance had
reached its limit. It was growing dark. After one look in
the direction of Dunfield, she took the opposite way, and ran
towards the Heath, ran till her breath failed and she had to
drop into a quick walk. Once more she was going to the
Upper Heath, and to the house which was the source of all
her misery. When she reached the quarry it was quite dark ;
at her approach she saw the shape of a man move away into
the shadow of the quarried rock, and an unreasoning fear
spurred her past the spot. Five minutes more and she was
at Dagworthy's gate. She rang the door-bell.

The servant told her that Mr. Dagworthy was at home ;
she declined to give her name, but said she must see him at
once. Speedily she was led into a room, where her enemy
sat alone.

He looked at her wonderingly, then with a deep flush—
for now he surely had gained his end,—he advanced towards
her without speaking.

' Where is my father ?' she asked ; the voice which dis-
abused him did not seem Emily's.

' Isn't he at home ?'

' He has not come home. What have you done ? '

' Not come home ? '

' Then he is free ? He is safe—my father ? You have
spared him ? '

Dagworthy inwardly cursed himself for shortsightedness.
Were he but able to answer ' Yes,' would she not yield him
anything ? Why had he not made trial of this policy ? Or
was it now too late ? But Hood had not returned home.
The man had gone forth from him in despair. As he gazed
at the girl, a suspicion, all but a fear, touched him. Why
should Hood remain away from his house ?

She was repeating her questions imploringly.

'He is free, as far as I am concerned, Emily.'

'You have forgiven him? Oh, you have had that mercy upon us?'

'Sit down, and let us talk about it,' said Dagworthy.

She did not seem to notice that he had taken her hand; but the next moment he was holding her in his arm, and with a cry she broke away.

'There are others in the house,' she exclaimed, her wild, fearful eyes seeking other exit than that which he stopped. 'I must call for their help. Can you not see that I am suffering— ill? Are you pitiless? But no—no—for you have spared him!'

Dagworthy mastered himself, though it cost him something, and spoke with an effort at gentleness.

'What thanks have you to give me, Emily?'

'My life's gratitude—but that will be your least reward.'

'Ay, but how is the gratitude going to be shown?'

Her keen sense found a fear in his manner of speaking.

'You have not said a word to him,' she asked, seeming to forget his question.

Of what ultimate use was it to lie? And she would not suffer him within reach of her.

'1 couldn't very well help doing that,' he replied, unable to resolve how it were best to speak, and uttering the first words that came, carelessly.

'Then he knows you have discovered——'

Her voice failed. Such explanation of her father's absence was a new terror.

'Yes, he knows,' Dagworthy answered, cruelty resuming its fascination. 'I couldn't keep him at the mill, you know, though I let him off his punishment.'

'You dismissed him?'

'J did. It's not too late to have him back, and something better.'

'Let me go!' she said hoarsely.

He moved from the door; sight of such misery vanquished even him.

When she reached home, her mother was standing with two or three neighbours in front of the house; at the sight of Emily there were exclamations of relief and welcome.

'My child, where can you have been?' Mrs. Hood cried, following the girl who passed the garden-gate without pausing.

'Is father come?' was the reply.

'No, not yet. But where have you been? Why, you were coming from the Heath, Emily, in the night air, and you so ill!'

'I have been to ask Mr. Dagworthy,' Emily said in a tired voice. 'He knows nothing of him.'

Her strength bore her into the parlour, then she sank upon the couch and closed her eyes. Mrs. Hood summoned the help of her friends. Unresisting, with eyes still closed, silent, she was carried upstairs and laid in her bed. Her mother sat by her. Midnight came, and Hood did not return. Already Mrs. Hood had begun to suspect something mysterious in Emily's anxiety; her own fears now became active. She went to the front door and stood there with impatience, by turns angry and alarmed. Her husband had never been so late. She returned to the bedroom.

'Emily, are you awake, dear?'

The girl's eyes opened, but she did not speak.

'Do you know any reason why your father should stay away?'

A slight shake of the head was the reply.

The deepest stillness of night was upon the house. As Mrs. Hood seated herself with murmured bewailing of such wretchedness, there sounded a heavy crash out on the staircase; it was followed by a peculiar ringing reverberation. Emily rose with a shriek.

'My love—hush! hush!' said her mother. 'It's only the clock-weight fallen. How that does shake my nerves! It did it only last week, and gave me such a start.'

Grasping her mother's hand, the girl lay back, death-pale. The silence was deeper than before, for not even the clock ticked. . . . .

Dagworthy could not sleep. At sunrise he had wearied himself so with vain efforts to lie still, that he resolved to take a turn across the Heath, and then rest if he felt able to. He rose and went into the still morning air.

The Heath was beautiful, seen thus in the purple flush of the dawn. He had called forth a dog to accompany him, and the animal careered in great circles over the dewy sward, barking at the birds it started up, leaping high from the ground, mad with the joy of life. He ran a race with it to the wall which bounded the top of the quarry. The exercise did him good, driving from his mind shadows which had clung about it in the night. Reaching the wall he rested his arms upon it, and looked over Dunfield to the glory of the rising sun. The smoke of the mill-chimneys, thickening as fires were coaled for the day's work, caught delicate reflection from the sky; the lofty spire of the church seemed built of some beautiful rose-hued stone. The grassy country round about wore a fresher green than it was wont to show; the very river, so foul in reality with the refuse of manufactures, gleamed like a pure current.

Dagworthy's eyes fixed themselves on the horizon, and grew wide with the sense of things half understood.

The dog had left him and was gone round into the quarry. A bark came from below. At a second bark Dagworthy looked down. The dog was snuffing at a man who lay between a big piece of quarried stone and a little grass-bordered pool. Asleep —was he? Yet it was not the attitude in which men sleep. The dog barked a third time.

He left his position, and followed the circuit which would bring him down to where the man lay. Whilst still a few yards off, he checked himself. If the man slept, his body was strangely distorted; one arm seemed to be beneath him, the other was extended stiffly; the face looked at the sky. A few steps, and Dagworthy, gazing upon the face, knew it.

A cold shudder thrilled him, and he drew back. His foot struck against something; it was a bottle. He picked it up, and read a word in large print on the white label.

The temptation to look full into the face again was irresistible, though horror shook him as he approached. The features were hideous, the eyes starting from their sockets, the lips drawn back over the teeth. He turned and walked away rapidly, followed by the dog, which roused the quarry echoes with its barking.

' My God ! I never thought of that.'

The words uttered themselves as he speeded on. Only at the garden-gate he stayed, and then seemed to reflect upon what he should do. The temptation was to return into the house and leave others to spread the news ; there would be workmen in the quarry in less than an hour. Yet he did not do this, but hurried past his own door to the house of a doctor not a hundred yards away. Him he called forth. . . . .

About midday a covered burden was brought in a cart to Banbrigg ; the cart stopped before the Hoods' house, and two men, lifting the burden, carried it through the gate and to he door. Mrs. Hood had already opened to them, and stood with her face half-hidden. The burden was taken into the parlour, and placed upon the couch. The outline was that of a man's form.

In the kitchen were two women, neighbours; as soon as the men had departed, and the front door was closed, they stole forward, one sobbing, the other pale with fear. They entered the sitting-room, and Mrs. Hood went in with them. She was strangely self-controlled. All three stood looking at the wrapped form, which was that of a man.

'I shan't dare to look at him!' Mrs. Hood whispered. 'The doctor told me I wasn't to. Oh, my husband!'

With the sublime love of woman, conquering all dread, she dropped to her knees and laid her head on the pillow of the couch by the side of that head so closely shrouded.

'Thank God, Emily can't see this!' she groaned.

'Hadn't I better go up to her?' one of the women asked. Both of them stood at a distance.

'Yes, perhaps you had. But you'll be wanted at home. Stay with me a minute, then I'll lock this door and go up myself.'

At the sound of a hand on the door all turned with a movement of surprise and affright. There entered Emily, hurriedly dressed, her hair loose upon her shoulders. She looked round the room, with half-conscious, pitiful gaze, then upon her mother, then at the form on the couch. She pointed to it.

'He has come?'

Her voice was unearthly. The sound gave her mother strength to run to her, and throw her arms about her, sobbing, terror-stricken.

She suffered herself to be led upstairs, and did not speak.

CHAPTER XIV.

NEWS AND COMMENTS.

As a man who took the world as he found **it, and on the** whole found it well worth accepting on such terms, Mr. Athel was not likely to allow his annoyance with Wilfrid to threaten the habitual excellence of his digestion. His disappointment was real enough. When of a sudden Wilfrid had announced that he could not accompany the family party to Switzerland, Mr. Athel was saved from undignified irresolution by a hearty outburst of temper, which saw him well over the Straits before it gave way to the natural reaction, under the influence of which he called himself a blockhead. He had, beyond a doubt, precipitated the marriage, when postponement was the only thing he really cared about. To abuse himself was one thing, the privilege which an Englishman is ready enough to exercise; to have his thoughts uttered to him by his sister with feminine neatness and candour was quite another matter. Mrs. Rossall had in vain attempted to stem the flood of wrath rushing Channelwards. Overcome, she clad herself in meaning silence, until her brother, too ingenuous man, was compelled to return to the subject himself, and, towards the end of the journey, rashly gave utterance to half a wish that he had not left 'that young fool' behind. Mrs. Rossall, herself a little too impetuous when triumph was no longer doubtful, made such pointed remarks on the neglect of good advice that the ire which was cooling shot forth flame in another direction. Brother and sister arrived at Geneva in something less than perfect amity. Their real affection for each other was quite capable of bearing not infrequently the strain of irritability on both sides. A day of mutual causticities had well prepared the ground for the return of good temper, when the arrival of Wilfrid, by astonishing both, hastened their complete reconciliation. Wilfrid was mysterious; for a week he kept his counsel, and behaved as if nothing unusual had happened. By that time Mr. Athel's patience had reached its limit; he requested to be told how matters stood. Wilfrid, determined not to compromise his dignity by speaking first, but glad enough when his father broached the topic, related the story

of his visit to Dunfield. Possibly he laid needless emphasis
on Emily's unselfish prudence.

'I fail to see the striking meritoriousness of all that,' Mr.
Athel observed, put into a good humour by the result, and
consequently allowing himself a little captiousness. 'It
merely means that she behaved as any woman who respected
herself would under the circumstances. Your own behaviour,
on the other hand—well, let it pass.'

'I don't see that I could have acted otherwise,' said Wilfrid, too contented to care about arguing the point.

'You of course saw her parents?'

Wilfrid had given no detailed account of the way in which
his interview with Emily had been obtained. He mentioned
it now, his father listening with the frowning smile of a man
who judges such puerilities from the standpoint of comfortable
middle age.

The tone between them returned before long to the friendliness never previously interrupted. Mr. Athel shortly wrote
a letter to Mr. Baxendale of Dunfield, whom he only knew
by name as Beatrice Redwing's uncle, and begged for private
information regarding Emily's family. He received a courteous reply, the details not of course wholly palatable, but
confirmatory of the modest hopes he had entertained. This
reply he showed to his sister. Mrs. Rossall raised her eyebrows resignedly, and returned the letter in silence.

'What one expected, I suppose?' said Mr. Athel.

'I suppose so. Mr. Baxendale probably thinks the man
has been applying for a position in your pantry.'

'Well, I was obliged, you know, to hint at my reasons for
seeking information.'

'You did? Then Beatrice knows all about it by this time.
As well that way as any other, I suppose.'

'We shall have to take the matter like reasonable beings,
Edith,' said her brother, a trifle annoyed by her failure to
countenance him.

'Yes; but you seem anxious that I should rejoice. That
would not be very reasonable.'

Something warned Mr. Athel that he had better abstain
from rejoinder. He pursed his lips and walked away.

Wilfrid had not spoken of the subject to his aunt since the
disclosure at The Firs, and Mrs. Rossall was offended by his
silence at least as much as by the prospect of his marrying
Miss Hood. Clearly he regarded the matter as no concern of

hers, whereas a woman claims by natural right a share in the matrimonial projects of all her male relatives with whom she is on a footing of intimacy. Perhaps the main cause of her displeasure in the first instance had been the fact that things should have got to such a pass without her having as much as suspected the imminence of danger; she regarded Emily as one that had outwitted her. Dearly would she have liked to be able to meet her brother with the assertion that she had suspected it all along; the impossibility of doing so—not from conscientious scruples, but because in that case it would clearly have been her duty to speak—exasperated her disappointment at the frustration of the match she desired. Now that she was getting used to the state of things, Wilfrid's behaviour to her became the chief ground of her offence. It seemed to her that at least he owed some kind of apology for the distress he had naturally caused her; in truth she would have liked him to undertake the task of winning her over to his side. Between her and her nephew there had never existed a warm confidence, and Wilfrid's present attitude was too much a confirmation of the feeling she had experienced now and then, that his affection was qualified with just a little contempt. She was not, she knew, a strong-minded woman, and on that very account cared more for the special dominion of her sex. Since Wilfrid had ceased to be a hobbledehoy, it would have become him to put a little more of the courtier into his manner towards her. For are there not countries in which their degree of kin is no bar to matrimony? Mrs. Rossall was of the women who like the flavour of respectful worship in all men who are neither father, brother, nor son. Wilfrid had fallen short of this, and hence the affectation with which she had persisted in regarding him as a schoolboy. His latest exploits were vastly more interesting to her than anything he had done in academic spheres, and she suffered a sense of exclusion in seeing him so determined to disregard her opinion.

She persuaded him to row her out one evening on a lake by which they were spending a few days. Wilfrid, suspecting that she aimed at a *tête-à-tête*, proposed that his father should accompany them. Mrs. Rossall overruled the suggestion.

'How wonderfully you are picking up,' she said, after watching him pull for a few minutes. 'Do you know, Wilf, your tendency is to stoutness; in a few years you will be portly, if you live too sedentary a life.'

He looked annoyed, and by so doing gratified her. She proceeded.

'What do you think I overheard one of our spectacled friends say this morning—"*Sehen Sie mal*,"—you were walking at a little distance—"*da haben Sie das Muster des englischen Aristokraten. O, der gute, schlichte Junge!*"'

Wilfrid had been working up his German. He stopped rowing, red with vexation.

'That is a malicious invention,' he declared.

'Nothing of the kind! The truth of the remark struck me.'

'I am obliged to you.'

'But, my dear boy, what is there to be offended at? The man envied you with all his heart; and it is delightful to see you begin to look so smooth about the cheeks.'

'I am neither an aristocrat, nor *schlicht*!'

'An aristocrat to the core. I never knew any one so sensitive on points of personal dignity, so intolerant of difference of opinion in others, so narrowly self-willed! Did you imagine yourself to have the air of a hero of romance, of the intense school?'

Wilfrid looked into her eyes and laughed.

'That is your way of saying that you think my recent behaviour incongruous. You wish to impress upon me how absurd I look from the outside?'

'It is my way of saying that I am sorry for you.'

He laughed again.

'Then the English aristocrat is an object of your pity?'

'Certainly; when he gets into a false position.'

'Ah!—well, suppose we talk of something else. Look at the moon rising over that shoulder of the hill.'

'That, by way of proving that you are romantic. No, we won't talk of something else. What news have you from England?'

'None,' he replied, regarding the gleaming drops that fell from his suspended oar.

'And you are troubled that the post brings you nothing?'

'How do you know?'

'Your emotions are on the surface.'

He made no reply.

'Ah!' Mrs. Rossall sighed, 'what a pity you are so independent. I often think a man's majority ought to come ten years later than it does. Most of you are mere boys till

thirty at least, and you go and do things that you repent all
the rest of your lives. Dare you promise to come to me in
ten years and tell me with complete frankness what you think
of—a certain step ? '

He smiled scornfully.

' Certainly ; let us register the undertaking.'

After pausing a moment, he continued with an outburst
of vehemence—a characteristic of Wilfrid's speech.

' You illustrate a thought I have often had about women.
The majority of you, at all events as you get into the world,
have no kind of faith in anything but sordid motives. You
are cynical beyond anything men can pretend to ; you scoff
at every suggestion of idealism. I suppose it is that which
makes us feel the conversation of most women of refinement
so intolerably full of hypocrisies. Having cast away all faith,
you cannot dispense with the show of it ; the traditions of
your sex must be supported. You laugh in your sleeves at
the very things which are supposed to constitute your claims
to worship ; you are worldly to the core. Men are very
Quixotes compared with you ; even if they put on cynicism
for show, they are ashamed of it within themselves. With
you, fine feeling is the affectation. I have felt it again and
again. Explain it now ; defend yourself, if you can. Show
me that I am wrong, and I will thank you heartily.'

' My word, what an arraignment ! ' cried Mrs. Rossall,
between amusement at his boldness and another feeling which
warmed her cheeks a little. ' But let us pass from broad
accusation to particulars. I illustrate all these shocking
things—poor me ! How do I illustrate them ? '

' In the whole of your attitude towards myself of late.
You pooh-pooh my feelings, you refuse to regard me as anything but a donkey, you prophesy that in a year or two I shall
repent having made a disinterested marriage. I observe the
difference between your point of view and my father's. The
worst of it is you are sincere : the circumstances of the case
do not call upon you for an expression of graceful sentiments,
and you are not ashamed to show me how meanly you regard
all that is highest and purest in life.'

' Shall I explain it ? Women are very quick to get at
realities, to see below the surface in conduct and profession.
We become, you say, worldly as soon as we get into the world.
Precisely because we have to be so wide awake to protect ourselves. We instinctively know the difference between the

ring of false and true, and as we hear the false so much
the oftener ! Your charge against us of want of real feeling is
the result of your ignorance of women ; you don't see below the
surface.'

'Well now, apply all this to the present instance. What
has your insight discerned in my proposed marriage to cause
you to regard it as a piece of folly ? '

'Simply this. You ally yourself with some one from a
class beneath your own. Such marriages very, very seldom
prove anything but miserable, and *always* bring a great many
troubles. You will say that Miss Hood is raised by education
above the class in which she was born ; but no doubt she has
relatives, and they can't be entirely got rid of. However, that
isn't the point I lay most stress on.'

'Well ? '

'I am quite sure you will make her miserable. You are
marrying too young. Your character is not fixed. In a few
years, before that, you will want to get rid of her.'

'Well, that is at all events intelligible. And your grounds
for the belief ? '

'You are inconstant, and you are ambitious. You might
marry a woman from a class higher than your own, and when
it is too late you will understand what you have lost.'

'Worldly advantages, precisely.'

'And how if your keen appreciation of worldly advantages
results in your wife's unhappiness ? '

'I deny the keen appreciation, in your sense.'

'Of course you do. Come to me in ten years and tell me
your opinion of women's ways of thinking.'

This was the significant part of their conversation.
Wilfrid came to land confirmed in his views ; Mrs. Rossall,
with the satisfaction of having prophesied uncomfortable
things.

She had a letter on the following morning on which she
recognised Beatrice Redwing's hand. To her surprise, the
stamp was of Dunfield. It proved that Beatrice was on a
visit to the Baxendales. Her mother, prior to going to the
Isle of Wight, had decided to accept an invitation to a house
in the midland counties which Beatrice did not greatly care
to visit ; so the latter had used the opportunity to respond to
a summons from her friends in the north, whom she had not
seen for four years. Beatrice replied to a letter from Mrs.
Rossall which had been forwarded to her.

After breakfast, Mrs. Rossall took her brother aside, and pointed out to him a paragraph in Beatrice's letter. It ran thus :—

'A very shocking thing has happened, which I suppose I may mention, as you will necessarily hear of it soon. Miss Hood's father has committed suicide, poisoned himself; he was found dead on a common just outside the town. Nobody seems to know any reason, unless it was trouble of a pecuniary kind. Miss Hood is seriously ill. The Baxendales send daily to make inquiries, and I am afraid the latest news is anything but hopeful. She was to have dined with us here the day after her father's death.'

There was no further comment ; the writer went on to speak of certain peculiarities in the mode of conducting service at St. Luke's church.

Mr. Athel read, and, in his manner, whistled low. His sister looked interrogation.

'I suppose we shall have to tell him,' said the former. 'Probably he has no means of hearing.'

'I suppose we must. He has been anxious at not receiving letters he expected.'

'How do you know ?'

'I had a talk with him last night.'

'Ah, so I thought. The deuce take it ! Of course he'll pack off on the moment. What on earth can have induced the man to poison himself ?'

Such a proceeding was so at variance with Mr. Athel's views of life that it made him seriously uncomfortable. It suggested criminality, or at least lunacy, both such very unpleasant things to be even remotely connected with. Poverty he could pardon, but suicide was really disreputable. From the philosophic resignation to which he had attained, he fell back into petulance, always easier to him than grave protest.

'The deuce take it !' he repeated.

Mrs. Rossall pointed to the words reporting Emily's condition at the time of writing.

'That was more than two days ago,' she said meaningly.

'H'm !' went her brother.

'Will you tell him ?'

'I suppose I must. Yes, it is hardly allowable even to postpone it. Where is he ?'

Wilfrid was found in the hotel garden.

'Your aunt has had a letter from Beatrice,' Mr. Athel

began, with the awkwardness of a comfortable Englishman
called upon to break bad news. 'She is staying in Dunfield.'

'Indeed?'

'There's something in the letter you ought to know.'

Wilfrid looked anxiously.

'It appears that Miss Hood's father has—don't let it be a
shock to you—has just died, and died, in fact, by his own
hands.'

'Has killed himself?' Wilfrid exclaimed, turning pale.

'Yes, I am sorry to say that is the report. Miss Hood is
naturally suffering from—from the shocking occurrence.'

'She is ill?' Wilfrid asked, when he had examined his
father's face for a moment.

'Yes, I am afraid she is. Beatrice gives no details.'

'You are not keeping anything from me?'

'Indeed, nothing. The words are that she is ill, and, it
is feared, seriously.'

'I must go at once.'

It was said with quiet decision. Wilfrid consulted his
watch, and walked rapidly to the hotel. He had to wait a
couple of hours, however, before he could start on his journey,
and he spent the time by himself. His father felt he could be
of no use, and Mrs. Rossall found a difficulty in approaching
her nephew under such circumstances.

'You will telegraph?' Mr. Athel said, at the station, by
way of expressing himself sympathetically.

The train moved away; and the long, miserable hours of
travelling had to be lived through. Wilfrid's thoughts were
all the more anxious from his ignorance of the dead man's
position and history. Even yet Emily had said very little of
her parents in writing to him; he imagined all manner of
wretched things to connect her silence with this catastrophe.
His fears on her own account were not excessive; the state of
vigorous health into which he had grown during late weeks
perhaps helped him to avoid thoughts of a desperate kind.
It was bad enough that she lay ill, and from such a cause; he
feared nothing worse than illness. But his uneasiness increased
as time went on; the travelling seemed intolerably tardy.
He had to decide what his course would be on reaching
Dunfield, and decision was not easy. To go straight to the
house might result in painful embarrassments; it would at
all events be better first to make inquiries elsewhere. Could he
have recourse to Beatrice? At first the suggestion did not

recommend itself, but nothing better came into his mind, and, as his impatience grew, the obstacles seemed so trifling that he overlooked them. He remembered that the address of the Baxendales was unknown to him; but it could easily be discovered. Yes, he would go straight to Beatrice.

Reaching London at ten o'clock in the morning, he drove directly to King's Cross, and pursued his journey northwards. Though worn with fatigue, excitement would not allow him more than a snatch of sleep now and then. When at length he stepped out at Dunfield, he was in sorry plight. He went to an hotel, refreshed himself as well as he could, and made inquiry about the Baxendales' address. At four o'clock he presented himself at the house, and sent in a card to Beatrice.

The Baxendales lived in St. Luke's, which we already know as the fashionable quarter of Dunfield. Their house stood by itself, with high walls about it, enclosing a garden; at the door were stone pillars, the lower half painted a dull red. It seemed the abode of solid people, not troubled with scruples of taste. It was with surprise that Wilfrid found himself in a room abundantly supplied with books and furnished in library fashion. His state of mind notwithstanding, he glanced along a few shelves, discovering yet more unexpected things, to wit, philosophical works. Unfortunately the corners of the room showed busts of certain modern English statesmen; but one looks for weaknesses everywhere.

Beatrice entered, rustling in a light, shimmery dress. Her face expressed embarrassment rather than surprise; after the first exchange of glances, she avoided his eager look. Her hand had lain but coldly in his. Wilfrid, face to face with her, found more difficulty in speaking than he had anticipated.

'I have come directly from Switzerland,' he began. 'You mentioned in a letter to my aunt that——'

His hesitation of a moment was relieved by Beatrice.

'You mean Miss Hood's illness,' she said, looking down at her hands, which were lightly clasped on her lap.

'Yes. I wish for news. I thought it likely you might know——'

Probably it was the effect of his weariness; he could not speak in his usual straightforward way; hesitancy, to his own annoyance, made gaps and pauses in his sentences.

'We heard this morning,' Beatrice said, looking past his

face to the window, 'that she is better. The danger seems to
be over.'

'There has been danger?'

'The day before yesterday she was given up.'

'So ill as that.' Wilfrid spoke half to himself, and indeed
it cost him an effort to make his voice louder. He began,
'Can you tell me——' and again paused.

'Have you heard nothing from any other quarter?'
Beatrice asked, after a silence of almost a minute.

He looked at her, wondering what she knew of his relations to Emily. It was clear that his interest occasioned her
no surprise.

'I came away immediately on hearing what your letter
contained. There is no one else with whom I could communicate. I hesitated to go to the house, not knowing——
Will you tell me what you know of this horrible event?'

Beatrice stroked one hand with the other, and seemed to
constrain herself to look up and to speak.

'I myself know nothing but the fact of Mr. Hood's death.
It took place some ten days ago, on Monday of last week. I
arrived here on the Wednesday.'

'Of course there was an inquest—with what results?'

'None, beyond the verdict of suicide. No definite cause
could be discovered. It is said that he suffered from very
narrow means. His body was found by Mr. Dagworthy.'

'Who is Mr. Dagworthy?'

'I thought you probably knew,' returned Beatrice, glancing
quickly at him. 'He was employed by Mr. Dagworthy as
clerk in a manufactory. He had just left for his summer
holiday.'

'What evidence did his employer give?'

'He only stated that Mr. Hood had been perfectly regular
and satisfactory at his work.'

'Then in truth it is a mystery?'

'Mr. Baxendale thinks that there had been a long struggle
with poverty, quite enough to account for the end.'

Wilfrid sat in gloomy silence. He was picturing what
Emily must have endured, and reproaching himself for not
having claimed a right to her entire confidence, when it was
in his power to make that hard path smooth, and to avert this
fearful misery. Looking up at length, he met the girl's eyes.

'I need not explain myself to you, Beatrice,' he said, finding at last a natural tone, and calling her by her Christian

name because he had much need of friendly sympathy. 'You appear to know why I have come.'

Sho answered rather hurriedly.

'I should not have known but for something that Mrs. Baxendale told me. Mr. Athel wrote a short time ago to ask for information about them—about the Hoods.'

'He wrote?'

Wilfrid heard it with a little surprise, but without concern.

'Do you know whether Mrs. Hood is alone—with her?' he went on to ask.

'I believe so.'

'And she is better?' He added quickly, 'Has she proper attendance? Have any friends been of aid?'

'The Baxendales have shown much kindness. My aunt saw her yesterday.'

'Will it be long before she is able to leave her room, do you know?'

'I am not able to say. Mrs. Baxendale hopes you will go upstairs and see her; she can tell you more. Will you go?'

'But is she alone? I can't talk with people.'

'Yes, she is alone, quite.'

He rose. The girl's eyes fixed themselves on him again, and she said:

'You look dreadfully tired.'

'I have not slept, I think, since I left Thun.'

'You left them all well?' Beatrice asked, with a change in her voice, from anxious interest which would have veiled itself, to the tone of one discharging a formal politeness.

Wilfrid replied with a brief affirmative, and they ascended the stairs together to a large and rather dim drawing-room, with a scent of earth and vegetation arising from the great number of growing plants arranged about it. Beatrice presented her friend to Mrs. Baxendale, and at once withdrew.

The lady with whom Wilfrid found himself talking was tall and finely made, not very graceful in her bearing, and with a large face, the singular kindness of which speedily overcame the first sense of dissatisfaction at its plainness. She wore a little cap of lace, and from her matronly costume breathed a pleasant freshness, akin to the activity of her frame. Having taken the young man's hand at greeting, she held it in both her own, and with large, grey eyes examined his face shrewdly. Yet neither the action nor the gaze was embarrassing to Wilfrid; he felt, on the contrary, something wonderfully soothing in the pressure of the warm, firm hands, and in her look an invitation to the repose of confidence which was new in his experience of women—an experience not extensive, by the bye, though his characteristic generalisations seemed to claim the opposite. He submitted from the first moment to an influence maternal in its spirit, an influence which his life had lacked, and which can perhaps only be fully appreciated either in mature reflection upon a past made sacred by death, or on a meeting such as this, when the heart is open to the helpfulness of disinterested sympathy. Mrs. Baxendale's countenance was grave enough to suit the sad thoughts with which she sought to commune, yet showed an under-smile, suggesting the consolation held in store by one much at home in the world's sorrows. As she smiled, each of her cheeks dimpled softly, and Wilfrid could not help noticing the marvellous purity of her complexion, as well as the excellent white teeth just visible between her lips.

'So you have come all the way from Switzerland,' she said, leading him to a chair, and seating herself by him. Her voice had a touch of masculine quality, even as her shape and features, but it chained attention, and impressed as the utterance of a large and strong nature. 'You are tired, too, with travel; I can see that. When did you reach Dunfield?'

'Half an hour ago.'

'And you came here at once. Beatrice and I were on the point of going to Hebsworth this afternoon; I rejoice that we did not. I'm continually afraid lest she should find the house dull. My husband and myself are alone. My eldest girl was married three months ago, my younger one is just gone to Germany, and my son is spending half a year in the United States; the mother finds herself a little forsaken. It was really more than kind of Beatrice to come and bury herself with me for a week or two.'

She passed by tactful transition to the matter in hand.

'Wasn't it a strange link that she should meet Miss Hood at your house! She has been so saddened. I never yet knew any one who could talk with Emily without feeling deep interest in her. My daughter Louisa, I am convinced, will never forget what she owes to her teacher. She and my youngest child used to be Miss Hood's pupils—perhaps you have heard? My own Emily—she is dead—was passionately fond of her namesake; she talked of her among the last words she ever spoke, poor little mite.'

'Miss Redwing tells me you saw her yesterday,' Wilfrid said.

' Yes, for the first time.'

' Was she conscious ? '

' Quite. But I was afraid to talk to her more than a minute or two; even that excited her too much. I fear you must not let her know yet of your presence.'

' I am glad I knew nothing of this till the worst was over. From the way in which she spoke of her father I should have feared horrible things. Did you know him with any intimacy ? '

' Only slightly, I am sorry to say. The poor man seems to have had a very hard life ; it is clear to me that sheer difficulty in making ends meet drove him out of his senses. Are you a student of political economy ? ' she asked suddenly, looking into Wilfrid's face with a peculiar smile.

' I am not. Why do you ask ? '

' It is the one subject on which my husband and I hold no truce. Mr. Baxendale makes it one of his pet studies, whilst I should like to make a bonfire of every volume containing such cruel nonsense. You must know, Mr. Athel, that I have an evil reputation in Dunfield; my views are held dangerous; they call me a socialist. Mr. Baxendale, when particularly angry, offers to hire the hall in the Corn Exchange, that I may say my say and henceforth spare him at home. Now think of this poor man. He had a clerkship in a mill, and received a salary of disgraceful smallness ; he never knew what it was to be free of anxiety. The laws of political economy will have it so, says my husband ; if Mr. Hood refused, there were fifty other men ready to take the place. He couldn't have lived at all, it seems, but that he owned a house in another town, which brought him a few pounds a year. I can't talk of such things with patience. Here's my husband offering himself as a Liberal candidate for Dunfield at the election coming on. I say to him : What are you going to do if you get into Parliament ? Are you going to talk political economy, and make believe that everything is right, when it's as wrong as can be ? If so, I say, you'd better save your money for other purposes, and stay where you are. He tells me my views are impracticable ; then, I say, so much the worse for the world, and so much the more shame for every rich man who finds excuses for such a state of things. It is dreadful to think of what those poor people must have

gone through. They were so perfectly quiet under it that
no one gave a thought to their position. When Emily used
to come here day after day, I've often suspected she didn't
have enough to eat, yet it was impossible for me to ask
questions, it would have been called prying into things that
didn't concern me.'

‘ She has told me for how much kindness she is indebted
to you,' Wilfrid said, with gratitude.

‘ Pooh ! What could I do ? Oh, don't we live absurdly
artificial lives ? Now why should a family who, through no
fault of their own, are in the most wretched straits, shut
themselves up and hide it like a disgrace ? Don't you think
we hold a great many very nonsensical ideas about self-respect and independence and so on ? If I were in want, I know
two or three people to whom I should forthwith go and ask
for succour ; if they thought the worse of me for it, I should
tell them they ought to be ashamed of themselves. We act,
indeed, as if we ourselves had made the world and were bound
to pretend it an admirable piece of work, without a screw
loose anywhere. I always say the world's about as bad a
place as one could well imagine, at all events for most people
who live in it, and that it's our plain duty to help each other
without grimacings. The death of this poor man has distressed me more than I can tell you ; it does seem such a
monstrously cruel thing. There's his employer, a man called
Dagworthy, who never knew what it was to be without
luxuries,—I'm not in the habit of listening to scandal, but
I believe there's a great deal of truth in certain stories told
about his selfishness and want of feeling. I consider Mr.
Dagworthy this poor man's murderer ; it was his bounden
duty to see that a man in his employment was paid enough
to live upon,—and Mr. Hood was not. Imagine what
suffering must have brought about such an end as this. A
sad case,—say people. I call it a case of crime that enjoys
impunity.'

Wilfrid listened gloomily. The broad question stirred
him to no strong feeling, but the more he heard the more
passionate was his longing to bear Emily away from the
scenes of such a past. With what devotion would he mould
his life to the one task of healing her memory ! Yet he knew
it must be very long before her heart could recover from the
all but deadly wound it had received. A feeling which one
may not call jealousy,—that were too inhuman,—but still

one of the million forms which jealousy assumes to torture us, drove him to ask himself what the effect of such a crisis in her life might be on Emily's love for him. There would always remain in her inmost soul one profound sadness in which he had no part, and which by its existence would impugn the supremacy of that bond which united him and her.

'How does Mrs. Hood bear it?' he asked, when he found Mrs. Baxendale again examining his face.

'I think Emily's illness has been her great help,—poor creatures that we are, needing one great grief to balance another. But she seems in a very weak state; I didn't like her look yesterday.'

'Will you describe her to me?' asked Wilfrid.

'She is not the kind of mother you would give to Emily. I'm afraid her miserable life has told upon her greatly, both in mind and body.'

'Emily never spoke of her, though so often of her father.'

'That is what I should have expected. Still, you must not think her quite unworthy. She speaks as an educated woman, and is certainly very devoted.'

'What of her present position? She must be in extreme difficulties.'

'No, she wants nothing for the present. Friends have been very anxious to help her. That's what I say,—only let your misery drive you out of the world, and people will find out all at once how very easily they might have saved you. A hundredth part of the interest that has been shown in the family since poor Mr. Hood's death would have found endless ways of making his life very different. All sorts of people have suddenly discovered that he really was a very deserving man, and that something ought long since to have been done for him. I don't know what has been told you of his history. He was once in independent business; I don't know exactly what. It was only utter failure that drove him to the miserable clerkship. How admirable it was of a man in such circumstances to have his daughter so well educated!'

Wilfrid smiled.

'Emily,' he said with gentle fervour, 'would have found her own way.'

'Ah, don't depreciate his care!' Mrs. Baxendale urged. 'You'll find out by degrees what a great deal of heathen doubt there is in me; among other things, I am impressed by the power of circumstances. Emily would always have been a remarkable girl, no doubt; but, without her education, you and I should not have been talking about her like this, even if we had known her. We can't dispense with these aids; that's where I feel the cruelty of depriving people of chances. Men and women go to their graves in wretchedness who might have done noble things with an extra pound a week to live upon. It does not sound lofty doctrine, does it? But I have vast faith in the extra pound a week. Emily had the advantage of it, however it was managed. I don't like to think of her as she might have been without it. What was it Beatrice called me yesterday? A materialist; yes, a materialist. It was a reproach, though she said it in the kindest way; I took it as a compliment. We can't get out of the world of material; how long will the mind support itself on an insufficient supply of dry bread?'

Wilfrid's intellectual sympathies were being aroused by his new friend's original way of talking. He began to feel a keen satisfaction at having her near him in these troubles.

'Do you think,' he asked, returning to his immediate needs, 'that I might write to her?'

'Not yet; you mustn't think of it yet.'

'Does Mrs. Hood——' he hesitated. 'Do you think Emily has told her mother—has spoken to her of me?'

Mrs. Baxendale looked surprised. 'I can't say; I took it for granted.'

'I wonder why she was reluctant to do so?' Wilfrid said, already speaking with complete freedom. 'Her father cannot have known; it would have relieved his worst anxieties; he would surely never have been driven to such things.'

'No; I think not. The poor girl will feel that, I fear. I suppose one can get a glimpse of her reasons for keeping silence?' She gave Wilfrid a friendly glance as she spoke.

'How glad I am,' he exclaimed, 'to be able to talk to you! I should have been in the utmost difficulties. Think of my position if I had been without a friend in the town. Then, indeed, but for Miss Redwing I should have heard nothing even yet.'

'She wrote to you?'

'Not to me; she mentioned the matter in a letter to my aunt, Mrs. Rossall.'

'Did Beatrice—you let me question?—did she know?'

'Only, she says, in consequence of a letter my father addressed to Mr. Baxendale.'

The lady smiled again.

'I ask because Beatrice is now and then a little mysterious to me. I spoke to her of that letter in the full belief that she must have knowledge of the circumstances. She denied it, yet, I thought, as if it were a matter of conscience to do so.'

'I think it more than likely that my aunt had written to her on the subject. And yet—no ; she would not have denied it to you. That would be unlike her.'

'Yes, I think it would.'

Mrs. Baxendale mused. Before she spoke again a servant entered the room with tea.

'You will be glad of a cup, I am sure,' said the lady. 'And now, what do you propose to do ? Shall you return to London ? '

'Oh, no! I shall stay in Dunfield till I am able to see her.'

'Very well. In that case you will not refuse our hospitality. The longer you stay the better pleased I shall be.'

She would hear of no difficulties.

'I wouldn't ask you,' she said, 'if I were not able to promise you any degree of privacy you like. A sitting-room is at your disposal—begging to be occupied since my boy Charlie went away. My husband is over head and ears in electioneering business, foolish man, and I can't tell you how I feel the need of someone to talk to on other subjects than the manufacture of votes. Where is your luggage ? '

Wilfrid named the hotel.

'It shall be fetched. And now I'll ask my niece to come and pour out tea for us.'

With the entrance of Beatrice the conversation naturally took a different turn. She heard with becoming interest of Wilfrid's establishment as a guest, and, after a little talk of Mrs. Rossall and the twins, led to the subject of certain 'revivalist' meetings then being held in Dunfield, an occasion of welcome excitement to such of the inhabitants as could not absorb themselves in politics. Mrs. Baxendale seemed to regard the religious movement dispassionately, and related a story she had from her husband of a certain prominent townsman driven to such a pass by his wife's perpetual absence from home on revivalist expeditions, that he at length fairly turned the key on her in her bedroom, and through the keyhole bade

her stay there till she had remembered her domestic duties.
He was that night publicly prayed for at a great meeting in
the Corn Exchange as one who, not content with losing his
own soul, did his best to hold back others from the way of
grace.

Beatrice affected to pay no heed to this anecdote.

'What is your side in politics?' she asked Wilfrid.
'Here we are all either Blues or Yellows.'

'What do they represent?' Wilfrid inquired.

'Oh, you shouldn't ask that,' said Mrs. Baxendale.
'Yellow is yellow, and Blue, blue; nothing else in the world.
I think it an excellent idea to use colours. Liberal and Conservative suggest ideas; names, therefore, quite out of place
in Dunfield politics—or any other politics, I dare say, if the truth
were known. My husband is a Yellow. It pleases him to
call himself a Liberal, or else a Radical. He may have been
a few months ago; now he's a mere Yellow. I tell him he's
in serious danger of depriving himself of two joys; in another
month a cloudless sky and the open sea will be detestable to
him.'

'But what are you, Mr. Athel?' Beatrice asked. 'A
Liberal or a Conservative? I should really find it hard to
guess.'

'In a Yellow house,' he replied, 'I am certainly Yellow.'

'Beatrice is far from being so complaisant,' said Mrs.
Baxendale. 'She detests our advanced views.'

'Rather, I know nothing of them,' the girl replied. The
quiet air with which she expressed her indifference evinced a
measure of spiritual pride rather in excess of that she was wont
to show. Indeed, her manner throughout the conversation was
a little distant to both her companions. If she jested with
Wilfrid it was with the idleness of one condescending to subjects below the plane of her interests. To her aunt she was
rather courteous than affectionate.

Whilst they still sat over tea, Mr. Baxendale came in.
Like his wife, he was of liberal proportions, and he had a
face full of practical sagacity; if anything, he looked too wide
awake, a fault of shrewd men, constitutionally active, whose
imagination plays little part in their lives. He wore an open
frock-coat, with much expanse of shirt-front. The fore part
of his head was bald, and the hair on each side was brushed
forward over his ears in a manner which gave him a singular
appearance. His bearing was lacking in self-possession; each

of his remarks was followed by a short laugh, deprecatory, apologetic. It seemed impossible to him to remain in a state of bodily repose, even with a cup of tea in his hand he paced the room. Constantly he consulted his watch—not that he had any special concern with the hour, but from a mere habit of nervousness.

He welcomed the visitor with warmth, at the same time obviously suppressing a smile of other than merely polite significance : then he began at once to speak of electioneering matters, and did so, pacing the carpet, for the next half hour. Wilfrid listened with such show of interest as he could command ; his thoughts were elsewhere, and weariness was beginning to oppress him.

Shortly after dinner fatigue passed the point at which it could be struggled against. Long waking, the harassment of fears at length consoled, and the exhaustion consequent upon his journey, besieged him with invincible drowsiness. Mrs. Baxendale, observing it, begged him to discard ceremony and go to rest. Gladly he suffered himself to be led to his room ; once there, he could not note the objects about him ; the very effort of taking off his clothes was almost beyond his strength. Sleep was binding his brows with oblivion, and relaxing every joint. His dearest concerns were nothing to him ; with a wave of the hand he would have resigned an eternity of love ; cry to him blood-chilling horrors, and his eyelids would make no sign. The feather-softness moulded itself to his limbs ; the pillows pressed a yielding coolness to his cheek ; his senses failed amid faint fresh odours. Blessed state ! How enviable above all waking joys the impotence which makes us lords of darkness, the silence which suffers not to reach our ears so much as an echo of the farce of life.

CHAPTER XV.

MRS. BAXENDALE'S GUESTS.

A SERVANT went to Banbrigg each morning for tidings ; Emily, so the report said, moved steadily towards recovery. On the second day after Wilfrid's arrival Mrs. Baxendale took him with her in the brougham, and let him wait for her whilst she made a call upon Mrs. Hood ; Wilfrid saw an upper window of which the blind was down against the sun, and would gladly have lingered within sight of it. Beatrice had excused herself from accompanying the two.

'I believe,' Mrs. Baxendale said on the way, 'she has gone to some special service at St. Luke's.' She was mistaken, though Beatrice had in truth been diligent at such services of late. 'Now there,' she added, 'is a kind of infatuation I find it difficult even to understand. How can a girl of her sense and education waste her time in that way? Don't think I have no religious belief, Mr. Athel; I'm not strong-minded enough for that. But this deliberate working of oneself into a state of nervous excitement seems to me, to speak plainly, indecent. Dr. Wardle, with whom I chat rather wickedly now and then, tells me the revivals are quite a windfall, subsequently, to him and his brethren. And, do you know, I begin to see bad results even in my niece. I certainly wouldn't have had her down just at this time if I had suspected her leanings that way. Didn't you notice how absent she was last night, and again at breakfast this morning? All revival, I assure you.'

'It's the want of a serious interest in life,' remarked Wilfrid, remembering, with a smile, a certain conversation between Beatrice and himself.

'Then it's so inconsistent,' continued the lady, 'for—you won't abuse my confidence—a more worldly girl I never knew. In her heart I am convinced she thinks nothing so important as the doings of fashionable society. She asked me, the first day she was here, how I lived without—what was it? I quite forget, but some paper or other which is full of what they call fashionable intelligence. "My dear," I said, "I know none of those people, and care not one grain of salt about their flutterings hither and thither, their marryings and givings in marriage, their dresses and their—never mind what." And what do you think she answered? "But you will care when my name begins to be mentioned." And she went off with—just so much—toss of the head; you know how Beatrice does it. Well, I suppose she really does to me an honour by coming down to my poor dull house; no doubt she's very brilliant in the world I know nothing about. I suppose you have seen her at her best? She won't waste her graces upon me, wise girl; only the—you know the movement—when I've shown my ignorance now and then. Did you ever dance with her?'

'Oh, yes; frequently.'

'I should like to see her in a ball-room. Certainly there are few girls more handsome; I suppose that is admitted?'

'Certainly; she queens it everywhere.'

'And her singing is lovely! Do you know a thought I often have? When I hear her singing it seems to me as if she were not quite the same person as at other times; she affects me, I can't quite tell you how; it's a sort of disenchantment to talk to her immediately afterwards.'

Wilfrid liked Mrs. Baxendale the more, the more he talked with her; in a day or two the confidence between them was as complete as if their acquaintance had been life-long. With her husband, too, he came to be on an excellent footing. Mr. Baxendale got him into the library when the ladies retired for the night, and expatiated for hours on the details of his electoral campaign. At first Wilfrid found the subject tedious, but the energy and bright intelligence of the man ended by stirring his interest in a remarkable way. It was new to Wilfrid to be in converse with such a strenuously practical mind; the element of ambition in him, of less noble ambition which had had its share in urging him to academic triumphs, was moved by sympathetic touches; he came to understand the enthusiasm which possessed the Liberal candidate, began to be concerned for his success, to feel the stirrings of party spirit. He aided Baxendale in drawing up certain addresses for circulation, and learned the difference between literary elegance and the tact which gets at the ear of the multitude. A vulgar man could not have moved him in this way, and Baxendale was in truth anything but vulgar. Through his life he had been, on a small scale, a ruler of men, and had ruled with conspicuous success, yet he had preserved a native sincerity and wrought under the guidance of an ideal. Like all men who are worth anything, either in public or private, he possessed a keen sense of humour, and was too awake to the ludicrous aspects of charlatanry to fall into the pits it offered on every hand. His misfortune was the difficulty with which he uttered himself; even when he got over his nervousness, words came to him only in a rough-and-tumble fashion; he sputtered and fumed and beat his forehead for phrases, then ended with a hearty laugh at his own inarticulateness. Something like this was his talk in the library of nights:

'There's a man called Rapley, an old-clothes dealer—

fellow I can't get hold of. He's hanging midway—what do you call it?—trimming, with an eye to the best bargain. Invaluable, if only I could get him, but a scoundrel. Wants pay, you know; do anything for pay; win the election for me without a doubt, if only I pay him; every blackguard in Dunfield hand and glove with him. Now pay I won't, yet I'm bound to get that man. Talked to him yesterday for two hours and thirty-five minutes by the parish church clock, just over his shop—I mean the clock is. The fellow hasn't a conviction, yet he can talk you blue; if I had his powers of speech —there it is I fail, you see. I have to address a meeting tomorrow; Rapley 'll be up at me, and turn me inside out. He'd do as much for the other man, if only I'd pay him. That isn't my idea; I'm going to win the election cleanhanded; satisfaction in looking back on an honest piece of work; what? I'll have another talk with him to-morrow. Now look at this map of the town; I've coloured it with much care. There you see the stronghold of the Blues. I'm working that district street by street—a sort of moral invasion. No humbug; I set my face against humbug. If a man's a rogue, or a sot, or a dirty rascal, I won't shake hands with him and pretend—you know—respect, friendship, how are your wife and children, so on. He's a vote, and I've only to deal with him as a vote. Can he see that two and two make four? Good; I'm at him by that side. There are my principles; what have you to urge against them? He urges damned absurdities. Good; I *prove* to him that they are damned absurdities.'

At times Wilfrid managed to lead the talk to other subjects, such as were suggested by the books around the room. Baxendale had read not a little, and entirely in the spheres of fact and speculation. Political economy and all that appertained to it was his speciality, but he was remarkably strong in metaphysics. Wilfrid had flattered himself that he was tolerably familiar with the highways of philosophy, but Baxendale made him feel his ignorance. The man had, for instance, read Kant with extraordinary thoroughness, and discussed him precisely as he did his electioneering difficulties; the problems of consciousness he attacked with hard-headed, methodical patience, with intelligence, moreover, which was seldom at fault. Everything that bore the appearance of a knot to be unravelled had for him an immense attraction. In mere mental calculation his power was amazing. He took

Wilfrid over his manufactory one day, and explained to him certain complicated pieces of machinery; the description was not so lucid as it might have been, owing to lack of words, but it manifested the completest understanding of things which to his companion were as hard as the riddle of the universe. His modesty, withal, was excessive; to Wilfrid's humane culture he deferred at all times; for all the learning which lay outside his own sphere he had boundless reverence. Wilfrid's gain by him was not only of a pleasant personal acquaintance; the intercourse extended his views, and in particular gave direction to much that had hitherto been vague potentiality in his character. In more than one sense this visit to Dunfield was to prove a turning point in his life.

Beatrice, in the meantime, held herself apart; Wilfrid had never before felt himself so little at ease in her presence. It was as though the short time which had elapsed since their last meeting had effected a permanent change in their mutual relations. Previously their intercourse had gone as far in familiarity as was possible if it were not to take quite a new colour; now all at once this past seemed to go for nothing. Beatrice was the active source of change. She was deliberately—he could not doubt it—extending the distance between them, annulling bygone intimacy, shifting into ineffective remoteness all manner of common associations. Things she would formerly have understood at a half-word she now affected to need to have explained to her. He was 'Mr. Athel' to an extent he had never been before; and even of his relatives she spoke with a diminished familiarity. She emphasised at every moment the characteristics which were alien to his sympathies, talked of the 'revival' *ad nauseam*, or changed with alarming suddenness from that to topics of excessive frivolousness. Wilfrid little by little ceased to converse with her, in the real sense of the word; he even felt uncomfortable in her presence. And Mrs. Baxendale had clear eyes for at all events the outward features of the situation.

On the fifth day of Wilfrid's presence in the house, Beatrice took the opportunity of being alone with her aunt to observe that she must go southwards by a certain train next morning.

'Oh, surely not!' protested Mrs. Baxendale. 'I can't spare you yet. And your mother is still in Berkshire.'

'Yes, but that makes no difference to me, you know,' said

Beatrice. 'I'm often at home by myself. Indeed I must go to-morrow.'

'Won't you stay if I beg you? It's four years since you were here, and who knows how long it will be before I entrap you again. You've already threatened me, you know, with the peerage, and I'm very sure you won't deign to honour me when that day comes. Now, there's a good girl—to the end of the week at least.'

It seemed as though Beatrice would persist.

'Now, if it were not such an unlikely thing,' said her aunt, 'I should be disposed to think it was Mr. Athel who is driving you away.'

'Mr. Athel!' the girl exclaimed, almost haughtily, and with a flush which disappeared as rapidly as it came, leaving the lovely face with a touch of exquisite paleness.

'I mean,' said Mrs. Baxendale quickly, averting her honest eyes, 'that I fear he has offended you.'

'How can Mr. Athel have offended me?' Beatrice asked, with a certain severity.

'I thought perhaps—a remark he made last night on the revival.'

Mrs. Baxendale felt ill at ease. Her first sentence had been inconsiderate; she knew it as soon as it was uttered, and indeed did not quite see what could have induced her to make such a remark. She had not the habit of nice conversation which endows with complete command of the tongue. But her wits had, as you see, come to her rescue.

'Mr. Athel's opinions on that subject are not likely to offend me,' Beatrice replied, with the shadow of a smile.

'I am so afraid lest he should suspect anything of the kind. I am sure it would grieve him dreadfully.'

The girl laughed outright, though not with much joyousness.

'Mr. Athel be grieved for such a cause! My dear aunt, you don't know him. He's as little sensitive as any man could be. Why, he holds it a duty to abuse people who do things he counts foolish.'

'You exaggerate,' returned her aunt, with a smile.

Beatrice continued, vivaciously.

'Oh, you don't know him as well as I do. We used to be always wrangling—in the days of my simplicity. I have been marvelling at his forbearance; it would have been nothing wonderful if he had called me an idiot. Frankness of that kind is the mark of his friendship—haven't you found that out? Hasn't he taken occasion yet to inform you that your life is conducted on an utterly mistaken principle, that you are shallow and inefficient, that you are worse than useless in the world, and ought, if properly constituted, to be a torment to yourself? None of these things he has said? Oh, then you are not admitted to Mr. Athel's intimacy; you are not of the inner circle.'

She spoke with a kind of reckless gaiety, a mocking merriment which her rich voice and command of facial expression made very effective. It startled her hearer, who, when the girl ceased, took one of her hands and patted it kindly.

'Why then,' she said, 'I have been altogether mistaken; for I did really think he had offended you. But now I'm sure you'll stay—won't you?'

'Rather than you should think I run away from Mr. Athel's high censure—certainly.'

Then she became silent, and shortly left the room. Mrs. Baxendale sat by herself musing.

She was a woman given to thoughtfulness, for all that she used her tongue freely when with those she liked. She did not greatly seek such society as Dunfield had to offer, and partly on that account, partly owing to alarms excited by her caustic comments on matters of popular interest, the ladies of the town left her abundance of leisure. She used it well. Though not a highly-educated woman, she read constantly, and books of a solid kind. Society in Dunfield had its book club, and Mrs. Baxendale enjoyed the advantage of choosing literature which her fellow-members were very willing to let her keep as long as she liked. Beatrice derived much amusement from her aunt's method of reading. Beatrice, with the run of Mr. Mudie's catalogues, would have half-a-dozen volumes in her lap at the same time, and as often as not get through them—*tant bien que mal*—in the same day. But to the provincial lady a book was a solid and serious affair. To read a chapter was to have provided matter for a day's reflection; the marker was put at the place where reading had ceased, and the book was not re-opened till previous matter had been thoroughly digested and assimilated. It was a slow method, but not without its advantages, I assure you.

Perhaps to relieve her worthy aunt of any lingering

anxiousness, Beatrice, throughout the day, wore an appearance of much contentment, and to Wilfrid was especially condescending, even talking with him freely on a subject quite unconnected with her pet interests. That evening two gentlemen, politicians, dined at the house; Beatrice, under cover of their loud discussions in the drawing-room, exchanged certain remarks with Wilfrid.

'My aunt was so good as to apologise to me on your behalf this morning,' she began.

'Apologise? What have I been guilty of?'

'Oh, nothing. She doesn't appreciate the freemasonry between us. It occurred to her that your remarks on my—well, my predilections, might have troubled me. Judge how amused I was!'

She did not look at him from the first, and appeared to be examining, even whilst she spoke, a book of prints.

'I sincerely hope,' Wilfrid replied, 'that I have uttered no thoughtless piece of rudeness. If I have, I beg you to forgive me.'

She glanced at him. He appeared to speak seriously, and it was the kind of speech he would never have dreamed of making to her in former days, at all events in this tone.

'You know perfectly well,' she answered, with slow voice, bending to look more closely at a page, 'that you never said anything to me which could call for apology.'

'I am not so sure of that,' Wilfrid replied, smiling.

'Then take my assurance now,' said Beatrice, closing her book, and rising to move towards her aunt. As she went, she cast a look back, a look of curious blankness, as if into vacancy.

She sang shortly after, and the souls of the politicians were stirred within them. For Wilfrid, he lay back with his eyes closed, his heart borne on the flood of music to that pale-windowed room of sickness, whose occupant must needs be so sadly pale. The security he felt in the knowledge that Emily grew better daily made him able to talk cheerfully and behave like one without preoccupation, but Emily in truth was never out of his mind. He lived towards the day when he should kneel at her feet, and feel once more upon his forehead those cold, pure lips. And that day, as he believed, was now very near.

To her aunt's secret surprise, Beatrice allowed the end of the week to come and go without any allusion to the subject of departure. It was all the more strange, seeing that the girl's show of easy friendliness with Wilfrid had not lasted beyond the day; she had become as distant and self-centred as before. But on the morning of the following Tuesday, as Mrs. Baxendale sat reading not long after breakfast, Beatrice entered the room in her light travelling garb, and came forward, buttoning her glove.

'You are going out?' Mrs. Baxendale asked, with some misgiving.

'Yes—to London. They are calling a cab. You know how I dislike preparatory miseries.'

Her aunt kept astonished silence. She looked at the girl, then down at her book.

'Well,' she said at length, 'it only remains to me to remember the old proverb. But when is the train? Are you off this moment?'

'The train leaves in five-and-twenty minutes. May I disturb uncle, do you think?'

'Ah, now I understand why you asked if he would be at home through the morning. I'll go and fetch him.'

She went quickly to the library. Mr. Baxendale sat there alone.

'Beatrice is going,' she said, coming behind his chair. 'Will you come and say good-bye?'

Mr. Baxendale jumped up.

'Going? Leaving?'

His wife nodded.

'Why? What is it? You haven't quarrelled with her about the prayer-meetings?'

'No. It's a fancy of hers, that's all. Come along; she's only twenty minutes to catch the train.'

When they reached the drawing-room, Beatrice was not there. Upon Mrs. Baxendale's withdrawal she had gone to Wilfrid's door and knocked at it. Wilfrid was pacing about in thought. It surprised him to see who his visitor was; yet more, when she advanced to him with her hand extended, saying a simple 'Good-bye.'

'Good-bye? Wherefore?'

Her attire explained. Beatrice possessed the beauty of form and face which makes profit of any costume; in the light-brown cape, and hat to match, her tall, lithe figure had a womanly dignity which suited well with the unsmiling expressiveness of her countenance. The 'good-bye' was uttered briefly and without emphasis, as one uses any insignificant form of speech.

Wilfrid resolved at once to accept her whim ; after all, it was but another instance of frequent eccentricities.

'Who is going to the station with you?' he asked.

'No one. I hate partings on the platform.'

She moved away almost as far as the door, then turned again.

'You will be in town before going back to Oxford?'

Wilfrid hesitated.

'Oh, never mind,' she said ; and was gone.

Ten minutes later Wilfrid went to the drawing-room. Mr. and Mrs. Baxendale were talking together ; they became silent as he entered.

'Has Miss Redwing gone?' he asked.

'She took leave of you, didn't she?' replied the lady.

'Yes. But it was so unprepared for, I half thought it might be a joke.'

'Oh, she's fond of these surprises,' Mrs. Baxendale said, in a tone of good-natured allowance. 'On the whole I sympathise with her ; I myself prefer not to linger over such occasions.'

Later in the day Mrs. Baxendale drove out to Banbrigg, this time alone. On her return, she sought Wilfrid and found him in his room. There was concern on her face.

'I have heard something very painful from Mrs. Hood,' she began. 'It seems that Emily is in ignorance of her father's death.'

Wilfrid looked at her in astonishment.

'I told you,' Mrs. Baxendale pursued, 'that she had not been altogether well just before it happened, but it now appears that the dreadful incident of her entering the room just when the body was brought in must have taken place when she was delirious. The poor woman has had no suspicion of that ; but it is proved by Emily's questions, now that she begins to talk. Of course it makes a new anxiety. Mrs. Hood has not dared to hint at the truth, but it cannot be concealed for long.'

'But this is most extraordinary,' Wilfrid exclaimed. 'What, then, was the origin of her illness?'

'That is the mystery. Mrs. Hood's memory seems to be confused, but I got her to allow that the feverish symptoms were declared even the night before the death was known.

I hardly like to hint it, but it really seemed to me as if she were keeping something back. One moment she said that Emily had been made ill by anxiety at her father's lateness in coming home that night, and the next she seemed, for some reason, unwilling to admit that it was so. The poor woman is in a sad, sad state, and no wonder. She wishes that somebody else might tell Emily the truth; but surely it will come most easily from her.'

Wilfrid was deeply distressed.

'It is the very worst that still remains,' he said, 'and we thought the worst was over. What does the doctor say? Can she bear it yet? It is impossible to let her continue in ignorance.'

It was at length decided that Mrs. Baxendale should visit the doctor, and hear his opinion. She had got into her mind a certain distrust of Mrs. Hood, and even doubted whether Emily ought to be left in her hands during convalescence; there was clearly no want of devotion on the mother's part, but it appeared to Mrs. Baxendale that the poor woman had been overtaxed, and was herself on the point of illness, perhaps of mental failure. From going well things had suddenly taken an anxious turn.

CHAPTER XVI.

RENUNCIATION.

WHEN Emily returned from the wastes of ravaged mind, and while yet the images of memory were hardly distinguished from the ghosts of delirious dream, the picture that haunted her with most persistency, with an objective reality the more impressive the clearer her thought became, was one which she could least comprehend or account for. She saw lying before her a closely muffled form, the outline seeming to declare it that of a man. The struggle of new-born consciousness was to associate such a vision with the events which had preceded her illness. Perchance for a day, perchance only for an hour, however long the unmeasured transition from darkness to the dawn of self-knowledge, she suffered the oppression of this mechanical questioning. At length the presence of her mother by the bedside became a fact, and it led on to the thought of her father. Her eyes moved in search for him.

The act of speech, in health a mere emphasis of thought, was only to be attained by repetition of efforts ; several times she believed herself to have spoken whilst silence still pressed her lips. Only when the recollection of her last waking day was complete, and when the absence of her father from the room linked itself to memory of her anguished waiting for him, did she succeed in uttering the words which represented her fear. Her mother was bending over her, aware of the new light in her questioning eyes.

'Where's father?' Emily asked.

'You shall see him, dear,' was the reply. 'Don't speak.'

'He came home?'

'Yes, he came home.'

Emily fell back into thought ; this great fear allayed, the past continued to rebuild itself within her mind. And now, only now, like an angel coming from afar over dark waters, there gleamed the image of her love. It had been expelled from memory by the all-possessing woe of those last hours ; it returned like a soothing warmth, an assuagement of pain. As though soul-easing music sounded about her, she again lost her hold on outward things and sank into a natural sleep.

Mrs. Hood feared the next waking. The question about her father, she attributed to Emily's incomplete command of her faculties, for she had not doubted that the muffled figure on the couch had been consciously seen by the girl and understood. Yet with waking the error prolonged itself ; it became evident at length that Emily knew nothing of her coming down to the sitting-room, and still had to learn that her father no longer lived. It was a new suffering under which the poor woman gave way. Already her natural affliction was complicated with a sense of painful mysteries ; in her delirium, Emily had uttered words which there was no explaining, but which proved that there had been some hidden connection between her mental trouble and her father's failure to return at the usual hour. Dagworthy's name she had spoken frequently, and with words which called to mind the sum of money her father had somehow procured. Mrs. Hood had no strength to face trials such as these. As long as her child's life seemed in danger, she strove with a mother's predominant instinct to defend it ; but her powers failed as Emily passed out of peril. Her outlook became blank; physical exhaustion joined with mental suffering began to render her incapable of further efforts. Fortunately, Mrs. Baxendale perceived this in time. A nurse was provided, in addition to the one who had assisted Mrs. Hood, and the mother became herself the object of care.

Emily had been told that her father was ill, but this fiction it was soon impossible to maintain. Three days after the last reported conversation between Wilfrid and Mrs. Baxendale, it was determined that the latter must take upon herself the office of telling Emily the truth. Mrs. Hood implored her to do so; the poor mother was sinking into a state which scarcely left her the command of her mind, and, though she could not sustain the duty herself, it was her harassing desire that it might quickly be performed. So at length the revelation was made, made with all the forbearance and strengthening tenderness of which a strong-souled woman is capable. But the first syllables prepared Emily for the whole truth. A secret dread, which she had not dared to confess to herself on that last evening, though probably it brought about the crisis in her suffering, and which the false assurances recently given her had perhaps not wholly overcome, rushed forth as soon as evil was hinted at. The softened statement that her father had been stricken down by a natural malady did not for a moment deceive her. She closed her eyes; the pillows which supported her were scarcely whiter than her face. But she was soon able to speak with perfect self-control.

'Was he brought home wrapped in something?' she asked. 'With his face covered?'

'He was, Emily.'

'How and where did I see him? For I know I did see him.'

'Your mother has told me that you rose from your bed, and went to the room below. She did not realise that you were unconscious; she believed that you knew of this.'

This was her dread vision. As if to protect herself from it, she raised her hand and laid it across her eyes. Then it fell again to the coverlet—thin, flower-like hand, which in its translucency of flesh seemed to have been created by spirit for its chosen abode.

When silence had lasted some moments—

'Now that I know he is dead,' Emily resumed—oh, the

sad music of the last word!—' I can bear to hear the manner
of it without disguise. Will you tell me the whole truth, Mrs.
Baxendale?'

It was spoken like herself. Ever clinging to sincerity,
ever ready to face the truth of things, in how many a matter
of less moment had the girl spoken with just this directness, inspiring respect in all who heard her clear, candid
voice.

Mrs. Baxendale sank her eyes, and hesitated.

'He died by his own hand,' Emily said, below her
breath.

The lady kept silence. Emily again closed her eyes, and,
as she so lay, felt warm lips touch her forehead.

Mrs. Baxendale believed for a moment that the sufferer
had lost consciousness, but the utterance of her name caused
Emily to raise her lids.

' Why did he do this?' she asked, regarding her friend
fixedly.

' No one can say, dear.'

Emily drew a deep sigh; a gleam passed over her face.

' There was an inquest?' she asked.

' Yes.'

' Is it possible for me to see a newspaper in which it was
reported?'

' If you really desire it,' said Mrs. Baxendale, with hesitation.

' I do; I wish to read it. Will you do me that great
kindness?'

' I will bring it you in a day or two. But would it not be
better to delay——'

' Is there anything,' Emily asked quickly, ' that you have
kept from me?'

' Nothing; nothing.'

'Then I need not put off reading it. I have borne the
worst.'

As Mrs. Baxendale left the house, she was passed at a
short distance along the road by a man on horseback. This
rider gave a sign to the coachman to stop, and a moment
after presented himself at the window of the brougham. It
was Dagworthy; he wished to have news of Mrs. and Miss
Hood. The lady gave him full information.

' I fear I could not see Mrs. Hood?' Dagworthy said.

' Oh, she is far too ill!' was the reply.

Having assured himself on this point, Dagworthy took his leave, and, when the carriage was remote, rode to the house. He made fast the reins to the gate, entered, and knocked at the door. A girl who did subordinate work for the nurses opened.

'I want you,' Dagworthy said, 'to give this note at once to Miss Hood. You understand?—to Miss Hood. Will you do so?'

'I will, sir.'

He went away, and, immediately after, Emily was reading these lines:

'I wish to tell you that no one has heard, and no one ever will, of the circumstances you would desire to have unknown. I send this as soon as you are able to receive it. You will know from whom it comes.'

She knew, and the message aided her. The shock of what she had just heard was not, in its immediate effect, as severe as others had feared it would be. Perhaps Emily's own sojourn at the gates of death lessened the distance between her and him who had passed them; perhaps the vast misery which lay behind her, the darkness threatening in the future, brought first to her mind death's attribute of deliverance. This, in the hours that followed, she strove to dwell upon; nothing could touch her father now, he was safe from trouble. But, as the current in her veins grew warmer, as life held her with a stronger hand and made her once more participant in his fears and desires, that apparition of the motionless veiled form haunted her with access of horror. If she slept it came into her dreams, and her waking thoughts strove with hideous wilfulness to unmuffle that dead face. When horror failed, its place was taken by a grief so intense that it shook the fabric of her being. She had no relapse in health, but convalescence was severed from all its natural joys; she grew stronger only to mourn more passionately. In imagination she followed her father through the hours of despair which must have ensued on his interview with Dagworthy. She pictured his struggle between desire to return home, to find comfort among those he loved, and the bitter shame which forbade it. How had he spent the time? Did he wander out of the town to lonely places, until daylight failed? Did he then come back under the shadow of the night, come back all but to the very door of his dwelling, make one last effort to face those within, pass on in blind agony? Was he on the

heath at the very hour when she crossed it to go to Dag-
werthy's house? Oh, had that been *his* figure which, as she
hurried past, she had seen moving in the darkness of the
quarry?

A pity which at times grew too vast for the soul to con-
tain absorbed her life, the pity which overwhelms and crushes,
which threatens reason. That he should have lived through
long years of the most patient endurance, keeping ever a
hope, a faith, so simple-hearted, so void of bitter feeling, so
kindly disposed to all men—only to be vanquished at length
by a moment of inexplicable weakness, only to creep aside,
and hide his shame, and die. Her father, whom it was her
heart's longing to tend and cherish through the brighter days
of his age—lying there in his grave, where no voice could
reach him, remote for ever from the solace of loving kindness,
his death a perpetuation of woe. The cruelty of fate had exhausted itself; what had the world to show more pitiful than
this?

No light ever came to her countenance; no faintest smile
ever touched her lips. Through the hours, through the days,
she lay heedless of things around her, solely occupied with
the past, with affliction, with remorse. Had it not been in
her power to save him? A word from her, and at this
moment he would have been living in cheerfulness such as
he had never known. She would have had but to turn her
head, and his smile would have met her; the rare laugh, so
touching to her always, would have become less rare; his
struggles would have been over. She had willed that he
should die, had sent him forth relentlessly to his last trial,
to his forsaken end. Without a leave-taking he had gone
forth; his last look had been at her blank windows. That
hour was passed into eternity, and with it the better part of
her life.

On the first day that she rose from her bed, she went,
with the nurse's aid, to her mother's room. What she saw
there was a new shock; her mother's face had aged incredibly,
and wore a look of such feeble intelligence that to meet her
eyes was more than painful. Upon the artificial maintenance
of her strength throughout Emily's illness had followed a
collapse of the vital powers; it seemed doubtful whether she
would ever regain her normal state of mind and body. She
knew her daughter, and, when Emily kissed her, the muscles
of her haggard face contracted in what was meant for a smile;

but she could not use her voice above a whisper, and her words were seldom consequent.

Two days later Mrs. Baxendale again paid a visit. Emily was sitting in her bed-room, unoccupied, on her countenance the sorrow-stricken gravity which never quitted it. The visitor, when she had made her inquiries, seemed to prepare herself to speak of some subject at once important and cheerful.

'For a fortnight,' she said, 'I have had staying with me someone whom you will be glad to hear of—your nearest friend.'

Emily raised her eyes slowly to the speaker's face; clearly she understood, but was accustoming herself to this unexpected relation between Mrs. Baxendale and Wilfrid.

'Mr. Athel came from Switzerland as soon as he heard of your illness.'

'How did he hear?' Emily inquired, gravely.

'My niece, Miss Redwing, whom you knew, happened to be visiting me. She wrote to Mrs. Rossall.'

Emily was silent. The lines of her mouth showed a slight tremor, but no colour sought her cheeks. The news was affecting her strongly, but only in the way in which she now received every impression; physical weakness had the effect of reducing outward demonstration of feeling, and her spiritual condition favoured passiveness.

'He has asked me to give you a letter, Emily,' pursued Mrs. Baxendale, saddened by the sight of such intense sadness.

Emily took the letter, and laid it on a table near her, murmuring her thanks.

'He is well?' she asked, as the other did not speak.

'Quite; his holiday has completely restored him. You can't think how glad I am to have come to know him, and to have him near me. Such excellent friends we are! You can think how anxious he has been; and his father scarcely less so. The inquiries have been constant. The others have just got home; Mr. Athel had a letter from London this morning. The little girls send you a message; I believe you will find the letter enclosed.'

At the mention of the twins, the slightest smile came upon Emily's lips.

'You are fond of them, I see,' said the lady. 'That they are fond of you, needs no telling. Oh, and Clara writes from

Germany to ask if she may write to you yet. Shall I let
her ? '

A few more words, and Mrs. Baxendale rose. Emily re-
tained her hand.

'You have not yet had from me one word of gratitude,
Mrs. Baxendale,' she said. 'Indeed, I have no words in
which to thank you.'

The lady kissed her forehead, pressed the thin hand again,
and went for a few moments to Mrs. Hood's room before de-
parting.

It was nearly an hour before Emily took up the letter to
open it. When at length she did so, she found that it
covered only a small sheet of notepaper. Enclosed was a
letter from Mr. Athel, announcing the family's arrival in
London, asking in a kind tone for the latest news, and repeating the message from the twins of which Mrs. Baxendale had
spoken. Wilfrid wrote with admirable delicacy and feeling ;
he forgot himself wholly in her affliction, and only in those
simplest words which can still be made the most powerful
uttered the tenderness which he hoped might speak some
comfort to her heart. He did not ask to see her ; would she
not bid him come to her in her own good time? And only if
her strength rendered it quite easy, he begged for one word of
reply. Mrs. Baxendale would visit her again very shortly,
and to her the answer could be given.

Emily returned the writings to their envelope, and sat
through the day as she had sat since morning, scarcely ever
moving, without heed of things that were said or done in the
room. Before quitting the chair for her bed, she went to
spend a quarter of an hour by her mother, whose hand she
held throughout the time. Mrs. Hood lay in the same state
of semi-consciousness alternating with sleep. In the night
she generally wandered a little. But she did not seem to
suffer pain.

To-night Emily could not sleep ; hitherto her rest had been
profound between sunset and early morning. As she had sat
through the day, so she lay now, her eyes fixed in the same
intent gaze, as on something unfolding itself before her.
When the nurses had ceased to move about, the house was
wrapped in a stillness more complete than of old, for the
clock had not been touched since the night when the weight
fell. In the room you might have heard now and then a deep
sigh, such sigh as comes from a soul overcharged.

Mrs. Baxendale allowed one day to intervene, then came again. She did not directly speak of Wilfrid, and only when she sat in significant silence, Emily said :

'To-morrow I shall go downstairs. Will you ask Mr. Athel to come and see me ? '

' Gladly I will. At what hour shall he come ? '

' I shall be down by eleven.'

Later in the day, Mrs. Cartwright and Jessie called. Hitherto Emily had begged that no one might be admitted save Mrs. Baxendale; she felt it would be unkindness to refuse her friends any longer, and the visitors came up and sat for a while with her. Both were awed by the face which met them; they talked scarcely above a whisper, and were sadly troubled by the necessity of keeping a watch upon their tongues.

Emily was now able to descend the stairs without difficulty. The first sight of the little parlour cost her a renewal of her keenest suffering. There was the couch on which his dead body had been placed ; that the chair in which he always rested after tea before going up to the laboratory ; in a little frame on the mantelpiece was his likeness, an old one and much faded. She moved about, laying her hand on this object and that ; she took the seat by the window where she had waited each evening, till she saw him at the gate, to rise at once and open to him. She had not shed tears since that last day of his life, and now it was only a passing mist that dimmed her eyes. Her sorrow was not of the kind which so relieves itself.

She had come down early, in order to spend some time in the room before Wilfrid's arrival She sat in her father's chair, once more in the attitude of motionless brooding. But her countenance was not as self-controlled as during the past days; emotions, struggles, at work within her found their outward expression. At times she breathed quickly, as if in pain ; often her eyes closed. In her worn face, the features marked themselves with strong significance ; it was beauty of a kind only to be felt by a soul in sympathy with her own. To others she would have appeared the image of stern woe. The gentleness which had been so readily observable beneath her habitual gravity was absorbed in the severity of her suffering and spiritual conflicts ; only a touching suggestion of endurance, of weakness bearing up against terrible fatality, made its plea to tenderness. Withal, she looked no older than in

the days of her happiness; a young life, a young heart,
smitten with unutterable woe.

When the sound of the opening gate made itself heard, she
lay back for a moment in the very sickness of pain; it recalled
the past so vividly, and chilled her heart with the fear of
what she had now before her. She stood, as soon as the
knock came at the front door, and kept the same position as
Wilfrid entered.

He was startled at the sight of her, but in an instant was
holding both her hands, gazing deep into her eyes with an
ecstasy of tenderness. He kissed her lips, and, as he did so,
felt a shudder in the hands he pressed. A few whispered
words were all that he could speak; Emily kept silence.
Then he sat near to her; her hand was still in his, but gave
no sign of responsive affection, and was very cold.

'It was kind to let me see you so soon,' he said. Her
fixed look of hard suffering began to impress him painfully,
even with a kind of fear. Emily's face at this moment was
that of one who is only half sensible to words spoken. Now
she herself spoke for the first time.

'You will forgive me that I did not write. It would have
been better, perhaps; it would have been easier to me. Yet
why should I fear to say to you, face to face, what I have to
say?'

The last sentence was like self-questioning uttered aloud;
her eyes were fixed on him, and with appeal which searched
his heart.

'Fear to say to me?' Wilfrid repeated, gravely, though
without apprehension. 'Has your suffering made strangers
of us?'

'Not in the way you mean, but it has so changed my life
that I cannot meet you as I should have done.' Her utterance quickened; her voice lost its steadiness. 'Will you be
very generous to me—as good and noble as it is in your heart
to be? I ask you to give me back my promise—to release
me.'

'Emily!'

He gazed at her in bewilderment. His thought was that
she was not herself; her manner since his entrance seemed to
confirm it; the tortured lines of her face seemed to express
illusory fears.

'Emily! Do you know what you say, dearest?'

'Yes; I know what I say, and I know how hard you find

it to believe me. If I could explain to you what it is that makes this change, you would not wonder at it, you would understand, you would see that I am doing the only thing I can do. But I cannot give you my reasons; that must be my sad secret to the end of my life. You feel you have a claim to hear the truth; indeed, indeed, you have; but you will be forbearing and generous. Release me, Wilfrid; I ask it as the last and greatest proof of the love you gave me.'

He rose with a gesture of desperation.

' Emily, I cannot bear this! You are ill, my own darling; I should have waited till you were stronger. I should have left you more time to turn your thoughts to me from these terrible things you have passed through.' He flung himself by her side, grasping her hands passionately. ' Dear one, how you have suffered! It kills me to look into your face. I won't speak; let me only stay by you, like this, for a few minutes. Will not my love calm you—love the purest and tenderest that man ever felt? I would die to heal your heart of its grief!'

With a great sob of uttermost anguish, she put back his hands, rose from the chair, and stood apart. Wilfrid rose and gazed at her in dread. Had the last calamity of human nature fallen upon her? He looked about, as if for aid Emily read his thoughts perfectly; they helped her to a desperate composure.

' Wilfrid,' she said, ' do I speak like one not in her perfect mind?'

' I cannot say. Your words are meaningless to me. You are not the Emily I knew.'

' I am not,' was her sad answer. ' If you can bring yourself to believe that truth, you will spare yourself and me.'

' What do you mean when you say that?' he asked, his voice intensified in suppression. ' If you are in full command of yourself, if your memory holds all the past, what can have made of you another being? We dare not play with words at a time such as this. Tell me at least one thing. Do I know what it was that caused your illness?'

' I don't understand you.'

Her eyes examined him with fear.

' I mean, Emily—was it solely due to that shock you received? Or was there any previous distress?'

' Has anything led you to think there was?' she asked, urgently.

' Mrs. Baxendale tells me you—Emily, why have I to pain you in this way ? '

' But tell me—tell me ! What did she say ? '

' That on coming to yourself you did not know of your father's death.'

' It is true ; I did not. My illness began before.'

Wilfrid stood with his eyes on the ground.

' Tell me, again,' she said. ' What else did Mrs. Baxendale say ? '

' Nothing. Her surprise when she heard this from your mother was as great as mine when it was repeated to me.'

' It is true,' Emily repeated, more calmly, as if relieved. ' I don't try to conceal that there is a reason I may not speak of. Will you not believe that it is strong enough to change my life ? If I did not tell you this, you might indeed refuse to listen to me, thinking I was not myself. I cannot tell you more—I cannot, I cannot ! '

She pressed her palms upon her forehead ; it throbbed with pain scarcely to be borne. Wilfrid, after a moment of wretched hesitation, said gravely :

' What *you* forbid me to ask, I may not even wish to know. I have come to regard your will as the seal upon everything that is true and right. Knowing this, seeing me here before you with my best hopes at stake, do you tell me that something has happened which makes the bond between us of no effect, which lays upon you a duty superior to that of the pledge you gave me ? '

She met his gaze, and answered firmly, ' I do.'

' Some duty,' he continued, with quivering voice, ' compared with which the sacredness of our love is nothing ? '

She trembled from head to foot ; then, as if clutching at a last help, said :

' I do not love you.'

And she waited with her head bowed. Wilfrid, taking up his hat, went to her and offered his hand. When hers was given :

' Raise your eyes and look at me, Emily.'

She did so.

' You are still in the shadow of a great grief, and it may well be that all other things seem trivial. I wish to respect you to the uttermost, and I will try to conceive that there is a motive high enough to justify you. But those last words must be repeated—when time has come to your aid—before I can regard them as final.'

He released her hand, and left her. . . .

What was her first sensation, when the door had closed, then the gate without, and Wilfrid in very deed was gone ? Was it hopeless misery, failure, dread foresight of the life which she still must live ?   Rather her mood was that of the martyr who has held firm to the last wrench of torture, who feels that agony is overcome and fear of self surpassed.   This possibility had there ever been in Emily, though associating with such variant instincts.   Circumstances had brought the occasion which weighed one part of her nature against the other, and with this result.

You may not judge her coldly; yet it is possible to indicate those points which connect her enthusiasm of sacrifice with the reasonings and emotions of the impartial mind.   In the moment that she heard of her father's self-destruction, she knew that her own destiny was cast ; the struggle with desire, with arguments of her self-love, with claims of others, this also she foresaw and measured.   Her resolve came of the interaction of intense feeling, feeling which only process of time could reduce from its morbid predominance, and that idealism which was the keynote of her personality.   It was not that she condemned herself for having refused to pay the price which would have saved her father ; she may have done so in her wildest paroxysms of grief, but in the silences which ensued she knew that there is an arbiter above natural affection, and that not with impunity could a life be purchased by the death of a soul.   She had refused ; it might be she would still have refused had she foreseen the worst ; but could she move on over her father's body to a life of joy ?   Not only did piety forbid it ; the compassionate voice of her heart cried against what she deemed such cruelty.   Her father was dead ; nothing that she did henceforth would concern him for good or ill ; none the less in her eyes was his claim upon her, the claim of one she had tenderly loved calling to her for pity from that desolate grave.   Which of us entirely out-reasons that surviving claim of the beloved dead ?   Which of us would, in his purest hour, desire to do so ?   She could not save him, but, as she valued her most precious human privileges, she dared not taste the fruits of life of which he was for ever robbed.   Between her and happiness loomed that agonising face.   She might disregard it, might close her eyes

and press on, might live down the old sacred pity and give
herself to absorbing bliss: what would be the true value of
that she gained? Nay, it was idle to affect that she had the
choice. She felt that the first memory of that face in the
midst of enjoyment would break her heart. Those last dark
hours of his she must live and relive in her own mind.
Dead? He was dead? Oh, did not the very tones of his
voice linger in the rooms where she sat? Could she not see
him enter, hold to her his hand, bend and kiss her? Did
she not fancy constantly that his foot sounded on the floor
above her, up in the bare little room, where she had parted
from him unkindly? Why, death meant but little, for at any
moment he was in truth standing by her. Years of unhappiness, and then to be put aside and forgotten as soon as the
heavy clods of earth had fallen upon him? To think of that
was to be driven almost to madness by the impotence of
grief. Rather than allow a joy to tempt her thought, she
would cast life from her and be his companion in that narrow
home.

And her character brought it about that the very strength
of her love for Wilfrid acted as another impulse to renunciation. Which had been the stronger motive in her refusal to
sacrifice herself—the preservation of her chaste womanhood,
or the inability to give up him she loved? Could she, at the
tribunal of her conscience, affirm that her decision had held
no mixture of the less pure? Nay, had she not known that
revolt of self in which she had maintained that the individual
love was supreme, that no title of inferiority became it? She
saw now more clearly than then the impossibility of distin-
guishing those two motives, or of weighing the higher and
the lower elements of her love. One way there was, and one
way only, of proving to herself that she had not fallen below
the worthiness which purest love demanded, that she had
indeed offered to Wilfrid a soul whose life was chastity—and
that must be utterly to renounce love's earthly reward, and
in spirit to be faithful to him while her life lasted. The pain
of such renunciation was twofold, for did she not visit him
with equal affliction? Had she the right to do that? The
question was importunate, and she held it a temptation of her
weaker self. Wilfrid would bear with her. He was of noble
nature, and her mere assurance of a supreme duty would out-
weigh his personal suffering. On him lay no obligation of
faithfulness to his first love; a man, with the world before

him, he would, as was right, find another to share his life.
To think that was no light test of steadfastness in Emily;
the image of Wilfrid loving and loved by another woman
wrung the sinews of her heart. That she must keep from
her mind; that was more than her strength could face and
conquer. It should be enough to love him for ever, without
hope, without desire. Faithfulness would cost her no effort;
to purify herself in ideal devotion would be her sustenance,
her solace.

What of her religion of beauty, the faith which had seen
its end in the nourishment of every instinct demanding loveliness within and without? What of the ideal which saw the
crown of life in passion triumphant, which dreaded imperfect-
ness, which allowed the claims of sense equally with those of
spirit, both having their indispensable part in the complete
existence? Had it not conspicuously failed where religion
should be most efficient? She understood now the timidity
which had ever lurked behind her acceptance of that view of
life. She had never been able entirely to divest herself of the
feeling that her exaltation in beauty-worship was a mood born
of sunny days, that it would fail amid shocks of misfortune
and prove a mockery in the hour of the soul's dire need. It
shared in the unreality of her life in wealthy houses, amid the
luxury which appertained only to fortune's favourites, which
surrounded her only by chance. She had presumptuously
taken to herself the religion of her superiors, of those to whom
fate allowed the assurance of peace, of guarded leisure
wherein to cultivate the richer and sweeter flowers of their
nature. How artificial had been the delights with which she
soothed herself! Here, all the time, was the reality; here in
this poor home, brooded over by the curse of poverty, whence
should come shame and woe and death. What to her now
were the elegance of art, the loveliness of nature? Beauty
had been touched by mortality, and its hues were of the corpse,
of the grave. Would the music of a verse ever again fill her
with rapture? How meaningless were all such toys of
thought to one whose path lay through the valley of desolation!

Thus did Emily think and feel in this sombre season, the
passionate force of her imagination making itself the law of
life and the arbiter of her destiny. She could not take counsel with time; her temperament knew nothing of that compromise with ardours and impulses which is the wisdom of

disillusion. Circumstances willed that she should suffer by
the nobleness of her instincts; those endowments which
might in a happier lot have exalted her to such perfection of
calm joy as humanity may attain, were fated to be the source
of misery inconceivable by natures less finely cast.

CHAPTER XVII.

THEIR SEVERAL WAYS.

As Wilfrid quitted the house, the gate was opened by Jessie
Cartwright, who, accompanied by one of her sisters, was
bringing Emily some fine grapes, purchased, in the Cartwright manner, without regard to expense. The girls naturally had their curiosity excited by the stranger of interesting,
even of aristocratic, appearance, who, as he hurried by, cast
at them a searching look.

'Now, who ever may that be?' murmured Jessie, as she
approached the door.

'A doctor, I dare say,' was her sister's suggestion.

'A doctor! Not he, indeed. He has something to do
with Emily, depend upon it.'

The servant, opening to them, had to report that Miss
Hood was too unwell to-day to receive visitors. Jessie would
dearly have liked to ask who it was that apparently had been
an exception, but even she lacked the assurance necessary to
the putting of such a question. The girls left their offering,
and went their way home; the stranger afforded matter for
conversation throughout the walk.

Wilfrid did not go straight to the Baxendales'. In his
distracted state he felt it impossible to sit through luncheon,
and he could not immediately decide how to meet Mrs. Baxendale, whether to take her into his confidence or to preserve
silence on what had happened. He was not sure that he
would be justified in disclosing the details of such an interview; did he not owe it to Emily to refrain from submitting
her action to the judgment of any third person? If in truth
she were still suffering from the effects of her illness, it was
worse than unkind to repeat her words; if, on the other hand,
her decision came of adequate motives, or such as her sound
intelligence deemed adequate, was it possible to violate the

confidence implied in such a conversation between her and himself? Till his mind had assumed some degree of calmness, he could not trust himself to return to the house. Turning from the main road at a point just before the bridge over the river, he kept on the outskirts of the town, and continued walking till he had almost made the circuit of Dunfield. His speed was that of a man who hastened with some express object; his limbs seemed spurred to activity by the gallop of his thoughts. His reason would scarcely accept the evidence of consciousness that he had indeed just heard such things from Emily's lips; it was too monstrous for belief; a resolute incredulity sustained him beneath a blow which, could he have felt it to be meant in very earnest, would have deprived him of his senses. She did not, she could not, know what she had said! Yet she spoke with such cruel appearance of reasoning earnestness; was it possible for a diseased mind to assume so convincingly the modes of rational utterance? What conceivable circumstances could bring her to such a resolution? Her words, 'I do not love you,' made horrible repetition in his ears; it was as though he had heard her speak them again and again. *Could they be true?* The question, last outcome of the exercise of his imagination on the track of that unimaginable cause, brought him to a standstill, physically and mentally. Those words had at first scarcely engaged his thought; it was her request to be released that seriously concerned him; that falsehood had been added as a desperate means of gaining her end. Yet now, all other explanations in vain exhausted, perforce he gave heed to that hideous chime of memory. It was not her father's death that caused her illness; that she admitted. Had some horrible complication intervened, some incredible change come upon her, since he left England? He shook off this suggestion as blasphemy. Emily? His high-souled Emily, upon whose faith he would stake the breath of his life? Was his own reason failing him?

Worn out, he reached the house in the middle of the afternoon, and went to his own sitting-room. Presently a servant came and asked whether he would take luncheon. He declined. Lying on the sofa, he still tormented himself with doubt whether he might speak with Mrs. Baxendale. That lady put an end to his hesitation by herself coming to his room. He sprang up.

'Don't move, don't move!' she exclaimed in her cheery

way. 'I have only come to ask why you resolve to starve yourself. You can't have had lunch anywhere ?'

'No; I am not hungry.'

'A headache?' she asked, looking at him with kind shrewdness.

'A little, perhaps.'

'Then at all events you will have tea. May I ask them to bring it here ?'

She went away, and, a few minutes after her return, tea was brought.

'You found Emily looking sadly, I'm afraid ?' she said, with one of the provincialisms which occasionally marked her language.

'Yes,' Wilfrid replied; 'she looked far too ill to be up.'

He had seated himself on the sofa. His hands would not hold the tea-cup steadily; he put it down by his side.

'I fear there is small chance of her getting much better in that house of illness,' said Mrs. Baxendale, observing his agitation. 'Can't we persuade her to go somewhere ? Her mother is in excellent hands.'

'I wish we could,' Wilfrid replied, clearly without much attention to his words.

'You didn't propose anything of the kind ?'

He made no answer. A short silence intervened, and he felt there was no choice but to declare the truth.

'The meeting was a very painful one,' he began. 'It is difficult to speak to you about it. Do you think that she has perfectly recovered ?—that her mind is wholly——'

He hesitated; it was dreadful to be speaking in this way of Emily. The sound of his voice reproached him; what words would not appear brutal in such a case ?

'You fear—— ?'

Wilfrid rose and walked across the room. It seemed impossible to speak, yet equally so to keep his misery to himself.

'Mrs. Baxendale,' he said at length, 'I am perhaps doing a very wrong thing in telling you what passed between us, but I feel quite unable to decide upon any course without the aid of your judgment. I am in a terrible position. Either I must believe Emily to speak without responsibility, or something inexplicable, incredible, has come to pass. She has asked me to release her. She says that something has happened which makes it impossible for her ever to fulfil her promise, something which must always remain her secret, which I may not hope to understand. And with such dreadful appearance of sincerity — such a face of awful suffering——'

His voice failed. The grave concern on Mrs. Baxendale's visage was not encouraging.

'Something happened?' the latter repeated, in low-toned astonishment. 'Does she offer no kind of explanation?'

'None—none,' he added, 'that I can bring myself to believe.'

Mrs. Baxendale could only look at him questioningly.

'She said,' Wilfrid continued, pale with the effort it cost him to speak, 'that she has no longer any affection for me.'

There was another silence, of longer endurance than the last. Wilfrid was the first to break it.

'My reason for refusing to believe it is, that she said it when she had done her utmost to convince me of her earnestness in other ways, and said it in a way—— How is it possible for me to believe it? It is only two months since I saw her on the Castle Hill.'

'I thought you had never been here before?'

'I have never spoken to you of that. I came and left on the same day. It was to see her before I went to Switzerland.'

'I am at a loss,' said Mrs. Baxendale. 'I can only suggest that she has had a terrible shock, and that her recovery, or seeming recovery, has been too rapid. Yet there is no trace of wandering in her talk with me.'

'Nor was there to-day. She was perfectly rational. Think of one's being driven to hope that she only *seemed* so!'

'Did you speak of correspondence?'

'No. I said that I could not agree to what she asked of me until she had repeated it after a time. I left her scarcely knowing what I spoke. What shall I do? How can I remain in doubt such as this? I said I wished for your help, yet how can you—how can anyone—help me? Have I unconsciously been the cause of this?'

'Or has anyone else consciously been so?' asked the lady, with meaning.

'What? You think—— ? Is it possible?'

'You only hinted that your relatives were not altogether pleased.'

Wilfrid, a light of anger flashing from his eyes, walked rapidly the length of the room.

'She admitted to me,' he said, in a suppressed voice, 'that her illness began before her father's death. It was not that that caused it. You think that someone may have interfered? My father? Impossible! He is a man of honour; he has written of her in the kindest way.'

But there was someone else. His father was honourable; could the same be said of Mrs. Rossall? He remembered his conversation with her on the lake of Thun; it had left an unpleasant impression on his mind—under the circumstances, explicable enough. Was his aunt capable of dastardly behaviour? The word could scarcely be applied to a woman's conduct, and the fact that it could not made disagreeably evident the latitude conceded to women in consideration of their being compelled to carry on warfare in underhand ways. Suppose an anonymous letter. Would not Mrs. Rossall regard that as a perfectly legitimate stratagem, if she had set her mind on resisting this marriage? Easy, infinitely easy was it to believe this, in comparison with any other explanation of Emily's behaviour. In his haste to seize on a credible solution of the difficulty, Wilfrid did not at first reflect that Emily was a very unlikely person to be influenced by such means, still more unlikely that she should keep such a thing secret from him. It must be remembered, however, that the ways of treachery are manifold, and the idea had only presented it to his mind in the most indefinite form. As it was, it drove him almost to frenzy. He could not find a calm word, nor was it indeed possible to communicate to Mrs. Baxendale the suspicion which occupied him. She, watching him as he stood at a distance, all but forgot her anxious trouble in admiration of the splendid passion which had transformed his features. Wilfrid looked his best when thus stirred—his best, from a woman's point of view. The pale cast of thought was far from him; you saw the fiery nature asserting itself, and wondered in what direction these energies would at length find scope. Mrs. Baxendale, not exactly an impressionable woman, had a moment of absent-mindedness.

'Come here and sit down,' she said, the motherly insistance of the tone possibly revealing her former thought.

He threw himself on the couch.

'Of course,' she continued, 'this must remain between Emily and yourself; my own relations to her must be precisely as they have been, as if I had heard nothing. Now I think we may conclude that the poor girl is perfectly aware of what she is doing, but I no more than yourself believe her explanation. In some way she has come to regard it as a duty to abandon you. Let Emily once think it a duty, and she will go through with it if it costs her life ; so much I know of her ; so much it is easy to know, if one has the habit of observing. May I advise you ? Do not try to see her again, but write briefly, asking her whether the mystery she spoke of in any way connects itself with you. You will know how to put it so as to exact the answer you require. Suppose you write such a note at once ; I will send it as soon as it is ready. You are in the torment of doubts ; no misery as bad as that. Does this plan recommend itself to you ? '

' Yes ; I will write.'

' Then I will take myself off whilst you do so. Ring the bell and send for me as soon as you are ready. It is only half-past four ; Emily will have your letter in an hour, and surely will reply at once.'

The letter was written, at greater length perhaps than was quite necessary, and Mrs. Baxendale speeded it on its way. Wilfrid begged that he might be excused from attendance at the dinner-table.

' By all means,' was Mrs. Baxendale's reply. ' The more so that we have politicians again, and I fear you would not be in the mood to make fun of them as you did the other night.'

' Make fun of them ? No, I was in earnest. I got interested in their subjects, and found I had more to say than I thought.'

' Well, well, that is your politeness. Now lie down again, poor boy. But you must promise to eat what I send you ; we have quite enough illness on our hands, remember.'

' I may have the answer before then,' Wilfrid said, moodily.

He had ; it came in less than two hours from the messenger's departure. He was alone when the servant brought it to him. Emily wrote :—

' Wilfrid,—The change is in myself, in my heart, in my life. Nothing have I heard against you ; nothing have I imagined against you ; the influence of which I spoke is in no way connected with you. Let this, I implore you, be final. Forgive me, forgive me, that I seem to inflict pain on you so heedlessly. I act as I must ; my purpose is unchangeable.'

Having been apprised of the messenger's return, Mrs. Baxendale entered Wilfrid's room as soon as she had dressed for dinner. He sat at the table, the letter lying open before him. As Mrs. Baxendale approached, he held the sheet to her.

'Then my last conjecture is fruitless,' she said, letting her hand fall. 'We cannot doubt her word.'

'Doubt it? No. There is nothing for me but to believe all she said.'

He let his face fall upon his hands; the bitterness of fate was entering his inmost heart.

'No, no, you shall not give way,' said his friend, just touching his fingers. 'It all looks very sad and hopeless, but I will not believe it is hopeless. Refuse to believe that one worst thing, the only thing for which there is no remedy. Come, defy yourself to believe it! You are strong enough for that; there is manhood in you for anything that is worth bearing, however hard.'

He could not reply to her encouragement; who cannot devise words of exhortation? and what idler than such words when the heart agonises?

'Try and listen to me, Wilfrid. If I make you angry with me, it is better than abandoning yourself to despondency. I firmly believe that this is a matter which time will bring right. Emily is acting hastily; I am convinced of that. Time is on your side; try and accept him as a friend. We are not living in a novel; there are no such things as mysteries which last a lifetime. Your part is to draw upon all the manliness you own, to have faith in yourself, and to wait. Have faith in her, too; there are few like her; some day you will see that this only made her better worth winning.—Now answer me a question.'

Wilfrid raised his head.

'Do you not in your heart believe that she is incapable of folly or wrongheadedness?'

'I believe that no truer woman lives.'

'And rightly, be sure of it. Believing that, you know she cannot break her word to you without some reason which you would yourself say was good and sufficient. She imagines she has such a reason; imagines it in all sincerity. Time will show her that she has been in error, and she will confess it. She has all her faculties, no doubt, but a trial such as this leads her to see things in ways we cannot realise.'

'You forget that it is *not* this shock that has so affected her.'

'Wilfrid, remember that her father's death is itself mysterious. She may know more of what led to it than anyone else does. She may very well have foreseen it; it may have distracted her, the cause, whatever it was. She could not disclose anything—some secret, perhaps—that nearly concerned her father; you know how strong were the ties between them.'

Perhaps it was inevitable that a suggestion of this kind should ultimately offer itself. Wilfrid had not hit upon the idea, for he had from the first accepted without reflection the reasons for Hood's suicide which were accepted by everyone who spoke of the subject. Mrs. Baxendale only delivered herself of the thought in fervour of kindly-devised argument. She paused, reviewing it in her mind, but did not like to lay more stress upon it. Wilfrid, also thoughtful, kept silence.

'Now, there's the gong,' Mrs. Baxendale continued, 'and I shall have to go to the politicians. But I think I *have* given you a grain of comfort. Think of a prosy old woman inciting *you* to endure for the sake of the greatest prize you can aim at? Keep saying to yourself that Emily cannot do wrong; if she did say a word or two she didn't mean—well, well, we poor women! Go to bed early, and we'll talk again after breakfast to-morrow.'

She gave him her hand, and hurried away. Even in his wretchedness, Wilfrid could not but follow her with his eyes, and *feel* something like a blessing upon her strong and tender womanhood.

Fortunate fellow, who had laid behind him thus much of his earthly journey without one day of grave suffering. Ah, something he should have sacrificed to the envious gods, some lesser joy, that the essential happiness of his life might be spared him. Wilfrid had yet to learn that every sun which rises for us in untroubled sky is a portent of inevitable gloom, that nature only prolongs our holiday to make the journey-work of misery the harder to bear. He had enjoyed the way of his will from childhood upwards; he had come to regard himself as exempt from ill-fortune, even as he was exempt from the degradation of material need; all his doings had prospered, save in that little matter of his overtaxed health, and it had grown his habit to map the future with a generous hand, saying: Thus and thus will I take my conquering course. Knowing love for the first time, he had met with love in return, love to the height of his desire, and with a wave of the hand he had swept the trivial obstacles from his path. Now that the very sum of his exultant youth offered itself like a wine-cup to his lips, comes forth the mysterious hand and spills relentlessly that divine draught. See how he turns, with the blaze of royal indignation on his brow ! Who of gods or men has dared thus to come between him and his bliss ? He is not wont to be so thwarted ; he demands that the cup shall be refilled and brought again ; only when mocking laughter echoes round him, when it is but too plain that the spirits no longer serve him, that where he most desires his power is least, does his resentment change by cold degrees to that chill anguish of the abandoned soul, which pays the debt of so many an hour of triumph. For the moment, words of kindness and sustaining hope might seem to avail him ; but there is the night waiting in ambush for his weakness, that season of the sun's silence, when the body denuded of vestment typifies the spirit's exposure to its enemies. Let him live through his fate-imposed trial in that torture-chamber of ancient darkness. He will not come forth a better man, though perchance a wiser ; wisdom and goodness are from of old at issue. Henceforth he will have eyes for many an ugly spot in his own nature, hidden till now by the veil of happiness. Do not pity him ; congratulate him rather that the inevitable has been so long postponed.

He put on a bold face at breakfast next morning, for he could not suppose that Mrs. Baxendale would feel any obligation to keep his secret from her husband, and it was not in his character to play the knight of the dolorous visage. You saw the rings round his eyes, but he was able to discuss the latest electioneering intelligence, and even to utter one or two more of those shrewd remarks by which he had lately been proving that politics were not unlikely to demand more of his attention some day. But he was glad when he could get away to the drawing-room, to await Mrs. Baxendale's coming. He tried to read in a volume of Boswell which lay out ; at other times the book was his delight, now it had the succulence of a piece of straw. He was in that state of mind when five minutes of waiting is intolerable. He had to wait some twenty before Mrs. Baxendale appeared. Only a clinging remnant of common-sense kept him from addressing her sourly. Wilfrid was not eminently patient.

'Well, what counsel has sleep brought?' she asked, speaking as if she had some other matter on her mind—as indeed she had—a slight difficulty which had just arisen with the cook.

'I should not be much advanced if I had depended upon sleep,' Wilfrid replied cheerlessly. Always sensitive, he was especially so at this moment, and the lady seemed to him unsympathetic. He should have allowed for the hour; matters involving sentiment should never be touched till the day has grown to ripeness. The first thing in the morning a poet is capable of mathematics.

'I fear you are not the only one who has not slept,' said Mrs. Baxendale.

Wilfrid, after waiting in vain, went on in a tone very strange to him:

'I don't know what to do; I am incapable of thought. Another night like the last will drive me mad. You tell me I must merely wait; but I cannot be passive. What help is there? How can I kill the time?'

Mrs. Baxendale was visibly harder than on the previous evening. A half-smile caused her to draw in her lips; she played with the watch-chain at her girdle.

'I fear,' she said, 'we have done all that can be done. Naturally you would find it intolerable to linger here.'

'I must return to London?'

'Under any other circumstances I should be the last to wish it, but I suppose it is better that you should.'

He was prepared for the advice, but unreason strove in him desperately against the facts of the situation. It was this impotent quarrel with necessity which robbed him of his natural initiative and made Mrs. Baxendale wonder at his unexpected feebleness. To him it seemed something to stand his ground even for a few minutes. He could have eased himself with angry speech. Remember that he had not slept, and that his mind was sore with the adversary's blows.

'I understand your reluctance,' Mrs. Baxendale pursued. 'It's like a surrendering of hope. But you know what I said last night; I could only repeat the same things now. Don't be afraid; I will not.'

'Yes,' he murmured, 'I must go to London.'

'It would be far worse if you had no friend here. You shall hear from me constantly. You have an assurance that the poor thing can't run away.'

In the expressive vulgar phrase, Wilfrid 'shook himself together.' He began to perceive that his attitude lacked dignity; even in our misery we cannot bear to appear ignoble.

'I will leave you to-day,' he said, more like his old self. 'But there are other things that we must speak of. What of Emily's practical position?'

'I don't think we need trouble about that. Mr. Baxendale tells me he has no doubt that the house in Barnhill can be sold at all events for a sum that will leave them at ease for the present. As soon as Mrs. Hood gets better, they must both go away. You can trust me to do what can be done.'

'It is my fear that Emily will find it difficult to accept your kindness.'

'It will require tact. Only experience can show what my course must be.'

'I sincerely hope the house *will* be sold. Otherwise, the outlook is deplorable.'

'I assure you it will be. My husband does not give up anything he has once put his hand to.'

'I shall keep my own counsel at home,' Wilfrid said.

'Do so, certainly. And you will return to Oxford?'

'I think so. I shall find it easier to live there—if, indeed, I can live anywhere.'

'I had rather you hadn't added that,' said Mrs. Baxendale with good-natured reproof. 'You know that you will only work the harder just to forget your trouble. That, depend upon it, is the only way of killing the time, as you said; if we strike at him in other ways we only succeed in making him angry.'

'Another apophthegm,' said Wilfrid, with an attempt at brightness. 'You are the first woman I have known who has that gift of neatness in speech.'

'And you are the first man who ever had discernment enough to compliment me on it. After that, do you think I shall desert your cause?'

Wilfrid made his preparations forthwith, and decided upon a train early in the afternoon. At luncheon, Mr. Baxendale was full of good-natured regrets that his visit could not be prolonged till the time of the election—now very near.

'When your constituents have sent you to Westminster,' said Wilfrid, 'I hope you will come and report to me the details of the fight?'

So he covered his retreat and retrieved in Mrs. Baxendale's eyes his weakness of the morning. She took him to the station in her brougham, but did not go on to the platform. Their parting was very like that of lovers, for it ended with mutual promises to 'write often.' Mrs. Baxendale was down-hearted as she drove home—in her a most unusual thing.

Two days later she went to Banbrigg, carrying the satisfactory news that at last a sale of the Barnhill property had been negotiated. To Emily this intelligence gave extreme relief; it restored her independence. Having this subject to speak of made the meeting easier on both sides than it could otherwise have been. Emily was restlessly anxious to take upon herself the task of nursing her mother; with the maid to help her, she declared herself able to bear all responsibilities, and persisted so strongly that Mrs. Baxendale had no choice but to assent to the nurse who had remained being withdrawn. She could understand the need of activity which possessed the girl, but had grave fears of the result of an undertaking so disproportioned to her strength.

'Will you promise me,' she said, 'to give it up and get help if you find it is trying you excessively?'

'Yes,' Emily replied, 'I will promise that. But I know I shall be better for the occupation.'

'And you will let me still come and see you frequently?'

'I should miss you very much if you ceased to,' was Emily's answer.

Both felt that a difficulty had been surmounted, though they looked at it from different sides.

October passed, and the first half of November. Mrs. Hood had not risen from her bed, and there seemed slight chance that she ever would; she was sinking into hopeless imbecility. Emily's task in that sick-room was one which a hospital nurse would have found it burdensome to support; she bore it without a sign of weariness or of failure in physical strength. Incessant companionship with bodily disease was the least oppressive of her burdens; the state of her mother's mind afflicted her far more. Occasionally the invalid would appear in full possession of her intellect, and those were the hardest days; at such times she was incessantly querulous; hours long she lay and poured forth complaints and reproaches. When she could speak no more for very weariness, she moaned and wept, till Emily also found

it impossible to check the tears which came of the extremity
of her compassion. The girl was superhuman in her patience;
never did she speak a word which was not of perfect gentleness; the bitterest misery seemed but to augment the tenderness of her devotion. Scarcely was there an hour of the day
or night that she could claim for herself; whilst it was
daylight she tended the sufferer ceaselessly, and her bed was
in the same room, so that it often happened that she lay
down only to rise before she could sleep. Her task was
lighter when her mother's mind strayed from the present;
but even then Mrs. Hood talked constantly, and was irritated
if Emily failed in attention. The usual subject was her
happiness in the days before her marriage; she would revive
memories of her school, give long accounts of her pupils, even
speak of proposals of marriage which she had had the pleasure
of declining. At no time did she refer to Hood's death, but
often enough she uttered lamentations over the hardships in
which her marriage had resulted, and compared her lot with
what it might have been if she had chosen this or that other
man. Emily was pained unspeakably by this revelation of
her mother's nature, for she knew that it was idle to explain
such tendencies of thought as the effect of disease; it was, in
truth, only the emphasising of the faults she had always
found it so hard to bear with. She could not understand the
absence of a single note of affection or sorrow in all these
utterances, and the fact was indeed strange, bearing in mind
Mrs. Hood's outburst of loving grief when her husband was
brought home, and the devotedness she had shown throughout Emily's illness. Were the selfish habits of years too
strong for those better instincts which had never found indulgence till stirred by the supreme shock? Thinking over
the problem in infinite sadness, this was the interpretation
with which Emily had to satisfy herself, and she saw in it
the most dreadful punishment which a life-long fault could
have entailed.

Though to her mother so sublimely forbearing, in her
heart she knew too well the bitterness of revolt against nature's
cruelty; her own causes of suffering became almost insignificant in her view of the tragedy of life. Was not this
calamity upon her surviving parent again a result of her own
action? Was it possible to avoid a comparison between this
blasted home and the appearance it might at this moment
have presented if she had sacrificed herself? What crime

had she ever been guilty of that such expiation could be demanded of her? She mocked at her misery for so questioning; as if causes and effects were to be thus discerned in fate's dealings. Emily had never known the phase of faith which finds comfort in the confession of native corruptness, nor did the desolation of her life guide her into that orthodox form of pessimism. She was not conscious of impurity, and her healthy human intelligence could only see injustice in the woe that had befallen her. From her childhood up she had striven towards the light, had loved all that is beautiful, had worshipped righteousness; out of this had it issued that her life was sunk in woe unfathomable, hopeless of rescue for ever. She was the sacrifice of others' wrong-doing; the evil-heartedness of one man, the thoughtless error of another, had brought this upon her.

Her character, like the elemental forces of earth, converted to beneficent energy the burden of corruption thrust upon it. Active at first because she dreaded the self-communings of idleness, she found in her labour and her endurance sources of stern inspiration; her indestructible idealism grasped at the core of spiritual beauty in a life even such as this. She did not reason with herself hysterically of evil passions to be purified by asceticism, of mysterious iniquities to be washed out in her very life's blood; but the great principles of devotion and renunciation became soothing and exalting presences, before which the details of her daily task lost their toilsome or revolting aspect in a hallowed purpose. Her work was a work of piety, not only to the living, but to the beloved dead. If her father could know of what she was now doing, he would be comforted by it; if he knew that she did it for his sake it would bring him happiness. This truth she saw: that though life be stripped of every outward charm there may yet remain in the heart of it, like a glorious light, that which is the source of all beauty—Love. She strove to make Love the essence of her being. Her mother, whom it was so hard to cherish for her own sake, she would and could love because her father had done so; that father, whose only existence now was in her own, she loved with fervour which seemed to grow daily. Supreme, fostered by these other affections, exalted by the absence of a single hope for self, reigned the first and last love of her woman-soul. Every hard task achieved for love's sake rendered her in thought more worthy of him whom she made the ideal man. He

would never know of the passion which she perfected to be
her eternal support; but, as there is a sense of sweetness in
the thought that we may be held dear by some who can
neither come near us nor make known to us their good-will,
so did it seem to Emily that from her love would go forth a
secret influence, and that Wilfrid, all unknowing, would be
blest by her faithfulness.

CHAPTER XVIII.

A COMPACT.

ON the last day of the year, a Sunday, Dagworthy sat by his
fireside, alone; luncheon had been removed, and decanters
stood within his reach. But the glass of wine which he had
poured out, on turning to the fire half an hour ago, was still
untasted, the cigar, of which he had cut the end, was still
between his fingers, unlighted. For the last three months
our friend had not lacked matter for thought; to do him
justice, he had exercised his mind upon it pretty constantly.
To-day he had received news which gave a fresh impulse to
his rumination.

Dagworthy had never, since the years of early manhood,
cared much for any of the various kinds of society open to
him in Dunfield, and his failure to show himself at the houses
of his acquaintance for weeks together occasioned no comment;
but during these past three months he had held so persistently
aloof that people had at length begun to ask for an explanation—at all events, when the end of the political turmoil
gave them leisure to think of minor matters once more. The
triumphant return of Mr. Baxendale had naturally led to
festive occasions; at one dinner at the Baxendales' house
Dagworthy was present, but, as it seemed, in the body only.
People who, in the provincial way, made old jokes last a very
long time, remarked to each other with a smile that Dagworthy
appeared to be in a mood which promised an item of interest
in the police reports before long. One person there was who
had special reason for observing him closely that evening,
and even for inducing him to converse on certain subjects;
this was Mrs. Baxendale. A day or two previously she had
heard a singular story from a friend of hers, which occupied

her thought not a little. It interested her to discover how Dagworthy would speak of the Hood family, if led to that topic. He did not seem to care to dwell upon it, and the lady, after her experiment, imagined that it had not been made altogether in vain.

With that exception Dagworthy had kept to his mill and his house. It was seldom that he had a visitor, and those persons who did call could hardly feel that they were desired to come again. Mrs. Jenkins, of the Doric tongue, ruled in the household, and had but brief interviews with her master; provided that his meals were served at the proper time, Dagworthy cared to inquire into nothing that went on—outside his kennels—and even those he visited in a sullen way. His child he scarcely saw; Mrs. Jenkins discovered that to bring the ' bairn ' into its father's presence was a sure occasion of wrath, so the son and heir took lessons in his native tongue from the housekeeper and her dependents, and profited by their instruction. Dagworthy never inquired about the boy's health. Once when Mrs. Jenkins, alarmed by certain symptoms of infantine disorder, ventured to enter the dining-room and broach the subject, her master's reply was: ' Send for the doctor then, can't you ? ' He had formerly made a sort of plaything of the child when in the mood for it; now he was not merely indifferent—the sight of the boy angered him. His return home was a signal for the closing of all doors between his room and the remote nursery. Once, when he heard crying he had summoned Mrs. Jenkins. ' If you can't stop that noise,' he said, ' or keep it out of my hearing, I'll send the child to be taken care of in Hebsworth, or somewhere else further off, and then I'll shut up the house and send you all about your business. So just mind what I say.'

Of late it had become known that he was about to take a partner into his business, a member of the Legge family—a name we remember. Dunfieldians discussed the news, and revived their pleasure in speculating on the sum total of Dagworthy's fortune. But it was as one talks of possible mines of treasure in the moon; practical interest in the question could scarcely be said to exist, for the chance of Dagworthy's remarriage seemed remoter than ever. The man was beginning to be one of those figures about whom gathers the peculiar air of mystery which ultimately leads to the creation of myths. Let him live on in this way for another twenty years, and stories would be told of him to children in the nursery. The case of assault and battery, a thing of the far past, would probably develop into a fable of manslaughter, of murder; his wife's death was already regarded very much in that light, and would class him with Bluebeard; his house on the Heath would assume a forbidding aspect, and dread whispers would be exchanged of what went on there under the shadow of night. Was it not already beginning to be remarked by his neighbours that you met him wandering about lonely places at unholy hours, and that he shunned you, like one with a guilty conscience? Let him advance in years, his face lose its broad colour, his hair grow scant and grey, his figure, perchance, stoop a little, his eyes acquire the malignity of miserly old age—and there you have the hero of a Dunfield legend. Even thus do such grow. . . .

But he is sitting by his fireside this New Year's Eve, still a young man, still fresh-coloured, only looking tired and lonely, and, in fact, meditating an attempt to recover his interest in life. He had admitted a partner to his business chiefly that he might be free to quit Yorkshire for a time, and at present he was settling affairs to that end. This afternoon he expected a visit from Mr. Cartwright, who had been serving him in several ways of late, and who had promised to come and talk business for an hour. The day was anything but cheerful; at times a stray flake of snow hissed upon the fire; already, at three o'clock, shadows were invading the room.

He heard a knock at the front door, and, supposing it to be Cartwright, roused himself. As he was stirring the fire a servant announced—instead of the father, the daughter. Jessie Cartwright appeared.

'Something amiss with your father?' Dagworthy asked, shaking hands with her carelessly.

'Yes; I'm sorry to say he has such a very bad sore-throat that he couldn't possibly come. Oh, what an afternoon it is, to be sure!'

'Why did *you* come?' was Dagworthy's not very polite inquiry. 'It wasn't so important as all that. Walked all the way?'

'Of course. I'm afraid the wet 'll drip off my cloak on to the floor.'

'Take it off, then, and put it here by the fire to dry.'

He helped her to divest herself, and hung the cloak on to the back of a chair.

' You may as well sit down. Shall I give you a glass of wine ? '

' Oh, indeed, no ! No, thank you ! '

' I think you'd better have one,' he said, without heeding her. ' I suppose you've got your feet wet ? I can't very well ask you to take your shoes off.'

' Oh, they're not wet anything to speak of,' said Jessie, settling herself in a chair, as if her visit were the most ordinary event. She watched him pour the wine, putting on the face of a child who is going to be treated to something reserved for grown-up persons.

' What do they mean by sending you all this distance in such weather ? ' Dagworthy said, as he seated himself and extended his legs, resting an elbow on the table.

' They didn't send me. I offered to come, and mother wouldn't hear of it.'

' Well—— ? '

' Oh, I just slipped out of the room, and was off before anyone could get after me. I suppose I shall catch it rarely when I get back. But we wanted to know why you haven't been to see us—not even on Christmas Day. Now that, you know, was too bad of you, Mr. Dagworthy. I said you must be ill. Have you been ? '

' Ill ? No.'

' Oh ! ' the girl exclaimed, upon a sudden thought. ' That reminds me. I really believe Mrs. Hood is dead ; at all events all the blinds were down as I came past.'

' Yes,' was the reply, ' she is dead. She died early this morning.'

' Well, I never ! Isn't poor Emily having a shocking Christmas ! I declare, when I saw her last week, she looked like a ghost, and worse.'

Dagworthy gazed at the fire and said nothing.

' One can't be sorry that it's over,' Jessie went on, ' only it's so dreadful, her father and mother dead almost at the same time. I'm sure it would have killed me.'

' What is she going to do ? ' Dagworthy asked, slowly, almost as if speaking to himself.

' Oh, I daresay it 'll be all right as soon as she gets over it, you know. She's a lucky girl, in one way.'

' Lucky ? ' He raised his head to regard her. ' How ? '

' Oh well, that isn't a thing to talk about. And then I

don't know anything for certain. It's only what people say you know.'

'*What* do people say?' he asked, impatiently, though without much sign of active interest. It was rather as if her manner annoyed him, than the subject of which she spoke.

'I don't see that it can interest you.'

No, I don't see that it can. Still, you may as well explain.'

Jessie sipped her wine.

'It's only that they say she's engaged.'

'To whom?'

'A gentleman in London—somebody in the family where she was teaching.'

'How do you know that?' he asked, with the same blending of indifference and annoyed persistency.

'Why, it's only a guess, after all. One day Barbara and I went to see her, and just as we got to the door, out comes a gentleman we'd never seen before. Of course, we wondered who he was. The next day mother and I were in the station, buying a newspaper, and there was the same gentleman, just going to start by the London train. Mother remembered she'd seen him walking with Mrs. Baxendale in St. Luke's, and then we found he'd been staying with the Baxendales all through Emily's illness.'

'How did you find it out? You don't know the Baxendales.'

'No, but Mrs. Gadd does, and she told us.'

'What's his name?'

'Mr. Athel—a queer name, isn't it?'

Dagworthy was silent.

'Now you're cross with me,' Jessie exclaimed. 'You'll tell me, like you did once before, that I'm no good but to pry into other people's business.'

'You may pry as much as you like,' was the murmured reply.

'Just because you don't care what I do?'

'Drink your wine and try to be quiet just for a little.'

'Why?'

He made no answer, until Jessie asked—

'Why does it seem to interest you so much?'

'What?—all that stuff you've been telling me? I was thinking of something quite different.'

'Oh!' exclaimed the girl, blankly.

There was a longer silence. Jessie let her eyes stray about the room, stealing a glance at Dagworthy occasionally. Presently he rose, poked the fire with violence, and drank his own wine, which had been waiting so long.

'I must have out the carriage to send you back,' he said, going to the window to look at the foul weather.

'The carriage, indeed!' protested the girl, with a secret joy. 'You'll do no such thing.'

'I suppose I shall do as I choose,' he remarked, quietly. Then he came and rang the bell.

'You're not really going to—— ?'

A servant answered, and the carriage was ordered.

'Well, certainly that's one way of getting rid of me,' Jessie observed.

'You can stay as long as you please.'

'But the carriage will be round.'

'Can't I keep it waiting half through the night if I choose? I've done so before now. I suppose I'm master in my own house.'

It was strictly true, that, of the carriage. Once the coachman had been five minutes late on an evening when Dagworthy happened to be ill-tempered. He bade the man wait at the door, and the waiting lasted through several hours.

The room was growing dusk.

'Aren't you very lonely here?' Jessie asked, an indescribable change in her voice.

'Yes, I suppose I am. You won't make it any better by telling me so.'

'I feel sorry.'

'I dare say you do.'

'Of course you don't believe me. All the same, I *do* feel sorry.'

'That won't help.'

'No?—I suppose it won't.'

The words were breathed out on a sigh. Dagworthy made no answer.

'I'm not much better off,' she continued, in a low-spirited voice.

'Nonsense!' he ejaculated, roughly, half turning his back on her.

Jessie fumbled a moment at her dress; then, succeeding in getting her handkerchief out, began to press it against her eyes furtively. Strangely, there was real moisture to be removed.

'What's the matter with you?' Dagworthy asked with surprise.

She no longer attempted concealment, but began to cry quietly.

'What the deuce has come to you, Jessie?'

'You—you—speak very unkindly to me,' she sobbed.

'Speak unkindly? I didn't know it. What did I say?'

'You won't believe when I say I'm sorry you feel lonely.'

'Why, confound it, I'll believe as much as you like, if it comes to that. Put that handkerchief away, and drink another glass of wine.'

She stood up, and went to lean on the mantelpiece, hiding her face. When he was near her again, she continued her complaints in a low voice.

'It's so miserable at home. They want me to be a teacher, and how can I? I never pretended to be clever, and if I'd all the lessons under the sun, I should never be able to teach French—and—arithmetic—and those things. But I wish I could; then I should get away from home, and see new people. There's nobody I care to see in Dunfield—nobody but one——'

She stopped on a sob.

'Who's that?' Dagworthy asked, looking at her with a singular expression, from head to foot.

She made no answer, but sobbed again.

'What Christmas presents have you had?' was his next question, irrelevant enough apparently.

'Oh, none—none to speak of—a few little things. What do I care for presents? You can't live on presents.'

'Can't live on them? Are things bad at home?'

'I didn't mean that. But of course they're bad; they're always bad nowadays. However, Barbara's going to be married in a week; she'll be one out of the way. And of course I haven't a dress fit to be seen in for the wedding.'

'Why then, get a dress. How much will it cost?' He went to a writing-table, unlocked a drawer, and took out a cheque-book. 'Now then,' he said, half jestingly, half in earnest, 'what is it to be? Anything you like to say—I'll write it.'

'As if I wanted money!'

'I can give you that. I don't see what else I can do. It isn't to be despised.'

'No, you can do nothing else,' she said, pressing each cheek with her handkerchief before putting it away. 'Will you help me on with my cloak, Mr. Dagworthy?'

He took it from the chair, and held it for her. Jessie, as if by accident, approached her face to his hand, and, before he saw her purpose, kissed his hard fingers. Then she turned away, hiding her face.

Dagworthy dropped the garment, and stood looking at her. He had a half contemptuous smile on his lips. At this moment it was announced that the carriage was coming round. Jessie caught at her cloak, and threw it over her shoulders. Then, with sunk head, she offered to shake hands.

'No use, Jessie,' Dagworthy remarked quietly, without answering her gesture.

'Of course, I know it's no use,' she said in a hurried voice of shame. 'I know it as well as you can tell me. I wish I'd never come.'

'But you don't act badly,' he continued.

'What do you mean?' she exclaimed, indignation helping her to raise her eyes for a moment. 'I'm not acting.'

'You don't mean anything by it—that's all.'

'No, perhaps not. Good-bye.'

'Good-bye. I'm going away before very long. I dare say I shan't see you again before then.'

'Where are you going to?'

'Abroad.'

'I suppose you'll bring back a foreign wife,' she said with sad scornfulness.

'No, I'm not likely to do that. I shouldn't wonder if I'm away for some time, though—perhaps a couple of years.'

'Years!' she exclaimed in astonishment.

He laughed.

'That startles you. I shan't be back in time for your wedding, you see.'

She sobbed again, averting her face.

'I shan't ever be married. I'm one of those wretched things nobody ever cares for.'

'You'll have to show you deserve it. Why, you couldn't give your word and keep it for two years.'

Through this extraordinary scene Dagworthy was utterly unlike himself. It was as if a man suffering physical agony should suddenly begin to jest and utter wild mirth; there was the same unreality in his behaviour. Throughout it all the lines of his face never lost their impress of gloom. Misery had its clutch upon him, and he was driven by an inexplicable spirit of self-mockery to burlesque the subject of his unhappiness. He had no sense of responsibility, and certain instincts were strongly excited, making a kind of moral intoxication.

Jessie answered his question with wide eyes.

'I couldn't?—Ah!'

She spoke under her breath, and with sincerity which was not a little amusing.

'It's New Year's Eve, isn't it?' Dagworthy pursued, throwing out his words at random. 'Be here this day two years—or not, as you like. I'm going to wander about, but I shall be here on that day—that is, if I'm alive. You won't though. Good-bye.'

He turned away from her, and went to the window. Jessie moved a little nearer.

'Do you mean that?' she asked.

'Mean it?' he repeated, 'why, yes, as much as I mean anything. Be off; you're keeping that poor devil in the snow.'

'Mr. Dagworthy, I shall be here, and you daren't pretend to forget, or to say you weren't in earnest.'

He laughed and waved his hand.

'Be off to your carriage!'

Jessie moved to the door reluctantly; but he did not turn again, and she departed.

CHAPTER XIX.

THE COMPLETION OF MISCHANCE.

UPON Emily had fallen silence. The tongue which for three months had incessantly sounded in her ears, with its notes of wailing, of upbraiding, of physical pain, of meaningless misery, was at rest for ever. As she stood beside the grave—the grave whose earth had not had time to harden since it received her father—she seemed still to hear that feeble, querulous voice, with its perpetual iteration of her own name;

the casting of clay upon the coffin made a sound not half so real. Returning home, she went up to the bedroom with the same hurried step with which she had been wont to enter after her brief absences. The bed was vacant; the blind made the air dim; she saw her breath rise before her.

There remained but a little servant-girl, who, coming to the sitting-room to ask about meals, stood crying with her apron held to her eyes. Emily spoke to her almost with tender kindness. Her own eyes had shed but few tears; she only wept on hearing those passages read which, by their promise of immortal life, were to her as mockery of her grief. She did not venture to look into the grave's mouth; she dreaded lest there might be visible some portion of her father's coffin.

Mrs. Baxendale, the Cartwrights, and one or two other friends had attended the funeral. At Emily's request no one accompanied her home. Mrs. Baxendale drove her to the door, and went on to Dunfield.

The last link with the past was severed—almost, it seemed, the last link with the world. A sense of loneliness grew about her heart; she lived in a vast solitude, whither came faintest echoes of lamentation, the dying resonance of things that had been. It could hardly be called grief, this drawing off of the affections, this desiccation of the familiar kindnesses which for the time seemed all her being. She forced herself to remember that the sap of life would flow again, that love would come back to her when the hand of death released her from its cruel grip; as yet she could only be sensible of her isolation, her forlorn oneness. It needs a long time before the heart can companion only with memories. About its own centre it wraps such warm folds of kindred life. Tear these away, how the poor heart shivers in its nakedness.

She was alone. It no longer mattered where she lived, for her alliances henceforth were only of the spirit. She must find some sphere in which she could create for herself a new activity, for to sit in idleness was to invite dread assaults. The task of her life was an inward one, but her nature was not adapted to quiescence, and something must replace the task which had come to an end by her mother's death. Already she had shaped plans, and she dared not allow needless time to intervene before practically pursuing them.

In the evening of that day Mrs. Baxendale again came to Banbrigg. She found Emily with writing materials before

her. Her object in coming was to urge Emily to quit this
lonely house.

'Come and stay with me,' she entreated. 'You shall be
as unmolested as here; no one but myself shall ever come
near you. Emily, I cannot go home and sleep with the
thought of you here alone.'

'You forget,' Emily replied, 'that I have in reality lived
alone for a long time; I do not feel it as you imagine. No, I
must stay here, but not for long. I shall at once find a
teacher's place again.'

'That is your intention?'

'Yes. I shall sell the furniture, and ask the landlord to
find another tenant as soon as possible. But till I go away I
wish to live in this house.'

Mrs. Baxendale knew that Emily's projects were not to be
combated like a girl's idle fancies. She did not persevere,
but let sad silence be her answer.

'Would you in no case stay in Dunfield?'

'No; I must leave Dunfield. I don't think I shall find it
difficult to get employment.'

Mrs. Baxendale had never ventured to ask for the girl's
confidence, nor even to show that she desired it. Emily was
more perplexing to her now than even at the time of Wilfrid
Athel's rejection. She consoled herself with the thought that
a period of active occupation was no doubt the best means of
restoring this complex nature to healthy views of life; that at
all events it was likely to bring about an unravelling of the
mysteries in which her existence seemed to have become
involved. You could not deal with her as with other girls;
the sources of her strength and her weakness lay too deep;
counsel to her would be a useless, an impertinent, interference
with her grave self-guiding. Mrs. Baxendale could but speak
words of extreme tenderness, and return whence she had
come. On going away, she felt that the darkest spot of night
was over that house.

Emily lived at Banbrigg for more than three weeks. After
the first few days she appeared to grow lighter in mind; she
talked more freely with those who came to see her, and gladly
accepted friendly aid in little practical matters which had to
be seen to. Half-way between Banbrigg and Dunfield lay the
cemetery; there she passed a part of every morning, sometimes in grief which opened all the old wounds, more often in
concentration of thought such as made her unaware of the

passage of time.   The winter weather was not severe ; not seldom a thin gleam of sunshine would pass from grave to grave, and give promise of spring in the said reign of the year's first month.   Emily was almost the only visitor at the hour she chose.   She had given directions for the raising of a stone at the grave-head ; as yet there was only the newly-sodded hillock.   Close at hand was a grave on which friends placed hot-house flowers, sheltering them beneath glass. Emily had no desire to express her mourning in that way ; the flower of her love was planted where it would not die.

But she longed to bring her time of waiting to an end. The steps she had as yet taken had led to nothing.   She had not requested Mrs. Baxendale to make inquiries for her, and her friend, thinking she understood the reason, did not volunteer assistance, nor did she hear any particulars of the correspondence that went on.   Ultimately, Emily communicated with her acquaintances in Liverpool, who were at once anxious to serve her.   She told them that she would by preference find a place in a school.   And at length they drew her attention to an advertisement which seemed promising ; it was for a teacher in a girls' school near Liverpool.   A brief correspondence led to her being engaged.

She was in perfect readiness to depart.   For a day or two she had not seen Mrs. Baxendale, and, on the afternoon before the day of her leaving Banbrigg, she went to take leave of her friends.   It was her intention to visit Mrs. Baxendale first, then to go on to the Cartwrights'.   As it rained, she walked to Pendal and took train for Dunfield.

At Dunfield station she was delayed for some moments in leaving the carriage by travellers who got out before her with complexities of baggage.   To reach the exit of the station she had to cross the line by a bridge, and at the foot of this bridge stood the porter who collected tickets.   As she drew near to him her eyes fell upon a figure moving before her, that of a young man, wearing thick travelling apparel and carrying a bag.   She did not need to see his face, yet, as he stopped to give up his ticket, she caught a glimpse of it.   The train by which she had travelled had also brought Wilfrid to Dunfield.

She turned and walked to a little distance away from the foot of the stairs.   There was no room that she could enter on this platform.   She dropped her black veil, and seated herself on a bench.   In truth she had a difficulty in standing, her body trembled so.

For five minutes she remained seated, calming herself and determining what course to take. She held it for certain that Wilfrid had come at Mrs. Baxendale's bidding. But would he go to that house first, or straight to her own? With the latter purpose he would probably have left the train at Pendal. She would have time to get home before he could come. At this moment a train was entering the station on the other side. She hurried over the bridge, and, without stopping to obtain a ticket, entered a carriage.

It was not without dread lest Wilfrid might have already arrived, and be waiting within for her return that she approached the house door. Her fears were groundless. The servant told her that no one had called.

'If anyone should call this evening,' she said, 'I cannot see them. You will say that I shall not be able to see any-one—anyone, whoever it is—till to-morrow morning.' . . .

At this same hour, Mrs. Baxendale, entering a shop in Dunfield, found Dagworthy making purchases.

'I shall not see you again for a long time,' he said, as he was leaving. 'I start to-morrow on a long journey.'

'Out of England?'

He did not specify his route, merely said that he was going far from England. They shook hands, and Mrs. Baxendale was left with a musing expression on her face. She turned her eyes to the counter; the purchase for which Dagworthy had just paid was a box of ladies' gloves. The shopman put them aside, to be made into a parcel and sent away.

When, half an hour later, she reached home, she was at once informed that Mr. Athel was in the drawing-room. The intelligence caused her to bite her lower lip, a way she had of expressing the milder form of vexation. She went first to re-move her walking apparel, and did not hasten the process. When she at length entered the drawing-room Wilfrid was pacing about in his accustomed fashion.

'You here?' she exclaimed, with a dubious shake of the head. 'Why so soon?'

'So soon! The time has gone more quickly with you than with me, Mrs. Baxendale.'

Clearly he had not spent the last three months in ease of mind. His appearance was too like that with which he had come from Oxford on the occasion of his break-down.

'I could bear it no longer,' he continued. 'I cannot let her go away without seeing her.'

'You will go this evening?'

'Yes, I must. You have nothing hopeful to say to me?'

Mrs. Baxendale dropped her eyes, and answered, 'Nothing.' Then she regarded him as if in preface to some utterance of moment, but after all kept silence.

'Has she heard of anything yet?'

'I believe not. I have not seen her since Tuesday, and then she told me of nothing. But I don't ask her.'

'I know—you explained. I think you have done wisely. How is she?'

'Well, seemingly.'

He let his feeling get the upper hand.

'I can't leave her again without an explanation. She *must* tell me everything. Have I not a right to ask it of her? I can't live on like this; I do nothing. The days pass in misery of idleness. If only in pity she will tell me all.'

'Don't you think it possible,' Mrs. Baxendale asked, 'that she has already done so?'

He gazed at her blankly, despairingly.

'You have come to believe that? Her words—her manner —seem to prove that?'

'I cannot say certainly. I only mean that you should be prepared to believe if she repeated it.'

'Yes, if she repeats it. I shall have no choice. Well, I wished to see you first; I will go to Banbrigg at once.'

Mrs. Baxendale seemed reluctant to let him go, yet at length she did. He was absent an hour and a half. At his return Mrs. Baxendale had friends with her in the drawing-room. Wilfrid ascertained it from the servant, and said that he would go to the sitting-room he had formerly occupied, and wait there till the lady was alone.

She came to him before very long, and learnt that he had not been able to see Emily; the servant had told him that she could see no one till the next morning.

Mrs. Baxendale sighed.

'Then you must wait.'

'Yes, I must wait.'

He passed the night at the house. Mr. Baxendale was in London, parliamentarily occupied. At eleven next morning he went again to Banbrigg. Again he was but a short time absent, and in his face, as he entered the drawing-room, Mrs. Baxendale read catastrophe.

'She has gone!' he said. 'She left very early this morn-

ing. The girl has no idea where she has gone to, but says
she won't return—that she has left for good. What does this
mean ? '

' What does it mean ? ' the lady repeated musingly. ' I
wonder, I wonder.'

' She knew I called yesterday; I left my name. She has
gone to avoid me.'

' That may be. But all her preparations were evidently
made.'

' But it may not be true. The girl of course would say
whatever she was bidden to. I don't believe that she has
really gone.'

' I do,' said Mrs. Baxendale, with quiet significance.

' On what grounds ? You know more than you will tell
me. Is there no one with common humanity ? Why
do you plot against me ? Why won't you tell me what you
know ? '

' I will, if you sit down there and endeavour to command
yourself. That is, I will tell you certain things that I have
heard, and something that I have seen. Then we will reason
about them.'

Wilfrid's brow darkened. He prepared to listen.

' About six weeks ago,' the lady began, ' I went to see a
friend of mine, a lady who was recovering from an illness,
someone who knows Emily, though not intimately. In her
illness she was nursed by the same woman who helped poor
Mrs. Hood when Emily was in her fever. This woman, it
appears, was induced to talk about Emily, and gave it as a
secret that Emily's illness had something to do with an
attachment between her and Mr. Dagworthy, her father's
employer. Her grounds for believing this were, first of all,
the fact of Emily frequently uttering his name in her delirium,
with words which seemed to refer to some mystery between
them ; then the circumstance of Mr. Dagworthy's having,
shortly after, left a note at the house, with special injunctions
to the servant that it should be given into Emily's own hands.
This story, you may imagine, surprised me not a little. A few
days later Mr. Dagworthy dined with us, and I took an opportunity of talking with him ; it seemed to me certain that
Emily had some special place in his thoughts. I know, too,
that he was particularly anxious throughout the time of her
illness, and that of her mother.'

The listener was paralysed.

' Why have you kept this from me ? ' he asked, indignation blending with his misery.

' Because it was no better than gossip and speculation. I had no right to report such things—at all events, so it seemed to me. Now I am going to add something which may be the wildest error, but which cannot trouble you much if you imagine that the story is true. Yesterday, just before I came home to find you here, I met Mr. Dagworthy by chance in a draper's shop, and he told me that he was going away to-day, leaving England.'

' To-day ? '

' Yes. And I saw that he had been buying a box of ladies' gloves.'

' What do you mean ? ' Wilfrid stammered out.

' I know that he has no female relatives—except his wife's, who live in another part of England, and are on bad terms with him.'

' His *wife*—you said ? '

' His late wife ; he is a widower. Now we may be imagining in the silliest way, but——'

' But why——' Wilfrid checked himself. ' Do I understand you ? You think Emily has gone with him—has gone to be married to him ? '

' It is almost impossible seriously to think it.'

' And you think she would shrink from being married here ? '

' For one or two reasons—at all events, so soon.'

' But is it possible to believe that she deliberately deceived you—made a pretence of seeking employment ? '

' I can't say. She never gave me any details of what she was doing. Another thing—she would not come to stay with me after her mother's funeral. Mr. Dagworthy lives on the Heath, only just beyond Banbrigg. You see to what things we can be led, if we begin interpreting shadows ; but Emily is a mystery to me, and, as I have begun, I must gossip to you all I know.'

Mrs. Baxendale was certainly doing more in the way of gossiping conjecture than perhaps she had ever done before ; the occasion excited her, and that coincidence of Dagworthy's purchase, together with his departure this very day, struck her with a force which unsettled her usual balance of thought. Wilfrid was as ready to believe ; to him there was a certain strange relief in feeling that he had at length reached the

climax of his sufferings. He had only to give credence to
Emily's own words. She had said that a change had come in
her heart, in her life, and that she no longer loved him.
Understand it he of course could not, nor ever would, unless
he lost all faith in woman's honour.

'But this can be either confirmed or refuted speedily,' he
exclaimed. 'Can you not make inquiries of this Mr. Dagworthy's friends? If they know nothing yet, they will soon
hear from him.'

'Yes, I can make such inquiries. But he has a peculiar
reputation in Dunfield; I think he scarcely has an intimate
friend.'

'Well, there is, at all events, Emily herself. If this story
is baseless, she will be writing to you.'

'I think so. Again we must wait. Poor Wilfrid! from
my heart I feel for you!'

It was decided that Wilfrid should remain in Dunfield for
a day or two, till news might be obtained. News came, however, sooner than was anticipated. In the afternoon a letter
was delivered, posted by Emily at Pendal in the morning.
She wrote to Mrs. Baxendale to say that she had left to take
a place in a school; then continued:

'I have a reason for leaving suddenly. A reason you will
understand. I should have come to say good-bye to you
yesterday, but something happened to prevent me. The same
reason has decided me to keep secret even from you, my dear
and honoured friend, the place to which I am going; in time
you shall hear from me, for I know I cannot have forfeited
your love, though I fear I have given you pain. Think of me
with forbearance. I do what I *must* do.'

That was all. No word for Wilfrid.

'This proves it,' Wilfrid said, with bitter coldness. 'All
she says is false. She does what she is ashamed of, and lies
to conceal it for a few days or weeks.'

'Do not let us even yet be sure,' said Mrs. Baxendale, who
was recovering her calmer judgment.

'I *am* sure! Why should she keep the place secret?
She fears that I should follow her? Could she not anywhere
keep me off by her mere bidding? Have I been brutally
importunate? What secret can exist that she might not
disclose to me—that she was not bound to disclose? I
thought her incapable of a breath of falsehood, and she must
have deceived me from the first, from the very first!'

' Wilfrid, that is impossible. I cannot abandon my faith in Emily. Now you speak in this way, it convinces me that we are wrong, utterly and foolishly mistaken. I believe what she says here ; she has *not* gone with him ! '

Wilfrid laughed scornfully.

' It is too late ; I can't twist my belief so quickly. I do not need that kind of comfort ; far easier to make up my mind that I have always been fooled—as I have ! '

He was beyond the stage at which reasoning is possible ; reaction, in full flood, beat down the nobler features of his mind and swamped him with the raging waters of resentment.

So here was a myth well on its way to establishment. For no one could afford Mrs. Baxendale satisfactory news of Dagworthy. She would not take the only step which remained, that of openly avowing to his partner the information she desired to obtain, and getting him to make inquiries ; his partner appeared to be the only person in direct communication with Dagworthy. It had to be remembered that Emily's own statement might be true ; she must not be spoken of lightly. It was said that Mr. Legge, the partner, pooh-poohed the idea that Dagworthy was secretly married. But Mr. Legge might know as little as other people.

There were circles in Dunfield in which another and quite a different myth grew up around the name of Emily Hood. The Cartwrights originated it. They too had received a mysterious note of farewell, and their interpretation was this : Emily, they held, had gone to London, there to be happily married to a certain Mr. Athel, a gentleman of aristocratic appearance and enormously wealthy. Mrs. Baxendale heard this story now and again ; she neither affirmed nor contradicted. Jessie Cartwright reflected much on Emily's slyness in keeping her affairs so secret. She was not as envious as she would have been but for a certain compact which she was determined should not—if it lay in her power to prevent it— be some day laughed away as a mere joke. And had she not received, on the very eve of Dagworthy's departure, a box of gloves, which could only come from one person ?

The second myth holds its ground, I believe, to the present day. The more mischievous fable was refuted before very long, but only when it had borne results for Wilfrid practically the same as if it had been a truth.

CHAPTER XX.

WILFRID THE LEGISLATOR.

LET time and change do their work for six years and six
months, their building and their destroying, their ripening for
love, their ripening for death.   Then we take our way to the
Capital, for, behold, it is mid-season; the sun of late June is
warm upon the many-charioted streets, upon the parks where
fashion's progress circles to the 'Io Triumphe' of regardant
throngs, even upon the quarters where life knows but one
perennial season, that of toil.   The air is voiceful; every
house which boasts a drawing-room gathers its five o'clock
choir; every theatre, every concert-room resounds beneath
the summer night; in the halls of Westminster is the culmination of sustained utterance.   There, last night, the young
member for a Surrey borough made his maiden speech; his
name, Mr. Wilfrid Athel.

The speech was better reported than such are wont to be,
for it contained clever things, and quite surprisingly resembled
in its tone of easy confidence and its mastery of relevant facts
the deliverances of men of weight in politics.   It had elicited
a compliment from a leader of the opposing party; it had
occasioned raisings of the eyebrows in capable judges, and
had led to remarks that a young man so singularly self-
possessed, so agreeably oracular, so remarkably long-headed,
might be expected, in the course of some five-and-twenty
years, to go far.   He was, to be sure, a child—not yet thirty
—but there were older children in the House decidedly of
less promise.   Mr. Wilfrid Athel might go home, and, if he
could, go to sleep, in the assurance that his career had
opened.

The next day, a Saturday, this finished little piece of talk
was the starting-point of a vast amount of less coherent speech
in a drawing-room within sight of Kensington's verdure.
Here Mrs. Ashley Birks did her friends the honour of receiving them; a lady well regarded in certain discriminating
circles.   A widow formerly, she had now been two years
married to a barrister new in silk.   We have the pleasure of
knowing her, for she once bore the name of Mrs. Rossall.

At half-past five Mrs. Ashley Birks' drawing-room contained some two dozen people, mostly ladies. Two of the
gentlemen present are not without interest for us. He whom
you observe standing, so to speak, the focus of a concave
mirror of three gracious dames, with his back somewhat diffi-
cultly bent, as if under ordinary circumstances he would be as
upright as any Briton who owes not a penny, with very
wholesome cheeks and lips which move in and out as he
forms his well-rounded periods, is, of course, Mr. Athel the
elder; he plays with his watch-guard, and is clearly in
hearty mood, not at all disliking the things that are being
said about a certain member of the legislature. The other is
as emphatically an Englishman, but of a different type; his
clothes are good, but he does not wear them with grace; he
is tall and solidly built, but he walks awkwardly, and is not
quite at home among these gracious ladies of the silvern
tongue, having much difficulty in expressing himself on
subjects which he perfectly understands, and absolutely without faculty for speech on subjects unfamiliar to him. When
we saw him last he was in the heat of a contested election;
there has been another election since then, but Mr. Baxendale
still represents Dunfield.

You see his wife at a little distance, still the same smooth-
skinned, well-preserved lady, with goodness declaring itself
upon her large and homely features. For three years now
she has been in the habit of spending her three months in
town, finding it lonely in Dunfield, and even nourishing a
late ambition, which has not been altogether futile; for there
are people who have a peculiar liking for the little room in
which she holds her modest gatherings. She is talking at
present with a lady who, by her costume, is of the house, a
lady of some seven-and-twenty years or a little more, and
strikingly beautiful. Beatrice Redwing has not yet changed
her name, though often enough solicited to do so; when her
mother died, now rather more than a year ago, she willingly
accepted the shelter of Mrs. Ashley Birks' roof, as she would
else have had to live alone. In one respect she has not
changed, her dress is exquisite; but to judge from her expression as she talks, she has become somewhat graver.
Visitors have a special reason for regarding her with glances
of curiosity and admiration. Though known to be extremely
wealthy, it was rumoured that she was about to appear before
the public as a vocalist, having prepared herself by a long

course of the most rigid study. Her first appearance was
looked forward to as an event of note in the musical world,
for her native gifts were unusual, and the results of her
training proportionately significant.

'It must be very gratifying to you,' Mrs. Baxendale had
said, as she came to a chair by her niece and began to talk of
Wilfrid's success.

'Yes, I am glad of it,' was the quiet reply.

'Will he be here this afternoon?'

'I'm not sure; I think so. Ah, there he is!'

For at that moment had come the announcement of the
name they had on their lips. Beatrice's exclamation was
made in a very subdued voice, but she moved slightly in her
chair, and it was not within her resources to subdue the
glister of her dark eyes and the warmth softly expanding
upon her cheek. Mrs. Birks floated towards her nephew
with airs of rightly-tuned welcome; she could not, of course,
make much of him, but her very familiarity made graceful
claim to a share in his glory. Wilfrid was sensibly changed
during the years we have allowed to pass silently by. To
begin with, he had grown a beard. His health seemed finally
to have established itself on a sound basis; his cheeks were
growing sunny, and he showed the proportions of a very
complete man. At the present moment, his consciousness of
regards fixed upon him heightened his colour; his fine eyes
danced in light; he checked a smile, and spoke sparingly
here and there. One part of his nature revelled in the joy of
this foretaste of distinction; he had looked forward to it, had
laboured for it, its sweetness was beyond all telling. Triumph
had been his aim as a schoolboy; he held it fitting that as a
man he should become prominent amongst his fellows. This
of politics was the easiest way. To be sure, he told himself
that it was a way he would once have sneered at, that it was
to rub shoulders with men altogether his inferiors in culture,
that, had he held to the ideals of his youth, a longer, a
wearier course would have been his, and the chance of a
simpler, nobler crown. But he had the gift of speech, and by
an effort could absorb himself as completely in blue-books as
in the pages of historian or poet. An hour such as this was
the first of his rewards.

Two there were in this assembly who turned their eyes
upon him with adoration which could scarcely have fallen short
of Wilfrid's utmost demands. They were his cousins, Minnie

and Patty Rossall. The twins were 'out,' very sweet girls, still too delicate in health, shadows of each other. Had they regarded Wilfrid as a mere mortal, both would have been dying for love of him; as it was they drooped before him the veiled eyes of worshippers; a word from him made their pulses tingle blissfully throughout the day. Such was their mutual love, that each schemed to win his kindness for the other, his brotherly kindness, for they never thought, had never dared to think, of anything else. Wilfrid was very gracious to them both.

He shook hands with Beatrice, but neither spoke. After a few words with Mrs. Baxendale, he passed on to other ladies. Wilfrid's manner was now all that could be desired in a young man who, destined to succeed in politics, would naturally make a figure in society. He was pliant, he struck the note of good-breeding, he was unsurpassed in phrasing; with ladies who chose to be 'superior,' he could find exactly the right tone, keeping clear of pedantry, yet paying her with whom he spoke the compliment of uttering serious opinions. With the more numerous class of ladies, who neither were nor affected to be anything but delightful chatterboxes, he could frolic on the lightest airs of society gossip. He was fast making of himself an artist in talk; woe to him, if he began to discover that exertion of his brain was waste of time, since his more obvious ends could be gained equally well without it. As yet, though hints of such a mood had come to him, he did not give way to the temptations of loquacious idleness; he still worked, and purposed to work still harder. Just of late he had spent a good deal of time in rooms not exactly arranged for purposes of study—but for this there was a special reason.

An hour later, when most of the visitors were departed, he went to Beatrice's corner of the room.

'When shall I call for you?' he asked, standing before her.

'Oh, but you will dine here?'

She leaned forward, looking up into his face. The gaze would have intoxicated most men; Wilfrid kept his calm smile.

'No, I am sorry to say I can't,' was his reply. 'I have things to see to at home. Will 8.15 do?'

'Quite well; I need not be at the hall before a quarter to nine.'

His father came up.

'Walking my way, Wilf?'

'Yes, and in a hurry. I think we must have a hansom.'

Father and son still lived together, in the same house as formerly. After a brief stretch of pavement, they hailed a conveyance.

'Going to St. James's Hall, I suppose?' Mr. Athel asked, as they drove on.

Wilfrid gave an affirmative.

'Is it the last time?'

The other laughed.

'I can't say. I fear it troubles you.'

Mr. Athel had, we know, long passed the time when the ardours of youth put him above the prejudices of the solid Englishman. When it was first announced to him that Beatrice was going to sing on a public platform, he screwed up his lips as if something acid had fallen upon them; he scarcely credited the story till his own eyes saw the girl's name in print. 'What the deuce!' was his exclamation. 'It would be all very well if she had to do it for her living, but she certainly owes it to her friends to preserve the decencies as long as there is no need to violate them.' The reasons advanced he utterly refused to weigh. Since then events had come to pass which gave him even a nearer interest in Miss Redwing, and his protests had grown serious.

'Why, yes,' he answered now, 'it does trouble me, and not a little. I very strongly advise you to put an end to it. Let her sing in her friends' houses; there's no objection to that. But to have her name on—great heavens!—on placards! No, no; it must stop, Wilf. Every day it becomes more imperative. Your position demands that she should become a private lady.'

Wilfrid knew well that the question could not be argued, and, in his secret mind, there was just a little tendency to take his father's view. He would never have allowed this shade of thought to appear in his speech; but was he not an Englishman and a member of Parliament?

This which had come about was inevitable. After his departure from Dunfield on that winter day, when his life seemed crushed, he had for a long time not even sought to hear of Emily. He did not write to Mrs. Baxendale, and from her had no letters. Correspondence between them only recommenced some ten months later, when Wilfrid had finally left Oxford, and then there was no mention on either side of the old troubles. Wilfrid began by writing that he had thoughts of taking up politics; his father advised him to the step, and other friends seconded the recommendation. ' I really believe I can talk,' he said, and Mrs. Baxendale smiled at the confession. Three months more went by; then Wilfrid at length asked plainly whether Emily had sent any news of herself, or whether the suspicions had proved grounded. The reply was this:—

' As I knew perfectly well, as soon as I came to my senses, Emily had told us the truth. I heard from her for the first time nearly half a year ago, but, as she appealed to my honour not to disclose the place of her abode, I thought it needless to speak to you on the subject before you yourself seemed desirous of hearing. She is teaching in a school, and I am convinced that the story we together concocted was based on some utter mistake; I don't think she was ever related to that man in the way we thought. But it is more than probable that there was some mystery about her father's death, in which Mr. D. was concerned. I cannot imagine what it could be. Something it was which, to Emily's mind, imposed upon her a necessity of breaking her engagement. I have spoken to her of you, have asked her directly if she still thinks her decision final; she assures me most solemnly that it is. I therefore advise you once for all to accept this; I am convinced she will never waver. Try to forget her; there is no choice. I don't think I am likely to see her again for a very long time, if ever, and our correspondence will be very slight, for I know she wishes it so. Let this, then, close a sad, sad story.'

There was indeed no choice, as far as outward relations went, but so profound a passion was not to be easily outgrown. The view which makes first love alone eternally valid derives from a conception of the nature of love which, out of the realm of poetry, we may not entertain; but it sometimes happens that the first love is that which would at any period of life have been the supreme one, and then it doubtless attains a special intensity of hold from the fact of its being allied with the earliest outburst of physical passion. Above all it is thus if the attachment has been brought about by other charms than those of mere personal beauty. Emily could not be called beautiful, in the ordinary acceptation of the word; for all that, her face grew to possess for Wilfrid a perfection

of loveliness beyond anything that he would ever again see in
the countenance of fairest woman. Had he been markedly
susceptible to female beauty, it is certain that he would have
fallen in love with Beatrice Redwing long before he ever saw
Emily, for Beatrice was fair to look upon as few girls are.
He had not done so; he had scarcely—a strange thing—been
tempted to think of doing so. That is to say, it needed something more to fire his instincts. The first five minutes that
he spent in Emily's presence made him more conscious of
womanhood than years of constant association with Beatrice.
This love, riveting itself among the intricacies of his being,
could not be torn out, and threatened to resist all piecemeal
extraction. Wilfrid regained the command of his mind, and
outwardly seemed recovered beyond all danger of relapse; but
he did not deceive himself into believing that Emily was
henceforth indifferent to him. He knew that to stand again
before her would be to declare again his utter bondage, body
and soul. He loved her still, loved her as his life; he desired
her as passionately as ever. She was not often in his thoughts;
no more is the consciousness of the processes whereby our
being supports itself. But he had only to let his mind turn to
her, and he scoffed at the hope that any other could ever be
to him what Emily had been, and was, and would be.

He saw very little of Beatrice, but it came to his ears that
her life had undergone a change in several respects, that she
spent hours daily in strenuous study of music, and was less
seen in the frivolous world. No hint of the purpose Beatrice
secretly entertained ever reached him till, long after, the purpose became action. He felt that she shunned him, and by
degrees he thought he understood her behaviour. Wilfrid
had none of the vulgarest vanity; another man would long
ago have suspected that this beautiful girl was in love with
him; Wilfrid had remained absolutely without a suspicion
of the kind. He had always taken in good faith her declared
aversion for his views; he had believed that her nature and
his own were definitely irreconcilable. This was attributable,
first of all to his actual inexperience in life, then to the
seriousness with which he held those views which Beatrice
vowed detestable. He, too, was an idealist, and, in many
respects, destined to remain so throughout his life; for he
would never become, on the one hand, the coldly critical man
who dissects motives—his own and those of others—to the
last fibre, nor yet the superficial cynic who professes, and

half-believes, that he can explain the universe by means of a few maxims of cheap pessimism. So he took, and continued to take, Beatrice's utterances without any grain of scepticism, and consequently held it for certain that she grew less friendly to him as she grew older.

Was it Mrs. Baxendale or Mrs. Birks who at length gave him the hint which set his mind at work in another direction? Possibly both about the same time, seeing that it was the occasion of Mrs. Baxendale's first making acquaintance with his aunt that dated the beginning of new reflections in Wilfrid. One or other of these ladies—of course it was managed so delicately that he really could not have determined to which of them he owed the impulse—succeeded in suggesting to him that he had missed certain obvious meanings in Beatrice's behaviour whilst he resided with her at Dunfield. Certainly, when he looked back at those days from his present standpoint, Beatrice did appear to have conducted herself singularly, the mode of her departure and leave-taking being above all curious. Was it possible that—— ? The question formed itself at last, and was the beginning of conviction. He sought Beatrice's society, at first merely for the sake of resolving his doubts, and behold, she no longer shrank from him as formerly. Of course he might take it for granted that she knew the details of his story, seeing that her closest intimates, Mrs. Baxendale and Mrs. Birks, were ignorant of none of them. Had she, then, waited for signs of his freedom? Did his revival of the old tone in their conversations strike her as something meant to be significant, meant to convey to her certain suggestions? It was so in point of fact, and Wilfrid could not be long, his eyes now open, without convincing himself that the girl loved him ardently, that it cost her struggles with herself to avoid a revelation of her feeling. How did it affect him?

Naturally, he was flattered. It afforded another instance of his lordship among men; a woman whom others longed for desperately and in vain was his when he chose to extend his hand to her. He saw, too, an appropriateness in the chance which offered him such a wife; Beatrice was in harmony with the future to which he aspired. Her property joined to his would make him so wealthy that he might aim almost at anything; political and social progress would aid each other, both rapid. Beatrice was in many respects brilliant; there was no station that she would not become;

she had the tastes and habits of society. He compared her with his career; she represented worldly success, the things which glitter on the outside—action, voice; even her magnificent powers of song he used as parallel—the gods forgive him!—to his own forensic abilities. Supposing he must marry early, and not rather expect the day when he might bid for a partner from a rank considerably above his own, Beatrice was clearly the one wife for him. She would devote herself with ardour to his worldly interests—for he began to understand that the divergence of her expressed views meant little in comparison with her heart's worship—and would enable him immediately to exchange the social inferiority of bachelor life for the standing of a man with his own very substantial roof-tree; she would have her drawing-room, which might be made a *salon*, where politics and art might rule alternately.

This was doing injustice to Beatrice, and Wilfrid felt it; but it was thus he regarded her as in distinction from the woman who should have been his wife. She typified his chosen career; that other path which had lain open to him, the path of intellectual endeavour, of idealism incompatible with loud talk, of a worship which knew no taint of time-serving, that for ever was represented by the image of the woman he had lost. Her memory was encompassed with holiness. He never heard the name she bore without a thrill of high emotion, the touch of exalted enthusiasm; 'Emily' was written in starlight. Those aspects of her face which had answered to the purest moments of his rapturous youth were as present as if she had been his daily companion. He needed no picture to recall her countenance; often he had longed for the skill of an artist, that he might portray that grave sweetness, that impassioned faith, to be his soul's altar-piece. Lost, lost! and, with her, lost the uncompromising zeal of his earliest manhood. Only too consciously he had descended to a lower level; politics tempted him because they offered a field in which he could exercise his most questionable faculty, and earn with it a speedy return of the praise to which he was so susceptible. It marks his position to state that, when politics began seriously to hold his thoughts, he was with difficulty able to decide to which party he should attach himself. To be sure, if names could be taken as sufficient, he was a Liberal, a Radical; but how different his interpretation of such titles from that they bore to men of affairs! Respect for the masses he had none; interest in their affairs he had none either. On the other hand, the tone of uninstructed Conservatism—that is to say, of the party so stamped—he altogether despised. The motive which ultimately decided him to declare himself a Liberal was purely of sentiment; he remembered what Mrs. Baxendale had said about the hardships of poor Hood, and consequently allied himself with those who profess to be the special friends of the toiling multitude.

From the first he talked freely with Beatrice of his projects; he even exaggerated to her the cynicism with which he framed and pursued them. He could never have talked in this way to Emily. With Beatrice the tone did not injure him in the least, partly because she did not take it altogether seriously, yet more owing to the habit of mind whereby women in general subordinate principle to the practical welfare of the individual. If Wilfrid found a sphere for the display of his talents, Beatrice cared nothing to dwell upon abstract points. Politics were a recognised profession for gentlemen, and offered brilliant prizes; that was enough. She was pleased, on the whole, that his line should be one of moderation; it was socially advantageous; it made things pleasant with friends of the most various opinions. That Wilfrid took her into his confidence was to her a great happiness. In secret she felt it would be the beginning of closer intimacy, of things which women—heaven be praised!—esteem of vastly more importance than intellectual convictions or the interest of party.

But it was long, very long, before Wilfrid could bring himself to pass the line which separates friendship from love-making. Of passion his nature had no lack, but it seemed to be absorbed in memory; he shrank from the thought of using to another those words he had spoken to Emily. One of the points of intense secret sympathy between Emily and himself was this chastity of temperament. Constitutionally incapable of vice, he held in repugnance even that degree of materialism in the view of sexual relations which is common to men who have grown their beards. Not only had a coarse word never passed his lips; he intensely disliked the frivolous way of discussing subjects which to him were more sacred than any other. When he had decided with himself that it was his destiny to wed Beatrice, he had a positive fear of taking this step from which there would be no return. Before he could do so, he must have utterly broken with the past, and how could that ever be ? He had not even moments of coldness in his thought of Emily; it was beyond his power to foresee the day when she would have become to him a mere symbol of something that was. Suppose that some day, when married, he again met her ? In spite of everything, he did not believe that she had ceased to love him; somewhere she still kept her faith, martyred by the incomprehensible fate which had torn her from his arms. To meet her again would be to forget every tie save that holiest which made one of his spirit and of hers.

One day—it was during the second season which Mrs. Baxendale passed in London—he went to his friend and asked her where Emily was. Mrs. Baxendale was too quick for him; Wilfrid thought he had put his question unexpectedly, but the lady was ready for such a question at any moment, and she replied, with appearance of absolute sincerity, that she had no knowledge of Emily's place of abode.

'Where was she last—when you last heard from her?' Wilfrid asked, in surprise at an answer so unanticipated.

Mrs. Baxendale named a town in Yorkshire. She had begun with a calculated falsehood, and had no scruple in backing it up by others.

'What can it concern you, Wilfrid?' she continued. 'Shall I confess my weakness ? I mentioned your name in a letter to her; the result was this complete ending of our correspondence. Now, will not even that satisfy you?'

He did not doubt what he was told; Mrs. Baxendale's character for veracity stood high. It was solely out of regard for Wilfrid that she allowed herself to mislead him, for by this time it seemed obvious that Beatrice was drawing near to her reward, and Mrs. Baxendale, with pardonable error, took this last inquiry about Emily for a piece of conscientiousness, which, once satisfied, Wilfrid would hold on his course to a happy haven. 'She has given him up,' was her self-justification. 'Beatrice now would suffer no less than she has done.'

'Then tell me one thing more,' Wilfrid pursued. 'What has become of that man Dagworthy?'

'That I can easily do. Long ago he married a young lady of Dunfield.'

'Then what did it mean ? what *did* it mean?'

Mrs. Baxendale merely shook her head.

A few months later, Beatrice astonished everyone by her first appearance as a public singer. Wilfrid had as little anticipated such a step as any other of Beatrice's friends. What was about to happen only became known a day or two in advance. Mrs. Ashley Birks was paralysed with horror; she implored, she reasoned, she put on her face of cold anger. Mr. Athel cried 'What the deuce!' and forthwith held a serious colloquy with his son. Wilfrid experienced a certain joy, only tempered with anxiety as to the result of the experiment. If it proved a success, he felt that the effect upon himself would be to draw him nearer to Beatrice; but it must be a great success. He calculated on imaginative influences as other men do on practical issues. Beatrice, acknowledged as more than an amateur, perchance publicly recognised as really a great singer, would impress him in a new way; he might overcome his impartial way of regarding her. The result, outwardly, answered his fullest hopes. Beatrice had not idly risked what would have been a deplorable fiasco; she had the encouragement of those who did not speak in vain, and her ambition had fired itself as she perceived the results of her conscientious labour. Her nervousness throughout the day of the concert was terrible, but little less than her life depended on the result, and at the hour of trial she was strong to conquer. Very far behind her, as she stepped out to that large audience, were the dilettante successes of drawing-room and charitable concerts; she smiled at all that now; since then she had unlearnt so much and wrought with such humility. But what she strove for was won; she knew it in the grasp of Wilfrid's hand when he led her to her carriage. Her veil was down; behind it she was sobbing.

'Am I nothing more than a frivolous woman now?' she said, leaning to him from the carriage.

Wilfrid could make no answer, and she was whirled away from him.

He went to her the next day, and asked her to be his wife. Beatrice looked him in the face long and steadily. Then she asked:

'Do you love me, Wilfrid?'

'I love you.'

Another word trembled on her tongue, but the temptation of her bliss was too great; the contained ardour of long years had its way, sweeping doubt and memory before it.

'For your sake I have done it all. What do I care for a

whole world's praise, compared with one word of recognition
from you! You remember the morning when you told me of
my faults, when we all but seemed to quarrel? Ah! I have
faults in abundance still, but have I not done one thing worth
doing, done it thoroughly, as not everyone could? I am
not only a woman of the world, of society and fashion? Do
I not know how contemptible that is? But only you could
raise me above it.'

He left her, in a bewildered state; she had excited, impassioned him; but how strange it all was after those other
scenes of love! It seemed so of the earth; the words he had
spoken rang over again in his ears, and stirred his blood to
shame. He could not say whether in truth he loved her or
not; was it enough to feel that he could cherish her with
much tenderness, and intoxicate himself in gazing on her
perfect face? Women are so different! Emily had scarcely
spoken when he made known to her his love; could he
ever forget that awe-struck face, dimly seen in the moonlight?
Her words to the end had been few; it was her eyes that
spoke. Beatrice was noble, and had a heart of gold; was
there not heaven in that ardour of hers, if only it had been
his soul's desire? Henceforth it must be; she loved him,
and he must not wrong her. Alas! the old name, the old
name alone, was still star-written. . . .

He passed with her the afternoon of each Sunday. Mrs.
Birks' house was a large one, and Beatrice had abundance of
room to herself. Thither Wilfrid took his way on the Sunday
which we have reached, the day following his drawing-room
triumph. Already he was a little ashamed of himself; he was
experiencing again the feeling which had come over him after
his first speech to a political meeting. As he went home that
night, a demon in his head kept crying ' Clap-trap! clap-trap!'
and there was no silencing the voice. He had talked to the
intelligence of the mob. Now his talk had been addressed to
—the representatives of the mob; if the demon did not cry
so loudly, it was only because he was weary of his thankless
task.

Beatrice was a superb coquette—but only for the man
she loved. For these Sunday afternoons she attired herself
divinely; Wilfrid had learnt to expect a new marvel at each
of his comings. To-day she wore her favourite colour, a
dark-blue. Her rising to meet him was that of a queen who
hath an honoured guest. The jewels beneath her long dark

lashes were as radiant as when first she heard him say, ' I love you.' All the impulses of her impetuous character had centred on this one end of her life. Her eccentricities had tamed themselves in the long discipline of frustrated desire. The breath of her body was love. About her stole a barely perceptible perfume, which invaded the senses, which wrapped the heart in luxury.

Wilfrid dropped on one knee before her and kissed her hand.

' You are in a happy mood,' Beatrice said. ' Who has been telling you the last flattery ? '

' I have seen no one to-day. If I look happy—should I not ? '

She drew her finger along the line of his eyebrow.

' How does your picture get on ? '

' I have to give two sittings next week. Thank goodness they are the last.'

' Oh ! why wasn't it in time for the Academy ! But it must go next year.'

Wilfrid laughed as he seated himself opposite to her.

' I am not sure, after all, that you are happy,' she said, leaning her head a little aside as she gazed at him. ' Now you are thoughtful. I suppose you will be more and more thoughtful.'

> ' Deep on his front engraven
> Deliberation sat, and public care——'

quoted Wilfrid, with a little wrying of the lips. ' This, you know, is one of the penalties of greatness.'

She seemed about to rise, but it was only to slip forward and sink upon her knees by his side, her arms embracing him. It was like the fall of fair waters, so gracefully impulsive, so self-abandoning.

' Not one kiss to-day ? ' she murmured, her voice like the dying of a flute.

And she raised to him a face lit from the inmost sanctuary of love.

' You are as beautiful,' he said, ' as any woman of whom fable ever told. Your beauty frightens me. It is sometimes more than human—as though the loveliest Greek goddess suddenly found breath and colour and the light of eyes.'

Beatrice threw her head far back, laughing silently ; he saw the laughter dance upon her throat.

' My love! my own!' she whispered. ' Say you love me!'

' Dearest, I love you!'

' Ah! the words make my heart flutter so! I am glad, glad that I have beauty; but for that you would never have loved me. Let me hide my face as I tell you. I used to ask myself whether I was not really fairer than other women—I thought—I hoped! But you were so indifferent. Wilfrid, how long, how long I have loved you! I was quite a young girl when I loved you first. That, I said, shall be my husband, or I will never have one. And I knew so little how to win your thought. How ashamed it makes me to think of things I said and did in those days!'

She was silent, leaning her head against his shoulder.

' Do you ever think of me as I was at Dunfield?' she asked presently, with timid utterance, hardly above her breath, risking what she had never yet dared.

' No,' he answered, ' I think of the present.'

His voice was a little hard, from the necessity of commanding it.

' You did not know that I loved you then? Think of me! Pity me!'

He made no answer. Beatrice spoke again, her face veiled against him, her arms pressing closer.

' You love me with perfect love? I have your whole heart?'

' I love you only, Beatrice.'

' And with love as great as you ever knew? Say that to me—Wilfrid, say that!' She clung to him with passion which was almost terrible. ' Forgive me! Only remember that you are my life, my soul! I cannot have less than that.'

He would have been cased in triple brass if music such as this had not melted into his being. He gave her the assurance she yearned for, and, in giving it, all but persuaded himself that he spoke the very truth. The need of affirming his belief drew from him such words as he had the secret of; Beatrice sighed in an anguish of bliss.

' Oh, let me die now! It is only for this that I have lived.'

Wilfrid had foreseen and dreaded this questioning. From any woman it was sooner or later to be expected, and Beatrice was as exacting as she was passionate. She knew herself, and strove hard to subdue those characteristics which might be displeasing to Wilfrid; her years of hopelessness, of perpetual self-restraint, were of aid to her now; three months had passed without a word from her which directly revived the old sorrows. Her own fear of trenching on indiscretion found an ally in Wilfrid's habitual gravity; her remark, at their meeting, on his mood was in allusion to a standing pleasantry between them; she had complained that he seldom looked really happy in her presence. It was true; his bearing as a rule was more than sober. Beatrice tormented herself to explain this. He was not in ordinary intercourse so persistently serious, though far more so than he had been in earlier years, the change dating, as Beatrice too well had marked, from the time of his supreme misery. With the natural and becoming gravity of mature age there mingled a very perceptible strain of melancholy. You felt it in his laugh, which was seldom hearty; it made his sprightliness in social hours more self-conscious than it might have been. Beatrice had always felt towards him a very real humility, even when the goading of her unrequited love drove her into a show of scornful opposition. Herself conscious of but average intelligence, and without studious inclinations, she endowed him with acquisitions as vast as they were vague to her discernment; she knew that it would always lie beyond her power to be his intellectual companion. Therefore she desired to be before everything womanly in his eyes, to make the note of pure sentiment predominate in their private relations to each other. She had but won him by her artistic faculty; she could not depend upon that to retain and deepen his affection. Her constant apprehension was lest familiarity should diminish her charm in his eyes. Wilfrid was no less critical than he had ever been; she suspected that he required much of her. Did he seek more than she would eventually be able to give? Was she outwearing the resources of her personal charm? Such thoughts as these made curious alternations in her manner towards him; one day she would endeavour to support a reserve which should surpass his own, another she lost herself in bursts of emotion. The very care which she bestowed upon her personal appearance was a result of her anxiety on this point; in the last resort she knew herself to be beautiful, and to her beauty he was anything but insensible. Yet such an influence was wretchedly insufficient; she must

have his uttermost love, and never yet had she attained full
assurance of possessing it.

Little did Wilfrid suspect the extent to which her thoughts
were occupied with that faint, far-off figure of Emily Hood.
It was her despair that she had known Emily so slightly; she
would have desired to study to the depths the woman who
had possessed such a secret of power. In personal charm
Emily could not compare with her; and yet—the distinction
struck her hard—that was perhaps only true if personal
charm merely meant charm of person, for she herself had
experienced something of the strange impressiveness which
men—men of imagination—submitted to in Emily's presence.
Where did it lie, this magic? It was indefinite, indefinable;
perhaps a tone of the voice represented it, perhaps a smile—
which meant, of course, that it was inseparable from her
being, from her womanhood. Could one attribute to Emily,
even after the briefest acquaintance, a thought, an instinct,
which conflicted with the ideal of womanly purity? Was not
her loveliness of the soul? Moreover, she was intellectual
beyond ordinary women; for Wilfrid that must have been a
rich source of attraction. Scarcely less than the image of
Wilfrid himself was that of Emily a haunting presence in
Beatrice's life. Recently she had spoken of her both with
Mrs. Birks and Mrs. Baxendale; it cost her something to do
so, but both of these had known Emily with intimacy, and
might perhaps tell her more than she herself remembered or
could divine. Mrs. Birks was disposed to treat Emily with
little seriousness.

'You make the strangest mistake,' she said, 'if you think
that was anything but a boy's folly. To be sure the folly got
very near the point of madness—that was because opposition
came in its way. Wilfrid has for years thought as little of
her as of the man in the moon's wife—if he has one. You
are surely not troubling yourself—what?'

Beatrice had thereupon retired into herself.

'You misunderstand me,' she said, rather coldly. 'It was
only a recollection of something that had seemed strange to
me at the time.'

Mrs. Baxendale held another tone, but even she was not
altogether sincere—naturally it was impossible to be so. To
begin with, she gave Beatrice to understand, even as she had
Wilfrid, that she had now for some time lost sight of Emily,
and, consequently, that the latter was less actually interest-

ing to her than was in fact the case. With her aunt Beatrice could be more unreserved; she began by plainly asking whether Mrs. Baxendale thought Wilfrid's regret had been of long endurance—a woman in Beatrice's position clearly could not, in talking to another, even suppose the case that the regret still endured. Her aunt honestly replied that she believed he had suffered long and severely.

'But,' she added, with characteristic tact, 'I did not need this instance, my dear, to prove to me that a first love may be only a preparation for that which is to last through life. I could tell you stories—but I haven't my grandmother's cap on at present.'

(Mrs. Baxendale was, in truth, a grandmother by this time, and professed to appreciate the authority she derived from the circumstance.)

That had drawn Beatrice out.

' She was strong-minded ? '

' Or very weak, I really don't know which.'

'Yes,' mused Beatrice, ' she was a problem to you. You never troubled yourself to puzzle over my character, aunt.'

' When a stream is of lovely clearness, Beatrice, we do not find it hard to determine the kind of ground it flows over.'

' I will owe you a kiss for that,' said the girl, blushing hot with very joy. 'But you are a flatterer, dear aunt, and just now I am very humble in spirit. I think great happiness should make us humble, don't you ? I find it hard to make out my claim to it.'

' Be humble still, dear, and the happiness will not be withdrawn.'

' I do like to talk with you,' Beatrice replied. ' I never go away without something worth thinking of.'

Humility she strove to nourish. It was a prime virtue of woman, and would sweeten her being. Unlike Emily, she was not inspired with an ardent idealism independently of her affections; with love had begun her conscious self-study, and love alone exalted her. Her many frivolous tendencies she had only overcome by dint of long endeavour to approach Wilfrid's standard. If in one way this was an item of strength, in another it indicated a very real and always menacing weakness. Having gained that to which her every instinct had directed itself, she made the possession of her bliss an indispensable factor of life; to lose it would be to fall into nether darkness, into despair of good. So widowed, there would be no support in herself; she knew it, and the knowledge at moments terrified her. Even her religious convictions, once very real and strong, had become subordinate; her creed—though she durst not confess it—was that of earthly love. Formerly she had been thrown back on religious emotion as a solace, an anodyne; for that reason the tendencies inherited from her mother had at one time reached a climax of fanaticism. Of late years, music had been her resource, the more efficient in that it ministered to hope. By degrees even her charitable activity had diminished; since her mother's death she had abandoned the habit of 'district visiting.' As confidence of the one supreme attainment grew in her, the mere accessories of her moral life were allowed to fall away. She professed no change of opinion, indeed underwent none, but opinion became, as with most women, distinct from practice. She still pretended to rejoice as often as she persuaded Wilfrid to go to church, but it was noticeable that she willingly allowed his preference for the better choral services, and seemed to take it for granted that the service was only of full efficacy when performed together with her. . . .

'Let me die now! It is only for this that I have lived!'

The cry came from her very heart. For once Wilfrid had been overcome, had thrown off his rather sad-coloured wooing, had uttered such words as her soul yearned for. Yet she had scarcely time to savour her rapture before that jealousy of the past mingled itself with the sensation. Even such words as these he must have used to *her*, and had they not perchance come more readily to his lips? Was he by nature so reserved? Or, the more probable thing, was it that she failed at other times to inspire him? How had *she* been used to behave, to speak?

In her incessant brooding upon the details of Wilfrid's first affection, Beatrice had found one point which never lost its power to distract her; it was the thought of all the correspondence that must have passed between him and Emily. What had become of those letters? Had they been mutually returned? It was impossible to discover. Not even to her aunt could she put such a question as that; and it might very well be that Mrs. Baxendale knew nothing certainly. If the story as she, Beatrice, had heard it was quite accurate, it seemed natural to suppose that Emily had requested to have her letters returned to her when she declared that the engagement must be at an end; but Wilfrid had refused to accept

that declaration, and would he not also have refused to let
the writing which was so precious to him leave his hands?
In that case he probably had the letters still; perhaps he still
read them at times. Would it be possible, even after marriage,
to speak of such a subject with Wilfrid? She had constantly
tried to assure herself that, even if he had kept the pledges
through all these years, a sense of honour would lead Wilfrid
to destroy them when he gave and received a new love. In
moments when it was her conscious effort to rise to noble
heights, to be as pure a woman as that other—for Beatrice
never sought the base comfort of refusing to her rival that
just homage—she would half persuade herself that no doubt
lingered in her mind, It was right to destroy the letters, and
whatever was right Wilfrid must have done. But she could
not live at all hours in that thin air; the defects of her blood
were too enduring. Jealousy came back from its brief exile,
and was more insinuating than ever, its suggestions more
maddening. By a sort of reaction, these thoughts assailed
her strongly in the moments which followed her outburst of
passion and Wilfrid's response. Yet she could not—durst
not—frame words to tell him of her suffering. It was to risk
too much; it might strike a fatal blow at his respect for her.
Even those last words she had breathed with dread, involun
tarily; already, perhaps, she had failed in the delicacy he
looked for, and had given him matter for disagreeable thought
as soon as he left her. She rose at length from her kneeling
attitude, and leaned back in her chair with a look of trouble
scarcely veiled.

Wilfrid did not notice it; he had already begun to think
of other matters.

'Beatrice,' he began, 'there's a subject I have avoided
speaking of, thinking you might perhaps be the first to mention it. Do you wish to continue your singing?'

She smiled, and did not seem to attach great importance
to the question,

'It is for you to decide,' she answered. 'You know why
I began it; I am ready to say my farewell whenever you bid
me.'

'But what is your own feeling? I suppose you would in
any case cease at our marriage?'

'You are not ashamed of it?'

'It is true,' he replied humorously, 'that I am a member
of the British House of Commons, but I beg you won't think

too meanly of me. I protest that I have still something of
my old self.'

'That means you are rather proud than ashamed. How
long,' she went on to ask, lowering her eyes, ' is the British
House of Commons likely to sit ? '

'Probably the talk will hold out for some seven or eight
weeks longer.'

'May I sing the two remaining engagements, if I take no
more after those ? '

'To be sure, you must. Let it stand so, then.'

She fell back into her brooding.

'Now I, too, have something to ask,' she said, after a short
silence.

'Whatever you ask is already granted.'

'Don't be too hasty. It's more than you think.'

'Well ? '

'I want you to give me some work to do for you—to let
me come and sit with you in your study some mornings and
write things for you.'

Wilfrid laughed cheerily.

'If I had a regard for my dignity,' he said, ' I certainly
shouldn't let you. What will become of my pretence of work
when you are let into the secrets ? But come, by all means.
You shall digest a blue-book for me.'

'When ? To-morrow morning ? '

'If you will.'

Beatrice was satisfied.

CHAPTER XXI.

DANGEROUS RELICS.

'BEATRICE is coming to act as my secretary this morning,'
Wilfrid said to his father, as they sat at breakfast on Monday.

'Is she ? ' remarked Mr. Athel, drily. 'It had struck me
that you were not very busy just now,' he added, by way of
natural comment.

The junior smiled.

'By the way, she has only two more engagements—then
it ceases.'

'I am glad to hear it,' said his father, with much satisfaction.

'After all,' observed Wilfrid, 'you must remember that everyone knows she doesn't sing for a living. Art, you know, is only contemptible when it supports the artist.

Well, well, file your epigrams by all means ; but we live in the world, Wilf. Criticise as smartly as you like ; the danger only begins when you act upon your convictions.'

At half-past ten Beatrice arrived. She came into the study with a morning colour on her cheeks, threw off her mantle and hat, and let Wilfrid draw off her gloves, which somehow took a long time in the doing. She was full of bright, happy talk, most of it tending to show that she had already given the attention to the morning's 'leaders' which was becoming in a politician's betrothed.

'Do you smoke whilst you are at work?' she asked, descending from those high themes.

'I allow myself a few cigarettes.'

'Cigarettes? Surely that is too frivolous an accompaniment!'

'O, it is only when I am musing upon the arguments of the Opposition.'

'I see.' Beatrice took the reply quite seriously. 'But where is the blue-book you want me to digest?'

Wilfrid shook his head, looking at her with a smile.

'You think me incompetent? But at least try me. I shan't spoil anything.'

'An illustration drawn from the art of millinery, I imagine.'

'Don't be unkind. I'm afraid you wouldn't let me write your letters?'

'By Jove! an excellent idea. Here's one of the free and independent electors of G—— writes to ask what my views are on the subject of compulsory vaccination. Do pen a reply and I'll sign it.'

'But what am I to say?'

'The ghost of Jenner alone knows! I offer it as an opportunity to show your fitness for this post. You have applied to me for work, Miss—Miss Redwing, I think your name is?' He assumed the air of one applied to.

'It is, sir.'

'Come, come; that's far too jaunty. You don't at all understand the position of the person applying for work. You must be profoundly depressed; there must be half a tear in your eye; you must look hungry.' ᵥ

'O dear—I had such an excellent breakfast!'

'Which clearly disqualifies you for the post you seek. However, Miss—Miss Redwing, I think you said?'

'I did, sir.'

'Vastly better. The applicant must always be a little ashamed of his name; they learn that, you know, from the way in which they are addressed by employers. Well, I'll give you a hint. Tell him he's an ass, or he wouldn't have needed to ask my opinion.'

'I am to put that into parliamentary language?'

'Precisely.'

'And say nothing more definite?'

'Really Miss—Miss Redwing, I begin to doubt the genuineness of your testimonials. You surely have learnt that the first essential of the art of public letter-writing is to say nothing whatever in as convincing a manner as possible.'

'But if I tell him he's a—a donkey?'

'You fear it will be deviating into truth. There's something in that. Say, then, that the matter is occupying my gravest attention, and that I hope to be able to reply definitely in the course of a few weeks.'

'Very well. Where may I sit? But I can't use a quill, dear boy.'

'Miss Redwing!'

'Oh, I forgot myself. Have you a nice, fine point, not too hard?'

'Let me see.'

Wilfrid unlocked one of the drawers in his desk. As he drew it out, Beatrice stole to him, and peeped into the drawer.

'How neat, Wilfrid!' she exclaimed. 'What a pretty pocket-book that is lying there. Do let me look at it.'

It was a morocco case, with an elastic band round it. Beatrice stretched her hand towards it, but he arrested her movement.

'No, no,' he said, playfully, 'we can't have prying. Here are the pens.'

'But do let me look at the case, Wilfrid.'

He began to close the drawer. Beatrice laid her hand on it.

'My aunt gave it me, long ago,' Wilfrid said, as if to dismiss the subject. 'Mind! I shall trap your fingers.'

'I'm sure you won't do that. But I *do* want to see it. The smell of morocco is so delicious. Just one whiff of it.'

'Then you want to smell it, not to see it. If you're good, you shall before you go away.'

'No, but now!—Wilfrid!'

He was pretending to squeeze her fingers in the shutting of the drawer. She would not undo her grasp.

'Why mayn't I, Wilfrid?'

She looked at him. His expression was graver than became the incident; he was trying to smile, but Beatrice saw that his eyes and lips were agitated.

'Why mayn't I?' she repeated.

'Oh, if you insist,' he exclaimed, moving back a step or two, 'of course you may.'

She took up the case, and looked at it on either side.

'There are letters in it?' she said, without raising her eyes.

'Yes, I believe there are letters in it.'

'Important, I suppose?'

'I daresay; I suppose I had some reason for putting them there.'

He spoke with apparent indifference, and turned to light a cigarette. Beatrice put back the case, and closed the drawer.

'Here is note-paper,' Wilfrid said, holding some to her.

She took it in silence, and seated herself. Wilfrid attempted to pursue the jest, but she could not reply. She sat as if about to write ; her eyes were drooped, and her mouth had set itself hard. Wilfrid affected to turn over papers in search for something, still standing before the table.

'You find it difficult to begin,' he said. 'Pray call him "dear sir." Society depends upon that "dear."'

'A word easily used,' remarked Beatrice, in a low voice, as if she were thinking.

He cast a glance at her, then seated himself. He was at the side of the table, she at the end. After a moment of silence, she leaned forward to him.

'Wilfrid,' she said, trying to smile, 'what letters are those, dear?'

'Of what possible moment can that be to you, Beatrice?'

'It seems—I can't help thinking they are—letters which you value particularly. Might I not know?'

He looked away to the window.

' Of course, if you tell me I am rude,' Beatrice continued, pressing her pen's point upon the table, ' I have no answer.'

' Well, yes,' he replied at length, as if having taken a resolve, ' they are letters of—that I have put apart for a special reason. And now, shall we forget them ? '

His tone was not altogether suave; about his nostrils there was a suspicion of defiance. He forced himself to meet her gaze steadily ; the effort killed a smile.

' We will cease to speak of them,' Beatrice answered, implying a distinction.

A minute later he saw that she laid down her pen and rose. He looked up inquiringly.

' I don't feel able to do anything this morning,' she said.

Wilfrid made no reply. She went to the chair on which her hat and mantle lay.

' You are not going ? ' he asked, in a tone of surprise.

' I think so ; I can't be of use to you,' she added, impulsively ; ' I have not your confidence.'

He let her throw the mantle over her shoulders.

' Beatrice, surely this is not the result of such a trifle ? Look ! ' He pulled open the drawer once more and threw the pocket-book on to the table. ' Suppose that had lain there when you came into this room alone. Should you have opened it and examined the contents ? '

' I should not—you know it.'

' Very well. You would simply have taken it for granted that I was to be trusted to look after my own affairs, until I asked someone else's aid or advice. Is not that the case at present ? '

A man more apt at dissimulation would have treated the matter from the first with joking irony, and might have carried his point, though with difficulty. Wilfrid had not the aptitude, to begin with, and he was gravely disturbed. His pulses were throbbing ; scarcely could he steady his voice. He dreaded a disclosure of what might well be regarded as throwing doubt upon his sincerity, the more so that he understood in this moment how justifiable such a doubt would be. After the merriment of a few minutes ago, this sudden shaking of his nerves was the harder to endure. It revived with painful intensity the first great agitations of his life. His way of speaking could not but confirm Beatrice's suspicions.

' We are not exactly strangers to each other,' she said, coldly.

'No, we are not; yet I think I should have forborne to press you on any matter you thought it needless to speak of.'

She put on her hat. Wilfrid felt his anger rising—our natural emotion when we are disagreeably in the wrong, yet cannot condemn the cause which has made us so. He sat to the table again, as if his part in the discussion were at an end.

Beatrice stood for some moments, then came quickly to his side.

'Wilfrid, have you secrets from me?' she asked, the tremor of her voice betraying the anguish that her suspicions cost her. 'Say I am ill-mannered. It was so, at first; I oughtn't to have said anything. But now it has become something different. However trifling the matter, I can't bear that you should refuse to treat me as yourself. There is nothing, nothing I could keep from you. I have not a secret in my life to hide from you. It is not because they are letters—or not only that. You put a distance between us; you say there are affairs of yours in which I have no concern. I cannot bear that! If I leave you, I shall suffer more than you dream. I thought we were one. Is not your love as complete as mine?'

He rose and moved away, saying—

'Open it! Look at the letters!'

'No, that I can't do. What can it be that troubles you so? Are they letters that I *ought* not to see?'

He could bear it no longer.

'Yes,' he answered, brusquely, 'I suppose they are.'

'You mean that you have preserved letters which, as often as you open that drawer, remind you of someone else?—that you purposely keep them so near your hand?'

'Beatrice, I had no right to destroy them.'

'No right!' Her eyes flashed, and her tongue trembled with its scorn. 'You mean you had no wish.'

'If I had no right, I could scarcely have the wish.'

Wilfrid was amazed at his own contemptible quibbling, but in truth he was not equal to the occasion. He could not defend himself in choice phrases; in a sort of desperate carelessness he flung out the first retort that offered itself. He was on the point of throwing over everything, of declaring that all must be at an end between them; yet courage failed for that. Nor courage only; the woman before him was very grand in her indignation, her pale face was surpassingly beautiful. The past faded in comparison with her; in his heart he doubted of its power.

Beatrice was gazing at him in resentful wonder.

' Why have you done this ? ' she asked. ' Why did you come to me and speak those words ? What necessity was there to pretend what you did not feel ? '

He met her eyes.

' I have not spoken falsely to you,' he said, with calmness which did not strengthen the impression his words were meant to convey.

' When you said that you loved me ? If it were true, you could not have borne to have those letters under your eyes. You say you had no right to destroy them. You knew that it was your duty to do so. *Could* you have kept them ? '

Wilfrid had become almost absent-minded. His heart was torn in two ways. He wished to take the letters from their case and destroy them at once ; probably it was masculine pride which now kept him from doing it.

' I think you must believe what I say, Beatrice,' was his answer. ' I am not capable of deliberately lying to you.'

' You are not. But you are capable of deceiving yourself; I accuse you of nothing more. You have deceived yourself, and I have been the cause of it ; for I had so little of woman's pride that I let you see my love ; it was as if I begged for your love in return. My own heart should have taught me better ; there can be no second love. You pitied me ! '

Wilfrid was in no state of mind to weigh phrases ; at a later time, when he could look back with calmness, and with the advantage of extended knowledge, he recognised in these words the uttermost confession of love of which a woman is capable. In hearing them, he simply took them as a reproach.

' If such a thing had been possible,' he said, ' it would have been a horrible injustice to you. I asked you to be my wife because I loved you. The existence of these letters is no proof that I misunderstood my own feeling. There are many things we cannot explain to another on the moment. You must judge the facts as you will, but no hasty and obvious judgment will hit the truth.'

She was not listening to him. Her eyes were fixed upon the letters, and over her heart there crept a desire which all but expelled other feeling, a desire to know what was there written. She would have given her hand to be alone in the room with that pocket book, now that she knew what it contained; no scruple would have withheld her. The impossibility that her longing could ever be satisfied frenzied her with jealousy.

'I will leave you with them,' she exclaimed, speaking her thought. 'You do not want me; I come between you and her. Read, and forget me; read them once more, and see then if you do not understand yourself. I know now why you have often been so cold, why it cost you an effort to reply to me. You shall never have that trouble again.'

She moved to quit the room. Wilfrid called her.

'Beatrice! Stay and listen to me. These letters are nothing, and mean nothing. Stay, and see me burn them.'

Irrational as it was, she could not bear to see them destroyed. In her distracted mind there was a sort of crazy hope that he would at last give them to her to burn; she might even perhaps have brought herself to take them away.

'That is childish,' she said. 'You know them by heart; the burning of the paper would alter nothing.'

'Then I can say and do no more.'

It had been like a rending of his heartstrings to offer to destroy these memories of Emily, though he at the same time persuaded himself that, once done, he would be a stronger and a happier man. In truth, they had made the chief strength of the link between him and the past; every day they had reminded him how much of the old feeling lingered in his being; the sanctity with which these relics were invested testified to the holiness of the worship which had bequeathed them. He had not opened the case since his betrothal to Beatrice, and scarcely a day passed that he did not purpose hiding it somewhere away for ever—not destroying. Beatrice's answer to his offer caused him half to repent that he had made it. He turned away from her.

She, after looking at the pocket-book still for some moments, seemed to force herself away. He heard her open the door, and did not try to stay her.

Half an hour later, Wilfrid restored the letters to their place in the drawer. If they were to be destroyed, it must now be in Beatrice's presence. With something like joy he turned the key upon them, feeling that they were preserved, that the last farewell was once again postponed. Wilfrid was not a very strong man where sacrifice was demanded of him.

He neither saw nor heard from Beatrice till the evening **of** the following day. Then it happened that they had to dine at the same house. On meeting her in the drawing-room, he gave her his hand as usual; hers returned no pressure. She seemed as cheerful as ever in her talk with others; him she kept apart from. He could not make up his mind to write. She had refused to accept such proof of his sincerity as it was in his power to offer, and Wilfrid made this an excuse—idle as he knew it to be—for maintaining a dignified silence. Dignified, he allowed himself to name it; yet he knew perfectly well that his attitude had one very ignoble aspect, since he all but consciously counted upon Beatrice's love to bring her back to his feet. He said to himself: Let her interpret my silence as she will; if she regard it as evidence of inability to face her—well, I make no objection. The conviction all the while grew in him that he did veritably love her, for he felt that, but for his knowledge of her utter devotedness, he would now be in fear lest he should lose her. Such fear need not occupy a thought; a word, and she flew to him. He enjoyed this sense of power; to draw out the misunderstanding a little would make reconciliation all the pleasanter. Then the letters should flame into ashes, and with them vanish even the regret for the blessedness they had promised.

Wednesday morning, and still no letter from Beatrice. Mr. Athel joked about her speedy resignation of the secretary-ship. Wilfrid joined in the joke, and decided that he would wait one more day, knowing not what a day might bring forth.

CHAPTER XXII.

HER PATH IN THE SHADOW.

YIELDING to the urgency of Beatrice, who was supported in her entreaty by Mrs. Birks, Wilfrid had, a little ere this, consented to sit for his portrait to an artist, a friend of the family, who had already made a very successful picture of Beatrice herself. The artist resided at Teddington. Wilfrid was due for a sitting this Wednesday morning, and he went down into the country, intending to be back for lunch and the House of Commons. But the weather was magnificent, and, the sitting over, truant thoughts began to assail the young legislator. Bushey Park was at hand, with its chestnut avenue leading to Hampton Court. A ramble of indefinite duration was, in his present frame of mind, much more attractive than the eloquence of independent members. He determined to take a holiday.

A very leisurely stroll across the park brought him to the King's Arms, and the sight of the hostelry suggested pleasant thoughts of sundry refreshing viands and cooling liquors. He entered and lunched. It was a holiday, and a truant holiday; he allowed himself champagne. When he came forth again, his intention to stroll through the galleries of the Palace had given way before the remembered shadow of the chestnuts; he returned to the park, and, after idly watching the fish in the shallow water of the round lake, strayed away into cool retreats, where the grass irresistibly invited to recumbency. He threw himself down, and let his eyes dream upon the delicate blades and stalks and leafage which one so seldom regards. If he chose to gaze further, there were fair tracts of shadowed sward, with sunny gleamings scattered where the trees were thinner, and above him the heaven of clustering leaves, here of impenetrable dark-green, there translucent-golden. A rustling whisper, in the air and on the ground, was the only voice that came thither.

He had set himself to think of Beatrice. He purposed writing her a long letter to-night, wherein he would do his best to make her understand the light in which the past appeared to him, and how little those memories had to do with the present and its love and its duty. To be sure, he could not use the words of very truth. He would much have preferred to speak with unflinching honesty, to confess that he *had*, even of late, often dwelt on the thought of Emily with tenderness, with something of heart-ache; but that the new love had, for all that, triumphed over the old, and would henceforth grow to perfectness. But the character of Beatrice would not allow this; in her, feeling was too predominant over intellect; she could not recognise in this very frankness the assurance of an affection which would end by being no less than the utmost she demanded. He had to seek for subtleties of explanation, for ingenuities of argument, which, unsatisfactory as they seemed to himself, might yet, he thought, help her to the reconciliation he knew she desired. He was scarcely less anxious for it. For Beatrice he would never

know that limitless passion, that infinite yearning alike of
spirit and of sense, which had been his love for Emily; but
she was very dear to him, and with all his heart he desired to
make her happiness. He imaged her beauty and her talent
with pride which made his veins warmer. Her husband, he
would be loyal to his last breath. Community of life would
establish that intimate alliance of heart and soul which every
year makes more enduring. Were they not young flesh and
blood, he and she? And could a bodiless ghost come between
them, a mere voice of long-vanished time, insubstantial,
unseizable, as the murmur in these chestnut-leaves?

He grew tired of the attitude which at first had been
reposeful, and rose to wander further. Someone else, it
seemed, had been tempted to this quiet corner, away from the
road; a woman was walking at a little distance, and reading
as she walked. The thought passed through his mind that a
woman never looked more graceful than when walking with
her head bent over a book. When he looked that way again,
he found that she had come much nearer, still very intent
upon her reading. She had, in truth, a comely figure, one
which suggested a face of the nobler kind. She would look
up presently.

Did not that form, that movement as she walked, stir
memories? Yes, he had known someone who might well
have paced thus beneath spreading trees, with her eyes upon
a book of poetry; not unlike this stranger, outwardly. In
what black, skyless, leafless town was she pursuing her lonely
life?—Lonely? why should it be so? Emily could not go on
her way without meeting one whom her sweetness and her
power would enthral, and the reasons, whatever they were,
that had forbidden her marriage six or seven years ago, were
not likely to resist time. He tried to hope that the happier
lot had by this solaced her. Do we not change so? His
own love—see how it had faded!

Half purposely, he had turned so as to pass near the
reader. At the distance of a few yards from her, he stayed
his step. A little nearer she came, then something made her
aware of his presence. She raised her eyes, the eyes of
Emily Hood.

Her hands fell, one still holding the book open. He, who
was prepared already, could watch her countenance change
from placid, if grave, thought, to the awakening of surprise,
to startled recognition; he could see the colour die upon her

cheeks, flee from her lips; he could observe the great heart-throbs which shook her and left her bosom quivering. He did not uncover his head; conventional courtesies have their season. It seemed very long before they ceased to look into each other's eyes, but at length hers fell.

'Is it possible that you are living in London?' were Wilfrid's first words. He could affect no distance of manner. To him all at once it was as though they had parted a few days ago.

'Yes,' she answered simply. 'In a far part of London.'

'And we meet here, where I seemed to find myself by the merest chance. I saw a stranger in the distance, and thought of yourself; I knew you long before you looked up from your reading.'

Emily tried to smile.

'How little you are changed!' Wilfrid continued, his voice keeping still its awed quietness, with under-notes of feeling. 'Rather, you are not changed at all.'

It was not true, but in the few minutes that he had gazed at her, past and present had so blended that he could not see what another would have noticed. Emily was appreciably older, and ill-health had set marks upon her face. A stranger looking at her now would have found it hard to imagine her with the light of joy in her eyes, her features had set themselves in sorrow. Her cheeks were very thin; her eyes were dark and sunken. Wilfrid saw only the soul in her gaze at him, and that was as it had ever been.

She was unable to speak; Wilfrid found words.

'Do you often walk here? Is your home near?'

'Not very near. I came by the river,' she answered.

'I am very glad that I have met you,' The words sounded insufficient, but Wilfrid was by this time at battle with himself, and succeeded in saying less than he felt. 'You will let me walk on a little way with you? We can't shake hands at once and say good-bye, can we, after such a long time?'

He spoke in the tone one uses to jest over bygone sadness. Emily made no verbal answer, but walked along by his side.

'You still have your old habits,' he said, casting an eye at the book. 'Are your tastes still the same, I wonder?'

'It is Dante,' she replied.

The name brought another to Wilfrid's consciousness; he averted his eyes for a moment, but spoke again without much delay.

'Still faithful to the great names. This is a lovely place to make one's study. Were you here when the chestnuts flowered?'

'Yes, once or twice.'

'I did not see them this year. And you have been walking here so often,' he added, wondering again, half to himself. 'I have been to Teddington several times lately, but only to-day came into the park.'

'I have not been here for a month,' Emily said, speaking at length with more ease. The shock had affected her physically more than she had allowed to be seen; it was only now that her voice was perfectly at her command. Her face remained grave, but she spoke in a tone free from suggestion of melancholy. 'I teach in a school, and to-day there is a holiday.'

'Do you live at the school?'

'No. I have my own lodgings.'

He was on the point of asking whether Mrs. Baxendale knew she was in London, but it seemed better to suppress the question.

'Have you been there long?' he asked instead.

'Half a year.'

As he kept silence, Emily continued with a question, the first she had put.

'What have you chosen for your life's work?'

Wilfrid could not overcome the tendency of blood to his cheeks. He was more than half ashamed to tell her the truth.

'You will laugh at me,' he said. 'I am in Parliament.'

'You are? I never see newspapers.'

She added it as if to excuse herself for not being aware of his public activity.

'Oh, I am still far from being a subject of leading-articles,' Wilfrid exclaimed. 'Indeed, I gave you no answer to your question. My life's work is non-existent. All my old plans have come to nothing, and I have formed no new ones, no serious plans. My life will be a failure, I suppose.'

'But you aim at success in politics?'

'I suppose so. I was thinking of the other things we used to speak of.'

Emily hazarded a glance at him, as if to examine him again in this new light.

'You used to say,' she continued, 'that you felt in many ways suited for a political life.'

'Did I? You mean at home, when I talked in a foolish way. It was not my serious thought. I never said it to you.'

She murmured a 'No.' They walked on in silence.

'You didn't read Italian then,' Wilfrid said. 'You, I feel sure, have not wasted your time. How much you must have read since we talked over our favourite authors.'

'I have tried to keep up the habit of study,' Emily replied, unaffectedly, 'but of course most of my time is occupied in teaching.'

Their walk had brought them from under the trees, and the lake was just before them.

'I will go on to the bridge,' Emily said. 'The boat I return by will leave shortly.'

She spoke as if expecting him to take leave of her. Wilfrid inwardly bade himself do so. He had seen her, had talked with her; what more for either? Yet it was beyond his power to stand here and see her walk away from him. Things were stirring in his heart and mind of which he refused to take cognisance; he would grant nothing more than a sense of pleasure in hearing once again a voice which had so long been buried, and there was no harm in that. Was not his strongest feeling merely surprise at having met her thus? Even yet he found a difficulty in realising that it was she with whom he spoke; had he closed his eyes and then looked round for her in vain it would only have appeared the natural waking from intense reverie. Why not dream on as long as he might?

'May I not walk as far as the bridge with you?' he asked. 'If I were not afraid of being tiresome I should even like to go by the boat; it would be the pleasantest way of getting back to town.'

'Yes, it is pleasant on the river,' Emily said rather absently.

They pursued their walk together, and conversed still much in the same way. Wilfrid learned that her school was in Hammersmith, a large day-school for girls; he led her to speak of the subjects she taught, and of her pupils.

'You prefer it,' he asked, 'to private teaching?'

'I think so.'

Once on the boat their talk grew less consecutive; the few words they exchanged now and then were suggested by objects or places passed. At length even these remarks ceased, and for the last half-hour they held silence. Other people close by were talking noisily. Emily sat with both hands holding the book upon her lap, her eyes seldom moving from a point directly before her. Wilfrid glanced at her frequently. He was more observant now of the traces of bodily weakness in her; he saw how meagre she had become, how slight her whole frame was. At moments it cost him a serious effort to refrain from leaning to her and whispering words—he knew not what—something kind, something that should change her fixed sadness. Why had he forced his company upon her? Certainly he brought her no joy, and presently he would take leave of her as any slight acquaintance might; how otherwise? It would have been better to part there by the lake where she offered the occasion.

The steamer reached Hammersmith. Only at this last moment he seemed to understand where he was and with whom, that Emily was sitting by him, in very deed here by his side, and directly would be gone—he knew not whither— scarcely to be met again. The silence between them had come of the difficulty they both had in realising that they were together, of the dreaminess so strange an event had cast upon them. Were they to fall apart again without a word, a sign? A sign of what, forsooth?

Wilfrid moved with her to the spot at which she would step from the deck; seeing him follow, Emily threw back one startled glance. The next moment she again turned, holding out her hand. He took it, held it, pressed it; nothing could restrain that pressure; his muscles closed upon her slight fingers involuntarily. Then he watched her walk hurriedly from the landing-stage. . . . .

Her we follow. She had a walk of nearly half an hour, which brought her at length to one of the streets of small lodging-houses which abound in this neighbourhood, and to a door which she opened with her latch-key. She went up-stairs. Here two rooms were her home. That which looked upon the street was furnished in the poor bare style which the exterior of the dwelling would have led one to expect. A very hideous screen of coloured paper hid the fireplace, and in front of the small oblong mirror—cracked across one corner—which stood above the mantelpiece were divers orna-ments such as one meets with in poor lodging-houses; certain pictures about the walls completed the effect of vulgarity.

Emily let herself sink upon the chintz-covered couch, and lay back, closing her eyes; she had thrown off her hat, but was too weary, too absent in thought, to remove her mantle. Her face was as colourless as if she had fainted ; she kept one hand pressed against her heart. Unconsciously she had walked home with a very quick step, and quick movement caused her physical suffering. She sat thus for a quarter of an hour, when there came a tap at the door.

Her landlady entered.

' Oh, I thought, Miss Hood,' she began, ' you'd maybe rung the bell as usual, and I hadn't heard it. I do sometimes think I'm getting a little hard of hearing ; my husband tell me of it. Will you have the tea made ? '

' Thank you, Mrs. Willis,' Emily replied, rising.

She opened a low cupboard beside the fireplace, took out a tea-pot, and put some tea into it.

' You'd have a long walk, I suppose,' continued the woman, ' and delightful weather for it, too. But you must mind as you don't over-tire yourself. You don't look very strong, if I may say it.'

' Oh, I am very well,' was the mechanical reply.

After a few more remarks the landlady took away the tea-pot. Emily then drew out a cloth from the cupboard, and other things needful for her evening meal. Presently the tea-pot returned filled with hot water. Emily was glad to pour out a cup and drink it, but she ate nothing. In a short time she rang the bell to have the things removed. This time a little girl appeared.

' Eh, Miss,' was the exclamation of the child, on examin- ing the state of the table, ' you haven't eaten nothing ! '

' No, I don't want anything just now, Milly,' was the quiet reply.

' Shall I leave the bread and butter out ? '

' No, thank you. I'll have some later.'

' Is there anything I could get you, Miss ? '

' Nothing, Milly. Take the things away, there's a good girl.'

Emily had seated herself on the couch again ; when the girl was gone she lay down, her hands beneath her head. Long, long since she had had so much to think of as to-night.

At first she had found Wilfrid a good deal altered. He looked so much older ; his bearded face naturally caused that. But before he had spoken twenty words how well she knew that the change was only of appearance. His voice was a little deeper, but the tone and manner of his speaking carried her back to the days when they had first exchanged words when she was a governess at The Firs in Surrey, and Wilfrid was the interesting young fellow who had overworked himself at college. The circumstances of to-day's meeting had reproduced something of the timidity with which he had approached her when they were strangers. This afternoon she had scarcely looked into his eyes, but she felt their gaze upon her, and felt their power as of old—ah, fifty-fold stronger!

Was he married? It was more than possible. Nothing had escaped him inconsistent with that, and he was not likely to speak of it directly. It would account for the nature of his embarrassment in talking with her; her keen insight distinguished something more than the hesitation which common memories would naturally cause. And that pressure of the hand at parting which had made her heart leap with such agony, might well be his way of intimating to her that this meeting would have no sequel. Was it to be expected that he should remain unmarried? Had she hoped it?

It could not be called hope, but for two or three years something had grown in her which made life a succession of alternating longings and despairs. For Emily was not so constituted that the phase of thought and feeling which had been brought about by the tragedy of her home could perpetuate itself and become her normal consciousness. When she fled from Dunfield she believed that the impulses then so strong would prevail with her to the end of her life, that the motives which were then predominant in her soul would maintain their ruling force for ever. And many months went by before she suspected that her imagination had deceived her; imagination, ever the most potent factor of her being, the source alike of her strength and her weakness. But there came a day when the poignancy of her grief was subdued, and she looked around her upon a world more desolate than that in which she found herself on the day of her mother's burial. She began to know once more that she was young, and that existence stretched before her a limitless tract of barren endurance.

The rare natures which are in truth ruled by the instinct of renunciation, which find in the mortification of sense a spring of unearthly joy brimming higher with each self-conquest, may experience temptation and relapse, but the former is a new occasion for the arming of the spirit, and the latter speedily leads to a remorse which is the strongest of all incen-

tives to ascetic struggle. Emily had not upon her the seal
of sainthood. It was certain that at some point of her life
asceticism would make irresistible claim upon the strongholds
of her imagination; none the less certain that it would be but
for a time, that it would prove but a stage in her development.
To her misfortune the occasion presented itself in connection
with her strongest native affections, and under circumstances
which led her to an irretrievable act. Had she been brought
up in a Roman Catholic country she would doubtless have
thrown herself into a convent, finding her stern joy in the
thought that no future wavering was possible. Attempting to
make a convent of her own mind, she soon knew too well
that her efforts mocked her, that there was in her an instinct
stronger than that of renunciation, and that she had condemned herself to a life of futile misery.

Her state of mind for the year following her father's death
was morbid, little differing from madness; and she came at
length to understand that. When time had tempered her
anguish, she saw with clear eyes that her acts had been
guided by hallucination. Never would sorrow for her parents
cease to abide with her, but sorrow cannot be the sustenance
of a life through those years when the mind is strongest and
the sensations most vivid. Had she by her self mortification
done aught to pleasure those dear ones who slept their last
sleep? It had been the predominant feature of her morbid
passion to believe that piety demanded such a sacrifice. Grief
may reach such a point that to share the uttermost fate of the
beloved one seems blessedness; in Emily's mind that moment
of supreme agony had been protracted till unreasoning desire
took to itself the guise of duty. Duty so represented cannot
maintain its sanction when the wounds of nature grow towards
healing.

She strove with herself. The reaction she was experiencing seemed to her a shameful weakness. Must she cease to
know the self-respect which comes of conscious perseverance
in a noble effort? Must she stand self-condemned, an ignoble
nature, incapable of anything good and great—and that, after
all her ambitions? Was she a mere waif, at the mercy of the
currents of sense? Never before had she felt this condemnation of her own spirit She had suffered beyond utterance,
but ever with a support which kept her from the last despair;
of her anguish had come inspiration. Now she felt herself
abandoned of all spiritual good. She came to loathe her life

as a polluted stream. The image of Wilfrid, the memory of her lost love, these grew to be symbols of her baseness. It was too much to face those with whom daily duty brought her in contact ; surely they must read in her face the degradation of which she was conscious. As much as possible she kept apart from all, nursing her bitter self-reproach.

Then it was that she sought relief in the schemes which naturally occur to a woman thus miserable. She would relinquish her life as a teacher, and bury her wretchedness beneath physical hardship. There was anguish enough in the world, and she would go to live in the midst of it, would undertake the hardest and most revolting tasks in some infirmary : thus might she crush out of herself the weakness which was her disgrace. It remained only a vision. That which was terribly real, the waste and woe of her heart, grew ever.

She yielded. Was not the true sin this that she tried to accomplish—the slaying of the love which cried so from her inmost being ? Glimpses of the old faith began to be once more vouchsafed her ; at moments she knew the joy of beautiful things. This was in spring-time. Living in the great seaport, she could easily come within sight of the blue line where heaven and ocean met, and that symbol of infinity stirred once more the yearnings for boundless joy which in bygone days she had taught herself to accept as her creed. Supposing that her father had still knowledge of the life she led, would it make him happy to know that she had deprived herself of every pleasure, had for his sake ruined a future which might have been so fair ? Not thus do we show piety to the dead ; rather in binding our brows with every flower our hands may cull, and in drinking sunlight as long as the west keeps for us one gleam.

She had destroyed herself. Joy could arise to her from but one source, and that was stopped for ever. For it never came to Emily as the faintest whisper that other love than Wilfrid's might bless her life. That was constancy which nothing could shake ; in this she would never fall from the ideal she had set before herself. She no longer tried to banish thoughts of what she had lost ; Wilfrid was a companion at all hours far more real than the people with whom she had to associate. She had, alas, destroyed his letters ; she had destroyed the book in which she wrote the secrets of her heart that he might some day read them. The lack of a single thing that had some to her from him made the more terribly real the severance of his life from hers. She anguished without hope.

Then there came to her the knowledge that her bodily strength was threatened by disease. She had fainting fits, and in the comfort administered by those about her she read plainly what was meant to be concealed. At times this was a relief; at least she might hope to be spared long years of weary desolation, and death, come when he might, would be a friend. In other hours the all but certainty of her doom was a thought so terrible that reason well-nigh failed before it. Was there no hope for her for ever, nothing but the grave to rest her tired heart? Why had fate dealt with her so cruelly? She looked round and saw none upon whom had fallen a curse so unrelieved.

At last the desire to go once more to the south of England grew overpowering. If she could live in London, she felt it might console her to feel that she was near Wilfrid; he would not seem, as now, in a world utterly remote. Perchance she might one day even see him. If she had knowledge of the approach of death, Wilfrid would not refuse to come and see her at the last, and with her hand in his how easy it would be to die. She sought for means of supporting herself in London; she still had money saved from that which the sale of her father's house had brought her, but she did not wish to use more of this than she could help, keeping it for a certain cherished purpose. After many months of fruitless endeavour, she found a place in a school in Hammersmith. . . .

And Wilfrid had sat by her, had looked at her with something of the old tenderness, had pressed her hand as no one else would. Far into the night she lay thinking over every word he had spoken. Sometimes she wept—poor Emily! He had not asked her where she lived; for that doubtless there was good reason. But it was much to have seen him this once. Again she wept, saying to herself that she loved him,—that he was lost to her,—that she must die.

CHAPTER XXIII

HER PATH IN THE LIGHT.

THAT Wilfrid did not at the last moment leap on shore and follow Emily seemed to him less the result of self-control than obedience to outward restraint; it was as though an actual hand lay on his shoulder and held him back. He went back to his seat, and again fell into dreaminess.

The arrival of the boat at Chelsea pier reminded him that he must land; thence he drove home. On reaching the house he found Mrs. Birks there; she had called to see his father, and was in the hall on the point of leaving as he entered. She stepped up to him, and spoke in a low voice.

'What is the matter with Beatrice?'

'The matter? How?'

'She seems out of sorts. Come round and see her, will you?'

'I really can't just now,' Wilfrid replied. 'Do you mean that she is not well?'

'Something seems to be upsetting her. Why can't you come and see her?'

'I can't this evening. I have an engagement.'

'Very well. But you had better come soon, I think.'

'I don't understand you,' said Wilfrid, with some show of impatience. 'Is she ill?'

'Not exactly ill, I suppose. Of course I mustn't interfere. No doubt you understand.'

'I will come as soon as I can,' Wilfrid said. And he added, 'Has she—spoken to you about anything?'

'I wish she had. She will speak neither to me nor to anyone else. It is too bad, Wilf, if you let her fret herself into a fever. She is just the girl to do it, you know.'

She nodded, smiled, and went off. Wilfrid, having committed himself to an engagement, loitered about in his dressing-room for a while, then, without seeing his father, betook himself to his club and dined there. After passing the early part of the evening in an uncomfortable way, with the help of newspapers and casual conversation, he went home again and shut himself in his study.

He sat long, without attempting to do anything. About midnight he rose as if to leave the room, but, instead of doing so, paced the floor for a few minutes; then he opened a certain drawer in his writing-table, and took out the morocco case which contained Emily's letters. He slipped off the band. The letters were still in their envelopes, and lay in the order in which he had received them. He drew forth the first and began to read it. He read them all.

Till the early daybreak he remained in the room, sometimes walking about, sometimes seating himself to re-read this letter and that. Twenty-four hours ago these written words would have touched his heart indeed, but only as does the memory of an irrecoverable joy; he could have read them, and still have gone to meet Beatrice as usual, or with but a little more than his ordinary reserve in her presence. It was otherwise now. The very voice had spoken again, and its tones lingering with him made the written characters vocal; each word uttered itself as it met his eye; Emily spoke still. The paper was old, the ink faded, but the love was of this hour. He grew fevered, and it was the fever of years ago, which had only been in appearance subdued; it had lurked still in his blood, and now asserted itself with the old dire mastery.

He marvelled that he had suffered her to leave him without even learning where she lived. He could not understand what his mood had been, what motives had weighed with him. He had not been conscious of a severe struggle to resist a temptation; the temptation had not, in fact, yet formed itself. What was her own thought? She had answered his questions freely, perhaps would have told him without hesitation the address of her lodgings. Clearly she no longer sought to escape him. But that, he reminded himself, was only the natural response to his own perfectly calm way of speaking; she could not suggest embarrassments when it was his own cue to show that he felt none. She was still free, it seemed, but what was her feeling towards him? Did she still love him? Was the mysterious cause which had parted them still valid?

When already it was daylight, he went upstairs and lay down on the bed. He was weary, but not with the kind of weariness that brings sleep. His mind was occupied with plans for discovering where Emily lived. Mrs. Baxendale had professed to have lost sight of her; Wilfrid saw now that there was a reason for concealing the truth, and felt that in all probability his friend had misled him; in any case, he could not apply to her. Was there a chance of a second meeting in the same place? Emily was sure to be free on Saturday afternoon; but only in one case would she go to the park again—if she desired to see him, and imagined a corresponding desire on his side. And that was an unlikely thing; granting she loved him, it was not in Emily's character to scheme thus, under the circumstances.

Yet why had she chosen to come and live in London?

Beatrice he had put out of his thoughts. He did not do it deliberately; he made no daring plans; simply he gave himself over to the rising flood of passion, without caring to ask whither it would bear him. Though it fevered him, there was a luxury in the sense of abandonment once more to desire which suffered no questioning. That he had ever really loved Beatrice he saw now to be more than doubtful; that he loved Emily was as certain as that he lived. To compare the images of the two women was to set side by side a life sad and wan with one which bloomed like a royal flower, a face whose lines were wasted by long desolation with one whose loveliness was the fit embodiment of supreme joy. But in the former he found a beauty of which the other offered no suggestion, a beauty which appealed to him with the most subtle allurements, which drew him as with siren song, which, if he still contemplated it, would inspire him with recklessness. He made no effort to expel it from his imagination; every hour it was sweeter to forget the facts of life and dream of what might be.

Through this day and that which followed he kept away from home, only returning late at night. No more news of Beatrice came. He saw that his father regarded him with looks of curiosity, but only conversation of the wonted kind passed between them. When Saturday arrived he was no longer in doubt whether to pursue the one faint hope of finding Emily again in Bushey Park; the difficulty was to pass the time till noon, before which it was useless to start. He was due for the last sitting in the studio at Teddington, but that was an ordeal impossible to go through in his present state of mind. He went to Hampton by train, lunched again at the King's Arms, though but hastily, and at length reached the spot in the park where his eyes had discovered Emily reading.

It was not such a day as Wednesday had been; the sun shone intermittently, but there was threatening of rain. A vehicle now and then drove along the avenue taking holiday-makers to the Palace, and, near the place where Wilfrid walked, a party was picnicking under the trees. But he in vain sought for one who wandered alone, one who, in the distance, could move him to uncertain hope.

Why had he come? Suppose he did again meet Emily, what had he to say to her? Long and useless waiting naturally suggested such thoughts, and the answer to them was a momentary failing at the heart, a touch of fear. Was he prepared to treat this temporary coldness between Beatrice and himself as a final rupture? Was his present behaviour exactly that of a man who recognises rules of honour? If he had no purpose in wishing to see Emily but the satisfaction of a desire about which he would not reason, was it not un-qualified treachery in which he was involving himself, treachery to two women and to one of them utter cruelty? He turned to walk towards the lake, desperate that his hope had failed, and at the same time—strange contradiction—glad in the thought that, having once yielded, he might overcome his madness. He passed the lake, and reached the exit from the park. At the same moment Emily was entering.

Her face expressed an agony of shame; she could not raise her eyes, could not speak. She gave him her hand mechanically, and walked on with her looks averted. Her distress was so unconcealed that it pained him acutely. He could not find words till they had walked a distance of twenty or thirty yards. Then he said:

'I came purposely to-day, in the hope that you might by chance be here. Do I annoy you?'

She half turned her face to him, but the effort to speak was vain.

A still longer silence followed. Wilfrid knew at length what he had done. That utterance of his had but one mean-ing, Emily's mute reply admitted of but one interpretation. His eyes dazzled; his heart beat violently. A gulf sank be-fore him, and there was no longer choice but to plunge into it. He looked at his companion, and—farewell the solid ground.

'Emily, is it your wish that I should leave you?'

She faced him, moved her lips, motioned 'no' with her head. She was like one who is led to death.

' Then I will not leave you. Let us walk gently on ; you shall speak to me when you feel able.'

He cared for no obstacle now. She was come back to him from the dead, and to him it was enough of life to hold her. Let the world go ; let all speak of him as they would ; this pale, weary-eyed woman should henceforth represent existence to him. He would know no law but the bidding of his sovereign love.

She spoke.

' Have I fallen in your eyes ? '

' You have always been to me the highest, and will be whilst I live.'

They had passed into the shadow of the trees ; he took her hand and held it. The touch seemed to strengthen her, for she looked at him again and spoke firmly.

' Neither was my coming without thought of you. I had no hope that you would be here, no least hope, but I came because it was here I had seen you.'

' Since Wednesday,' Wilfrid returned, ' I have read your letters many times. Could you still speak to me as you did then ? '

' If you could believe me.'

' You said once that you did not love me.'

' It was untrue.'

' May you tell me now what it was that came between us ? '

She fixed upon him a gaze of sad entreaty, and said, under her breath, ' Not now.'

' Then I will never ask. Let it be what it might ; your simple word that you loved me is all I need.'

' I will tell you,' Emily replied, ' but I cannot now. It seemed to me at the time that that secret would have to die with me ; I thought so till I met you here. Then I knew that, if you still loved me and had been faithful to me so long, I could say nothing to myself which I might not speak to you. My love for you has conquered every other love and everything that I believed my duty.'

' Is it so, Emily ? ' he asked, with deepest tenderness.

' When I tell you all, you will perhaps feel that I have proved my own weakness. I will conceal from you nothing I have ever thought ; you will see that I tried to do what my purest instincts urged, and that I have been unable to persevere to the end. Wilfrid——'

' My own soul ! '

'When I tell you all that happened at that time, I shall indeed speak to you as if your soul and mine were one. It may be wrong to tell you—you may despise me for not keeping such things a secret for ever. I cannot tell whether I am right or wrong to do this. Is your love like mine?'

'I would say it was greater, if you were not so above me in all things.'

'Wilfrid, I was dying in my loneliness. It would not have been hard to die, for, if I was weak in everything else, at least my love for you would have grown to my last breath. If I speak things which I should only prove in silence, it is that you may not afterwards judge me hardly.'

'You shall tell me,' Wilfrid replied, 'when you are my wife. Till then I will hear nothing but that you are and always have been mine.'

They came to a great tree about the trunk of which had been built a circular seat. The glades on every side showed no disturbing approach.

'Let us sit here,' said Wilfrid. 'We have always talked with each other in the open air, haven't we?'

He drew her to him and kissed her face passionately. It was the satisfying of a hunger of years. With Beatrice his caresses had seldom been other than playful; from the first moment of re-meeting with Emily, he had longed to hold her to his heart.

'Can I hope to keep you now? You won't leave me again, Emily?'

'If I leave you, Wilfrid, it will be to die.'

Again he folded her in his arms, and kissed her lips, her cheeks, her eyes. She was as weak as a trembling flower.

'Emily, I shall be in dread through every moment that parts us. Will you consent to whatever I ask of you? Once before I would have taken you and made you my wife, and if you had yielded we should have escaped all this long misery. Will you now do what I wish?'

She looked at him questioningly.

'Will you marry me as soon as it can possibly be? On Monday I will do what is necessary, and we can be married on Wednesday. This time you will not refuse?'

'Wednesday?'

'Yes. One day only need intervene between the notice and the marriage; it shall be at the church nearest to you.'

'Wilfrid, why do you——'

Fear had taken hold upon her; she could not face the thought. Wilfrid checked her faint words with his lips.

'I wish it,' he said, himself shaken with a tempest of passion which whelmed the last protest of his conscience. 'I shall scarcely tear myself from you even till then. Emily, Emily, what has my life been without your love? Oh, you will be the angel that raises me out of the ignoble world into which I have fallen! Hold me to you—make me feel and believe that you have saved me! Emily, my beautiful, my goddess! let me worship you, pray to you! Mine now, mine, love, for ever and ever!'

She burst into tears, unable to suffer this new denizen of her heart, the sure and certain hope of bliss. He kissed away the tears as they fell, whispering love that was near to frenzy. There came a sob that shook her whole frame, then Wilfrid felt her cheek grow very cold against his; her eyes were half closed, from her lips escaped a faint moan. He drew back and, uncertain whether she had lost consciousness, called to her to speak. Her body could not fall, for it rested against a hollow part of the great trunk. The faintness lasted only for a few moments; she once more gazed at him with the eyes of infinite sadness.

'It is so hard to bear happiness,' were her first words.

'My dearest, you are weak and worn with trouble. Oh, we will soon leave that far behind us. Are you better, my lily? Only give me your hands to hold, and I will be very still. Your hands are so light; they weigh no more than leaves. Do you suffer, dear?'

'A little pain—there;' she touched her heart.

Wilfrid looked into her face anxiously.

'Have you often that pain?'

'No, not often. I don't feel it now. Wilfrid! Every day I have spoken that name, have spoken it aloud.'

'So have I often spoken yours, dear.'

They gazed at each other in silence.

'And it is to be as I wish?' Wilfrid said gently.

'So very soon?'

'So very long! This is only Saturday. If I had known this morning, it could have been on Monday.'

'Your wife, Wilfrid? Really your wife?'

'How your voice has changed! Till now you spoke so sadly. Those words are like the happiest of our old happy time. Three long days to bo passed, but not one day more. You promise me ? '

' I do your bidding, now and always, always ! '

For the moment she had forgotten everything but love and love's rapture. It was as though life spread before her in limitless glory; she thought nothing of the dark foe with whose ever-watchful, ever-threatening presence she had become so familiar.

They talked long; only the lengthening and deepening shadow of the trees reminded them at length that hours had passed whilst they sat here.

' The boat will have gone,' Emily said.

' Never mind. We will get a conveyance at the hotel. And you must have refreshment of some kind. Shall we see what they can give us to eat at the King's Arms ? To be sure we will. It will be our first meal together.'

They rose.

' Emily ! '

' Yes, Wilfrid ? '

' I can trust you ? You will not fail me ? '

' Not if I am living, Wilfrid.'

' Oh, but I shall of course see you before Wednesday. To-morrow is Sunday   '

He checked himself. Sunday was the day he always gave to Beatrice. But he durst not think of that now.

' On Sunday there are so many people about,' he continued. ' Will you come here again on Monday afternoon ? '

Emily promised to do so.

' I will write to you to-morrow, and again a letter for Tuesday, giving you the last directions. But I may have to see you on Tuesday. May I call at your lodgings ? '

' If you need to. Surely you may ? My—my husband ?'

' My wife ! '

They walked to the hotel, and thence, when dusk was falling, started to drive homewards. They stopped at the end of Emily's street, and Wilfrid walked with her to the door.

' Till Monday afternoon,' he said, grasping her hand as if he clung to it in fear

Then he found another vehicle. It was dark when he reached home.

CHAPTER XXIV.

THE UNEXPECTED.

LATE in the evening Wilfrid received a visit from his father. Mr. Athel had dined with his sister, and subsequently accompanied his nieces to a concert. Beatrice should have sung, but had broken her engagement on the plea of ill-health.

' Been at home all the evening ? ' Mr. Athel began by asking.

' I got home late,' Wilfrid answered, rising from his chair.

His father had something to say which cost him hesitation. He walked about with his hands between the tails of his coat.

' Seen Beatrice lately ? ' he inquired at length.

' No ; not since last Monday.'

' I'm afraid she isn't well. She didn't sing to-night. Didn't dine with us either.'

Wilfrid kept silence.

' Something wrong ? ' was his father's next question.

' Yes, there is.'

' I'm sorry to hear that.'

Wilfrid went to the fireplace and leaned his arm upon the mantelpiece. As he did not seem disposed to speak, his father continued—

' Nothing serious, I hope ? '

' Yes ; something serious.'

' You don't mean that ? Anything you can talk about ? '

' I'm afraid not. I shall go and see Beatrice as usual to-morrow. I may be at liberty to tell you after that, though probably not for a few days.'

Mr. Athel looked annoyed.

' I hope this is not of your doing,' he said. ' They tell me the girl is causing them a good deal of anxiety. For the last few days she has been sitting alone, scarcely touching food, and refusing to speak to anyone. If this goes on she will be ill.'

Wilfrid spoke hoarsely.

' I can't help it. I shall see her to-morrow.'

' All right,' observed his father, with the impatience which was his way of meeting disorders in this admirable universe.

'Your aunt asked me to tell you this; of course I can do no more.'

Wilfrid made no reply, and Mr. Athel left him.

It was an hour of terrible suffering that Wilfrid lived through before he left the study and went to lay his head on the pillow. He had not thought very much of Beatrice hitherto; the passion which had spurred him blindly on made him forgetful of everything but the end his heart desired. Now that the end was within reach, he could consider what it was that he had done. He was acting like a very madman. He could not hope that any soul would regard his frenzy even with compassion; on all sides he would meet with the sternest condemnation. Who would recognise his wife? This step which he was taking meant rupture with all his relatives, perchance with all his friends; for it would be universally declared that he had been guilty of utter baseness. His career was ruined. It might happen that he would have to leave England with Emily, abandoning for her sake everything else that he prized.

How would Beatrice bear the revelation? Mere suspense had made her ill; such a blow as this might kill her. Never before had he been consciously guilty of an act of cruelty or of wrong to any the least valued of those with whom he had dealt; to realise what his treachery meant to Beatrice was so terrible that he dared not fix his thought upon it. Her love for him was intense beyond anything he had imagined in woman; Emily had never seemed to him possessed with so vehement a passion. Indeed he had often doubted whether Emily's was a passionate nature; at times she was almost cold—appeared so, in his thought of her—and never had she given way to that self-forgetful ardour which was so common in Beatrice. Sweat broke out upon his forehead as he saw the tragic issues to which his life was tending. There was no retreat, save by a second act of apostasy so unspeakably shameful that the brand of it would drive him to self-destruction. He had made his choice, or had been driven upon it by the powers which ruled his destiny; it only remained to have the courage of his resolve and to defy consequences. At least it was in no less a cause than that of his life's one love. There was no stamp of turpitude on the end for which he would sacrifice so much and occasion so much misery.

He passed the time in his own rooms till the afternoon of the following day; then, at the customary hour, he set forth

to visit Beatrice. Would she see him? In his heart he hoped
that she would refuse to; yet he dreaded lest he should be
told that she was too unwell. It was a new thing in Wilfrid's
experience to approach any door with shame and dread; between his ringing the bell and the servant's answer he learnt
well what those words mean.

He was admitted as usual, the servant making no remark.
As usual, he was led to Beatrice's room.

She was sitting in the chair she always occupied, and was
dressed with the accustomed perfection. But her face was an
index to the sufferings she had endured this past week. As
soon as the door had closed, she stood to receive him, but not
with extended hand. Her eyes were fixed upon him steadily,
and Wilfrid, with difficulty meeting them, experienced a shock
of new fear, a kind of fear he could not account for. Outwardly she was quite calm; it was something in her look, an
indefinable suggestion of secret anguish, that impressed him
so. He did not try to take her hand, but, having laid down
his hat, came near to her and spoke as quietly as he could.

'May I speak to you of what passed between us last
Monday?'

'How can we avoid speaking of it?' she replied, in a low
voice, her eyes still searching him.

'I ought to have come to see you before this,' Wilfrid continued, taking the seat to which she pointed, whilst she also
sat down. 'I could not.'

'I have been expecting you,' Beatrice said, in an emotion-
less way.

The nervous tension with which he had come into her
presence had yielded to a fit of trembling. Coldness ran along
his veins; his tongue refused its office; his eyes sank before
her gaze.

'I felt sure you would come to-day,' Beatrice continued,
with the same absence of pronounced feeling. 'If not, I must
have gone to your house. What do you wish to say to me?'

'That which I find it very difficult to say. I feel that after
what happened on Monday we cannot be quite the same to
each other. I fear I said some things that were not wholly true.'

Beatrice seemed to be holding her breath. Her face was
marble. She sat unmoving.

'You mean,' she said at length, 'that those letters represented more than you were willing to confess?'

It was calmly asked. Evidently Wilfrid had no outbreak

of resentment to fear. He would have preferred it to this dreadful self-command.

'More,' he answered, 'than I felt at the time. I spoke no word of conscious falsehood.'

'Has anything happened to prove to you what you then denied?'

He looked at her in doubt. Could she in any way have learnt what had come to pass? Whilst talking, he had made up his mind to disclose nothing definitely; he would explain his behaviour merely as arising from doubt of himself. It would make the rest easier for her to bear hereafter.

'I have read those letters again,' he answered.

'And you have learnt that you never loved me?'

He held his eyes down, unable to utter words. Beatrice also was silent for a long time. At length she said—

'I think you are keeping something from me?'

He raised his face.

'Has nothing else happened?' she asked, with measured tone, a little sad, nothing more.

The truth was forced from him, and its utterance gave him a relief which was in itself a source of new agitation.

'Yes, something else has happened.'

'I knew it.'

'How did you—— ?'

'I felt it. You have met her again.'

Again he was speechless. Beatrice asked—

'Does she live in London?'

'She does.'

'You have met her, and have—have wished that you were free?'

'Beatrice, I have done worse. I have acted as though I were free.'

She shook, as if a blow had fallen upon her. Then a smile came to her lips.

'You have asked her again to be your wife?'

'I have.'

'And she has consented?'

'Because I deceived her at the same time that I behaved dishonourably to you.'

She fixed upon him eyes which had a strange inward look, eyes veiled with reverie, vaguely troubled, unimpassioned. It was as though she calmly readjusted in her own mind the relations between him and herself. The misery of Wilfrid's situation was mitigated in a degree by mere wonder at her mode of receiving his admissions. This interview was no logical sequence upon the scene of a week ago ; and the issue then had been, one would have thought, less provocative of demonstration than to-day's.

Directness once more armed her gaze, and again he was powerless to meet it. Still no resentment, no condemnation. She asked—

'It is your intention to marry soon ? '

He could not reply.

' Will you let me see you once more before your marriage?' she continued. 'That is, if I find I wish it. I am not sure. I may or may not.'

It was rather a debate with herself than an address to him.

'May I leave you now, Beatrice ? ' he said, suddenly. ' Every drop of blood in me is shame-heated. In telling you this, I have done something which I thought would be beyond my force.'

' Yes,' she murmured, ' it will be better if we part now.'

She rose and watched him as he stepped to the table and took his hat. There was a moment's hesitation on either side, but Beatrice did not offer her hand. She stood superbly, as a queen might dismiss one from whom her thoughts were already wandering. He bowed, with inward self-mockery, and left her.

Some hours later, when already the summer evening had cloaked itself, Wilfrid found himself wandering by the river, not far from Hammersmith. The influence of a great water flowing from darkness into darkness was strong upon him ; he was seeking for a hope in the transitoriness of all things earthly. Would not the hour come when this present anguish, this blood-poisoning shame, would have passed far away and have left no mark ? Was it not thinking too grandiosely to attribute to the actions of such a one as himself a tragic gravity ? Was there not supernal laughter at the sight of him, Wilfrid Athel, an English gentleman, a member of the Lower House of the British Parliament, posing as the arbiter of destinies ? What did it all come to ? An imbroglio on the threshold of matrimony; a temporary doubt which of two women was to enjoy the honour of styling herself Mrs. Athel. The day's long shame led to this completeness of self-contempt. As if Beatrice would greatly care ! Why, in his very behaviour he had offered the cure for her heartburn ; and her calmness showed how effective the remedy would be. The very wife whom he held securely had only been won by keeping silence ; tell her the story of the last few days, and behold him altogether wifeless. He laughed scornfully. To this had he come from those dreams which guided him when he was a youth. A commonplace man, why should he not have commonplace experiences ?

He had walked in this direction with the thought of passing beneath Emily's window before he returned home, yet, now that he was not more than half an hour's walk from her, he felt weary and looked aside for a street which should lead him to the region of vehicles. As he did so, he noticed a woman's form leaning over the riverside parapet at a short distance. A thought drew him nearer to her. Yes, it was Emily herself.

'You were coming to see me ?' she asked.

Love in a woman's voice—what cynicism so perdurable that it will bear against that assailant ? In the dusk, he put her gloved hand against his lips, and the touch made him once more noble.

'I had meant to, beautiful, but it seemed too late, and I was just on the point of turning back. You always appear to me when I most need you.'

'You wanted to speak to me, Wilfrid ?'

'When do I not ? My life seems so thin and poor ; only your breath gives it colour. Emily, I shall ask so much of you. I have lost all faith in myself ; you must restore it.'

They stood close to each other, hand in hand, looking down at the dark flow.

'If I had not met you, Wilfrid,' she said, or whispered, 'I think my end must have been there there, below us. I have often come here at night. It is always a lonely place, and at high tide the water is deep.'

His hand closed upon hers with rescuing force.

'I am carrying a letter,' Emily continued, 'that I was going to post before I went in. I will give it you now, and I am glad of the opportunity ; it seems safer. I have written what I feel I could never say to you. Read it and destroy it, and never speak of what it contains.'

She gave him the letter, and then he walked with her homewards.

On the morrow, shortly after breakfast, he was sitting in his study, when a knock came at the door. He bade enter, and it was Beatrice. She came towards him, gave her hand mechanically, and said—

' Can you spare me a few minutes ? '

He placed a chair for her. Her eyes had not closed since they last looked at him ; he saw it, though the expression of her features was not weariness.

' There is one thing, Wilfrid, that I think I have a right to ask you. Will you tell me why she left you, years ago ? '

Her tone was that of one continuing a conversation. There might have been no break between yesterday and to-day. We cannot always gather from the voice what struggle has preceded utterance.

Wilfrid turned away. On the table lay that letter of Emily's ; he had read it many times, and was reading it when the knock disturbed him. With a sudden movement, he took up the sheet of paper and held it to Beatrice.

' It is there—the reason. I myself have only known it a few hours. Read that. I have no right to show it you—and no right to refuse.'

Beatrice held the letter for a brief space without turning her eyes upon it. Wilfrid walked to a distance, and at length she read. Emily had recounted every circumstance of her father's death, and told the history of her own feelings, all with complete simplicity, almost coldly. Only an uncertainty in the hand-writing here and there showed the suffering it had cost her to look once more into the very eyes of the past. Yet it was of another than herself that she wrote ; she felt that even in her memory of woe.

They faced each other again. Beatrice's eyes were distended ; their depths lightened.

' I am glad ! I am glad you met her before it was too late ! '

Her voice quivered upon a low, rich note. Such an utterance was the outcome of a nature strong to the last limit of self-conquest. Wilfrid heard and regarded her with a kind of fear ; her intensity passed to him ; he trembled.

' I have nothing to pardon,' she continued. ' You were hers long before my love had touched your heart. You have tried to love me ; but this has come soon enough to save us both.'

And again—

' If I did not love you, I should act selfishly ; but self is all gone from me. In this moment I could do greater things to help you to happiness. Tell me : have you yet spoken to—to the others ? '

' To no one.'

' Then do not. It shall all come from me. No one shall cast upon you a shadow of blame. You have done me no wrong ; you were hers, and you wronged her when you tried to love me. I will help you—at least I can be your friend. Listen ; I shall see her. It shall be I who have brought you together again—that is how they shall all think of it. I shall see her, and as your friend, as the only one to whom you have yet spoken. Do you understand me, Wilfrid ? Do you see that I make the future smooth for her and you ? She must never know what *we* know. And the others—they shall do as I will ; they shall not dare to speak one word against you. What right have they, if *I* am—am glad ? '

He stood in amaze. It was impossible to doubt her sincerity ; her face, the music of her voice, the gestures by which her eagerness expressed herself, all were too truthful. What divine nature had lain hidden in this woman ! He gazed at her as on a being more than mortal.

' How can I accept this from you ? ' he asked hoarsely.

' Accept ? How can you refuse ? It is my right, it is my will ! Would you refuse me this one poor chance of proving that my love was unselfish ? I would have killed myself to win a tender look from you at the last moment, and you shall not go away thinking less of me than I deserve. You know already that I am not the idle powerless woman you once thought me ; you shall know that I can do yet more. If *she* is noble in your eyes, can *I* consent to be less so ? '

Passion the most exalted possessed her. It infected Wilfrid. He felt that the common laws of intercourse between man and woman had here no application ; the higher ground to which she summoned him knew no authority of the conventional. To hang his head was to proclaim his own littleness.

' You are not less noble, Beatrice,' his voice murmured.

' You have said it. So there is no longer a constraint between us. How simple it is to do for love's sake what those who do not know love think impossible. I will see her, then the last difficulty is removed. That letter has told me where she lives. If I go there to-day, I shall find her ? '

' Not till the evening,' Wilfrid replied under his breath.

' When is your marriage ? '

He looked at her without speaking.

' Very soon ?   Before the end of the session ? '

' The day after to-morrow.'

She was white to the lips, but kept her eyes on him steadily.

' And you go away at once ? '

' I had thought '—he began ; then added, ' Yes, at once ; it is better.'

' Yes, better.   Your friend stays and makes all ready for your return.   Perhaps I shall not see you after to-day, for that time.   Then we are to each other what we used to be. You will bring her to hear me sing ?   I shall not give it up now.'

She smiled, moved a little away from him, then turned again and gave her hand for leave-taking.

' Wilfrid ! '

' Beatrice ? '

' She would not grudge it me.   Kiss me—the last time—on my lips ! '

He kissed her.   When the light came again to his eyes, Beatrice had gone.

In the evening Emily sat expectant.   Either Wilfrid would come or there would be a letter from him; yes, he would come ; for, after reading what she had written, the desire to speak with her must be strong in him.   She sat at her window and looked along the dull street.

She had spent the day as usual—that is to say, in the familiar school routine ; but the heart she had brought to her work was far other than that which for long years had laboriously pulsed the flagging moments of her life.   Her pupils were no longer featureless beings, the sole end of whose existence was to give trouble ; girl-children and budding womanhood had circled about her ; the lips which recited lessons made unconscious music ; the eyes, dark or sunny, laughed with secret foresight of love to come.   Kindly affection to one and all grew warm within her ; what had been only languid preferences developed in an hour to little less than attachments, and dislikes softened to pity.   The girls who gave promise of beauty and tenderness she looked upon with the eyes of a sister ; their lot it would be to know the ecstasy of whispered vows, to give and to receive that happiness which is not to be named lest the gods become envious. Voices singing together in the class practice which had ever

been a weariness, stirred her to a passion of delight; it was
the choral symphony of love's handmaidens. Did they see a
change in her? Emily fancied that the elder girls looked at
each other and smiled and exchanged words in an undertone
—about her.

It was well to have told Wilfrid all her secrets, yet in the
impatience of waiting she had tremors of misgiving; would
he, perchance, think as she so long had thought, that to speak
to anyone, however near, of that bygone woe and shame was
a sin against the pieties of nature, least of all excusable when
committed at the bidding of her own desires? He would
never breathe to her a word which could reveal such a thought,
but Wilfrid, with his susceptibility to the beautiful in character, his nature so intensely in sympathy with her own, might
more or less consciously judge her to have fallen from fidelity
to the high ideal. Could he have learnt the story of her life,
she still persevering on her widowed way, would he not have
deemed her nobler? Aid against this subtlety of conscience
rose in the form of self-reproof administered by that joyous
voice of nature which no longer timidly begged a hearing, but
came as a mandate from an unveiled sovereign. With what
right, pray, did she desire to show in Wilfrid's eyes as other
than she was? That part in life alone becomes us which is
the very expression of ourselves. What merit can there be in
playing the votary of an ascetic conviction when the heart is
bursting with its stifled cry for light and warmth, for human
joy, for the golden fruit of the tree of life? She had been
sincere in her renunciation; the way of worthiness was to
cherish a sincerity as complete now that her soul flamed to
the bliss which fate once more offered her.

The hours passed slowly; how long the night would be if
Wilfrid neither wrote to her nor came. But he had written;
at eight o'clock the glad signal of the postman drew her to the
door of her room where she stood trembling whilst someone
went to the letter-box, and—oh, joy! ascended the stairs. It
was her letter; because her hands were too unsteady to hold
it for reading, she knelt by a chair, like a child with a new
picture-book, and spread the sheet open. And, having read it
twice, she let her face fall upon her palms, to repeat to herself the words which danced fiery like before her darkened eyes.
He wrote rather sadly, but she would not have had it otherwise, for the sadness was of love's innermost heart, which is
the shrine of mortality.

As Emily knelt thus by the chair there came another knock at the house-door, the knock of a visitor. She did not hear it, nor yet the tap at her own door which followed. She was startled to consciousness by her landlady's voice.

'There's a lady wishes to see you, Miss Hood.'

'A lady?' Emily repeated in surprise. Then it occurred to her that it must be Mrs. Baxendale, who knew her address and was likely to be in London at this time of the year. 'Does she give any name?'

No name. Emily requested that the visitor should be introduced.

Not Mrs. Baxendale, but a face at first barely remembered, then growing with suggestiveness upon Emily's gaze until all was known save the name attached to it. A face which at present seemed to bear the pale signs of suffering, though it smiled; a beautiful visage of high meanings, impressive beneath its crown of dark hair. It smiled and still smiled; the eyes looked searchingly.

'You do not remember me, Miss Hood?'

'Indeed, I remember you—your face, your voice. But your name——? You are Mrs. Baxendale's niece.'

'Yes; Miss Redwing.'

'O, how could I forget!'

Emily became silent. The eyes that searched her so wore surely kind, but it was the time of fears. Impossible that so strange a visit should be unconnected with her fate. And the voice thrilled upon her strung nerves ominously; the lips she watched were so eloquent of repressed feeling. Why should this lady come to her? Their acquaintance had been so very slight.

She murmured an invitation to be seated.

'For a moment,' returned Beatrice, 'you must wonder to see me. But I think you remember that I was a friend of the Athels. I am come with Mr. Athel's leave—Mr. Wilfrid.'

Emily was agitated and could not smooth her features.

'Oh, don't think I bring you bad news!' pursued the other quickly, leaning a little forward and again raising her eyes. She had dropped them on the mention of Wilfrid's name. 'I have come, in fact, to put Mr. Athel at ease in his mind.' She laughed nervously. 'He and I have been close friends for a very long time, indeed since we were all but children, and I—he—you won't misunderstand? He has told me—me alone as yet—of what has happened, of the great good fortune that has come to him so unexpectedly. If you knew the terms of our friendship you would understand how natural it was for him to take me into his confidence, Miss Hood. And I begged him to let me visit you, because '—again she laughed in the same nervous way—'because he was in a foolish anxiety lest you might have vanished ; I told him it was best that he should have the evidence of a very practical person's senses that you were really here and that he hadn't only dreamt it. And as we did know each other, you see—— You will construe my behaviour kindly, will you not ? '

' Surely I will, Miss Redwing,' Emily responded warmly. ' How else could I meet your own great kindness ? '

' I feared so many things ; even at the door I almost turned away. There seemed so little excuse for my visit. It was like intruding upon you. But Mr. Athel assured me that I should not be unwelcome.'

Emily, overcome by the sense of relief after her apprehensions, gave free utterance to the warm words in which her joy voiced itself. She forgot all that was strange in Beatrice's manner or attributed it merely to timidity. Sympathy just now was like sunshine to her ; she could not inquire whence or why it came, but was content to let it bathe her in its divine solace.

' If you knew how it has flattered me ! ' Beatrice continued, with a semblance of light-hearted goodness which her hearer had no thought of criticising. ' It is the final proof of Mr. Athel's good opinion. You know his poor opinion of conventional people and conventional behaviour. He is determined that no one shall be told till—till after Wednesday— making me the sole exception, you see. But seriously I am glad he did so, and that I have been able to meet you again just at this time. Now I can assure him that you are indeed a living being, and that there is no danger whatever of your disappearing.'

Emily did not join the musical laugh, but her heart was full, and she just laid her hand on that of Beatrice.

' It was only for a moment,' the latter said, rising as she felt the touch. ' This is no hour for paying visits, and, indeed, I have to hurry back again. I should like to only to say that you have my very kindest wishes. You forgive my coming ; you forgive my hastening away so ? '

' I feel I ought to thank you more,' broke from Emily's lips. ' To me, believe, it is all very like a dream. O, it was

kind of you to come! You can't think,' she added, with only
apparent irrelevance, ' how often I have recalled your beautiful singing; I have always thought of you with gratitude for
that deep pleasure you gave me.'

' O, you shall hear me sing again!' laughed Beatrice. ' Ask
Mr. Athel to tell you something about that. Indeed, it must
be good-bye.'

They took each other's hands, but for Emily it was not
sufficient; she stepped nearer, offering her lips.

Beatrice kissed her.

CHAPTER XXV.

A FAMILY CONCLAVE.

AT eleven o'clock on Wednesday morning Beatrice called at
the Athels' house. Receiving the expected information that
Wilfrid was not at home, she requested that Mr. Athel senior
might not be disturbed and went to Wilfrid's study.

Alone in the room, she took from her hand-bag a little
packet addressed to Wilfrid on which she had written the
word ' private,' and laid it on the writing-table.

She appeared to have given special attention to her toilet
this morning; her attire was that of a lady of fashion, rich,
elaborate, devised with consummate art, its luxury draping
well the superb form wherein blended with such strange
ardour the flames of heroism and voluptuousness. Her
moving made the air delicate with faint perfume; her attitude
as she laid down the packet and kept her hand upon it for a
moment was self-conscious, but nobly so; if an actress, she
was cast by nature for the great parts and threw her soul into
the playing of them.

She lingered by the table, touching objects with the tips
of her gloved fingers, as if lovingly and sadly; at length she
seated herself in Wilfrid's chair and gazed about the room
with languid, wistful eyes. Her bosom heaved; once or
twice a sigh trembled to all but a sob. She lost herself in
reverie. Then the clock near her chimed silverly half-past
eleven. Beatrice drew a deep breath, rose slowly, and slowly
went from the room.

A cab took her to Mrs. Baxendale's. That lady was at home and alone, reading in fact; she closed her book as Beatrice entered, and a placid smile accompanied her observation of her niece's magnificence.

'I was coming to make inquiries,' she said. 'Mrs. Birks gave me a disturbing account of you yesterday. Has your headache gone?'

'Over, all over,' Beatrice replied quietly. 'They make too much of it.'

'I think it is you who make too little of it. You are wretchedly pale.'

'Am I? That will soon go. I think I must leave town before long. Advise me; where shall I go?'

'But you don't think of going before—— ?'

'Yes, quite soon.'

'You are mysterious,' remarked Mrs. Baxendale, raising her eyebrows a little as she smiled.

'Well, aunt, I will be so no longer. I want to cross-examine you, if you will let me. Do you promise to answer?'

'To the best of my poor ability.'

'Then the first question shall be this,—when did you last hear of Emily Hood?'

'Of Emily Hood?'

Mrs. Baxendale had the habit of controlling the display of her emotions, it was part of her originality. But it was evident that the question occasioned her extreme surprise, and not a little trouble.

'Yes, will you tell me?' said Beatrice, in a tone of calm interest.

'It's a strange question. Still, if you really desire to know, I heard from her about six months ago.'

'She was in London then?'

Mrs. Baxendale had quite ceased to smile. When any puzzling matter occupied her thought she always frowned very low; at present her frown indicated anxiety.

'What reason have you to think she was in London, Beatrice?'

'Only her being here now.'

Beatrice said it with a show of pleasant artfulness, holding her head aside a little and smiling into her aunt's eyes. Mrs. Baxendale relaxed her frown and looked away.

'Have you seen her lately?' Beatrice continued.

'I have not seen her for years.'

' Ah ! But you have corresponded with her ? '

' At very long intervals.'

Before Beatrice spoke again, her aunt resumed.

' Don't lay traps for me, my dear. Suppose you explain at once your interest in Emily Hood's whereabouts.'

' Yes, I wish to do so. I have come to you to talk about it, aunt, because I know you take things quietly, and just now I want a little help of the kind you can give. You have guessed, of course, what I am going to tell you,—part of it at least. Wilfrid and she have met.'

' They have met,' repeated the other, musingly, her face still rather anxious. ' In what way ? '

' By chance, pure chance.'

' By chance ? It was not, I suppose, by chance that you heard of the meeting ? '

' No. Wilfrid told me of it. He told me on Sunday——'

Her voice was a little uncertain.

' Give me your hand, dear,' said Mrs. Baxendale. ' There, now tell me the rest.'

Beatrice half sobbed.

' Yes, I can now more easily,' she continued, with hurried utterance. ' Your hand is just what I wanted ; it is help, dear help. But you mustn't think I am weak ; I could have stood alone. Yes, he told me on Sunday. And that of course was the end.'

' At his desire ? '

' His and mine. He was honest with me. It was better than such discoveries when it would have been too late.'

' And he is going to marry her ? '

' They were married an hour ago.'

Mrs. Baxendale looked with grave inquiry into Beatrice's face. Incredulity was checked by what she saw there. She averted her eyes again, and both were silent for awhile.

' So it is all well over, you see,' Beatrice said at length, trying at light-heartedness.

' Over, it seems. As to the well or ill, I can't say.'

' Surely well,' rejoined Beatrice. ' He loves her, and he would never have loved me. We can't help it. She has suffered dreadful things ; you see it in her face.'

' Her face ? '

' I went to see her on Monday evening,' Beatrice explained, with simplicity, though her lips quivered. ' I asked leave of Wilfrid to do so ; he had told me all her story, as he had just heard it from herself, and I—indeed I was curious to see her again. Then there was another reason. If I saw her and brought her to believe that Wilfrid and I were merely intimate friends, as we used to be—how much easier it would make everything. You understand me, aunt?'

Mrs. Baxendale was again looking at her with grave, searching eyes, eyes which began to glimmer a little when the light caught them. Beatrice's hand she held pressed more and more closely in both her own. She made no reply to the last question, and the speaker went on with a voice which lost its clearness, and seemed to come between parched lips.

'You see how easy that makes everything? I want your help, of course; I told Wilfrid that this was how I should act. It is very simple; let us say that I prefer to be thought an unselfish woman: anyone can be jealous and malicious. You are to think that I care as little as it would seem; I don't yet know how I am to live, but of course I shall, it will come in time. It was better they should be married in this way. Then he must come back after the holidays, and everything be smooth for him. That will be our work, yours and mine, dear aunt. You understand me? You will talk to Mrs. Birks; it will be better from you; and then Mr. Athel shall be told. Yes, it is hard for me, but perhaps not quite in the way you think. I don't hate her, indeed I don't. If you knew that story, which you never can! No, I don't hate her. I kissed her, aunt, with my lips—indeed. She couldn't find me out; I acted too well for that. But I couldn't have done it if I had hated her. She is so altered from what she was. You know that I liked her years ago. She interested me in a strange, strange way; it seems to me now that I foresaw how her fate would be connected with mine. I knew that Wilfrid loved her before anyone else had dreamt of such a thing. Now promise your help.'

'Have they gone away?' her aunt asked.

'I don't know. It is likely.'

Her face went white to the lips, for a moment she quivered.

'Beatrice, stay with me,' said Mrs. Baxendale, 'Stay with me here for a day or two.'

'Willingly. I wished it. Mrs. Birks is all kindness, but I find it hard to talk, and she won't let me be by myself. Don't think I am ill—no, indeed no! It's only rest that I want. It seems a long time since Sunday. But you haven't yet promised me, aunt. It will be much harder if I have to do everything myself. I promised him that everything should be made smooth. I want to show him that my—that my love was worth having. It's more than all women would do, isn't it, aunt? Of course it isn't only that; there's the pleasure of doing something for him. And he cannot help being grateful to me as long as he lives. Suppose I had gone and told her! She would never have married him. She was never beautiful, you know, and now her face is dreadfully worn, but I think I understand why he loves her. Of course you cannot know her as well as I do. And you will help me, aunt?'

'Are you perfectly sure that they have been married this morning?' Mrs. Baxendale asked, with quiet earnestness.

'Sure, quite sure.'

'In any other case I don't know whether I should have done as you wish.'

'You would have tried to prevent it? Oh no, you are too wise! After all this time, and he loves her as much as ever. Don't you see how foolish it would be to fret about it? It is fate, that's all. You know we all have our fate. Do you know what I used to think mine would be? I feared madness; my poor father—— But I shall not fear that now; I have gone through too much; my mind has borne it. But I must have rest, and I can only rest if I know that you are helping me. You promise?'

'I will do my best, dear.'

'And your best is best indeed, aunt. You will go to Mrs. Birks and tell her where I am? The sooner you speak to her the better. I will lie down. If you knew how worn-out I feel!'

She rose, but stood with difficulty. Mrs. Baxendale put her arm about her and kissed her cheek. Then she led her to another room.

Tension in Beatrice was nearing the point of fever. She had begun the conversation with every appearance of calmness; now she was only to be satisfied by immediate action towards the end she had in view, every successive minute of delay was an added torment. She pressed her aunt to go to Mrs. Birks forthwith; that alone could soothe her. Mrs. Baxendale yielded and set out.

But it was not to Mrs. Birks that she paid her first visit. Though it was clear that Beatrice firmly believed all she said, Mrs. Baxendale could not accept this as positive assurance;

before taking upon herself to announce such a piece of news she felt the need of some further testimony. She had a difficulty in reconciling precipitate action of this kind with Wilfrid's character as it had of late years developed itself, political, even social, ambition had become so pronounced in him that it was difficult to imagine him turning with such sudden vehemence from the path in which every consideration of interest would tend to hold him. The best of women worship success, and though Mrs. Baxendale well knew that Wilfrid's aims had suffered a degradation, she could not, even apart from her feeling for Beatrice, welcome his return to the high allegiance of former days, when it would surely check or altogether terminate a brilliant career. The situation had too fantastic a look. Could it be that Beatrice was suffering from some delusion? Had a chance discovery of Emily Hood's proximity, together perhaps with some ambiguous behaviour on Wilfrid's part, affected her mind? It was an extreme supposition, but on the whole as easy of acceptance as the story Beatrice had poured forth.

In pursuit of evidence Mrs. Baxendale drove to the Athels'. It was about luncheon-time. She inquired for Wilfrid, and heard with mingled feelings that he was at home. She found him in his study; he had before him a little heap of letters, the contents of a packet he had found on his table on entering a quarter of an hour before.

Mrs. Baxendale regarded him observantly. The results of her examination led her to come to the point at once.

'I have just left Beatrice,' she said. 'She has been telling me an extraordinary story. Do you know what it was?'

'She has told you the truth,' Wilfrid replied, simply.

'And you were married this morning?'

Wilfrid bent his head in assent.

Mrs. Baxendale seated herself.

'My dear Wilfrid,' were her next words, 'you have been guilty of what is commonly called a dishonourable action.'

'I fear I have. I can only excuse myself by begging you to believe that no other course was open to me. I have simply cut a hard knot. It was better than wasting my own life and others' lives in despair at its hopelessness.'

Wilfrid was collected. The leap taken, he felt his foot once more on firm ground. He felt, too, that he had left behind him much of which he was heartily ashamed. He was in no mood to feign an aspect of contrition.

'You will admit,' observed the lady, 'that this cutting of the knot makes a rather harsh severance.'

'It would be impertinent to say that I am sorry for Beatrice. Her behaviour to me has been incredibly magnanimous, and I feel sure that her happiness as well as my own has been consulted. I don't know in what sense she has spoken to you——'

'Very nobly, be sure of it.'

'I can only thank her and reverence her.'

Mrs. Baxendale remained for a moment in thought.

'Well,' she resumed, 'you know that it is not my part to make useless scenes. I began with my hardest words, and they must stand. Beatrice will not die of a broken heart, happily, and if your wife is one half as noble you are indeed a fortunate man. Perhaps we had better talk no more at present; it is possible you have acted rightly, and I must run no risk of saying unkind things. Is your father informed?'

'Not yet.'

'You are leaving town?'

'This afternoon.'

'To go to a distance?'

'No. I shall be in town daily.'

'You doubtless inform your father before you leave?'

'I shall do so.'

'Then we will say good-bye.'

Mrs. Baxendale gave her hand. She did not smile, but just shook her head as she looked Wilfrid steadily in the face.

It was later in the afternoon when she called upon Mrs. Birks. She was conducted to that lady's boudoir, and there found Mr. Athel senior in colloquy with his sister. The subject of the conversation was unmistakable.

'You know?' asked Mrs. Birks, with resignation, as soon as the door was closed behind the visitor.

'I have come to talk it over with you.'

Mr. Athel was standing with his hands clasped behind him; he was rather redder in the face than usual, and had clearly been delivering himself of ample periods.

'Really, Mrs. Baxendale,' he began, 'I have a difficulty in expressing myself on the subject. The affair is simply monstrous. It indicates a form of insanity. I—uh—I—uh—in truth I don't know from what point to look at it.'

'Where is Beatrice?' Mrs. Birks asked.

'She will stay with me for a day or two,' replied Mrs. Baxendale.

'How—how is she?' inquired Mr. Athel, sympathetically.

'Upset, of course, but not seriously, I hope.'

'Really,' Mrs. Birks exclaimed, 'Wilfrid might have had some consideration for other people. Here are the friendships of a lifetime broken up on his account.'

'I don't know that that is exactly the point of view,' remarked her brother, judicially. 'One doesn't expect such things to seriously weigh—I mean, of course, when there is reason on the man's side. What distresses me is the personal recklessness of the step.'

'Perhaps that is not so great as it appears,' put in Mrs. Baxendale, quietly.

'You defend him?' exclaimed Mrs. Birks.

'I'm not sure that I should do so, but I want to explain how Beatrice regards it.'

'*She* defends him?' cried Mr. Athel.

'Yes, she does. At present there is only one thing I fear for her, and that is a refusal on your part to carry out her wishes. Beatrice has made up her mind that as little trouble as possible shall result. I bring, in fact, the most urgent request from her that you, Mr. Athel, and you, Mrs. Birks, will join in a sort of conspiracy to make things smooth for Wilfrid. She desires—it is no mere whim, I believe her health depends upon it—that no obstacle whatever may be put in the way of Wilfrid's return to society with his wife. We are to act as though this old engagement had come to an end by mutual agreement, and as approving the marriage. This is my niece's serious desire.'

'My dear Mrs. Baxendale!' murmured the listening lady. 'How very extraordinary! Are you quite sure——'

'Oh, this surely is out of the question,' broke in her brother. 'That Beatrice should make such a request is very admirable, but I—uh—I really——'

Mr. Athel paused, as if expecting and hoping that someone would defeat his objections.

'I admit it sounds rather unreal,' pursued Mrs. Baxendale, 'but fortunately I can give you good evidence of her sincerity. She has visited the lady who is now Mrs. Athel, and that with the express purpose of representing herself as nothing more than a friend of Wilfrid's. You remember she had a slight acquaintance with Miss Hood. After this I don't see how we can refuse to aid her plan.'

'She visited Miss Hood?' asked Mrs. Birks, with the mild amazement of a lady who respects her emotions. 'Does Wilfrid know that?'

'Beatrice asked his permission to go.'

'This is altogether beyond me,' confessed Mr. Athel, drawing down his waistcoat and taking a turn across the room. 'Of course, if they have been amusing themselves with a kind of game, well, we have nothing to do but to regret that our invitation to join in it has come rather late. For my own part, I was disposed to take a somewhat more serious view. Of course it's no good throwing away one's indignation. I—uh—but what is your own attitude with regard to this proposal, Mrs. Baxendale?'

'I think I must be content to do my niece's bidding,' said the lady addressed.

'There's one thing, it seems to me, being lost sight of,' came from Mrs. Birks, in the disinterested tone of a person who wishes to deliver with all clearness an unpleasant suggestion. 'We are very much in the dark as to Miss Hood's —I should say Mrs. Athel's—antecedents. You yourself,' she regarded Mrs. Baxendale, 'confess that her story is very mysterious. If we are asked to receive her, really—doesn't this occur to you?'

At this moment the door opened and amid general silence Beatrice came forward. Mrs. Birks rose quickly and met her. Mrs. Baxendale understood at a glance what had brought her niece here. Agitation had grown insupportable. It was not in Beatrice's character to lie still whilst others decided matters in which she had supreme interest. The more difficult her position the stronger she found herself to support it. The culmination of the drama could not be acted with her behind the scenes.

Mrs. Birks, with a whispered word or two, led her to a seat. Beatrice looked at her aunt, then at Mr. Athel. The proud beauty of her face was never more impressive. She smiled as if some pleasant trifle were under discussion.

'I heard your voice as I came in,' she said to Mrs. Birks, bending towards her gracefully. 'Were you on my side?'

'I'm afraid not, dear, just then,' was the reply, given in a corresponding tone of affectionateness.

'You will tell me what you were saying?'

Mr. Athel looked as uncomfortable as even an English gentleman can in such a situation. Mrs. Baxendale seemed to be finding amusement in observing him. The lady appealed to plucked for a moment at her sleeve.

'May I make a guess?' Beatrice pursued. 'It had something to do with the private circumstances of the lady Mr. Wilfrid Athel has married?'

'Yes, Beatrice, it had.'

'Then let me help you over that obstacle, dear Mrs. Birks. I have heard from herself a full explanation of what you are uneasy about, and if I were at liberty to repeat it you would know that she has been dreadfully unhappy and has endured things which would have killed most women, all because of her loyalty and purity of heart. I think I may ask you to give as much effect to my words as if you knew everything. Mrs. Athel is in every respect worthy to become a member of your family.'

Her voice began to express emotion.

'Mr. Athel, *you* are not against me? It is so hard to find no sympathy. I have set my heart on this. Perhaps I seem to ask a great deal, but I—have I not some little——'

'My dear Miss Redwing,' broke in Mr. Athel; then, correcting himself, 'My dear Beatrice, no words could convey the anxiety I feel to be of service to you. You see how difficult it is for me to speak decidedly, but I assure you that I could not possibly act in opposition to your expressed desire. Perhaps it would be better for me to withdraw. I am sure these ladies——'

His speech hung in mid-air, and he stood nervously tapping his fingers with his eyeglass.

'No, please remain,' exclaimed Beatrice. 'Aunt, you are not against me? Mrs. Birks, you won't refuse to believe what I have told you?'

The two ladies glanced at each other. In Mrs. Baxendale's look there was appeal.

'Indeed, I believe you implicitly, my dear Beatrice,' said Mrs. Birks. 'My brother is the one to decide. You are mistaken in thinking I oppose your wish. How could I?'

The last words were very sweetly said. With a smile which did not pass beyond her lips, Beatrice rose from her seat and held her hand to Mr. Athel.

'Then it is understood? When Wilfrid brings his wife to you, you receive her with all kindness. I have your promise?'

Mr. Athel drew himself up very straight, pressed the offered hand and said:

'It shall be as you wish.' . . . .

Beatrice returned with Mrs. Baxendale. Her desire to be alone was respected during the rest of the day. Going to her the last thing at night, her aunt was reassured; weariness had followed upon nervous strain, and the beautiful eyes seemed longing for sleep.

But in the morning appearances were not so hopeful. The night had after all been a troubled one: Beatrice declined breakfast and, having dressed with effort, lay on a sofa, her eyes closed.

At noon Mrs. Baxendale came near and said gently:

'Dear, you are not going to be ill?'

The sufferer stirred a little, looked in her aunt's face, rose to a sitting position.

'Ill?' She laughed in a forced way. 'O, that would never do! Ill after all? Why, that would spoil everything. Are you going out this morning?'

'Certainly not. I should only have done some idle shopping.'

'Then you shall do the shopping, and I will go with you. Yes, yes, I will go! It is the only way. Let us go where we shall see people; I wish to. I will be ready in five minutes.'

'But, Beatrice——'

'O, don't fear my looks; you shall see if I betray myself! Quick, quick,—to Regent Street, Bond Street, where we shall see people! I shall be ready before you.'

They set forth, and Beatrice had no illness.

CHAPTER XXVI.

MID-DAY.

Once more at The Firs. Wilfrid had decided to make this his abode. It was near enough to London to allow of his going backwards and forwards as often as might be necessary; his father's town house offered the means of change for Emily, and supplied him with a *pied-à-terre* in time of session. By limiting his attendance at the House as far as decency would allow, he was able to enjoy with small interruption the quiet of his home in Surrey, and a growing certainty that the life of the present Parliament would be short encouraged him in looking forward to the day when politics would no longer exist for him.

He and Emily established themselves at The Firs towards the end of December, having spent a week with Mr. Athel on their return from the Continent. Emily's health had improved, but there was no likelihood that she would ever be other than a delicate flower, to be jealously guarded from the sky's ruder breath by him to whom she was a life within life. Ambition as he formerly understood it had no more meaning for Wilfrid; the fine ardour of his being rejected grosser nourishment and burned in altar-flame towards the passion-pale woman whom he after all called wife. Emily was an unfailing inspiration; by her side the nobler zeal of his youth renewed itself; in the light of her pure soul he saw the world as poetry and strove for that detachment of the intellect which in Emily was a gift of nature.

She, Emily—Emily Athel, as she joyed to write herself—moved in her new sphere like a spirit humbled by victory over fate. It was a mild winter; the Surrey hills were tender against the brief daylight, and gardens breathed the freshness of evergreens. When the sun trembled over the landscape for a short hour, Emily loved to stray as far as that hollow on the heath where she had sat with Wilfrid years ago, and heard him for the first time speak freely of his aims and his hopes. That spot was sacred; as she stood there beneath the faint blue of the winter sky, all the exquisite sadness of life, the memory of those whom death had led to his kindly haven, the sorrows of new-born love, the dear heartache for woe passed into eternity, touched the deepest fountains of her nature and made dim her eyes. She would not have had life other than it was given to her, for she had learned the secrets of infinite passion in the sunless valleys of despair.

She rested. In the last few months she had traversed a whole existence; repose was needful that she might assimilate all her new experiences and range in due order the gifts which joy had lavishly heaped upon her. The skies of the south, the murmur of blue seas on shores of glorious name, the shrines of Art, the hallowed scenes where earth's greatest have loved and wrought, these were no longer a dream; with her bodily eyes she had looked upon Greece and Italy, and to have done so was a consecration, it cast a light upon her brows. 'Talk to me of Rome;' those were always her words when Wilfrid came to her side in the evening. 'Talk to me of Rome, as you alone can.' And as Wilfrid recalled their life in the world's holy of holies, she closed her eyes for the full rapture of the inner light, and her heart sang praise.

Wilfrid was awed by his blessedness. There were times when he scarcely dared to take in his own that fine-moulded hand which was the symbol of life made perfect; Emily uttered thoughts which made him fear to profane her purity by his touch. She realised to the uttermost his ideal of womanhood, none the less so that it seemed no child would be born of her to trouble the exclusiveness of their love. He clad her in queenly garments and did homage at her feet. Her beauty was all for him, for though Emily could grace any scene she found no pleasure in society, and the hours of absence from home were to Wilfrid full of anxiety to return. All their plans were for solitude; life was too short for more than the inevitable concessions to the outside world.

But one morning in February, Emily's eye fell upon an announcement in the newspaper which excited in her a wish to go up to town. Among the list of singers at a concert to be given that day she had caught the name of Miss Beatrice Redwing. It was Saturday; Wilfrid had no occasion for leaving home and already they had enjoyed in advance the two unbroken days.

'But I should indeed like to hear her,' Emily said, 'and she seems to sing so rarely.'

'She has only just returned to England,' Wilfrid remarked

They had heard of Beatrice having been in Florence a week or two prior to their own stay there. She was travelling with the Baxendales. Emily was anxious to meet her, and Wilfrid had held out a hope that this might come about in Italy, but circumstances had proved adverse.

'Have you seen her?' Emily inquired.

Her husband had not. He seemed at first a little disinclined to go up for the concert, but on Emily's becoming silent he hastened to give a cheerful acquiescence.

'Couldn't we see her to-morrow?' she went on to ask.

'No doubt we can. It's only the facing of my aunt's drawing-room on a Sunday afternoon.

'O, surely that is needless, Wilfrid? Couldn't we go and see her quietly? She would be at home in the morning, I should think.'

'I should think so. We'll make inquiries to-night.'

They left home early in the afternoon and procured tickets on their way from the station to Mr. Athel's. Their arrival being quite unexpected, they found that Mr. Athel had left town for a day or two. It was all that Emily needed for the completing of her pleasure; her father-in-law was scrupulously polite in his behaviour to her, but the politeness fell a little short as yet of entire ease, and conversation with him involved effort. She ran a risk of letting Wilfrid perceive the gladness with which she discovered an empty house; he did, in fact, attribute to its true cause the light-heartedness she showed as they sat together at dinner, and smiled to think that he himself shared in the feeling of relief. There were reasons why he could not look forward to the evening with unalloyed happiness, but the unwonted gaiety which shone on Emily's face, and gave a new melody to her voice, moved him to tenderness and gratitude. He felt that it would be well to listen again to the music of that strong heart whose pain had been his bliss. He overcame his ignoble anxieties and went to the concert as to a sacred office.

Their seats, owing to lateness in applying for them, were not in the best part of the hall; immediately behind them was the first row of a cheaper section, and two men of indifferent behaviour were seated there within ear-shot; they were discussing the various names upon the programme as it for the enlightenment of their neighbours. When Emily had been sitting for a few minutes, she found that it had been unwise to leave her mantle in the cloak-room; there was a bad draught. Wilfrid went to recover it. Whilst waiting, Emily became aware that the men behind her were talking of Miss Redwing; she listened

'She's married, I think, eh?' said one.

'Was to have been, you mean. Why, wasn't it you told me the story? O no, it was Drummond. Drummond knows her people, I think.'

'What story, eh?'

'Why, she was to have married a Member of Parliament; what the deuce was his name? Something that reminded me of a race-horse, I remember. Was it Blair? No—Athol! That's the name.'

' Why didn't it come off, then ? '

' Oh, the honourable member found somebody he liked better.'

It was not the end of the conversation, but just then the conductor rose in his place and there was ' hushing.' Wilfrid returned at the same moment. He noticed that Emily shivered as he put the covering on her shoulders. When he was seated she looked at him so strangely that he asked her in a whisper what was the matter. Emily shook her head and seemed to fix her attention on the music.

Beatrice Redwing was the third singer to come forward. Whilst she sang Emily frequently looked at her husband. Wilfrid did not notice it, he was absorbed in listening. Towards the end Emily, too, lost thought of everything save the magic with which the air was charged. There was vociferous demand for an encore and Beatrice gave another song.

When the mid-way interval was reached Emily asked her husband if he would leave the hall. She gave no reason and Wilfrid did not question her. When they were in the carriage she said the draught had been too severe. Wilfrid kept silence; he was troubled by inexplicable misgivings.

Servants hastened to light the drawing-room on their arrival earlier than was expected. Emily threw off her wraps and seated herself near the fire.

' Do you suffer from the chill ? ' Wilfrid asked, approaching her as if with diffidence.

She turned her face to him, gazing with the sadness which was so much more natural to her than the joy of two hours ago.

' It was not the draught that made me come away,' she said with gentle directness. ' I must tell you what it was, Wilfrid. I cannot keep any of my thoughts from you.'

' Tell me,' he murmured, standing by her.

She related the substance of the conversation she had overheard, always keeping her eyes on him.

' Is it true ? '

' It is true, Emily.'

Between him and her there could be no paltry embarrassments. A direct question touching both so deeply could be answered only in one way. If Emily had suffered from a brief distrust, his look and voice, sorrowful but frank as though he faced Omniscience, restored her courage at once. There might be grief henceforth, but it was shared between them.

He spoke on and made all plain. Then at the last:

'I felt it to be almost impossible that you should not some day know. I could not tell you, perhaps on her account as much as on my own. But now I may say what I had no words for before. She loved me, and I believed that I could return her love. When I met you, how could I marry her? A stranger sees my conduct—you have heard how. It is you who alone can judge me.'

'And she came to me in that way,' Emily murmured. 'She could not only lose *you*, but give her hand to the woman who robbed her!'

'And take my part with everyone, force herself to show a bright face, do her best to have it understood that it was she herself who broke off the marriage—all this.'

'Dare I go to her, Wilfrid? Would it be cruel to go to her? I wish to speak—oh, not one word that would betray my knowledge, but to say that I love her. Do you think I may go?'

'I cannot advise you, Emily. Wait until the morning and do then what you think best.'

She decided to go. Beatrice still lived with Mrs. Birks, and it was probable that she would be alone on Sunday morning. It proved to be so.

Wilfrid waited more than an hour for Emily's return. When at length she entered to him, he saw that there was deep content on her countenance. Emily embraced her husband and laid her head upon his breast. He could hear her sigh gently.

'She wishes to see you, Wilfrid.'

'She received you kindly?'

'I will tell you all when I have had time to think of it. But she was sorry you did not come with me. Will you go? She will be alone this afternoon.'

They held each other in silence. Then Emily, raising an awed face, asked softly:

'Where does she find her strength? Is her nature so spotless that self-sacrifice is her highest joy? Wilfrid, I could have asked pardon at her feet; my heart bled for her.'

'Dearest, you least of all should wonder at the strength which comes of high motive.'

'Oh, but to surrender you to another and to witness that other's happiness! Was not my self-denial perhaps a form of selfishness? I only shrank from love because I dreaded the reproaches of my own heart; I did good to no one, was only anxious to save myself. She—I dare not think of it! My nature is so weak. Take your love from me and you take my life.'

Wilfrid's heart leaped with the wild joy of a mountain torrent.

'She will not always be alone,' he said, perhaps with the readiness of the supremely happy to prophesy smooth things for all. There came the answer of gentle reproach:

'After loving you, Wilfrid?'

'Beautiful, that is how it seems to you. There is second love, often truer than the first.'

'Then the first was not love indeed! If I had never seen you again, what meaning would love have ever had for me apart from your name? I only dreamed of it till I knew you, then it was love first and last. Wilfrid, my own, my husband —my love till I die!' . . . .

Notes to the Text

Page 3, line 5:
Fate, free-will, foreknowledge absolute: 'Others apart sat on a hill retire'd,/In thoughts more elevate, and reason'd high/Of providence, foreknowledge, will, and fate,/Fix'd fate, free will, foreknowledge absolute,/And found no end, in wand'ring mazes lost.' Milton, *Paradise Lost*, Book II, lines 557-60.

Page 3, lines 39-40:
She passed to George Herbert and the 'Christian Year': George Herbert (1593-1633), the metaphysical poet, author of *The Temple*, which was very popular in the seventeenth century and came to be regarded as piety rather than poetry until Coleridge founded Herbert's modern reputation. *The Christian Year* (1827) is a collection of verse by John Keble (1792-1866). He was eminent in the High Church Tractarian movement in the 1830s and 1840s. The book enjoyed considerable popularity in Victorian times. In *The Odd Women*, Alice and Virginia Madden offer a copy of *The Christian Year* to their sister Monica in an equally derisive context.

Page 4, lines 38-39:
Hieratic: a style of ancient Egyptian writing which consisted of abridged forms of hieroglyphics. *Scarabs* were gems cut in the form of a beetle which were worn as signet-rings or attached on a chain hung round the neck. They were common among Egyptians and people of Western Asia. Demotic, as opposed to *hieratic*, applied to the popular form of the ancient Egyptian script.

Page 4, line 40:
Champollion or Brugsch: Jean-François Champollion (1790-1832), the French orientalist who first succeeded in deciphering Egyptian

xxxi

hieroglyphics. — Heinrich Karl Brugsch (1827-1894), Egyptologist who pioneered in deciphering demotic, the simplified script of the later Egyptian periods.

Page 20, line 1:
Guardami ben ... Beatrice! Look at me well, I am, I am indeed Beatrice. Dante, *Purgatorio*, Canto XXX, line 73. The same quotation appears in part in Ch. IX of *The Crown of Life*.

Page 26, line 41:
The 'spirit of the age': William Hazlitt's collection of essays, *The Spirit of the Age*, was published in 1825. The phrase has become a commonplace one, but the quotation marks clearly indicate that Gissing had Hazlitt in mind.

Page 32, line 14:
Humanising ruffians by the influence of music: this notion was to be developed in an authorial digression in *The Nether World* (Ch. XII).

Page 32, lines 20-22:
Napoleon the Great ... Napoleon the Little: of course Napoleon I (1769-1821) and Napoleon III (1808-1873). The distinction between the Great and the Little was popularized by Victor Hugo in his 1852 lampoon, 'Napoléon le Petit'.

Page 36, line 24:
A sitting upon: the OED records 'to sit upon' as slang as early as 1865 with the sense of 'rebuke, express contempt'. Mrs. Lynnn Linton used it in *Paston Carew* (1886): 'My lady felt rebuked, and, as she afterwards expressed it, sat upon'.

Page 44, line 2:
The Spectator: the well-known weekly periodical started in 1828 by Robert Stephen Rintoul.

Page 49, line 35:
The Knightes Tale: one of Chaucer's *Canterbury Tales*. Gissing's copy of the book is signed and dated April 1879 (Coustillas collection).

Page 51, line 36:
The holy of holies: a Hebraism meaning 'the most holy place' and, figuratively, 'a place of special sacredness'. The phrase occurs again on p. 344, line 6.

Page 64, line 28:
The fourth circle of Inferno: in the fourth circle (*Inferno*, Canto VII) Dante places the 'Avaricious' and the 'Prodigal'. Gissing was reading Dante in the original at the time he wrote *A Life's Morning*. His three-volume copy of the *Divina Commedia* contains many passages marked in pencil (Couscillas collection).

Page 66, line 27:
On her way to school: as P.F. Kropholler has noted, Emily's action in defending a dog that is being tortured is reminiscent of Marcella Moxey's defence of a horse that was being beaten by its owner (*Born in Exile*, Part VII, Ch. I).

Page 67, line 2:
Mosheim's 'Ecclesiastical History': Johann von Mosheim (1694-1755), Lutheran theologian, who founded the pragmatic school of church historians, insisted on objective, critical treatment of original sources. His *Ecclesiastical History* was first published in Latin in 1755. — Emanuel Swedenborg (1688-1772), the Swedish theosophist and visionary.

Page 67, line 42:
Lorenzo the Magnificent: Lorenzo I (1449-1492), statesman and poet, one of the early Medici. He reigned over Florence during the last twenty-three years of his life.

Page 68, line 20:
Her prayer was for 'beauty of the inward soul': Gissing quotes from Socrates' prayer in the *Phaedrus*. In Ch. XII of *Demos* he quotes again at greater length from the same source. The longer quotation occurs in *Extracts from my Reading*, one of Gissing's notebooks.

Page 70, line 5:
Its 'lordly pleasure-house': an allusion to Tennyson's 'The Palace of

Art', where the poet wrote 'I built my soul a lordly pleasure-house,/Wherein at ease for aye to dwell' (first stanza).

Page 70, line 23:
The fitness of things: a playful use of a phrase extensively used in the eighteenth century with reference to the ethical theory of Clarke, in which the quality of moral rightness is defined as consisting in a 'fitness' to the relations inherent in the nature of things (OED).

Page 73, line 41:
The land of milk and honey: a land flowing with milk and honey (*Exodus*, III.8).

Page 84, line 14:
Put money in thy purse: from *Othello*, I, iii, 345.

Page 99, line 12:
The Union: Union House or workhouse. A fairly common sense in the nineteenth century. Hardy uses it in Ch. XXX of *Far from the Madding Crowd*: 'I wonder sometimes if I am doomed to die in the Union.'

Page 108, line 38:
Like that woman did to Henry the Eighth: probably Anne Boleyn who said to the King: 'I would rather lose my life than give encouragement to your addresses' (see Patrick Fraser Tytler, *Life of Henry the Eighth*, Edinburgh: Oliver & Boyd, 1837, p. 241).

Page 111, line 31:
An ounce of civet: from *King Lear*, IV, iv, 133 ('Give me an ounce of civet, good apothecary, to sweeten my imagination').

Page 112, line 26:
The still voice within spoke clearly amid the hush: and after the fire a still small voice (I *Kings*, XIX.12).

Page 112, line 39:
To tend the garden of her mind: an echo from Ch. XXX of *Candide*, where Voltaire wrote: 'Cela est bien dit, répondit Candide, mais il faut cultiver notre jardin.'

Page 129, line 14:
The working of the very means of grace: a reminiscence from the *Book of Common Prayer*, A General Thanksgiving: From the means of grace, and for the hope of glory.

Page 132, line 35:
(The clerk) seized a ruler, and began a species of sword-play about Hood's head: as P.F. Kropholler has noted, in Ch. VII of *The Nether World*, Samuel Byass, also a clerk, plays the same curious 'game'.

Page 141, line 17:
If only he could bring himself to the lie direct and shameless: an echo from *As You Like It* (V, iv,96): 'the retort courteous ... the quip modest ... the lie circumstantial ... the lie direct.'

Page 164, line 2:
All is vanity, Ecclesiastes, I.2.

Page 164, line 12:
Effort was weary and unprofitable: a reminiscence from *Hamlet* (I,ii,133): 'How weary, stale, flat and unprofitable/Seem to me all the uses of this world.'

Page 165, line 39:
The Moonlight Sonata: by Beethoven, Opus 27, no. 2. See also p. 170.

Page 172, line 22:
The tenor of her life: 'They kept the noiseless tenor of their way.' Thomas Gray, *Elegy Written in a Country Churchyard*, XIX.

Page 172, line 36:
It was the means offered to Isabel of rescuing her brother Claudio: a reference to *Measure for Measure*.

Page 174, line 11:
The crown of life: an early use of this phrase by Gissing before he used it as a title for one of his later novels and came across its French equivalent in Victor Hugo. The phrase occurs again on page 239, line 13.

Page 174, line 43:
Her life must have seemed to her a weary pilgrimage: probably an echo from *O God of Bethel*, a hymn by Philip Doddridge (1702-1751): 'O God of Bethel ... Who through this weary pilgrimage/Hast all our fathers led.'

Page 191, line 13:
Nether Circle: Dante reserved the Nether Circle of his Inferno for traitors.

Page 196, line 13:
With the sublime love of woman, conquering all dread, she dropped to her knees: 'thy love to me was wonderful, passing the love of woman' (2 *Samuel*, I.26).

Page 200, lines 4-6:
'Sehen Sie mal ... Junge!' Look a bit ... there you have the model of English aristocrats. O the good, simple young man!

Page 200, line 21:
The intense school: for this phrase the OED quotes Mackintosh (1830), who defined 'the intense school' as always using the strongest possible word on every possible occasion.

Page 215, line 22:
Sleep was binding his brows with oblivion: probably an echo from *Henry IV*, Part 2, I, i, 150: 'Now bind my brow with iron.'

Page 218, line 37:
Kant: Immanuel Kant, the German philosopher (1724-1804), to whose works Eduard Bertz had introduced Gissing in the late 1870s. Gissing's copy was a present from Bertz, bought at Tübingen on April 4, 1877 and given to his friend in London on February 1879 (Coustillas collection).

Page 221, line 35:
Mr Mudie's catalogues: the catalogues of the well-known circulating library founded by Charles Edward Mudie (1818-1890) in the early 1840s. See Guinevere Griest, *Mudie's Circulating Library and the Victorian Novel* (1970).

Page 221, line 37:
Tant bien que mal: somehow or other.

Page 223, line 15:
The old proverb: perhaps 'more haste less speed.'

Page 242, line 11:
You found Emily looking sadly: the OED records this sense as
meaning 'in bad health, ill, poorly' and now dialectal. The examples
quoted are from Swift, George Eliot and Mrs Humphry Ward.

Page 244, line 34:
The pale cast of thought: 'And thus the native hue of resolution/is
sicklied o'er with the pale cast of thought' (*Hamlet*, III, i, 84).

Page 248, line 21:
*He will not come forth a better man, though perchance a wiser; wisdom
and goodness are from of old at issue*: reminiscence of Coleridge and
Shakespeare are combined here: 'A sadder and a wiser man,/He rose
the morrow morn'/ (*The Ancient Mariner*, part VII) and 'Wisdom
and goodness to the vile seem vile' (*King Lear*, IV, ii, 38).

Page 248, line 30:
The knight of the dolorous visage: an allusion to Don Quixote whom
Smollett, in his translation of Cervantes' book, called the Knight of
the sorrowful countenance.

Page 248, line 37:
Boswell: James Boswell (1740-1795), Samuel Johnson's biographer,
and one of Gissing's favourite authors.

Page 249, line 10:
The first thing in the morning a poet is capable of mathematics: Gissing
is thinking here of his own childhood experiences as recorded in *The
Private Papers of Henry Ryecroft* (Summer XI) where he says he
could apply himself with gusto to mathematics at five o'clock in the
morning although he hated the subject at any other time.

Page 272, line 6:
Io Triumphe: an exclamation of triumph uttered by the soldiers and

the crowd while the Roman troops and their victorious general filed through Rome to the Capitol.

Page 285, lines 25-26:
'Deep on his front ...': Milton, *Paradise Lost*, Book II, line 302.

Page 329, line 27:
The golden fruit of the tree of life: a phrase with biblical and Goethean connotations, from *Genesis*, II.9 ('the tree of life') and *Studienzimmer* ('All theory, dear friend is grey, but the golden tree of actual life springs ever green').

Historical and
Topographical Notes

It was in *A Life's Morning* that Gissing drew most upon Wakefield, his hometown: Dunfield stands for Wakefield; Hebsworth for Leeds; Banbrigg for Agbrigg and Belle Vue; St. Luke's for St. John's; and the Heath for Heath Common and the village of Heath. Of the five houses in Dunfield referred to in the story three were occupied at different times by Mrs. Gissing, the novelist's mother, and the other two were the residences of Robert and Alexander Mackie. Except for Mr. Baxendale the characters do not appear to have been based on identifiable persons, and if some of the details of Emily Hood's life are similar to some others concerning Gissing's two sisters, it is hardly conceivable that he modelled such an unsympathetic woman as Mrs. Hood on his mother.

Page 6, line 4:
The last to enter the room was the governess, Miss Emily Hood.
George Gissing's elder sister was called Margaret Emily and it seems likely that she spent a period as a governess. Later she and her younger sister opened a Boys' Preparatory School in Wakefield in 1898. Her age at the time the book was written was the same as Emily Hood's at the beginning of the story. There had been another Emily in the family, Emily Williams by whose will Gissing and each of his brothers had received £500, which in his case had helped him to pay for the publication of his first novel.

Page 10, line 18:
'*We used to go to a seaside place in Lincolnshire called Cleethorpes*'.
Wakefield families more commonly chose Blackpool in Lancashire or Scarborough in Yorkshire rather than Cleethorpes in Lincolnshire, all three being within a hundred miles from the town.

Page 63, line 8:

The house which was the end of Emily's journey was situated two miles outside the town of Dunfield. Belle Vue and Agbrigg are more than a mile from the centre of Wakefield on the main route to Doncaster and the South. In Gissing's lifetime there was little open land between Wakefield and Belle Vue although the change to a rural landscape was abrupt beyond Agbrigg. *A row of two-storied dwellings built of glazed brick ... opposite an ecclesiastical edifice ... stone-built ... presenting a corner to the highway* existed until a dozen years ago, easily identified both by its description and its position relative to St. Catherine's, a daughter church of St. Helen's, Sandal. Most of the houses in Belle Vue and Agbrigg were spread along Doncaster Road except for a small development which included *Regent Street*, crossed by Oxford Street. Except for half a dozen old buildings including the 'Graziers' Arms', most of the property had been erected after the publication of the town map of 1848.

After this first mention of the Hoods' home Gissing transferred the house out of Belle Vue some two hundred yards to 2 Stoneleigh Terrace, Agbrigg, a stone house with a garret under the roof on a third floor (see page 96, line 26), where his mother was living. The house was turned into a hotel in 1977.

Page 64, line 14 and page 66, line 9:

Hither her parents came to live when she was thirteen years old ... Education she did get by hook or by crook ... Each morning going into Dunfield ... she must walk her couple of miles – it was at least so far to the school. Margaret and Ellen Gissing were amongst the first intake of pupils when Wakefield Girls' High School opened in 1878. Margaret left the school in April 1880 (school records — 'because of ill-health') a few months before Mrs. Gissing moved from Stamp Office Yard, Wakefield, to the newly-built Stoneleigh Terrace, Agbrigg. Then Ellen who was thirteen, like Emily, had a two-mile walk to school until she left at Christmas 1884.

Page 65, line 30:

Rents were lower in Banbrigg, and it was beyond the range of certain municipal taxings. Agbrigg was in the Sandal Local Board administrative area, separate from Wakefield. For a few weeks in 1885 Gissing's brother, Algernon, was a member of the Sandal Local Board until he left to take employment in Richmond, North Yorkshire.

Page 66, lines 37 and 42:
Fortunately there was the library of the Mechanics' Institute ... Books which came down to her from the shelves. Wakefield Mechanics' Institute had the largest library in the town and not only was Gissing's father, Thomas Waller Gissing, its Honorary Librarian from 1868 to his death in 1870, but his brother, Algernon, held the post from 1884 to 1885. Each of them produced new catalogues, important requirements when borrowers were not allowed access to the shelves.

Page 68, line 39 and page 72, line 26 to page 79:
As a young child she had walked in her sleep ... crossed the narrow footing of a canal lock ... 'I thought we might have a turn over the Heath'. Stoneleigh Terrace was the last building before the open country. A railway bridge (with a modern one by its side) and the canal (closed and filled-in since 1945) are no more than two hundred yards beyond Mrs. Gissing's home. Heath Common is exactly as described in the novel. It has never been enclosed and at the best is rough grazing land. It was important for a later stage in the plot that Emily and her father did not take the more likely way to the village of Heath, which is at the upper end of the common, by passing over the canal lock and following an old, paved path up the eastern boundary of the common. Instead they walked along the middle one of three roads that branch just beyond the canal. This ploy enabled Gissing to introduce the stone quarries, at the side of the road, where Mr. Hood later was to die. From the head of the quarries, now grassed over, nineteenth-century Wakefield with the lone prominence of its parish church, the tallest in Yorkshire, could be seen on the opposite side of the valley worn out by the River Calder. Nine miles further away the *murkiness* would be caused by the industrial smoke of Leeds, which Gissing called Hebsworth, a name very like Hemsworth, which is a mining township five miles away in the opposite direction. The village of Heath is exceptional in that its thirty or so buildings are scattered about at the upper end of the common as if children's bricks had been thrown onto a hearth rug. The most impressive were the Elizabethan Heath Old Hall, the even larger Heath Hall, Heath House and a dower-house. The Manor House identified as Dagworthy's is nearest the quarries and has a strange stable-like outbuilding, apparently a set of superior dog-kennels. It appears that the Hoods walked across the village in the direction of

St. John's colliery to Kirkthorpe Church, and there turned right onto a path which by a semi-circular route brought them back into Heath alongside the boundary of the Manor House occupied at that time by Alexander Mackie.

Page 86, line 2 and page 92, line 38:
The village of Pendal, where stand the remains of an ancient castle ... '*When was this castle destroyed?*' Sandal Castle ruins have existed exactly in the form described at least since 1722 when Samuel Buck made a well-known engraving. The castle is the location of Shakespeare's *Henry VI*, Part III, Act I, Scenes 2, 3 and 4, and it was destroyed by Cromwellian troops in 1645 after a long siege.

Page 94, lines 11 and 19:
'*I must go as far as Pendal station*' ... *They stood together under the station shed.* Sandal station, which comprised little more than an open shelter, was the first stop from Wakefield on the line to London. Before the electric trams and later 'buses, passengers used it for the two-mile journey to Wakefield as did Emily, page 265, line 28. Gissing stretched facts when he arranged that the long distance train bringing Wilfrid from the south should stop there to pick her up.

Page 98, line 11:
A train was passing a quarter of a mile away. This is further confirmation that the Hoods' house was in Stoneleigh Terrace and not opposite the *chapel of ease*. From the garret window can be seen Sandal Castle ruins, and houses by Sandal railway station.

Page 98, lines 25 to 36:
Mrs. Cartwright and her five grown-up daughters ... *lived* ... *in an abode consisting of six rooms.* The two Cartwright homes mirror the fortunes of Mrs. Gissing in the years around 1870. Until T.W. Gissing's death the family had occupied the chemist's shop, 60 Westgate, and for at least five years the whole of the Georgian house attached to it; a total of about a dozen rooms excluding cellars. They then lived in All Saints Parish but on the boundary of St. John's Ward, which T.W. Gissing represented as a town councillor for his last three years. The portion around St. John's Church was the most select in Wakefield, but Westgate was five hundred yards

away amongst commercial property. After his death the family moved to Stamp Office Yard, a meaner area only a hundred yards away and about the same distance from South Parade, an important set of town houses. Pictures of Stamp Office Yard show run-down six-roomed houses; but the view out of the *uppermost windows* is a unique one from the rooms above the chemist's shop looking across Westgate through the gap caused by Market Street. Like Mrs. Cartwright who spent much of her time as a grass widow, Mrs. Gissing had five children.

Page 107, line 29 and page 120, line 35:
The garden ... was ... ten minutes' walk from the house ... (Dagworthy) *was standing at the window of his private room, which was on the first floor of the mill.* These gardens appear on the town map of 1848 and Morley Roberts in *The Private Life of Henry Maitland* said that the Gissings had such a garden; of course neither of their houses had one. They were in a plot across the road from the cattle market and bounded along one edge by the 'Ninety-Nine Arches'. By the cattle market was a two-storied building, not a worsted mill but a mill carrying the sign 'J. Fawcett & Son, Corn Mill, Grinding & For Hire', and from the upper floor an observer could have watched Emily in a garden only fifty yards away.

Page 149, line 35 and page 150, line 37:
On the embankment beyond this bridge ... (Dagworthy) *could see the whole track of the lane.* Gissing here used poetic licence. There is a railway embankment from which Dagworthy could have overlooked Stoneleigh Terrace, and at that point it is parallel to the road that Emily would have taken to Sandal Castle. Also, half way to the castle the road twists under a railway bridge at Sandal station, but the two places are on different routes, so that Dagworthy could not have trailed her without leaving the embankment.

Page 185, line 12:
In the afternoon, and again in the evening, the single bell of the chapel at *played for worshippers.* Below is one of several references to the female members of the Gissing family attending St. Catherine's Church: *Wakefield Herald*, 30 December, 1882. 'Sale of work at St. Catherine's, Belle Vue. The General stall was presided over by the Misses Gissing (and others).'

Page 205, line 15, page 209, line 33 and page 219, line 1:
The Baxendales lived in St. Luke's ... 'Here's my husband offering himself as a Liberal candidate for Dunfield' ... (Mr. Baxendale) took Wilfrid over his manufactory. Gissing had in mind St. John's House, a mansion built at the same time as St. John's Church as part of a grand speculation in 1790 and which was then out of the town. It stands at the end of, and at right angles to, a terrace, so that from the entrance gate in its high garden wall it appears to be detached. Gissing knew its occupant, Robert Bownas Mackie, M.P., who was elected to Parliament on his second attempt, in 1880. He was a second generation corn merchant who had interests much in common with Gissing's father, particularly in the management of the local Liberal party and Mechanics' Institute. He was a guarantor when T.W. Gissing took out a second mortgage on his shop, and a pall-bearer at his funeral.

Page 209, line 23:
'Mr. Baxendale, when particularly angry, offers to hire the hall in the Corn Exchange'. This building, opposite T.W. Gissing's shop, could seat six hundred people and was used for the most important political occasions.

Page 213, line 34:
Led to the subject of certain 'revivalist meetings'. Gissing also used the same combination of an election campaign and a wife affected by revivalist meetings in *Denzil Quarrier*.

Page 218, line 14:
'I'm going to win the election clean-handed'. Parliamentary elections in Wakefield were notoriously corrupt and many results were challenged, three successfully. After the 1865 election at which the Liberal candidate had won the seat there was a government enquiry; T.W. Gissing and R.B. Mackie were named amongst the ten Liberals who had chosen the candidate and organised his campaign.

Page 221, line 28:
Society in Dunfield had its book club. T.W. Gissing was Secretary of Wakefield Book Society as well as being Honorary Librarian of the Mechanics' Institution.

Page 241, line 4:
Turning from the main road at a point just before the bridge over the river. There is a path that starts from that spot and follows the River Calder, but rather than *almost ma(king) a circuit* of Wakefield, it is an alternative way from Wakefield to Heath. In those days it ended at the canal lock beyond Stoneleigh Terrace.

Page 251, line 8:
Two days later (Mrs. Baxendale) went to Banbrigg, carrying the satisfactory news that at last a sale of the Barnhill property had been negotiated. For this detail as well, there is a parallel in the life of the Gissing family. After a first, abortive, attempt to sell the chemist's shop the latter was bought by J.L. Chaplin with the help of a mortgage provided by Robert and Alexander Mackie.

Page 254, line 8, page 257, line 26 and page 264, line 40:
On the last day of the year ... 'I really believe Mrs. Hood is dead' ... Half way between Banbrigg and Dunfield lay the cemetery. T.W. Gissing was buried on the *last day* of 1870 in Wakefield town cemetery, which lies in Belle Vue, a short distance from Stoneleigh Terrace. Samuel Bruce, a friend of his, said after the funeral 'he saw one little lad whose eyes were almost rubbed to a sore. He knew how much that lad was to his father and the father to the lad because he had witnessed them in private.'

Page 265, line 31:
To reach the exit of the station. Passengers from London still cross the line at Westgate station by a wood-and-iron footbridge to leave the station.

The Manuscript: A Note

Most of the manuscripts of Gissing's novels are in institutional libraries, but no clue whatever to the fate of the others has ever been found. The manuscripts of *The Unclassed*, *The Odd Women*, *Sleeping Fires* and *The Paying Guest* are not known to be in private hands or to have been sold since the writer's death. Nor have they been reported by his family to have been destroyed. *A Life's Morning* is an intermediate case — one chapter of the manuscript survives, that of Chapter III, eleven leaves numbered 26 to 37, and it is not even complete since p. 35 is missing. For some sixty years it awaited Gissing scholars in a most unexpected repository, the Library of the Royal Society for the Protection of Birds in London, where it was, together with eight letters from Gissing to W.H. Hudson, among Hudson's papers. Under what circumstances this fragment of the story passed into the hands of Gissing's old friend is a matter for conjecture. True, Hudson, as is testified by his correspondence with both George and Algernon Gissing (soon to be published), was in touch with George until his death and was also one of Algernon's familiars until about 1912, but Hudson is not known to have been a collector of literary relics — rather, he was a destroyer of many that were in his possession — and it is altogether impossible to account for the presence among his papers of this fragment of the manuscript of *A Life's Morning*. One can only note a coincidence which may well be irrelevant to the matter: Algernon began to dispose of the manuscripts of George's novels about the time he lost contact with Hudson. Perhaps, for some obscure reason, he sent Hudson these eleven leaves and they were never returned.

Although of limited interest, the eleven leaves extant offer some information on the composition of the story in the autumn of 1885 and on its revision two years later when Gissing read the proofs of his novel for the serialization in the *Cornhill*.

First of all, this chapter, composed on paper measuring 24.8 x 20 cm, has no title, and the text is only preceded by III in Roman numerals. Gissing was following the practice he had inaugurated in *Isabel Clarendon*, and it would seem that titles for the chapters were requested by James Payn at the same time as he asked for a new title for the book. Considering that 37 MS pages corresponded to 51 printed pages in the one-volume edition, the whole manuscript must have been about 250 pages long. That the fragment under consideration is unquestionably part of it and not a discarded portion of a previous version of the story is confirmed by the limited number of discrepancies between the manuscript and the printed story, and even more conspicuously by the compositors' names in the margins of pp. 26 (Crabbe), 28 (Rew), 31 (Pothill), 33 (Argent) and 36 (Crabbe). The absence of p. 35 is all the more to be regretted as it conceals the most part of the most substantial difference between the manuscript and the printed text: the first paragraph on p. 49 of the present edition originally ended as follows: '... words must be upon our lips when we wrestle with fate. And what though the blessing be bestowed in mockery?'

Three kinds of variants may be distinguished chronologically. First the alterations made in the course of composition when a word, a group of words or a sentence was crossed out and replaced by other words on the same line; secondly, the interlinear alterations made at some stage prior to printing; thirdly, the discrepancies between the manuscript and the printed text that are indicative of changes at proof stage. The first category is most difficult to evaluate as cancellation usually makes the first version undecipherable. Two legible examples occur on p. 41 of the book. At the end of the first paragraph, an uncompleted sentence read: 'led to his partial self-revelation in their ...'. Lower down, Mr. Athel was 'just finishing', not 'relating' a story of his early wanderings in Egypt. The second category of alterations is equally difficult to assess for the same reason: Gissing's aim in such cases was sometimes to avoid a repetition ('a choice of literature' became 'a change of reading' on p. 35, lines 3-4), or to use a better and, as a rule, simpler phrase ('quick recruiting' was replaced by 'perfect repose' in line 10 of p. 37), or to be more accurate (the last but one complete sentence on p. 38 originally began with 'On his first return home from Oxford ...'). The third kind of variant results from changes made in the autumn of 1887 when batches of proofs began to reach an author who, having partly forgotten his own work, saw it with fairly critical eyes. The extent of alterations was doubtless limited by a provision in the memorandum of agreement regarding authorial modifications. Here is a list of the main ones (the version given is that of the manuscript:

p. 34, line 6 from bottom: ... the twins still kept her company to their hour of bedtime.

p. 35, line 3: It fettered her perhaps a little, the fact that her choice of reading ...

p. 35, line 17: ... attractive for savour.

p. 36 and p. 37: no paragraphs after 'his speech' and 'very tolerable'.

p. 38, line 30: and that one of which they altogether approved.

p. 39, line 6: regarded as militating against matrimony.

p. 40, line 11: Emily was untainted by that kind of radicalism ...

p. 40, line 24: the forces of her soul.

p. 40, line 27: apart from the superficialities of intercourse.

p. 40, line 41: the Yorkshire manufacturing town.

p. 41, line 20: profundity of the summer midnight ...

p. 41, line 23: with a kind of spiritual ecstasy ...

p. 41, line 26: superficial intercourse ...

p. 41, line 37: the latter two ...

p. 43, line 14: it showed deep emotion ...

p. 43, line 15: its loveliness, its force, its pleading entered the soul.

p. 43, line 18: from the first rich, sustained note one felt that ...

p. 43, line 21: which ordinarily the superficial complexities ...

p. 43, line 24: this rapture of harmony.

p. 43, line 26: this magic power.

p. 43, line 27: technical excellence ...

p. 43, line 36: her gaze ...

p. 44, line 3: just now.

p. 44, line 17: the air was full of moonlight ...

p. 44, line 21: the orb of brightness ...

p. 44, line 29: showed at once graceful and dignified ...

p. 46, line 6: it was of less than ten minutes.

p. 46, line 40: an excessive severity of maidenhood in reliving, instant by instant ...

p. 47, line 7: the haunting actuality ...

p. 47, line 14: Ah, there was no need ...

p. 47, line 24: the beginning of bliss ...

p. 47, line 27: all that her soul could comprehend.

p. 49, line 20: in awe of the solemn beauty which illumined her countenance ...

p. 49, line 30: one of her fair hands ...

p. 49, line 33: gave no audible sound ...

p. 49, line 36: 'Will you not let me hear you speak my own?'/She took courage upon her lips and uttered it. They passed on ...

p. 50, line 8. *honours as these* ...

p. 50, line 15: the little ones ...

p. 50, line 26: it is infinitely preferable ...

p. 50, line 36: as she looked up. Those eyes filled him with worship.

p. 51, line 12: Oh, yes; it is far better.

p. 51, line 14: your friends. Let everything be complete.

p. 51, line 15: 'My fair wise one!' he said, tenderly.

Close scrutiny of these changes leaves one in no doubt as to Gissing's intentions. His suppression of some superfluous adjectives and sentences, his striving after greater stylistic sobriety, his quest for the right word all show that he was learning his trade. Had his hand been altogether free, above all had Smith, Elder given him a serious chance of revising his story — a chance like that he was given for *Thyrza* — he would have made the definitive version of *A Life's Morning* as different from the original one as are the two versions of *The Unclassed*, an earlier novel which benefited from the exercise of his maturer thoughts on the art of fiction.

Bibliography

I — Reviews of the first edition
(*indicates a reprint in *Gissing: The Critical Heritage*).

Scotsman, 26 November 1888, p. 3
Saturday Review, 1 December 1888, p. 650*
Public Opinion, 7 December 1888, p. 722
Athenaeum, 8 December 1888, p. 770*
Manchester Guardian, 10 December 1888, p. 6
Pall Mall Gazette, 12 December 1888, p. 5
Whitehall Review, 13 December 1888, p. 20
Glasgow Herald, 20 December 1888, p. 9
Daily Telegraph, 25 December 1888, p. 7
Standard, 28 December 1888, p. 2
Court Journal, 29 December 1888, p. 1516*
Graphic, 5 January 1889, p. 19
Guardian (London weekly), 23 January 1889, p. 136*
Morning Post, 30 January 1889, p. 2
Dublin Review, January 1889, pp. 170-71
Murray's Magazine, January 1889, p. 143
Spectator, 9 February 1889, p. 204*
Scottish Review, April 1889, p. 446
Vanity Fair, 15 June 1889, p. 454

II — Articles on *A Life's Morning*

Anon., 'A Novelist's Picture of Wakefield', *Wakefield Free Press*, 10 March 1888, p. 5
Anon., 'George Gissing', *Outlook* (London), 30 January 1904, p. 19. See also the article entitled 'George Gissing' in the number for 2 January 1904, pp. 649-50

Morley Roberts, Introduction to the Nash and Grayson edition of
   A Life's Morning (1927)

Anon., 'Novels in Brief', *Nation and Athenaeum*, 14 April 1928,
   p. 54

William Plomer, Introduction to the Home & Van Thal edition of
   A Life's Morning (1947)

Arthur Nash, 'An Author Who Died Too Soon', *John o'London's
   Weekly*, 31 October 1947, p. 667

Arthur Calder-Marshall, 'George Gissing', *Tribune*, 7 November
   1947, p. 20

V.S. Pritchett, 'Books in General', *New Statesman and Nation*,
   8 November 1947, p. 372

F. Hadland Davis, 'Letters: George Gissing', *John o'London's
   Weekly*, 14 November 1947, p. 703

Anon., 'Letters', *John o'London's Weekly*, 28 November 1947,
   p. 729

Anon., 'A Life's Morning', *Notes and Queries*, 13 December 1947,
   p. 550

Anon., 'A Life's Morning', *Sunday Times*, 28 December 1947, p. 3

[Walter Allen], 'The Permanent Stranger', *Times Literary Supple-
   ment*, 14 February 1948, p. 92

George-a-Green, 'Looking Around', *Wakefield Express*, 25 October 1952, p. 7

Clifford Brook, 'A View of *A Life's Morning* from Wakefield',
   Gissing Newsletter, April 1975, pp. 1-12. See also July 1975, p. 21

G.O. Morse, 'An Appreciation of *A Life's Morning*', *Gissing
   Newsletter*, October 1982, pp. 1-24

III — Books containing material on *A Life's Morning*

Baker, Ernest A., *The History of the English Novel*, vol. IX (1936)

Brook, Clifford, *George Gissing and Wakefield* (1980)

Coustillas, P. (ed.), *Collected Articles on George Gissing* (1968)

Coustillas, P. and Partridge, C. (eds.), *Gissing: The Critical Heritage*
   (1972)

Coustillas, P. (ed.), *George Gissing: Essays and Fiction* (1970)

Coustillas, P. (ed.), *London and the Life of Literature in Late
   Victorian England, the Diary of George Gissing, Novelist* (1978)

Davis, Oswald H., *George Gissing. A Study in Literary Leanings*
   (1966, reprinted 1975)

Donnelly, Mabel Collins, *George Gissing, Grave Comedian* (1954)

Gapp, Samuel Vogt, *George Gissing, Classicist* (1936)

Gettmann, Royal A. (ed.), *George Gissing and H.G. Wells* (1961)

Gissing, Algernon and Ellen (eds.), *Letters of George Gissing to Members of His Family* (1927)

Goode, John, *George Gissing: Ideology and Fiction* (1978)

Gordan, John D., *George Gissing 1857-1903: An Exhibition from the Berg Collection* (1954)

Halperin, John, *Gissing: A Life in Books* (1982)

Irwin, Michael, *Picturing: Description and Illusion in the Nineteenth-Century Novel* (1979)

Korg, Jacob, *George Gissing, a Critical Biography* (1963, reprinted 1965 and 1980)

McKay, Ruth Capers, *George Gissing and his Critic Frank Swinnerton* (1933)

Michaux, Jean-Pierre (ed.), *George Gissing: Critical Essays* (1981)

Pritchett, V.S., *Books in General* (1953)

Roberts, Morley, *The Private Life of Henry Maitland* (1912, reprinted 1923 and 1958)

Selig, Robert L., *George Gissing* (1983)

Spiers, J. and Coustillas, P., *The Rediscovery of George Gissing* (1971)

Swinnerton, Frank, *George Gissing, a Critical Study* (1912, reprinted 1923 and 1966)

Tindall, Gillian, *The Born Exile: George Gissing* (1974)

Van Thal, Herbert, *The Tops of the Mulberry Trees* (1971)

Weber, Anton, *George Gissing und die soziale Frage* (1932, reprinted 1967)

Wolff, Joseph, *George Gissing: An Annotated Bibliography of Writings about Him* (1974)

Young, Arthur C. (ed.), *The Letters of George Gissing to Eduard Bertz* (1961)

IV — Other related material

Allen, Walter, *The English Novel* (1954)

Bridgwater, Patrick, *Gissing and Germany* (1981)

Calder, Jenni, *Women and Marriage in Victorian Fiction* (1976)

Cunningham, Gail, *The New Woman and the Victorian Novel* (1978)

Ford, Boris (ed.), *From Dickens to Hardy* (1958)

Hellerstein, Erna Olafson, *et al*, *Victorian Women* (1981)

Kanner, Barbara (ed.), *The Women of England* (1980)

Kennard, Jean E., *Victims of Convention* (1978)

Korg, Jacob and Cynthia (eds.), *George Gissing on Fiction* (1978)

Korg, Jacob (ed.) *George Gissing's Commonplace Book* (1962)

Pollard, Arthur (ed.), *The Victorians* (1970)

Poole, Adrian, *Gissing in Context* (1975)

Speak, Harold, and Forrester, Jean, *Old Wakefield in Photographs* (1972)

Stubbs, Patricia, *Women and Fiction: Feminism and the Novel 1880-1920* (1979)

Taylor, Kate (compiler), *Wakefield District Heritage*, vols. I and II (1976 and 1979)

Thomson, Patricia, *The Victorian Heroine: A Changing Ideal 1837-1873* (1956)

Walker, J.W., *Wakefield, Its History and People*, 2 vols. (1939)

West, Katharine, *Chapter of Governesses* (1949)

Williams, Raymond, *Culture and Society 1780-1950* (1958)